Garfield

BY JIM DAVIS ®

VOLUME 9

ROSS RICHIE CEO & Founder • MATT GAGNON Editor-in-Chief • FILIP SABLIK President of Publishing & Marketing • STEPHEN CHRISTY President of Development • LANCE KREITER VP of Licensing & Merchandising
PHIL BARBARO VP of Finance • BRYCE CARLSON Managing Editor • MEL CAYLO Marketing Manager • SCOTT NEWMAN Production Design Manager • IRENE BRADISH Operations Manager
SIERRA HAHN Senior Editor • DAFNA PLEBAN Editor • SHANNON WATTERS Editor • ERIC HARBURN Editor • WHITNEY LEOPARD Associate Editor • JASMINE AMIRI Associate Editor
CHRIS ROSA Associate Editor • ALEX GALER Assistant Editor • CAMERON CHITTOCK Assistant Editor • MARY GUMPORT Assistant Editor • MATTHEW LEVINE Assistant Editor • KELSEY DIETERICH Production Designer
JILLIAN CRAB Production Designer • MICHELLE ANKLEY Production Design Assistant • GRACE PARK Production Design Assistant • AARON FERRARA Operations Coordinator • ELIZABETH LOUGHRIDGE Accounting Coordinator
JOSÉ MEZA Sales Assistant • JAMES ARRIOLA Mailroom Assistant • HOLLY AITCHISON Operations Assistant • STEPHANIE HOCUTT Marketing Assistant • SAM KUSEK Direct Market Representative

kaboom!

GARFIELD Volume Nine, September 2016. Published by KaBOOM!, a division of Boom Entertainment, Inc. Garfield is © 2016 PAWS,
INCORPORATED. ALL RIGHTS RESERVED. "GARFIELD" and the GARFIELD characters are registered and unregistered trademarks of Paws,
Inc. Originally published in single issue form as GARFIELD No. 33-36. Copyright © 2015 PAWS, INCORPORATED. ALL RIGHTS RESERVED.
KaBOOM!™ and the KaBOOM! logo are trademarks of Boom Entertainment, Inc., registered in various countries and categories. All characters,
events, and institutions depicted herein are fictional. Any similarity between any of the names, characters, persons, events, and/or institutions in
this publication to actual names, characters, and persons, whether living or dead, events, and/or institutions is unintended and purely coincidental.
KaBOOM! does not read or accept unsolicited submissions of ideas, stories, or artwork.

A catalog record of this book is available from OCLC and from the KaBOOM! website, www.kaboom-studios.com, on the Librarians Page.

BOOM! Studios, 5670 Wilshire Boulevard, Suite 450, Los Angeles, CA 90036-5679. Printed in China. First Printing.

ISBN: 978-1-60886-847-6, eISBN: 978-1-61398-518-2

BY JIM DAVIS

WRITTEN BY
SCOTT NICKEL

INTRODUCTIONS ILLUSTRATED BY
ANDY HIRSCH
WITH COLORS BY
LISA MOORE

LETTERS BY
STEVE WANDS

PART ONE

"CAVE CAT"

ART BY
DAVID DeGRAND

COLORS BY
LISA MOORE

"KING CAT"

ART BY
K. LYNN SMITH

COLORS BY
LISA MOORE

PART TWO

"PIRATE CAT"

ART & LETTERS BY
ROGER LANGRIDGE

COLORS BY
LISA MOORE

"COWBOY CAT"

ART BY
YEHUDI MERCADO

COLORS BY
LISA MOORE

PART THREE

"SUPER CAT"

ART BY
BRITTNEY WILLIAMS

"SAM SPAYED"

ART BY
ANDY HIRSCH

PART FOUR

"LAB CAT"

ART BY
FRAZER IRVING

"SPACE CAT"

ART BY
GENEVIEVE FT

DESIGNER
GRACE PARK

ASSOCIATE EDITOR
CHRIS ROSA

COLLECTED EDITION EDITOR
SIERRA HAHN

ORIGINAL SERIES EDITORS
REBECCA TAYLOR & SHANNON WATTERS

GARFIELD CREATED BY
JIM DAVIS

SPECIAL THANKS TO SCOTT NICKEL, DAVID REDDICK, AND THE ENTIRE PAWS, INC. TEAM.

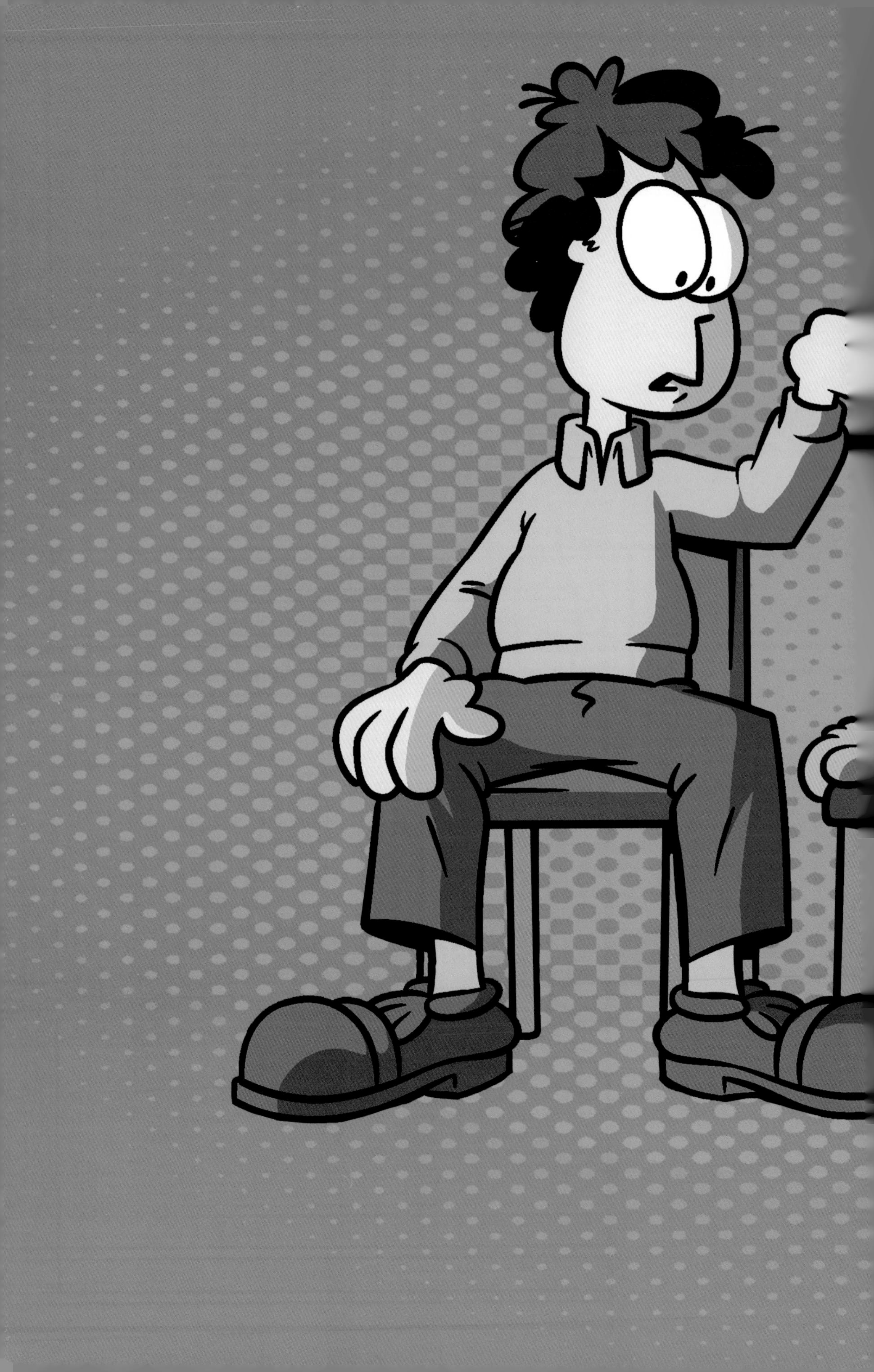

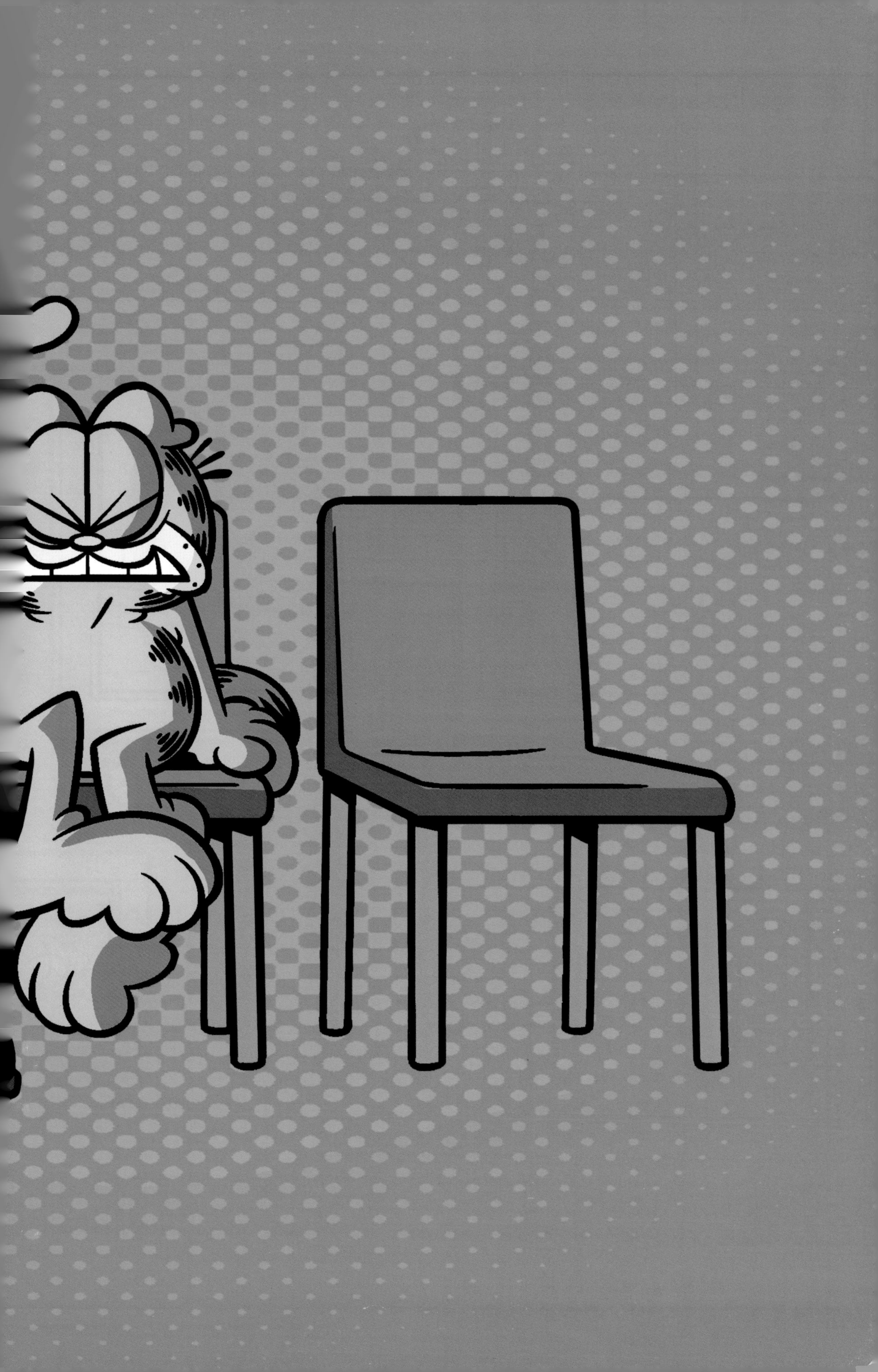

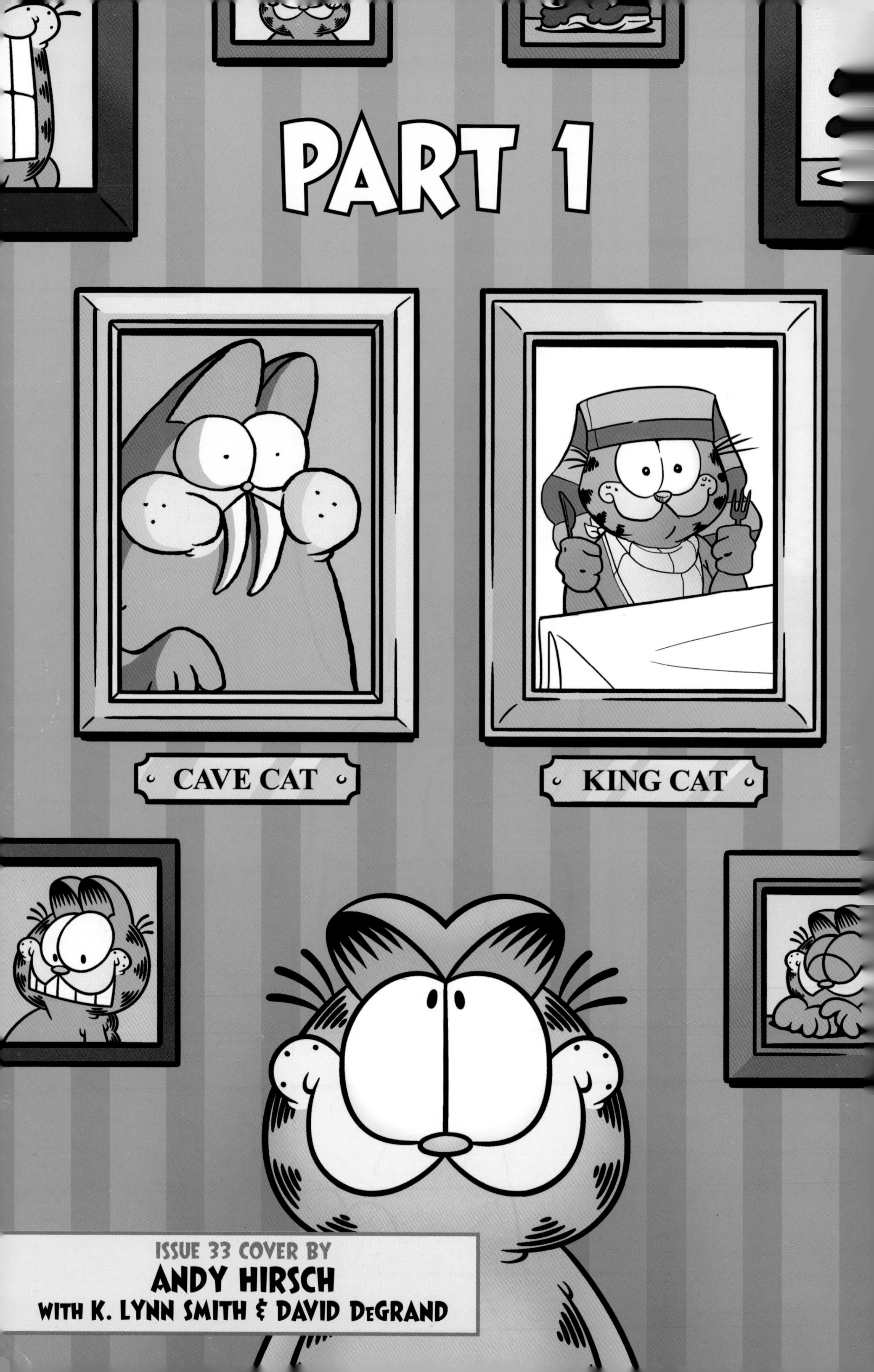
PART 1
CAVE CAT
KING CAT
ISSUE 33 COVER BY
ANDY HIRSCH
WITH K. LYNN SMITH & DAVID DEGRAND

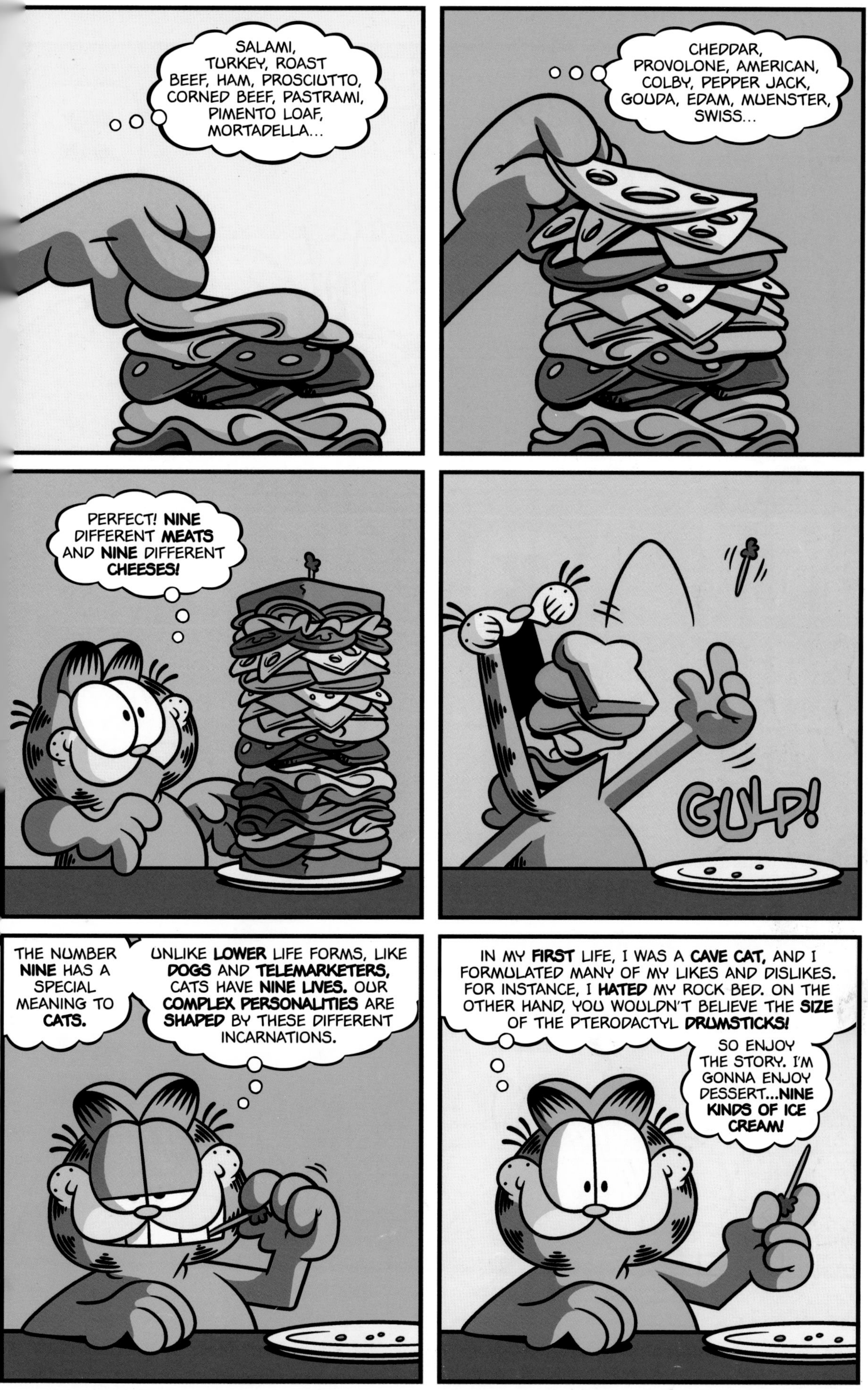
SALAMI, TURKEY, ROAST BEEF, HAM, PROSCIUTTO, CORNED BEEF, PASTRAMI, PIMENTO LOAF, MORTADELLA...
CHEDDAR, PROVOLONE, AMERICAN, COLBY, PEPPER JACK, GOUDA, EDAM, MUENSTER, SWISS...
PERFECT! **NINE** DIFFERENT **MEATS** AND **NINE** DIFFERENT **CHEESES!**
GULP!
THE NUMBER **NINE** HAS A SPECIAL MEANING TO **CATS.**
UNLIKE **LOWER** LIFE FORMS, LIKE **DOGS** AND **TELEMARKETERS,** CATS HAVE **NINE LIVES.** OUR **COMPLEX PERSONALITIES** ARE **SHAPED** BY THESE DIFFERENT INCARNATIONS.
IN MY **FIRST** LIFE, I WAS A **CAVE CAT,** AND I FORMULATED MANY OF MY LIKES AND DISLIKES. FOR INSTANCE, I **HATED** MY ROCK BED. ON THE OTHER HAND, YOU WOULDN'T BELIEVE THE **SIZE** OF THE PTERODACTYL **DRUMSTICKS!**
SO ENJOY THE STORY. I'M GONNA ENJOY DESSERT...**NINE KINDS OF ICE CREAM!**

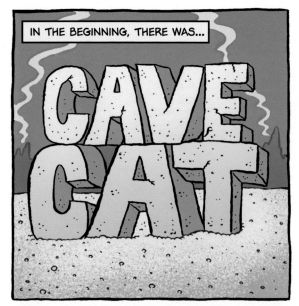

IN THE BEGINNING, THERE WAS... CAVE CAT

LIKE ALL CATS, CAVE CAT LOVED TO **SLEEP.**

Z

AND SLEEP...

Z

AND SLEEP...

Z

AND SLEEP...

Z

AND THEN SLEEP SOME **MORE**...

Z

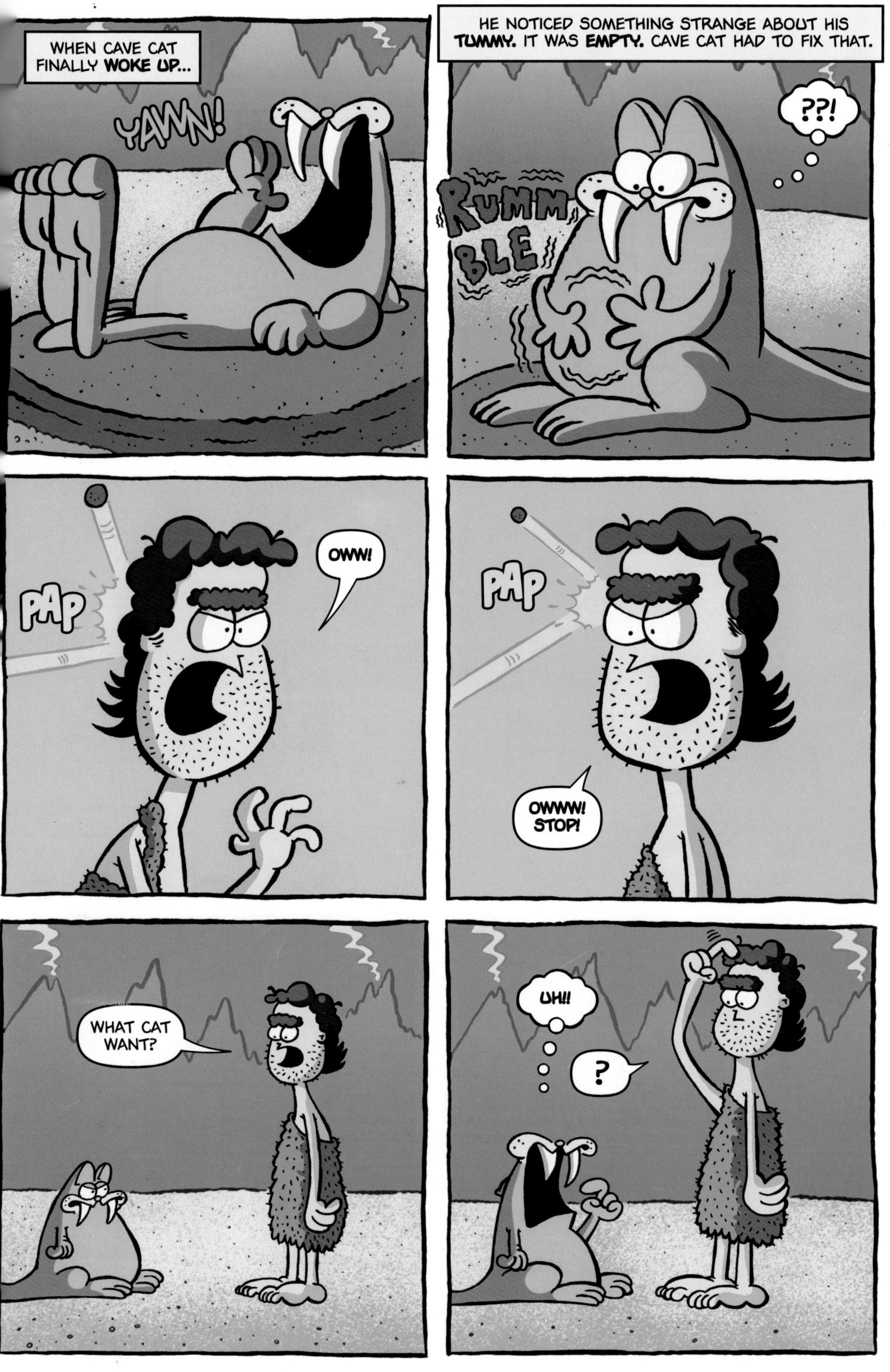
WHEN CAVE CAT FINALLY **WOKE UP**...
YAWN!
HE NOTICED SOMETHING STRANGE ABOUT HIS **TUMMY.** IT WAS **EMPTY.** CAVE CAT HAD TO FIX THAT.
RUMMBLE
??!
PAP
OWW!
PAP
OWWW! STOP!
WHAT CAT WANT?
UH!!
?

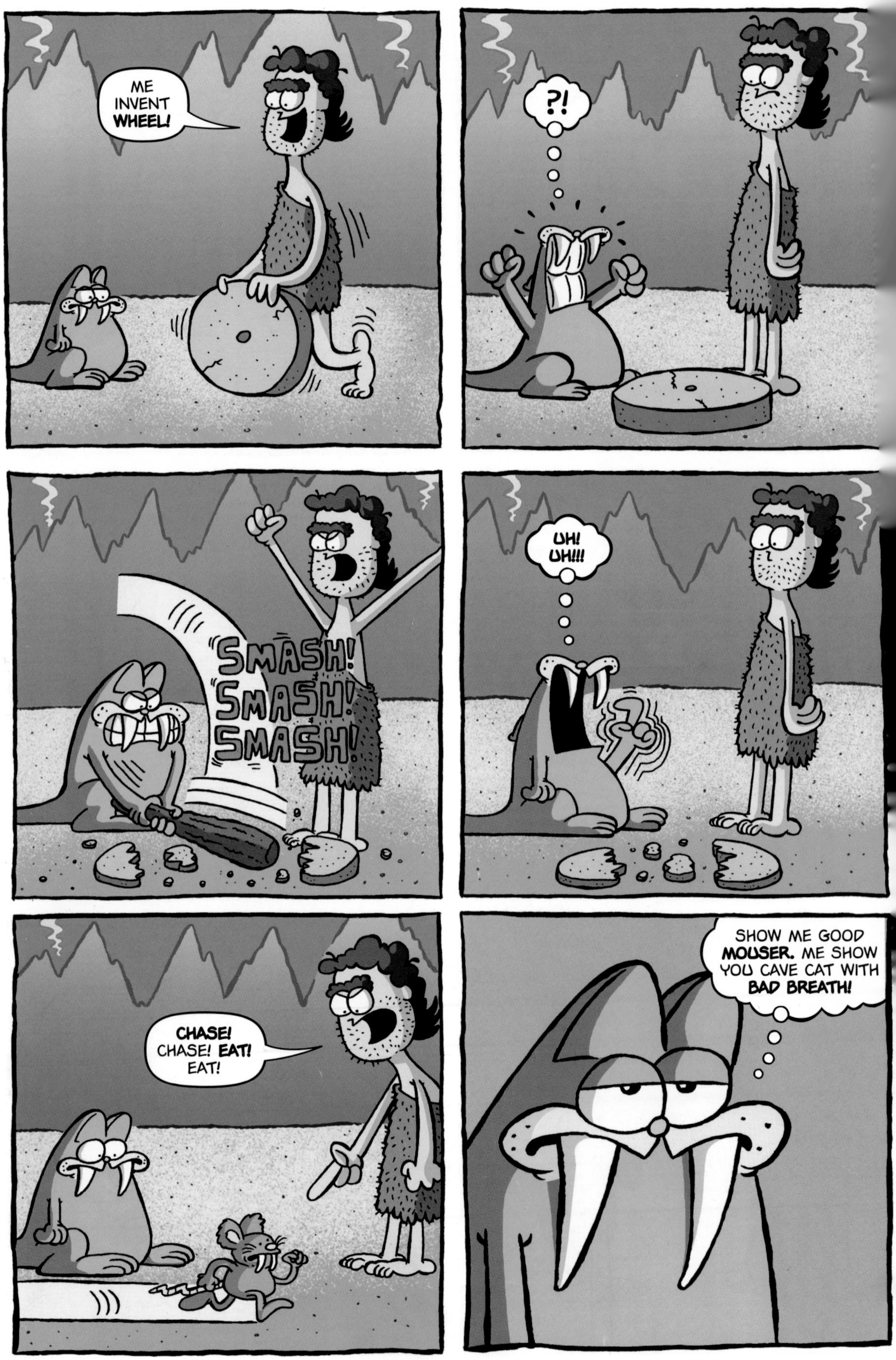

ME INVENT WHEEL!
?!
SMASH! SMASH! SMASH!
UH! UH!!!
CHASE! CHASE! EAT! EAT!
SHOW ME GOOD MOUSER. ME SHOW YOU CAVE CAT WITH BAD BREATH!

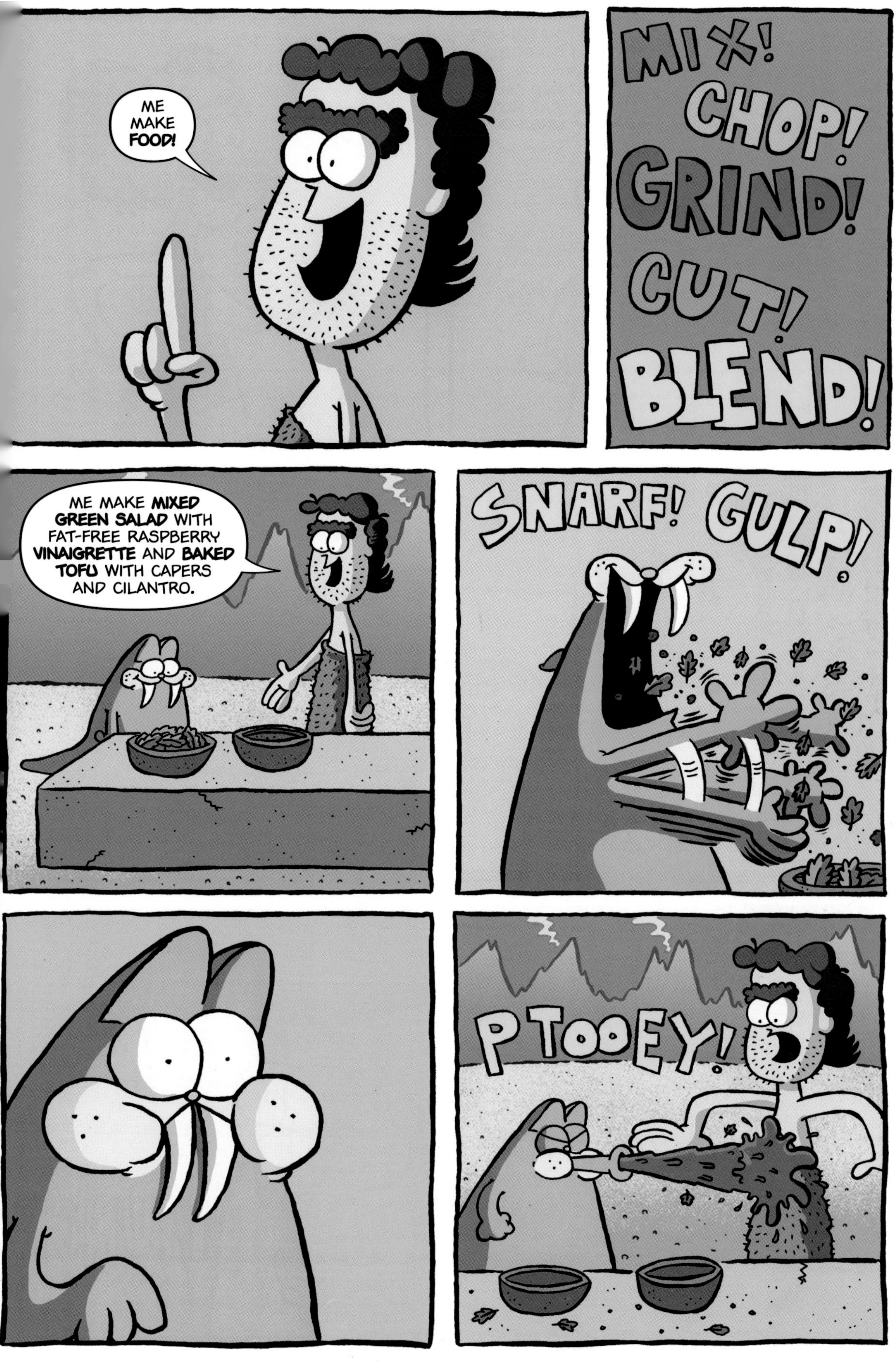
ME MAKE **FOOD!**
MIX! CHOP! GRIND! CUT! BLEND!
ME MAKE **MIXED GREEN SALAD** WITH FAT-FREE RASPBERRY **VINAIGRETTE** AND **BAKED TOFU** WITH CAPERS AND CILANTRO.
SNARF! GULP!
PTOOEY!

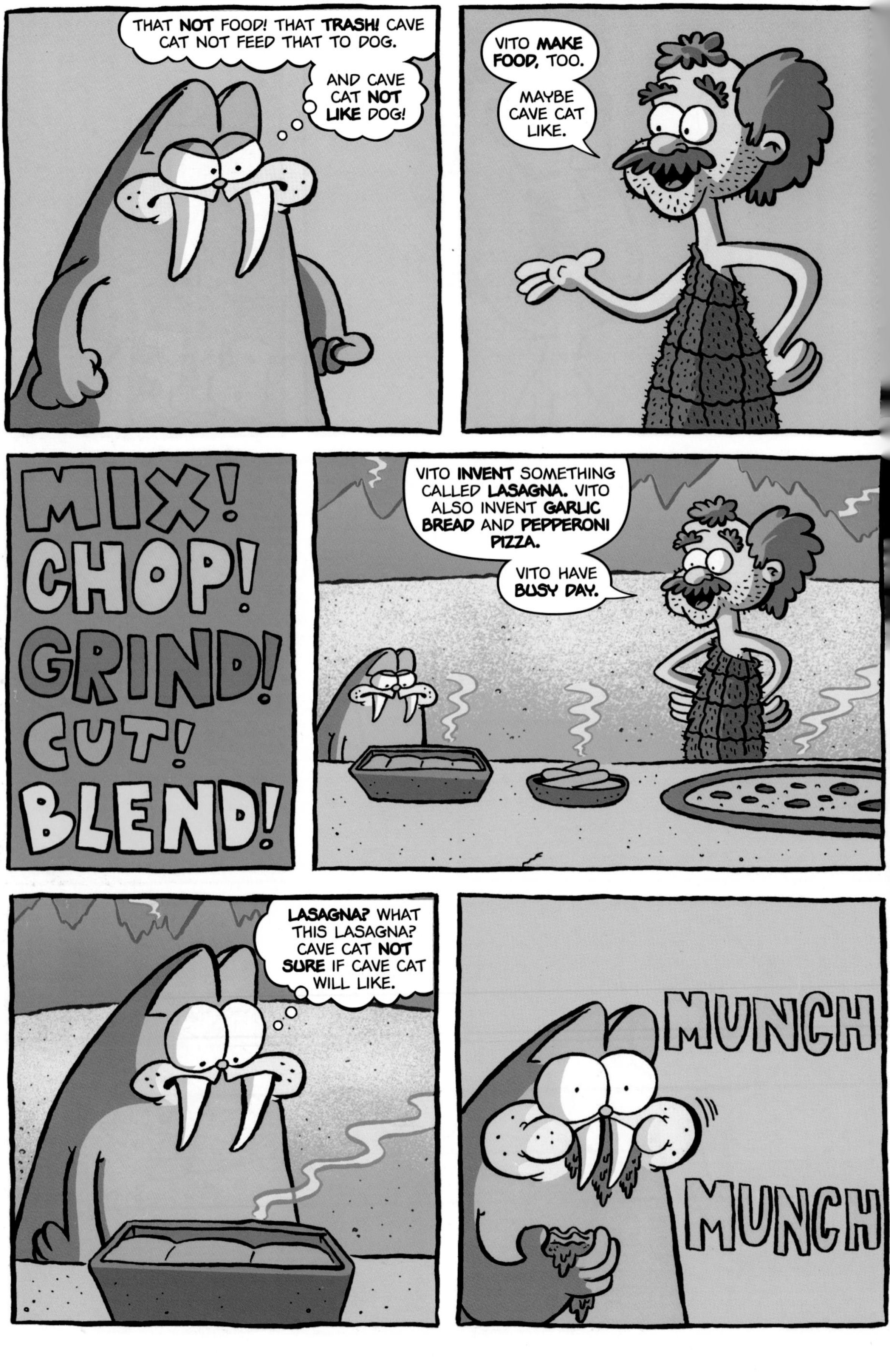
THAT NOT FOOD! THAT TRASH! CAVE CAT NOT FEED THAT TO DOG.
AND CAVE CAT NOT LIKE DOG!
VITO MAKE FOOD, TOO.
MAYBE CAVE CAT LIKE.
MIX! CHOP! GRIND! CUT! BLEND!
VITO INVENT SOMETHING CALLED LASAGNA. VITO ALSO INVENT GARLIC BREAD AND PEPPERONI PIZZA.
VITO HAVE BUSY DAY.
LASAGNA? WHAT THIS LASAGNA? CAVE CAT NOT SURE IF CAVE CAT WILL LIKE.
MUNCH
MUNCH

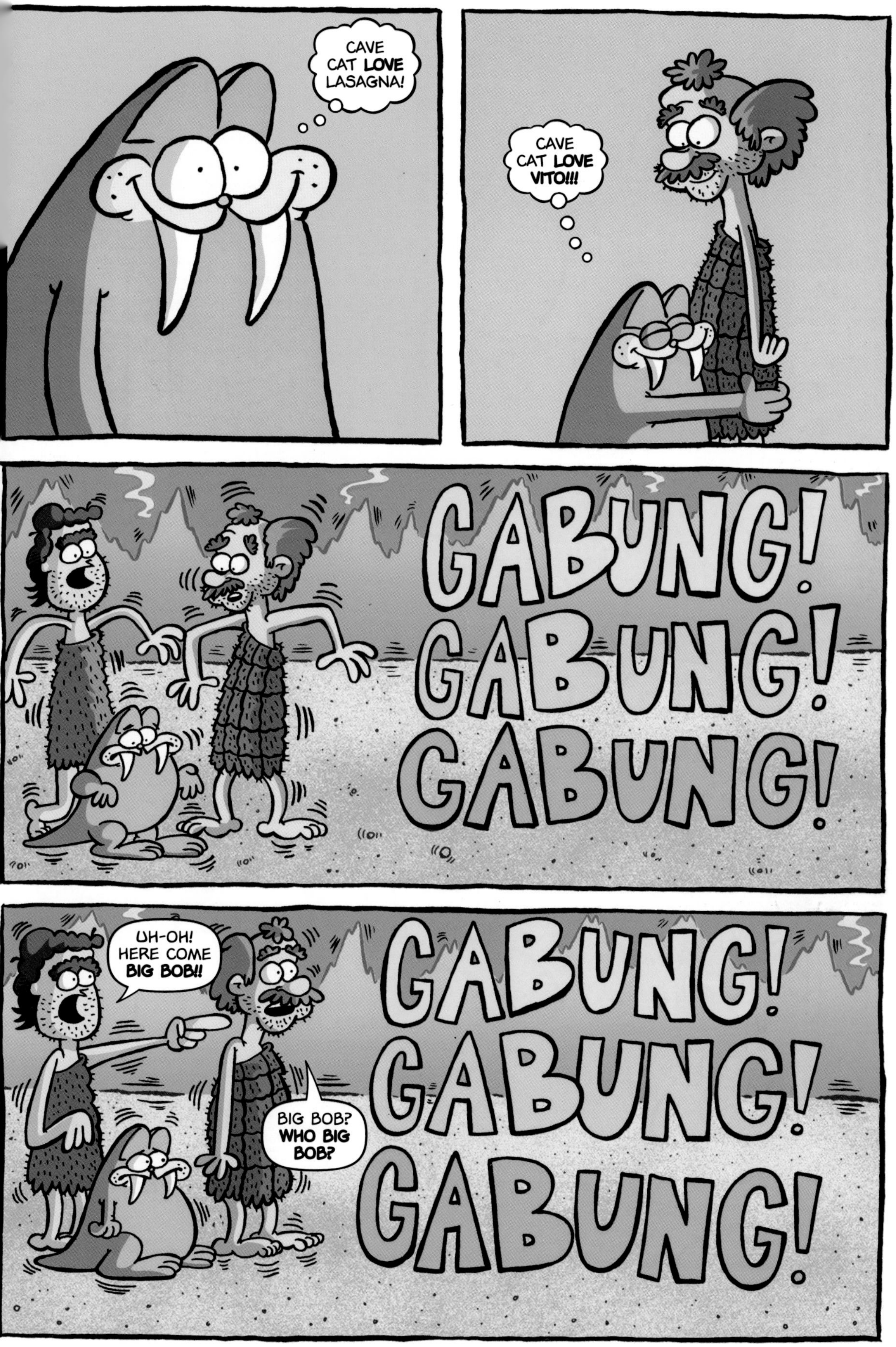
CAVE CAT LOVE LASAGNA!
CAVE CAT LOVE VITO!!!
GABUNG! GABUNG! GABUNG!
UH-OH! HERE COME BIG BOB!!
BIG BOB? WHO BIG BOB?
GABUNG! GABUNG! GABUNG!

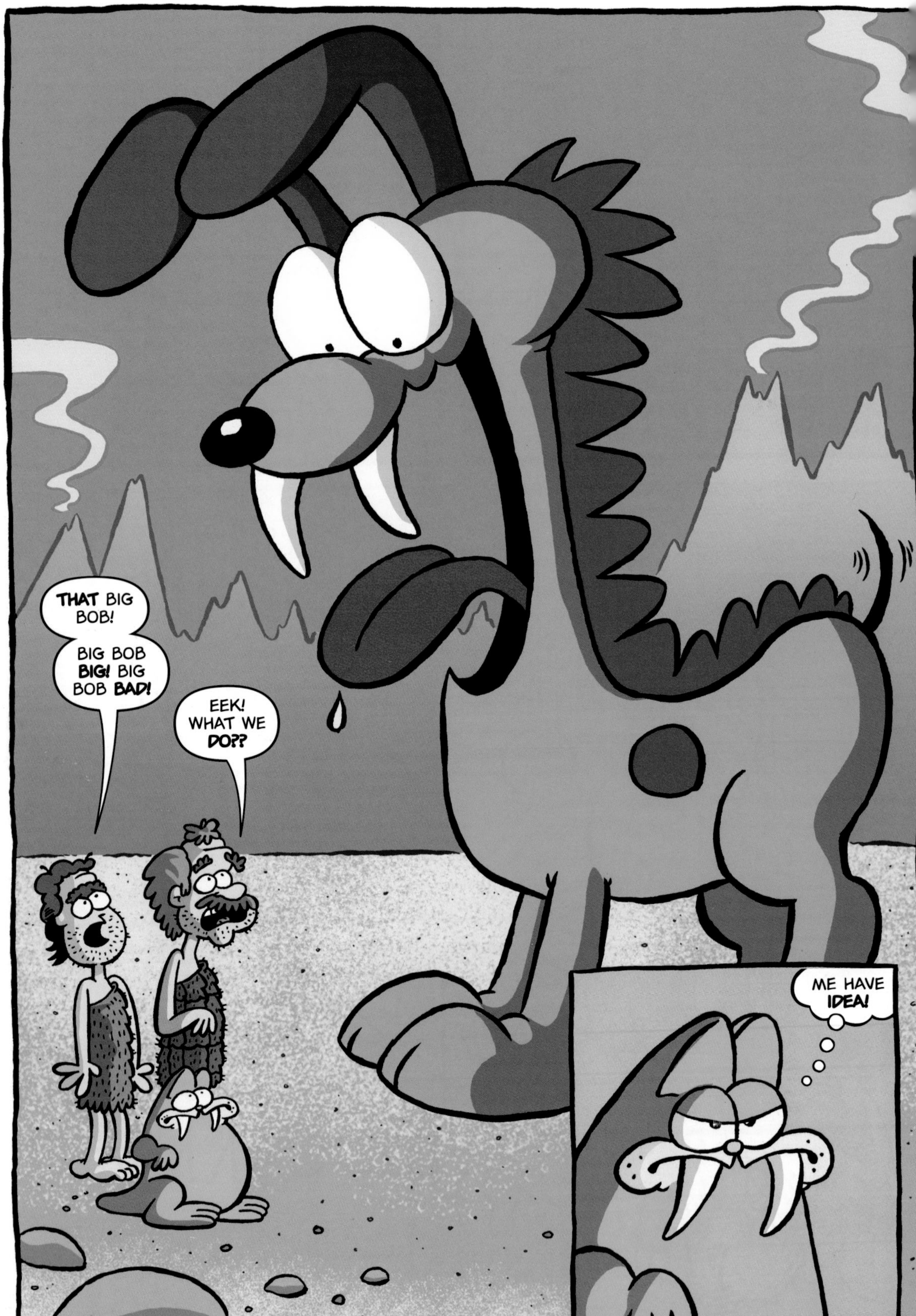
THAT BIG BOB!
BIG BOB BIG! BIG BOB BAD!
EEK! WHAT WE DO??
ME HAVE IDEA!

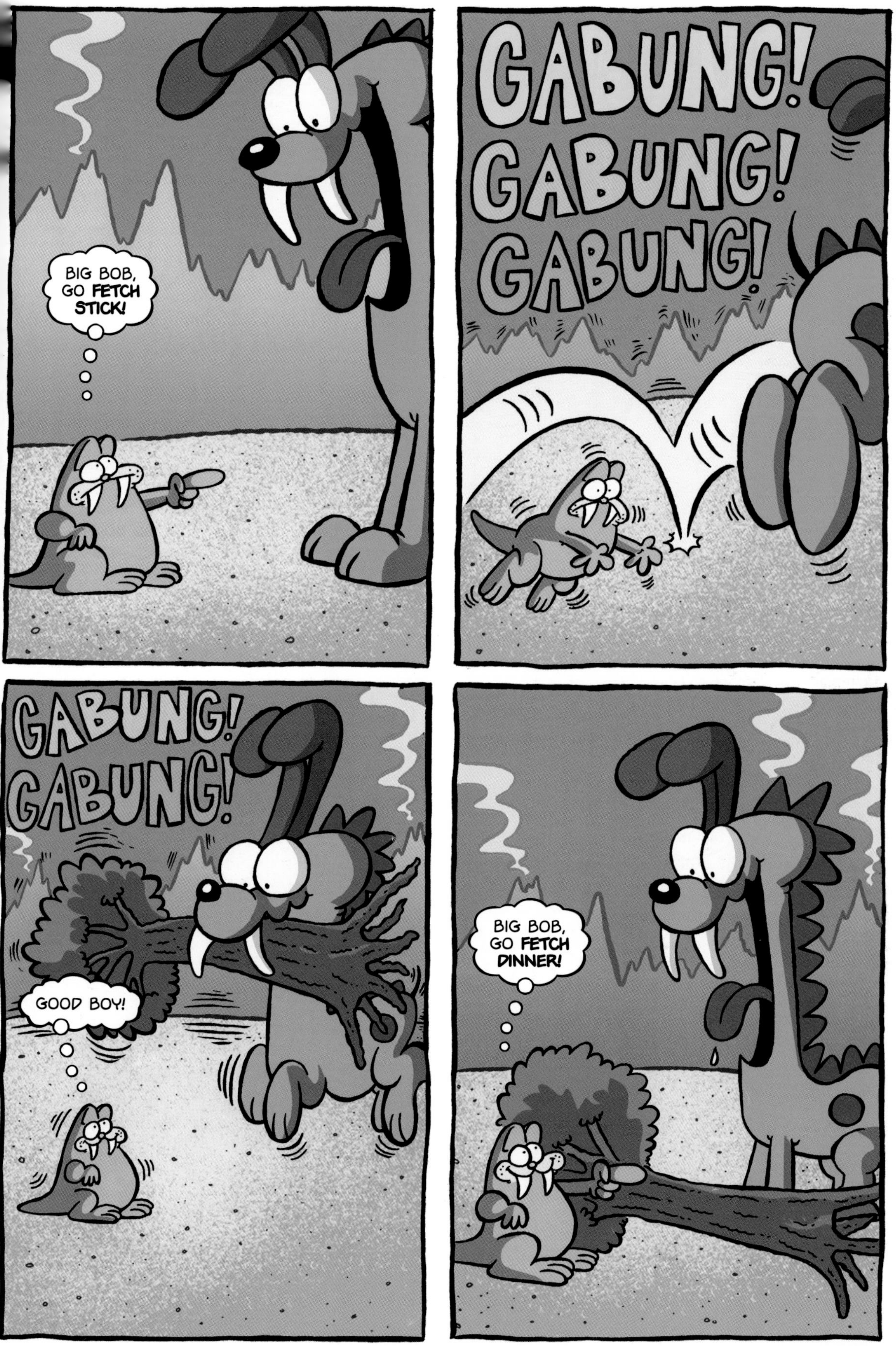
BIG BOB, GO FETCH STICK!
GABUNG! GABUNG! GABUNG!
GABUNG! GABUNG!
GOOD BOY!
BIG BOB, GO FETCH DINNER!

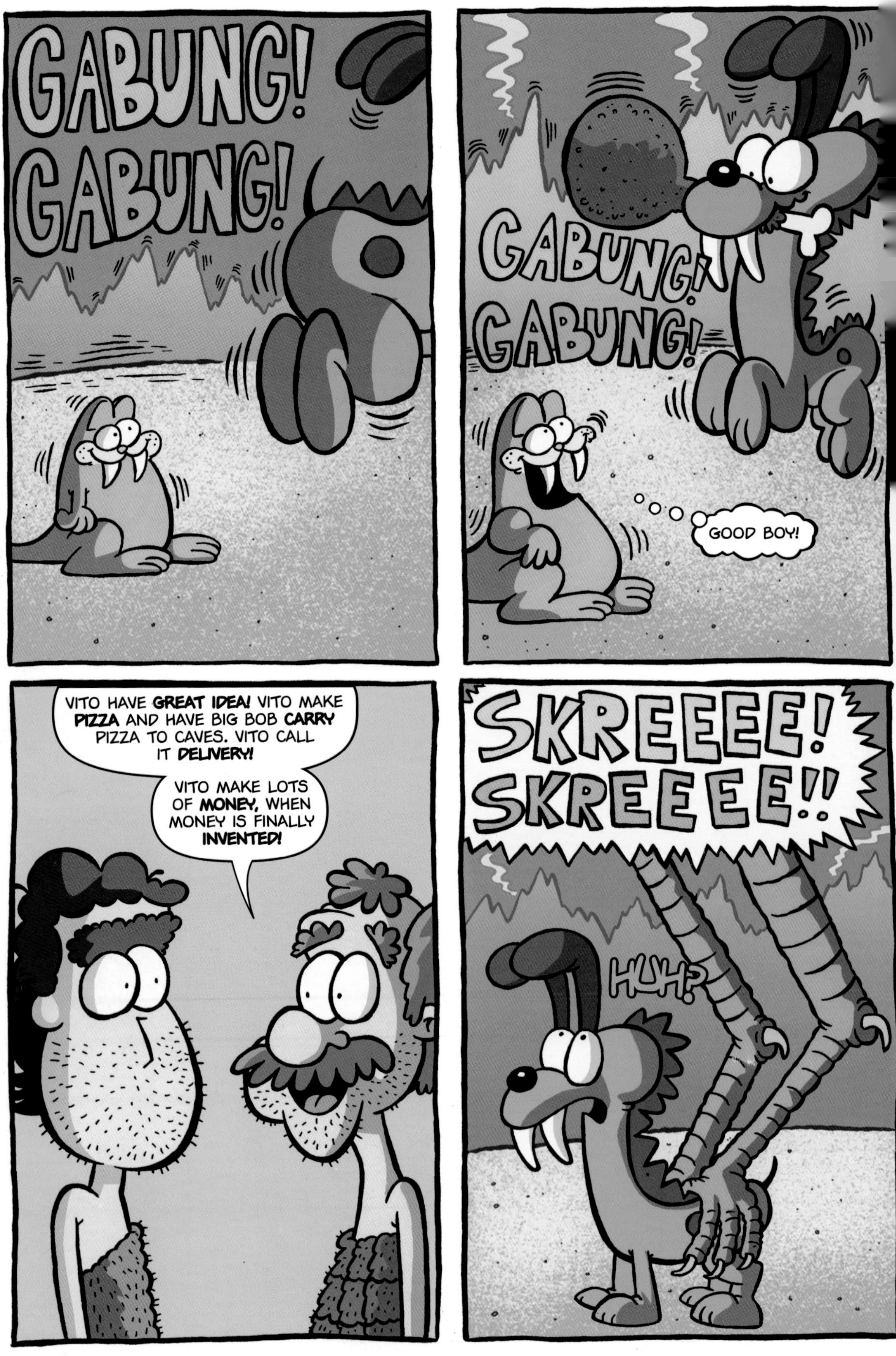
GABUNG! GABUNG!
GABUNG! GABUNG!
GOOD BOY!
VITO HAVE GREAT IDEA! VITO MAKE PIZZA AND HAVE BIG BOB CARRY PIZZA TO CAVES. VITO CALL IT DELIVERY!
VITO MAKE LOTS OF MONEY, WHEN MONEY IS FINALLY INVENTED!
SKREEEE! SKREEEE!!
HUH?

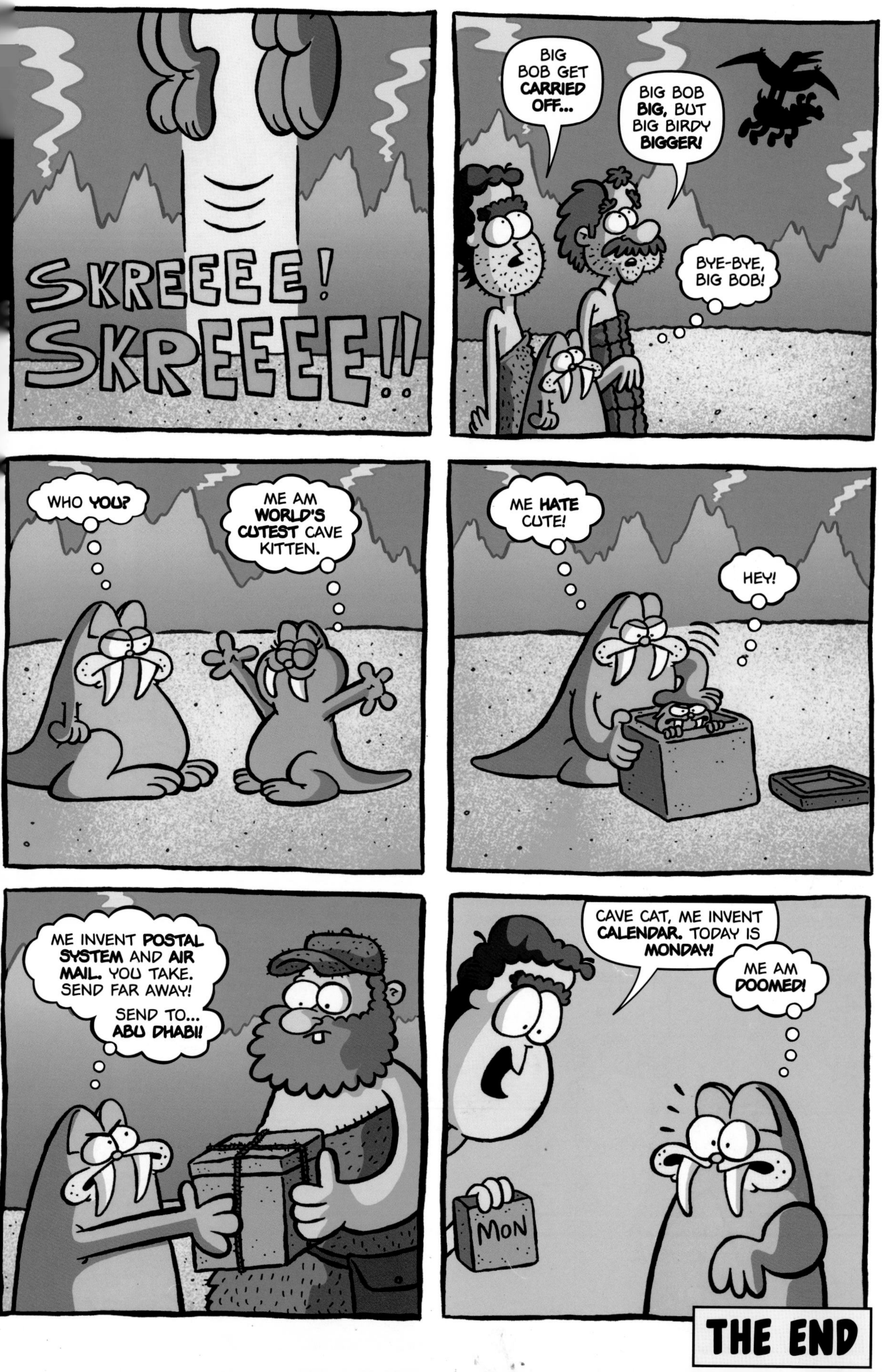
SKREEEE!
SKREEEE!!
BIG BOB GET CARRIED OFF...
BIG BOB BIG, BUT BIG BIRDY BIGGER!
BYE-BYE, BIG BOB!
WHO YOU?
ME AM WORLD'S CUTEST CAVE KITTEN.
ME HATE CUTE!
HEY!
ME INVENT POSTAL SYSTEM AND AIR MAIL. YOU TAKE. SEND FAR AWAY!
SEND TO... ABU DHABI!
CAVE CAT, ME INVENT CALENDAR. TODAY IS MONDAY!
ME AM DOOMED!
MON
THE END

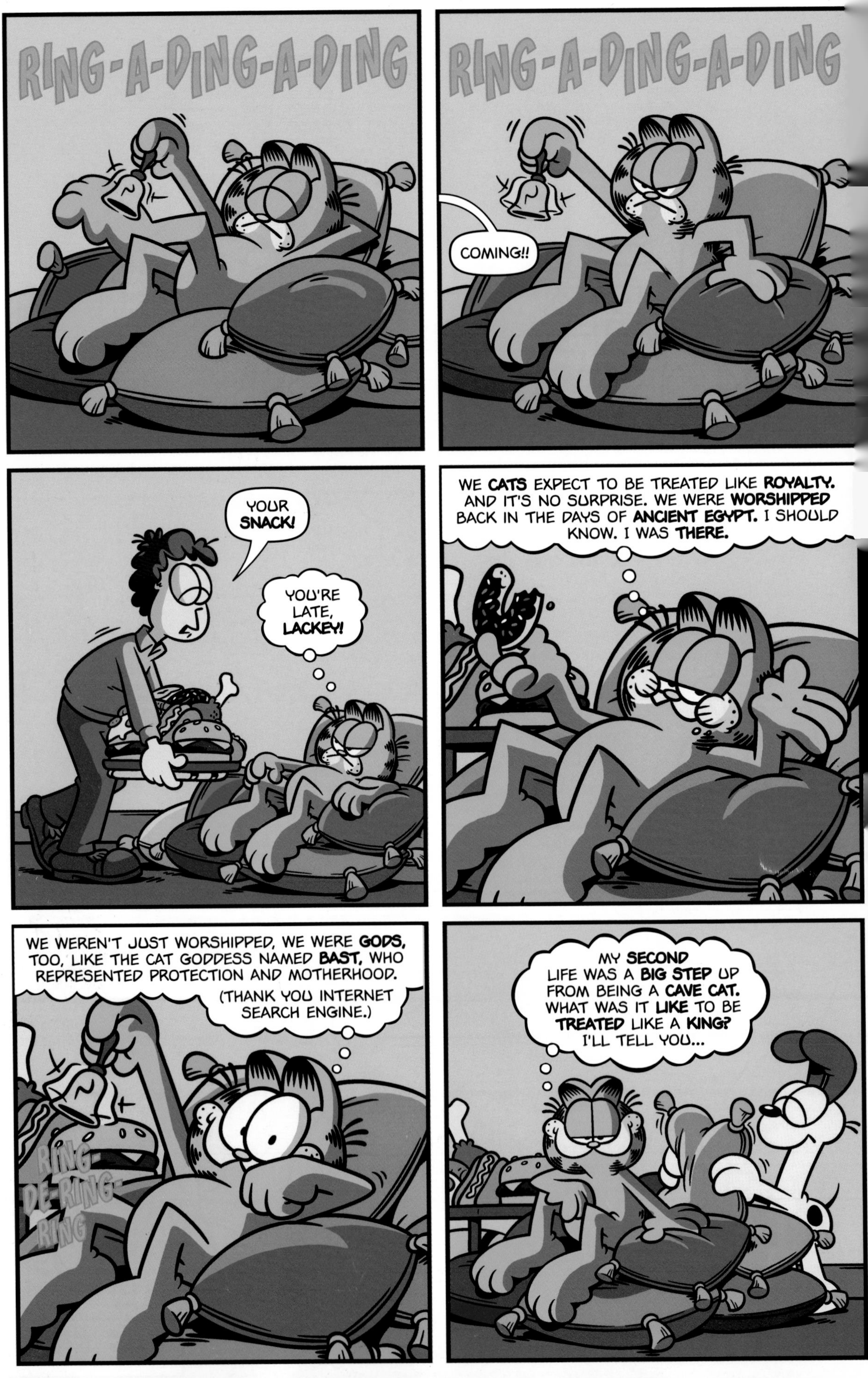
RING-A-DING-A-DING
RING-A-DING-A-DING
COMING!!
YOUR SNACK!
YOU'RE LATE, LACKEY!
WE CATS EXPECT TO BE TREATED LIKE ROYALTY. AND IT'S NO SURPRISE. WE WERE WORSHIPPED BACK IN THE DAYS OF ANCIENT EGYPT. I SHOULD KNOW. I WAS THERE.
WE WEREN'T JUST WORSHIPPED, WE WERE GODS, TOO, LIKE THE CAT GODDESS NAMED BAST, WHO REPRESENTED PROTECTION AND MOTHERHOOD.
(THANK YOU INTERNET SEARCH ENGINE.)
RING DE-RING-RING
MY SECOND LIFE WAS A BIG STEP UP FROM BEING A CAVE CAT. WHAT WAS IT LIKE TO BE TREATED LIKE A KING? I'LL TELL YOU...

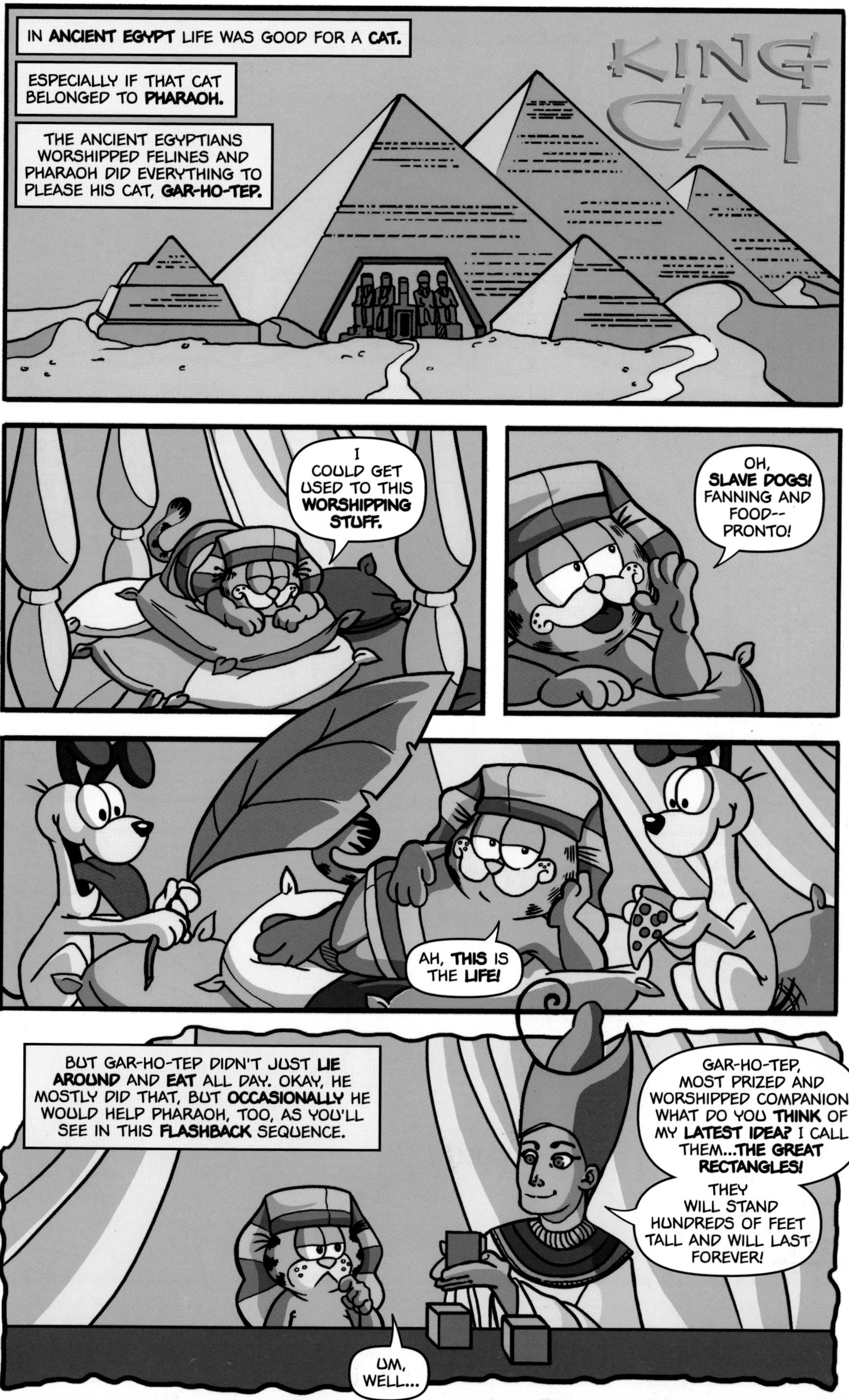
KING CAT
IN ANCIENT EGYPT LIFE WAS GOOD FOR A CAT.
ESPECIALLY IF THAT CAT BELONGED TO PHARAOH.
THE ANCIENT EGYPTIANS WORSHIPPED FELINES AND PHARAOH DID EVERYTHING TO PLEASE HIS CAT, GAR-HO-TEP.
I COULD GET USED TO THIS WORSHIPPING STUFF.
OH, SLAVE DOGS! FANNING AND FOOD-- PRONTO!
AH, THIS IS THE LIFE!
BUT GAR-HO-TEP DIDN'T JUST LIE AROUND AND EAT ALL DAY. OKAY, HE MOSTLY DID THAT, BUT OCCASIONALLY HE WOULD HELP PHARAOH, TOO, AS YOU'LL SEE IN THIS FLASHBACK SEQUENCE.
GAR-HO-TEP, MOST PRIZED AND WORSHIPPED COMPANION, WHAT DO YOU THINK OF MY LATEST IDEA? I CALL THEM...THE GREAT RECTANGLES!
THEY WILL STAND HUNDREDS OF FEET TALL AND WILL LAST FOREVER!
UM, WELL...

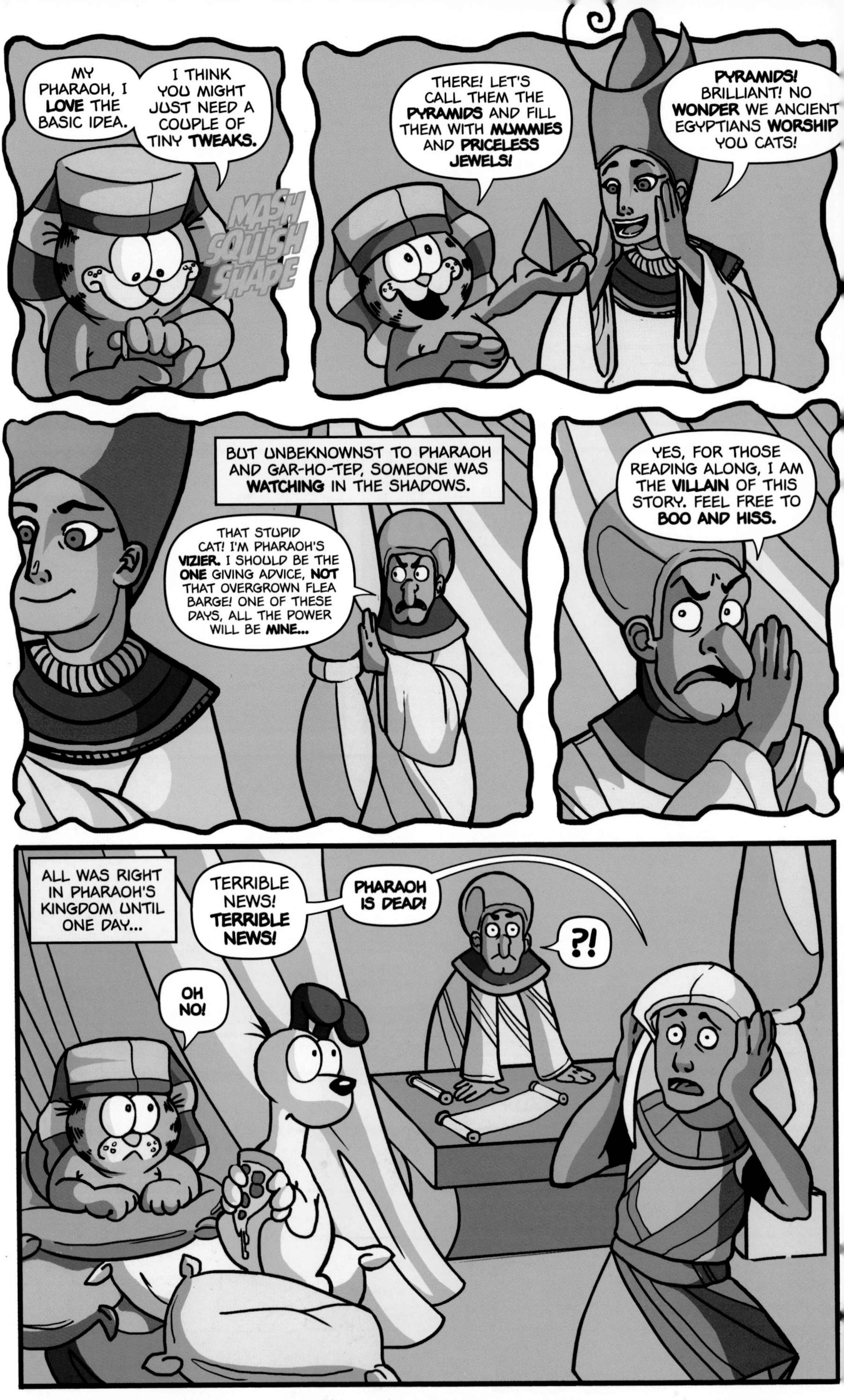

MY PHARAOH, I **LOVE** THE BASIC IDEA.
I THINK YOU MIGHT JUST NEED A COUPLE OF TINY **TWEAKS.**
MASH SQUISH SHAPE
THERE! LET'S CALL THEM THE **PYRAMIDS** AND FILL THEM WITH **MUMMIES** AND **PRICELESS JEWELS!**
PYRAMIDS! BRILLIANT! NO **WONDER** WE ANCIENT EGYPTIANS **WORSHIP** YOU CATS!
BUT UNBEKNOWNST TO PHARAOH AND GAR-HO-TEP, SOMEONE WAS **WATCHING** IN THE SHADOWS.
THAT STUPID CAT! I'M PHARAOH'S **VIZIER.** I SHOULD BE THE **ONE** GIVING ADVICE, **NOT** THAT OVERGROWN FLEA BARGE! ONE OF THESE DAYS, ALL THE POWER WILL BE **MINE...**
YES, FOR THOSE READING ALONG, I AM THE **VILLAIN** OF THIS STORY. FEEL FREE TO **BOO AND HISS.**
ALL WAS RIGHT IN PHARAOH'S KINGDOM UNTIL ONE DAY...
TERRIBLE NEWS! **TERRIBLE NEWS!**
PHARAOH IS DEAD!
?!
OH NO!

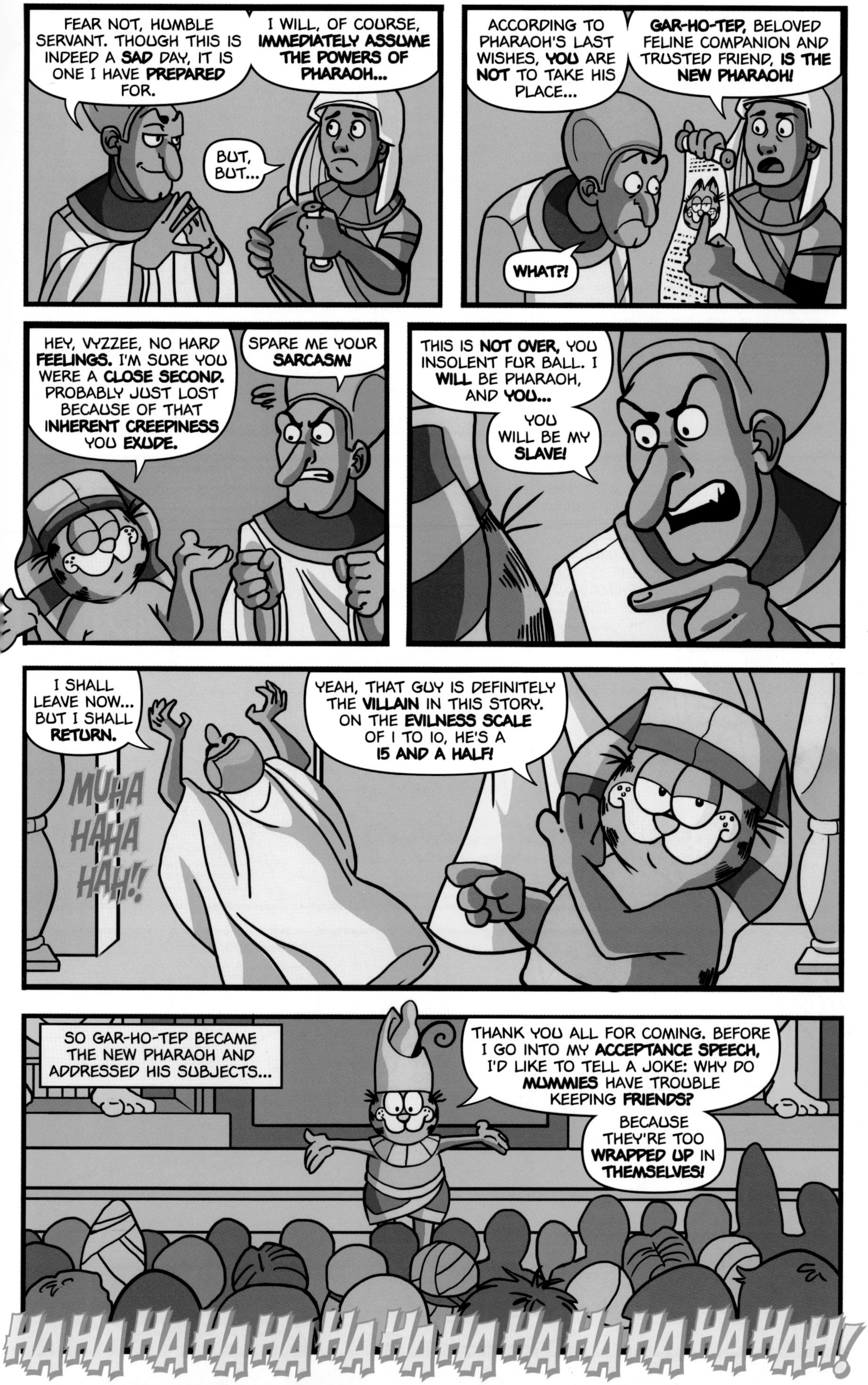
FEAR NOT, HUMBLE SERVANT. THOUGH THIS IS INDEED A SAD DAY, IT IS ONE I HAVE PREPARED FOR.
I WILL, OF COURSE, IMMEDIATELY ASSUME THE POWERS OF PHARAOH...
BUT, BUT...
ACCORDING TO PHARAOH'S LAST WISHES, YOU ARE NOT TO TAKE HIS PLACE...
GAR-HO-TEP, BELOVED FELINE COMPANION AND TRUSTED FRIEND, IS THE NEW PHARAOH!
WHAT?!
HEY, VYZZEE, NO HARD FEELINGS. I'M SURE YOU WERE A CLOSE SECOND. PROBABLY JUST LOST BECAUSE OF THAT INHERENT CREEPINESS YOU EXUDE.
SPARE ME YOUR SARCASM!
THIS IS NOT OVER, YOU INSOLENT FUR BALL. I WILL BE PHARAOH, AND YOU...
YOU WILL BE MY SLAVE!
I SHALL LEAVE NOW... BUT I SHALL RETURN.
MUHA HAHA HAH!!
YEAH, THAT GUY IS DEFINITELY THE VILLAIN IN THIS STORY. ON THE EVILNESS SCALE OF 1 TO 10, HE'S A 15 AND A HALF!
SO GAR-HO-TEP BECAME THE NEW PHARAOH AND ADDRESSED HIS SUBJECTS...
THANK YOU ALL FOR COMING. BEFORE I GO INTO MY ACCEPTANCE SPEECH, I'D LIKE TO TELL A JOKE: WHY DO MUMMIES HAVE TROUBLE KEEPING FRIENDS?
BECAUSE THEY'RE TOO WRAPPED UP IN THEMSELVES!
HA HA HA HA HA HA HA HA HA HA HA HA HAH!

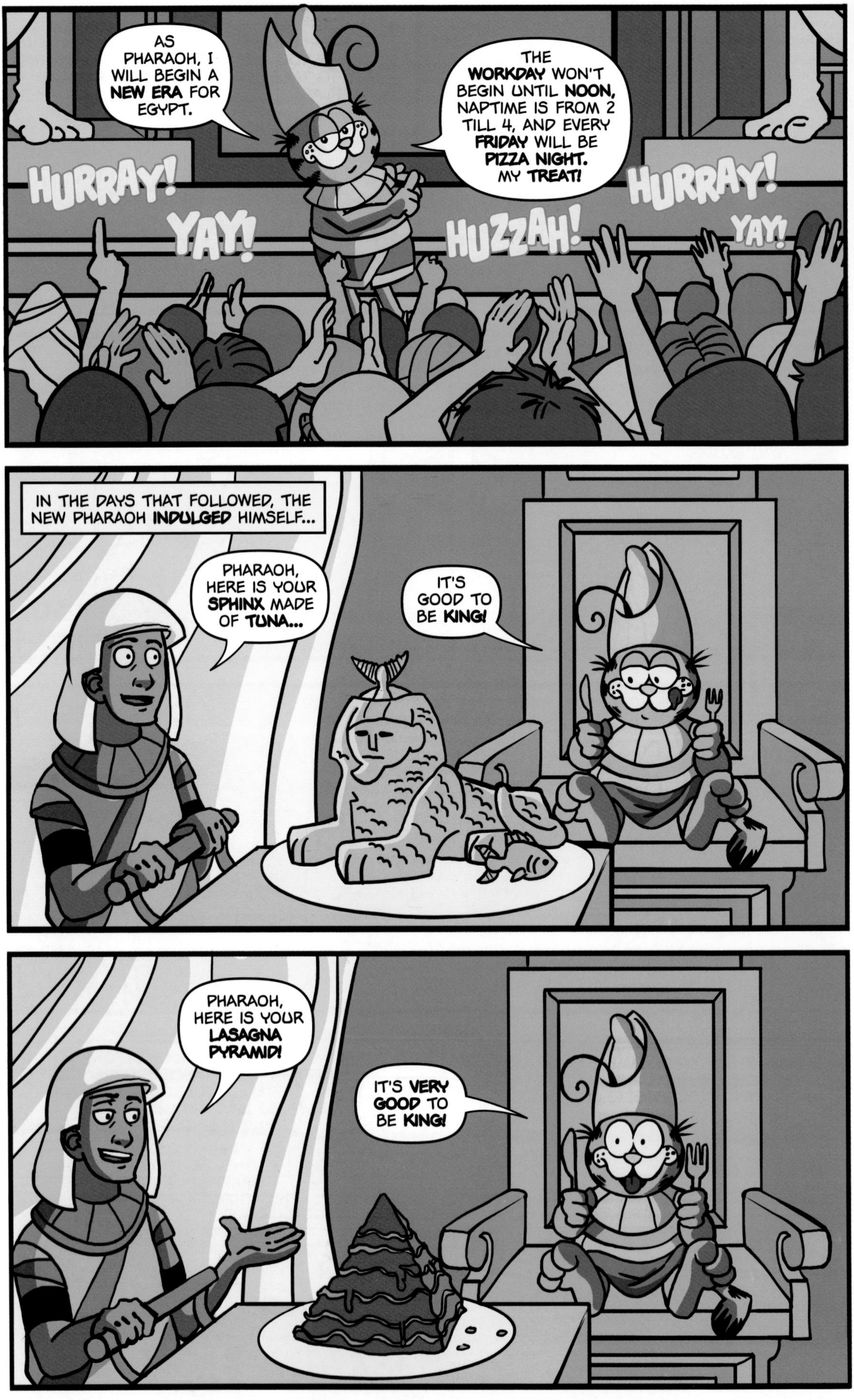
AS PHARAOH, I WILL BEGIN A NEW ERA FOR EGYPT.
THE WORKDAY WON'T BEGIN UNTIL NOON, NAPTIME IS FROM 2 TILL 4, AND EVERY FRIDAY WILL BE PIZZA NIGHT. MY TREAT!
HURRAY!
YAY!
HUZZAH!
HURRAY!
YAY!
IN THE DAYS THAT FOLLOWED, THE NEW PHARAOH INDULGED HIMSELF...
PHARAOH, HERE IS YOUR SPHINX MADE OF TUNA...
IT'S GOOD TO BE KING!
PHARAOH, HERE IS YOUR LASAGNA PYRAMID!
IT'S VERY GOOD TO BE KING!

BUT WHILE KING CAT WAS SNACKING, THE VIZIER WAS DEEP IN THE **ROYAL TOMB**...

THERE IT IS!

AT LAST! I'VE FOUND IT!!

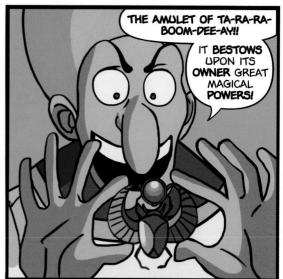

THE AMULET OF TA-RA-RA-BOOM-DEE-AY!!

IT BESTOWS UPON ITS **OWNER** GREAT MAGICAL **POWERS!**

I CALL UPON YOU, OH MIGHTY AMULET, GRANT ME MY **WISH.** BRING FORTH THE **SLUMBERING DENIZENS** FROM THE LAND OF THE DEAD...

MEANWHILE AT THE PALACE OF GAR-HO-TEP...

SO WE HAVE **PIZZA FRIDAYS.** HOW ABOUT **TACO TUESDAYS** OR **MEATLOAF MONDAYS**...NO I **HATE** MONDAYS...

RRRAAARRRRR!!

IS THAT **MONDAY SNEAKING UP** ON ME??!

??!

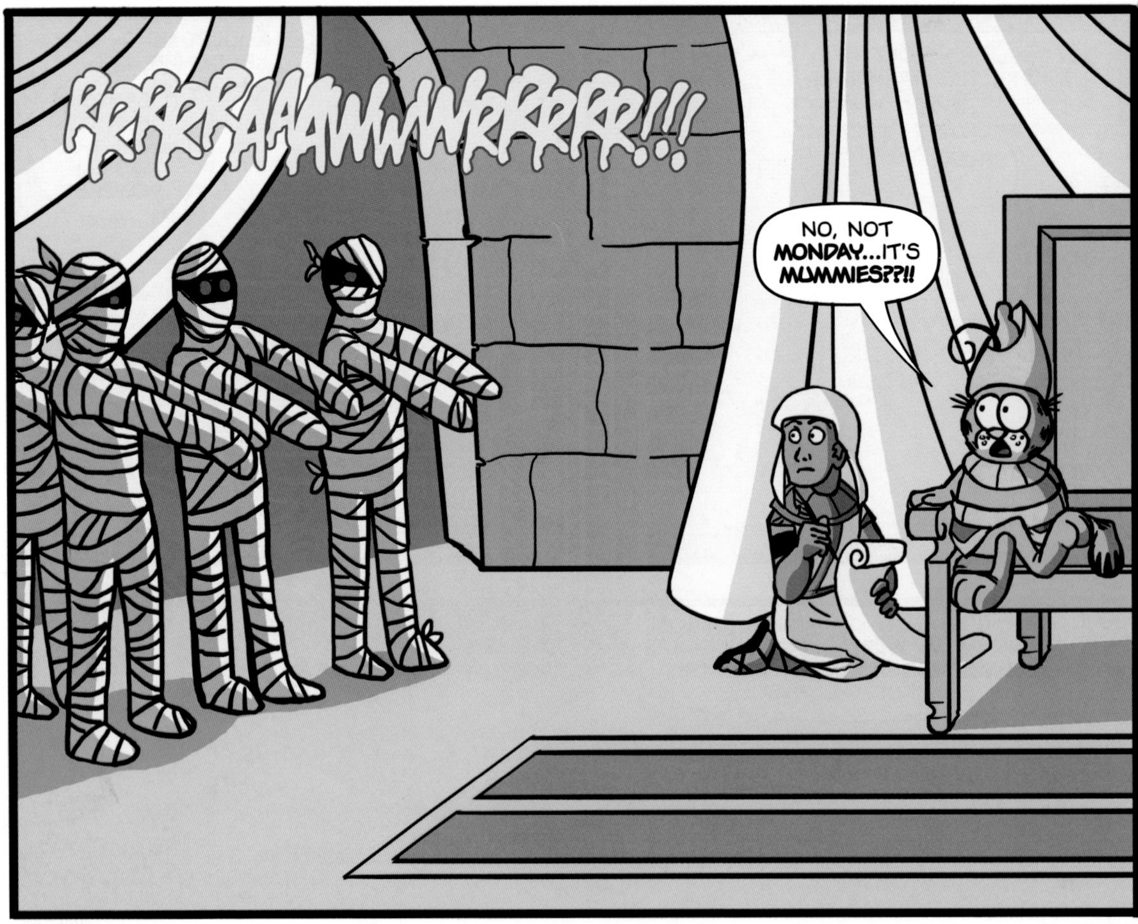
RRRRRAAAWWWRRRRR!!!
NO, NOT MONDAY...IT'S MUMMIES??!!

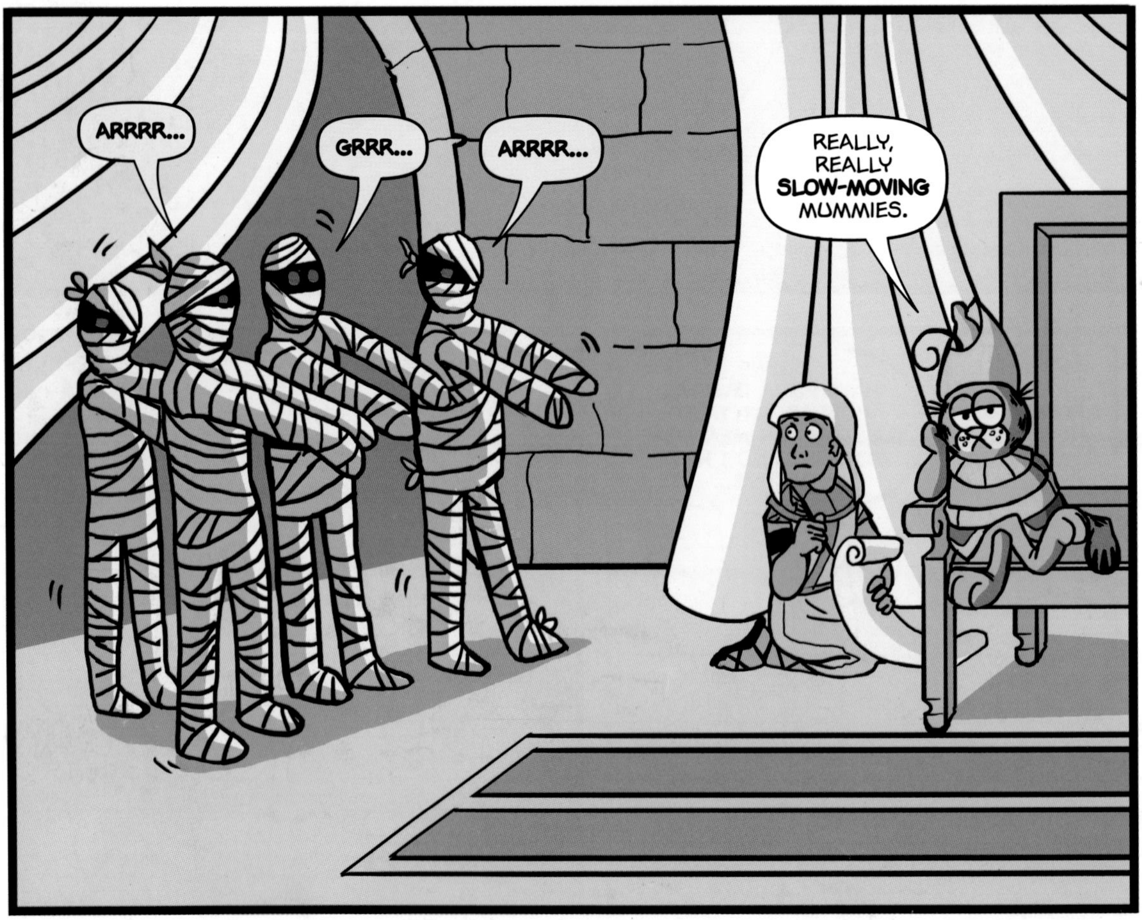
ARRRR...
GRRR...
ARRRR...
REALLY, REALLY SLOW-MOVING MUMMIES.

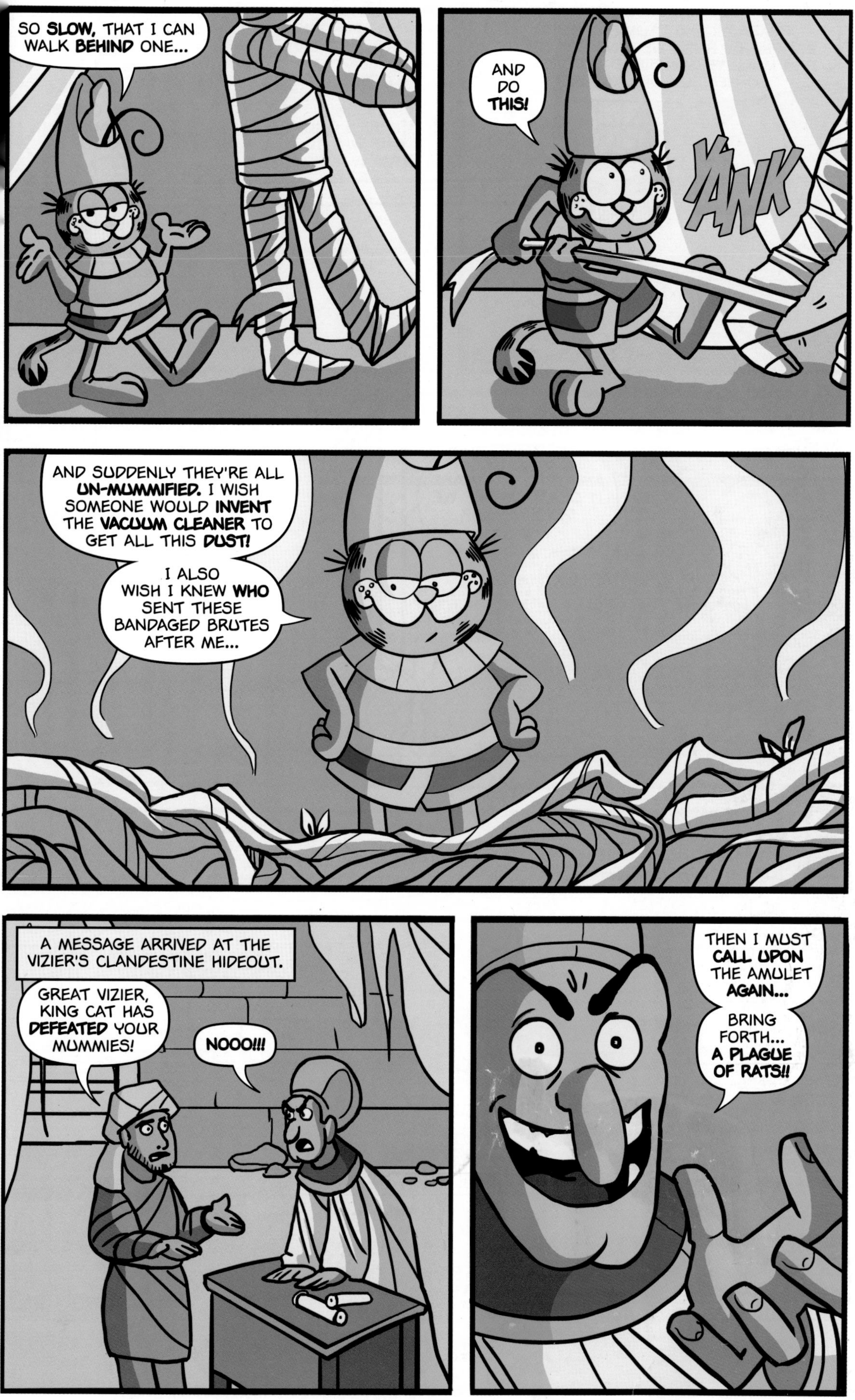
SO SLOW, THAT I CAN WALK BEHIND ONE...
AND DO THIS!
YANK
AND SUDDENLY THEY'RE ALL UN-MUMMIFIED. I WISH SOMEONE WOULD INVENT THE VACUUM CLEANER TO GET ALL THIS DUST!
I ALSO WISH I KNEW WHO SENT THESE BANDAGED BRUTES AFTER ME...
A MESSAGE ARRIVED AT THE VIZIER'S CLANDESTINE HIDEOUT.
GREAT VIZIER, KING CAT HAS DEFEATED YOUR MUMMIES!
NOOO!!!
THEN I MUST CALL UPON THE AMULET AGAIN...
BRING FORTH... A PLAGUE OF RATS!!

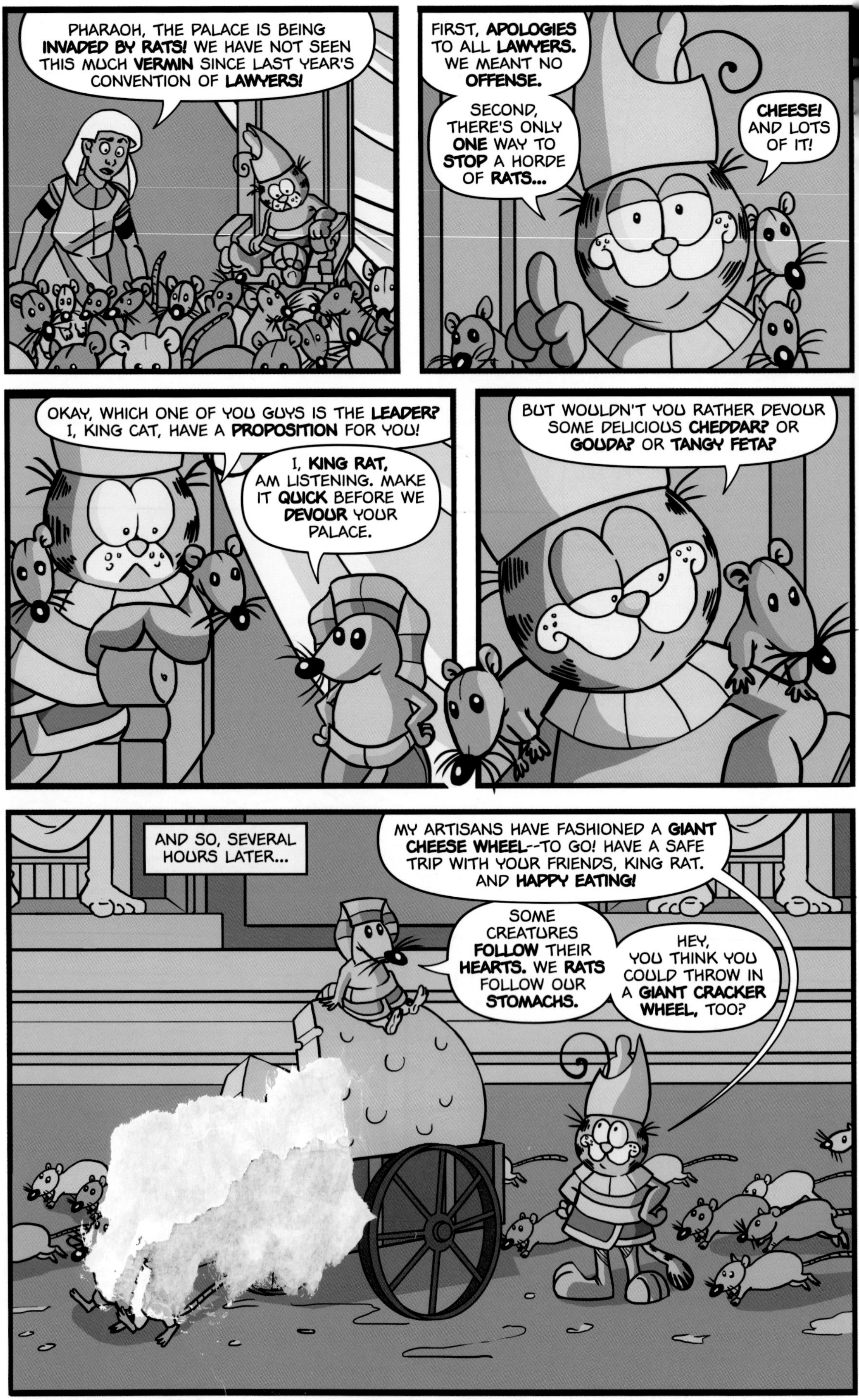
PHARAOH, THE PALACE IS BEING INVADED BY RATS! WE HAVE NOT SEEN THIS MUCH VERMIN SINCE LAST YEAR'S CONVENTION OF LAWYERS!
FIRST, APOLOGIES TO ALL LAWYERS. WE MEANT NO OFFENSE.
SECOND, THERE'S ONLY ONE WAY TO STOP A HORDE OF RATS...
CHEESE! AND LOTS OF IT!
OKAY, WHICH ONE OF YOU GUYS IS THE LEADER? I, KING CAT, HAVE A PROPOSITION FOR YOU!
I, KING RAT, AM LISTENING. MAKE IT QUICK BEFORE WE DEVOUR YOUR PALACE.
BUT WOULDN'T YOU RATHER DEVOUR SOME DELICIOUS CHEDDAR? OR GOUDA? OR TANGY FETA?
AND SO, SEVERAL HOURS LATER...
MY ARTISANS HAVE FASHIONED A GIANT CHEESE WHEEL--TO GO! HAVE A SAFE TRIP WITH YOUR FRIENDS, KING RAT. AND HAPPY EATING!
SOME CREATURES FOLLOW THEIR HEARTS. WE RATS FOLLOW OUR STOMACHS.
HEY, YOU THINK YOU COULD THROW IN A GIANT CRACKER WHEEL, TOO?

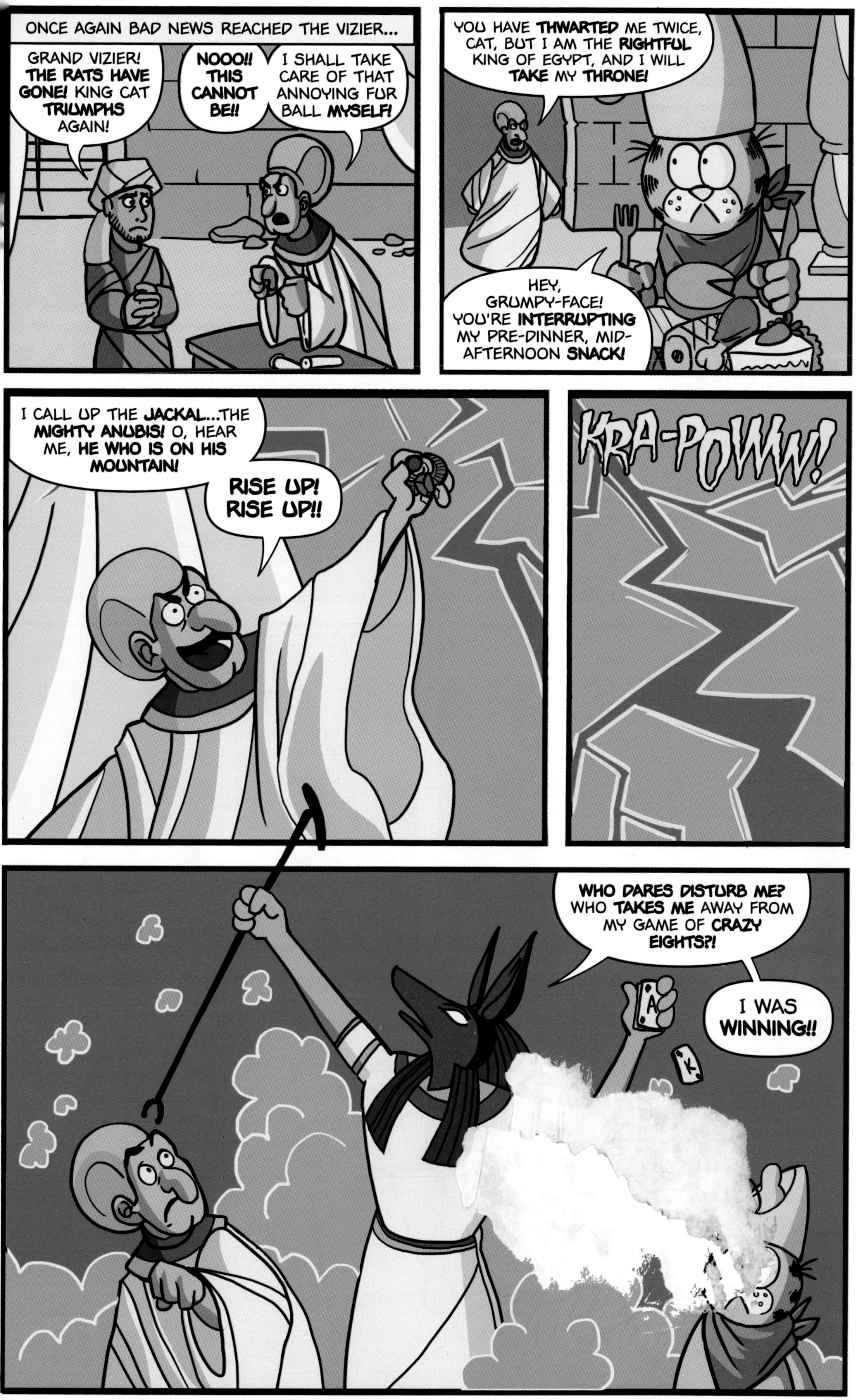

ONCE AGAIN BAD NEWS REACHED THE VIZIER...
GRAND VIZIER! THE RATS HAVE GONE! KING CAT TRIUMPHS AGAIN!
NOOO!! THIS CANNOT BE!!
I SHALL TAKE CARE OF THAT ANNOYING FUR BALL MYSELF!
YOU HAVE THWARTED ME TWICE, CAT, BUT I AM THE RIGHTFUL KING OF EGYPT, AND I WILL TAKE MY THRONE!
HEY, GRUMPY-FACE! YOU'RE INTERRUPTING MY PRE-DINNER, MID-AFTERNOON SNACK!
I CALL UP THE JACKAL...THE MIGHTY ANUBIS! O, HEAR ME, HE WHO IS ON HIS MOUNTAIN!
RISE UP! RISE UP!!
KRA-POWW!
WHO DARES DISTURB ME? WHO TAKES ME AWAY FROM MY GAME OF CRAZY EIGHTS?!
I WAS WINNING!!

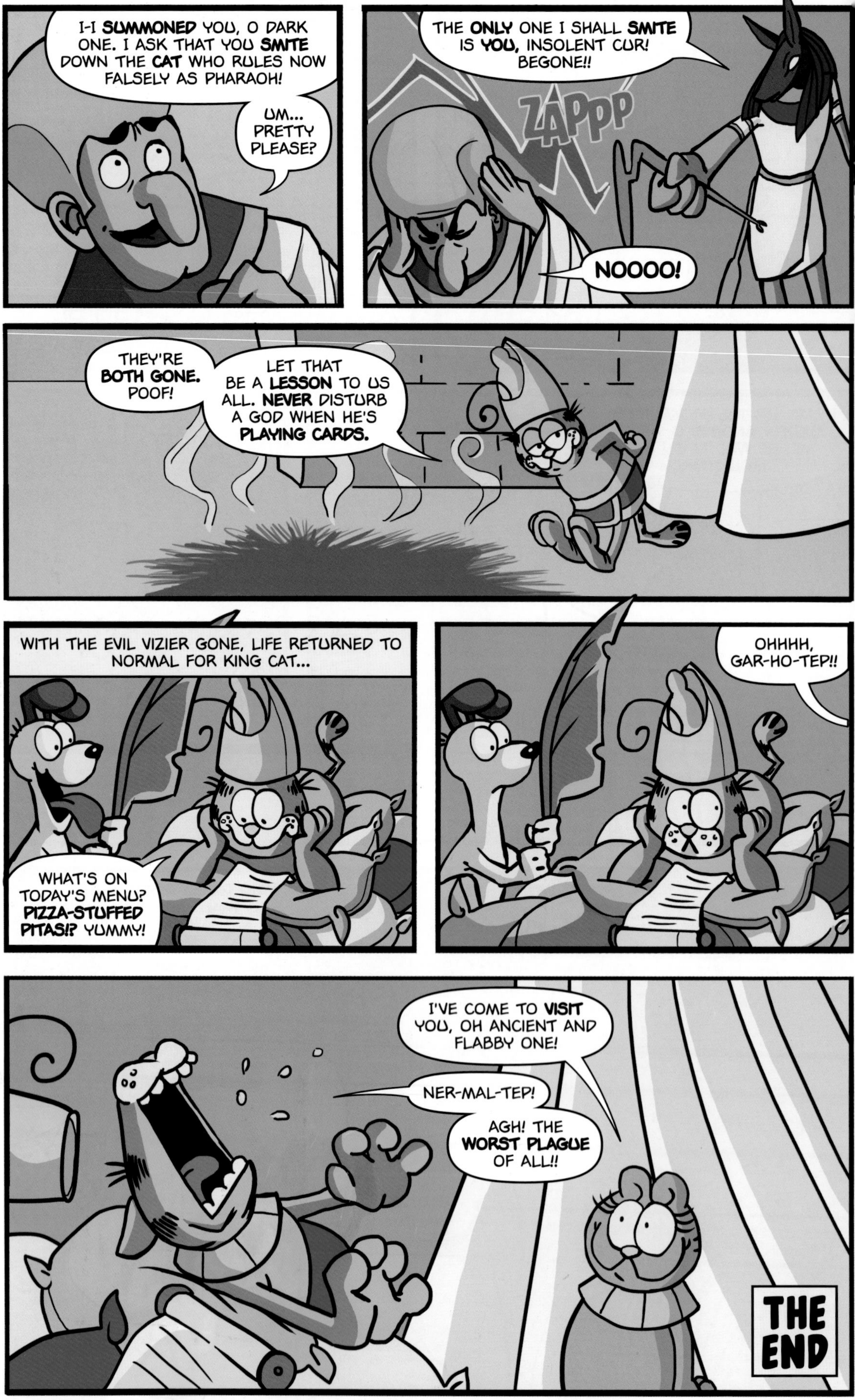

I-I SUMMONED YOU, O DARK ONE. I ASK THAT YOU SMITE DOWN THE CAT WHO RULES NOW FALSELY AS PHARAOH!
UM... PRETTY PLEASE?
THE ONLY ONE I SHALL SMITE IS YOU, INSOLENT CUR! BEGONE!!
ZAPPP
NOOOO!
THEY'RE BOTH GONE. POOF!
LET THAT BE A LESSON TO US ALL. NEVER DISTURB A GOD WHEN HE'S PLAYING CARDS.
WITH THE EVIL VIZIER GONE, LIFE RETURNED TO NORMAL FOR KING CAT...
WHAT'S ON TODAY'S MENU? PIZZA-STUFFED PITAS!? YUMMY!
OHHHH, GAR-HO-TEP!!
I'VE COME TO VISIT YOU, OH ANCIENT AND FLABBY ONE!
NER-MAL-TEP!
AGH! THE WORST PLAGUE OF ALL!!
THE END

PART 2

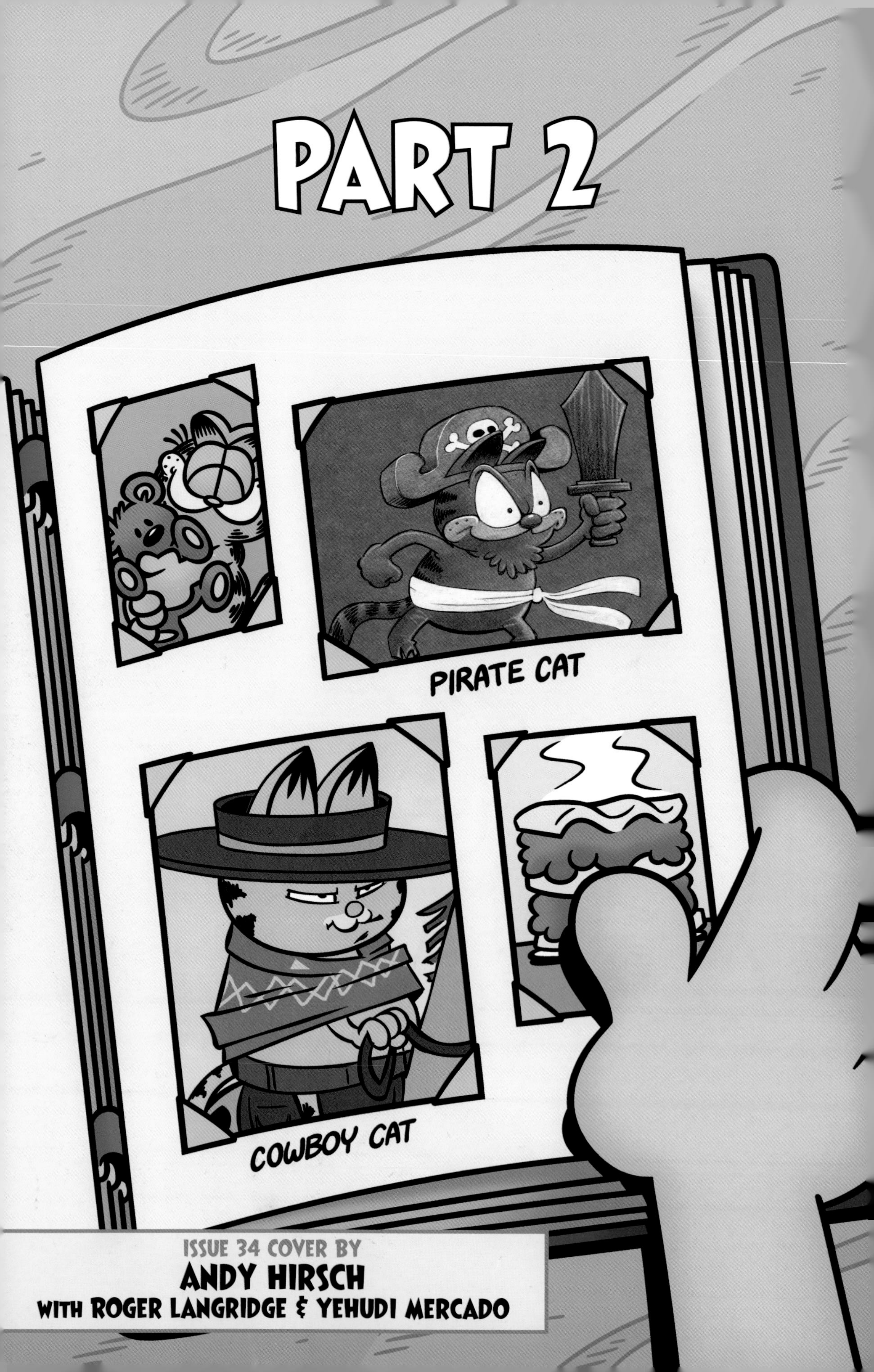
PIRATE CAT
COWBOY CAT

ISSUE 34 COVER BY
ANDY HIRSCH
WITH ROGER LANGRIDGE & YEHUDI MERCADO

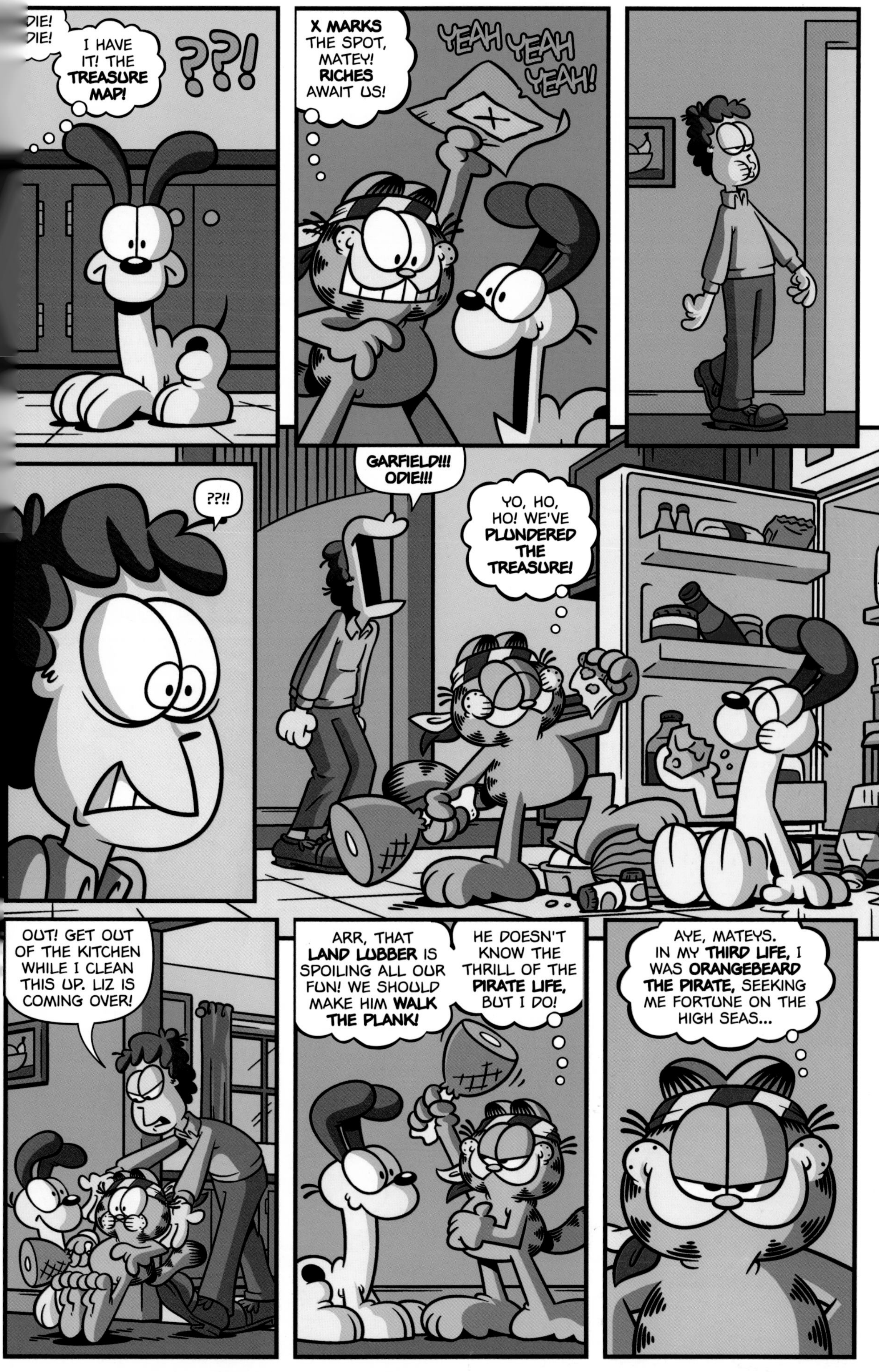
DIE!
DIE!
I HAVE IT! THE TREASURE MAP!
??!
X MARKS THE SPOT, MATEY! RICHES AWAIT US!
YEAH YEAH YEAH!
??!!
GARFIELD!!! ODIE!!!
YO, HO, HO! WE'VE PLUNDERED THE TREASURE!
OUT! GET OUT OF THE KITCHEN WHILE I CLEAN THIS UP. LIZ IS COMING OVER!
ARR, THAT LAND LUBBER IS SPOILING ALL OUR FUN! WE SHOULD MAKE HIM WALK THE PLANK!
HE DOESN'T KNOW THE THRILL OF THE PIRATE LIFE, BUT I DO!
AYE, MATEYS. IN MY THIRD LIFE, I WAS ORANGEBEARD THE PIRATE, SEEKING ME FORTUNE ON THE HIGH SEAS...

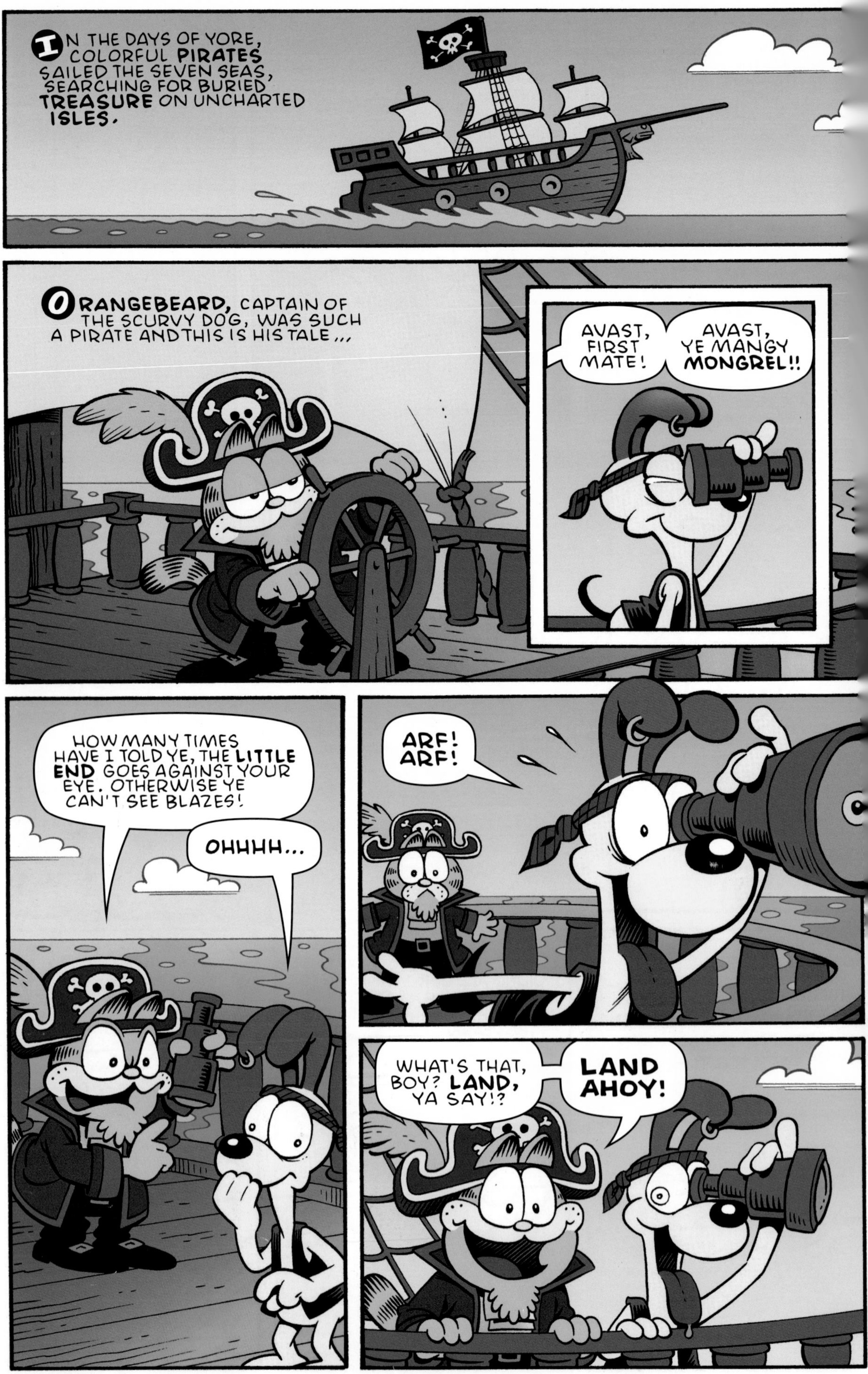

IN THE DAYS OF YORE, COLORFUL **PIRATES** SAILED THE SEVEN SEAS, SEARCHING FOR BURIED **TREASURE** ON UNCHARTED **ISLES**.
ORANGEBEARD, CAPTAIN OF THE SCURVY DOG, WAS SUCH A PIRATE AND THIS IS HIS TALE...
AVAST, FIRST MATE!
AVAST, YE MANGY **MONGREL**!!
HOW MANY TIMES HAVE I TOLD YE, THE **LITTLE END** GOES AGAINST YOUR EYE. OTHERWISE YE CAN'T SEE BLAZES!
OHHHH...
ARF! ARF!
WHAT'S THAT, BOY? **LAND**, YA SAY!?
LAND AHOY!

THEN WE'VE FINALLY MADE IT TO THE **ISLAND OF MISFIT TOYS!**

ISLAND of MISFIT TOYS

WAIT! THAT BE THE **WRONG MAP!**

ISLAND of MISFIT TOYS

AH, HERE IT BE! **THE ISLAND OF LOST RICHES!**

FOR YEARS, SEAFARING TYPES SPOKE IN WHISPERS OF THE **FABLED ISLAND** WHERE PRICELESS **TREASURE** — RICHES BEYOND IMAGINATION — WAS **BURIED.**

ISLAND of LOST RICHES

"I **WON** THE MAP **FAIR AND SQUARE** IN A POKER GAME AGAINST **LONG JON SLIVER...**"

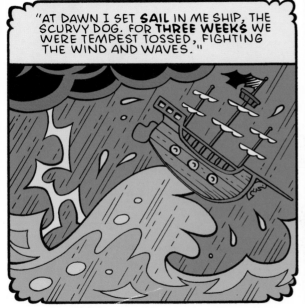

"AT DAWN I SET **SAIL** IN ME SHIP, THE **SCURVY DOG**. FOR **THREE WEEKS** WE WERE TEMPEST TOSSED, FIGHTING THE WIND AND WAVES."

NOW, AT **LAST,** THAT TREASURE WILL BE **MINE!**

CAPTAIN ORANGEBEARD? WHY ARE YOU **TALKING TO YOURSELF?**

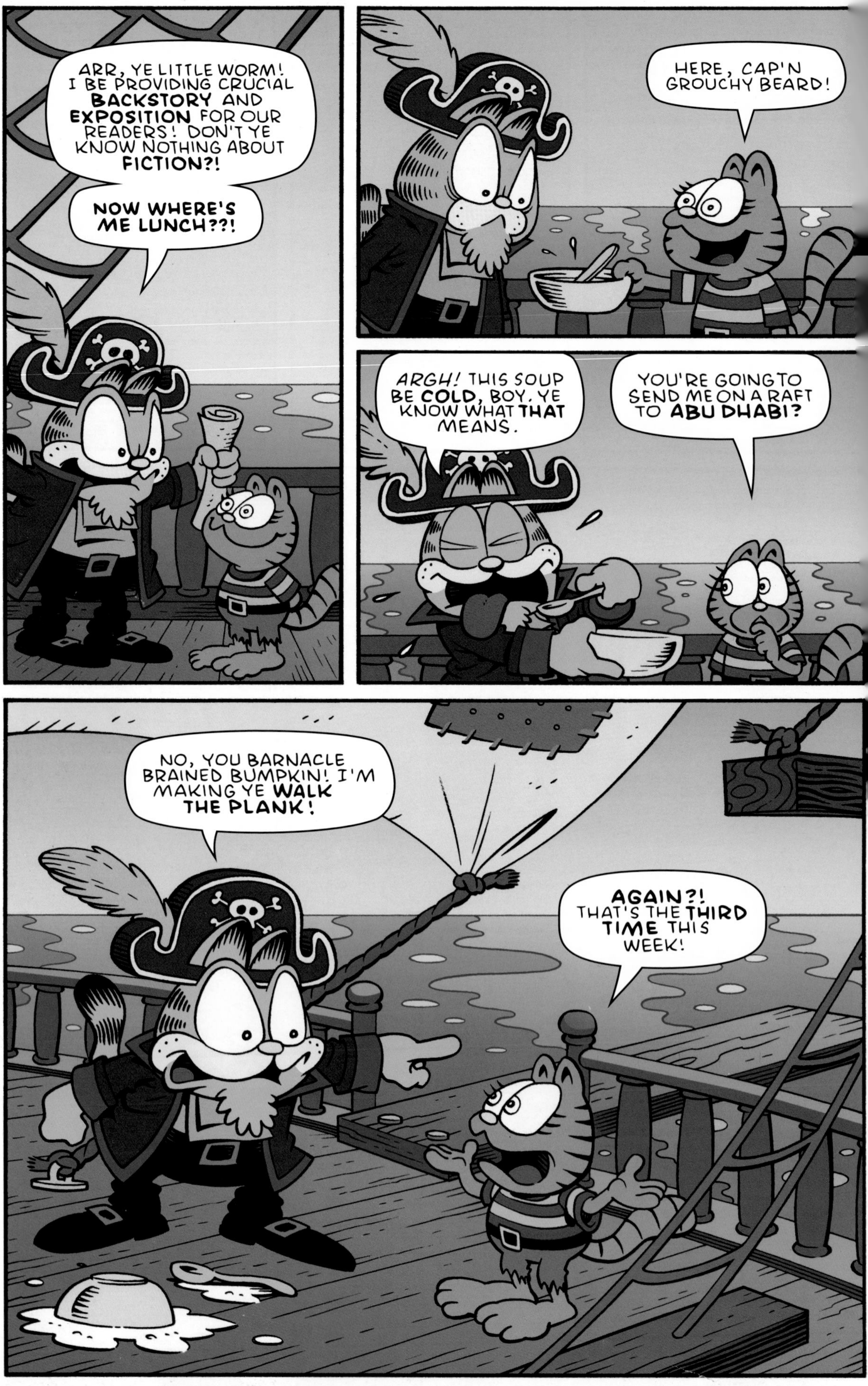
ARR, YE LITTLE WORM! I BE PROVIDING CRUCIAL BACKSTORY AND EXPOSITION FOR OUR READERS! DON'T YE KNOW NOTHING ABOUT FICTION?!
NOW WHERE'S ME LUNCH??!
HERE, CAP'N GROUCHY BEARD!
ARGH! THIS SOUP BE COLD, BOY. YE KNOW WHAT THAT MEANS.
YOU'RE GOING TO SEND ME ON A RAFT TO ABU DHABI?
NO, YOU BARNACLE BRAINED BUMPKIN! I'M MAKING YE WALK THE PLANK!
AGAIN?! THAT'S THE THIRD TIME THIS WEEK!

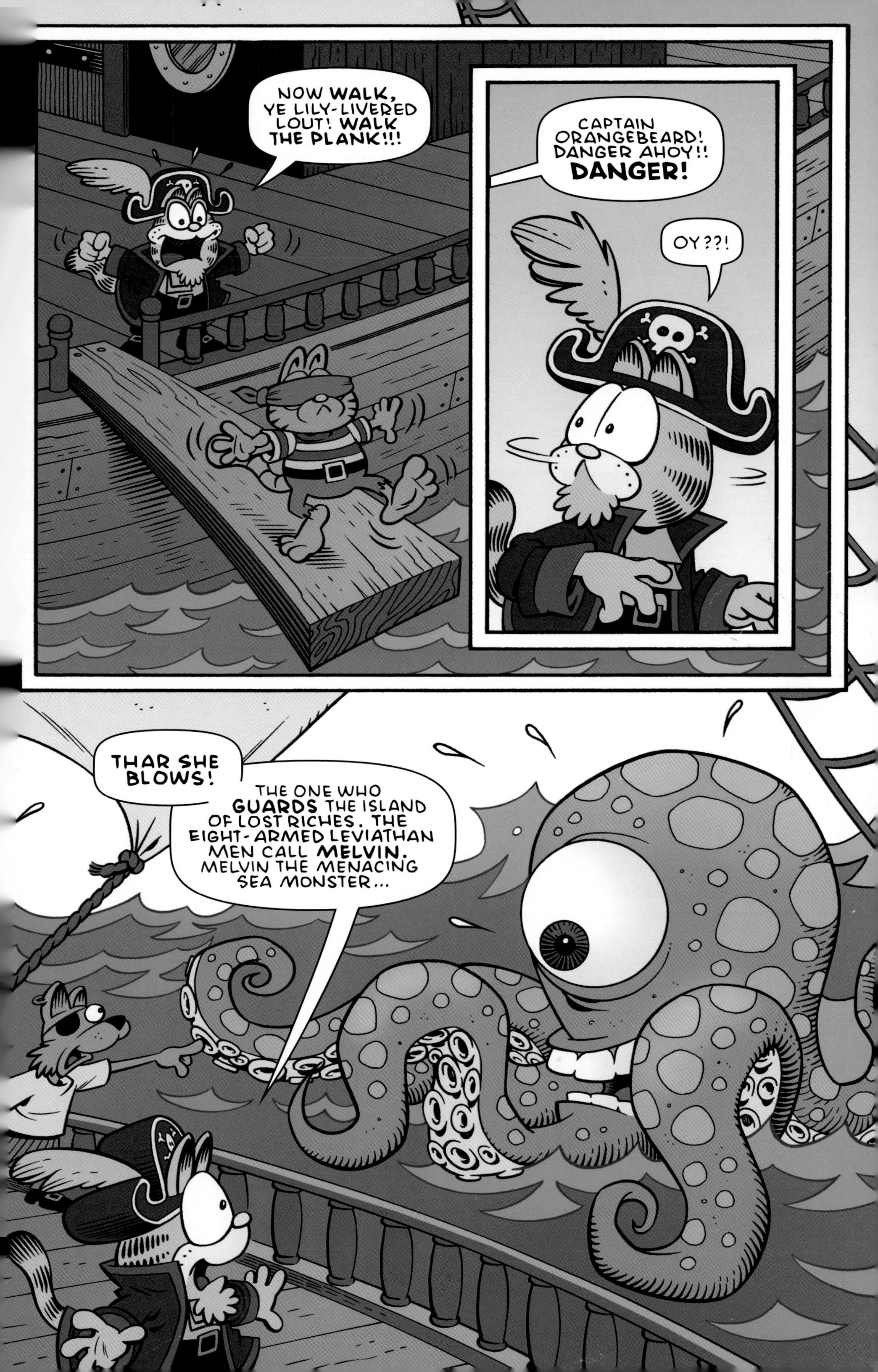
NOW WALK, YE LILY-LIVERED LOUT! WALK THE PLANK!!!
CAPTAIN ORANGEBEARD! DANGER AHOY!! DANGER!
OY??!
THAR SHE BLOWS!
THE ONE WHO GUARDS THE ISLAND OF LOST RICHES. THE EIGHT-ARMED LEVIATHAN MEN CALL MELVIN. MELVIN THE MENACING SEA MONSTER...

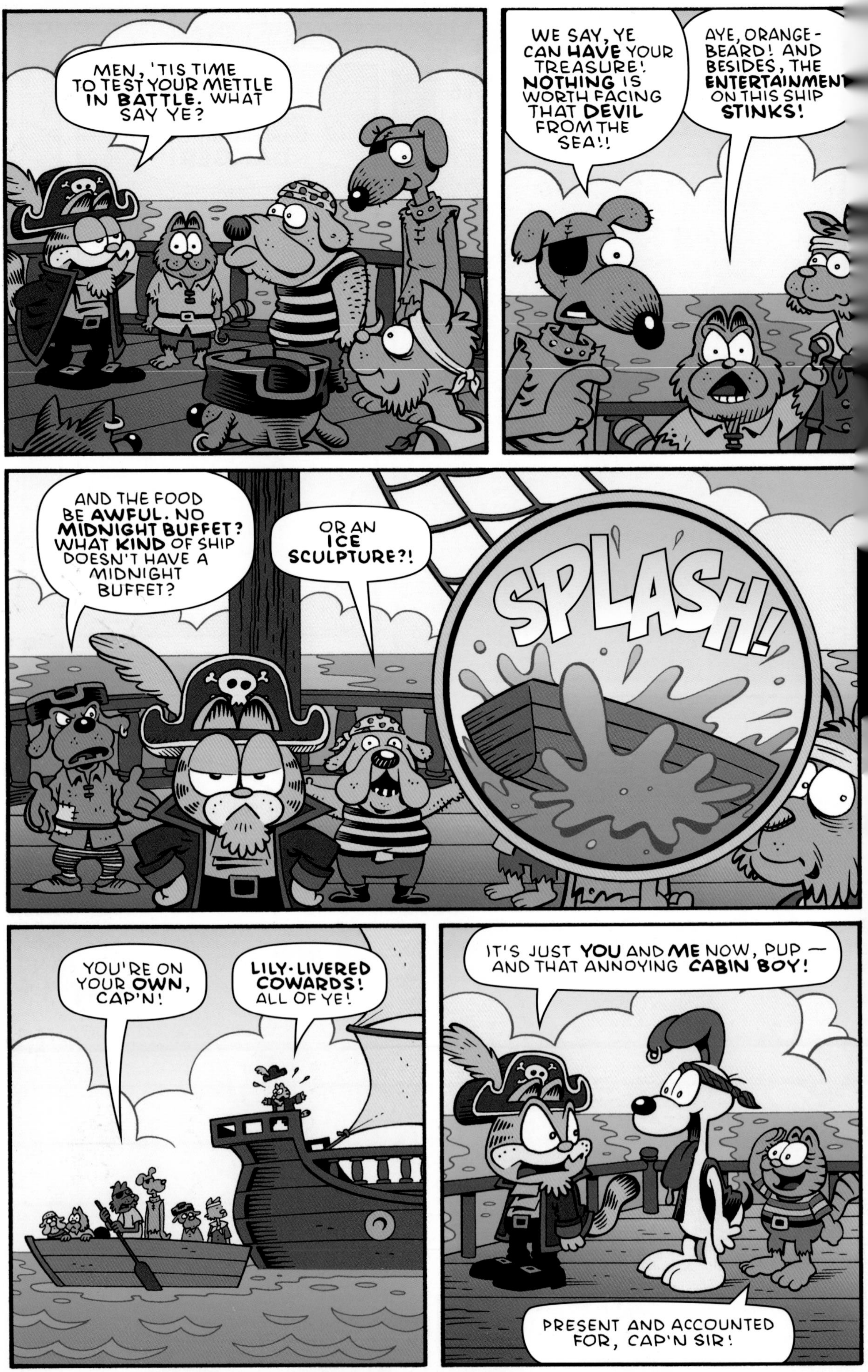

MEN, 'TIS TIME TO TEST YOUR METTLE IN BATTLE. WHAT SAY YE?
WE SAY, YE CAN HAVE YOUR TREASURE! NOTHING IS WORTH FACING THAT DEVIL FROM THE SEA!!
AYE, ORANGE-BEARD! AND BESIDES, THE ENTERTAINMENT ON THIS SHIP STINKS!
AND THE FOOD BE AWFUL. NO MIDNIGHT BUFFET? WHAT KIND OF SHIP DOESN'T HAVE A MIDNIGHT BUFFET?
OR AN ICE SCULPTURE?!
SPLASH!
YOU'RE ON YOUR OWN, CAP'N!
LILY-LIVERED COWARDS! ALL OF YE!
IT'S JUST YOU AND ME NOW, PUP — AND THAT ANNOYING CABIN BOY!
PRESENT AND ACCOUNTED FOR, CAP'N SIR!

WE'RE SAILING **RIGHT FOR** THAT EIGHT-ARMED DEMON OF THE DEEP!

AVAST!!!

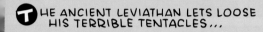
THE ANCIENT LEVIATHAN LETS LOOSE HIS TERRIBLE TENTACLES...

RRRAWRR!

... SNARING THE SCURVY DOG AND ITS COWERING CREW OF THREE.

FLING!

WITH GREAT MENACE — OR GREAT STUPIDITY — MELVIN HURLS THE PIRATE SHIP...

... WHICH SAILS THROUGH THE AIR...

SAIL!

YAAAAAGHH!

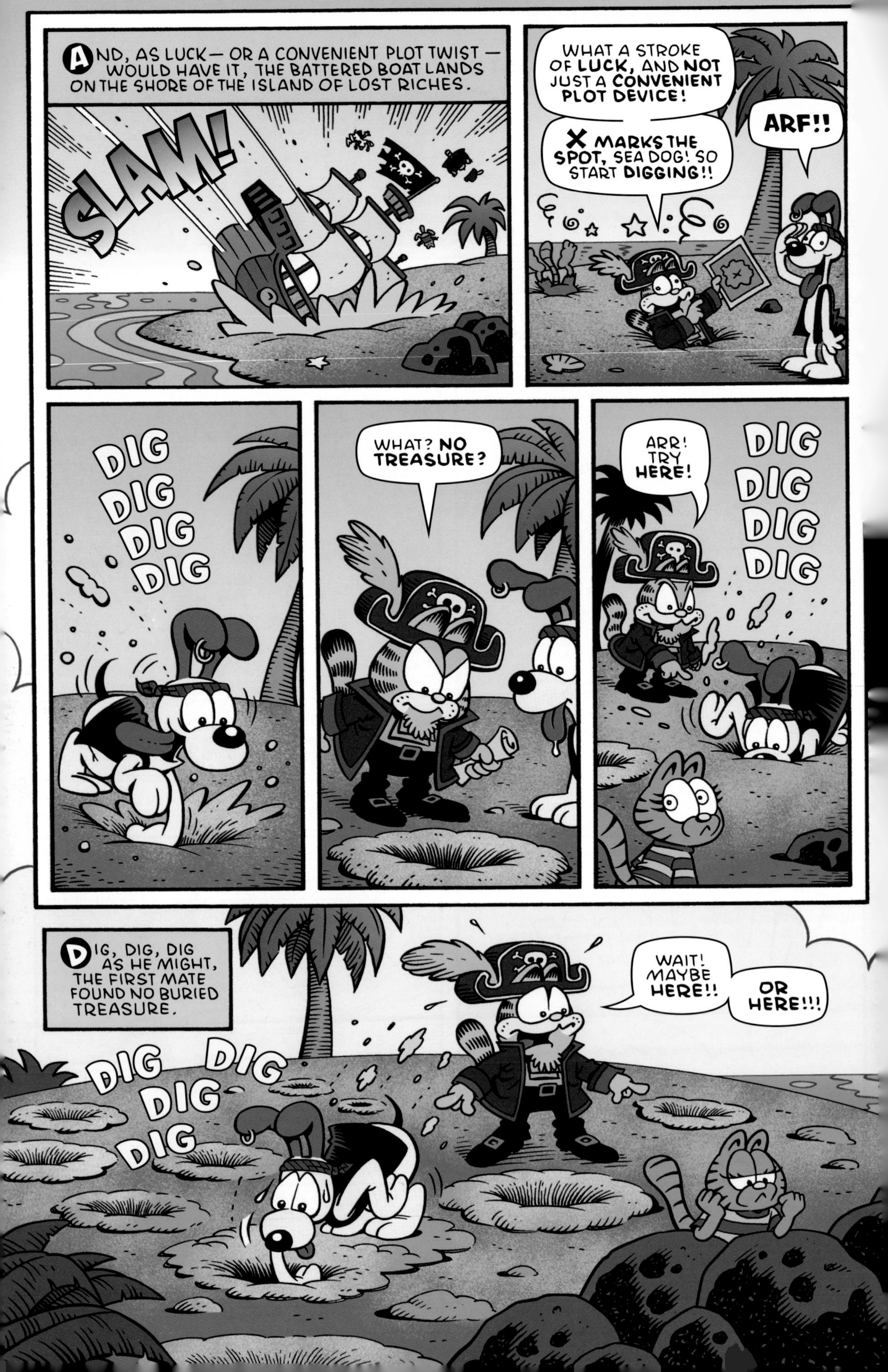
AND, AS LUCK— OR A CONVENIENT PLOT TWIST — WOULD HAVE IT, THE BATTERED BOAT LANDS ON THE SHORE OF THE ISLAND OF LOST RICHES.
SLAM!
WHAT A STROKE OF LUCK, AND NOT JUST A CONVENIENT PLOT DEVICE!
X MARKS THE SPOT, SEA DOG! SO START DIGGING!!
ARF!!
DIG DIG DIG DIG
WHAT? NO TREASURE?
ARR! TRY HERE!
DIG DIG DIG DIG
DIG, DIG, DIG AS HE MIGHT, THE FIRST MATE FOUND NO BURIED TREASURE.
DIG DIG DIG DIG
WAIT! MAYBE HERE!!
OR HERE!!!

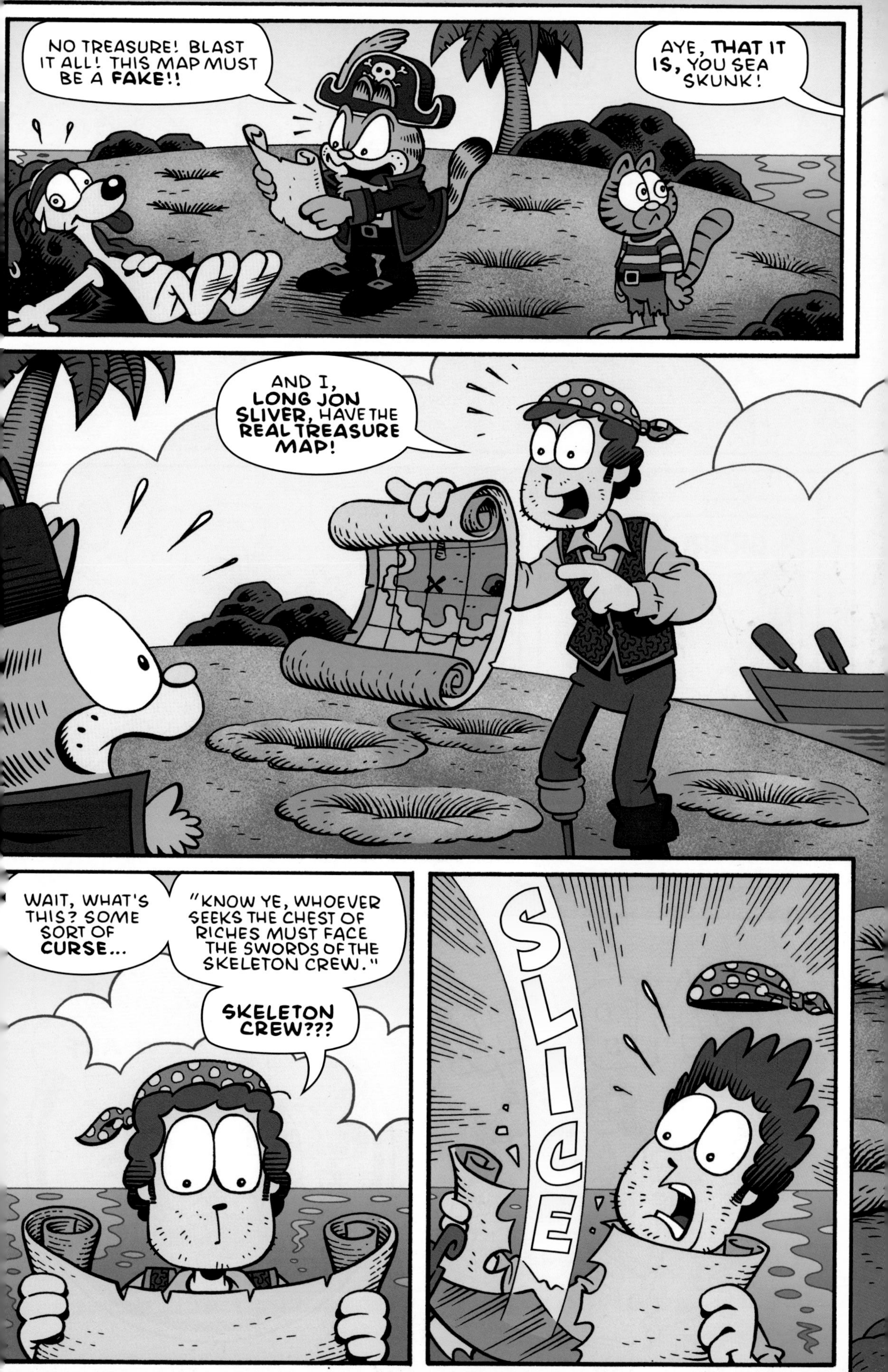
NO TREASURE! BLAST IT ALL! THIS MAP MUST BE A **FAKE!!**
AYE, **THAT IT IS,** YOU SEA SKUNK!
AND I, **LONG JON SLIVER,** HAVE THE **REAL TREASURE MAP!**
WAIT, WHAT'S THIS? SOME SORT OF **CURSE...**
"KNOW YE, WHOEVER SEEKS THE CHEST OF RICHES MUST FACE THE SWORDS OF THE SKELETON CREW."
SKELETON CREW???
SLICE

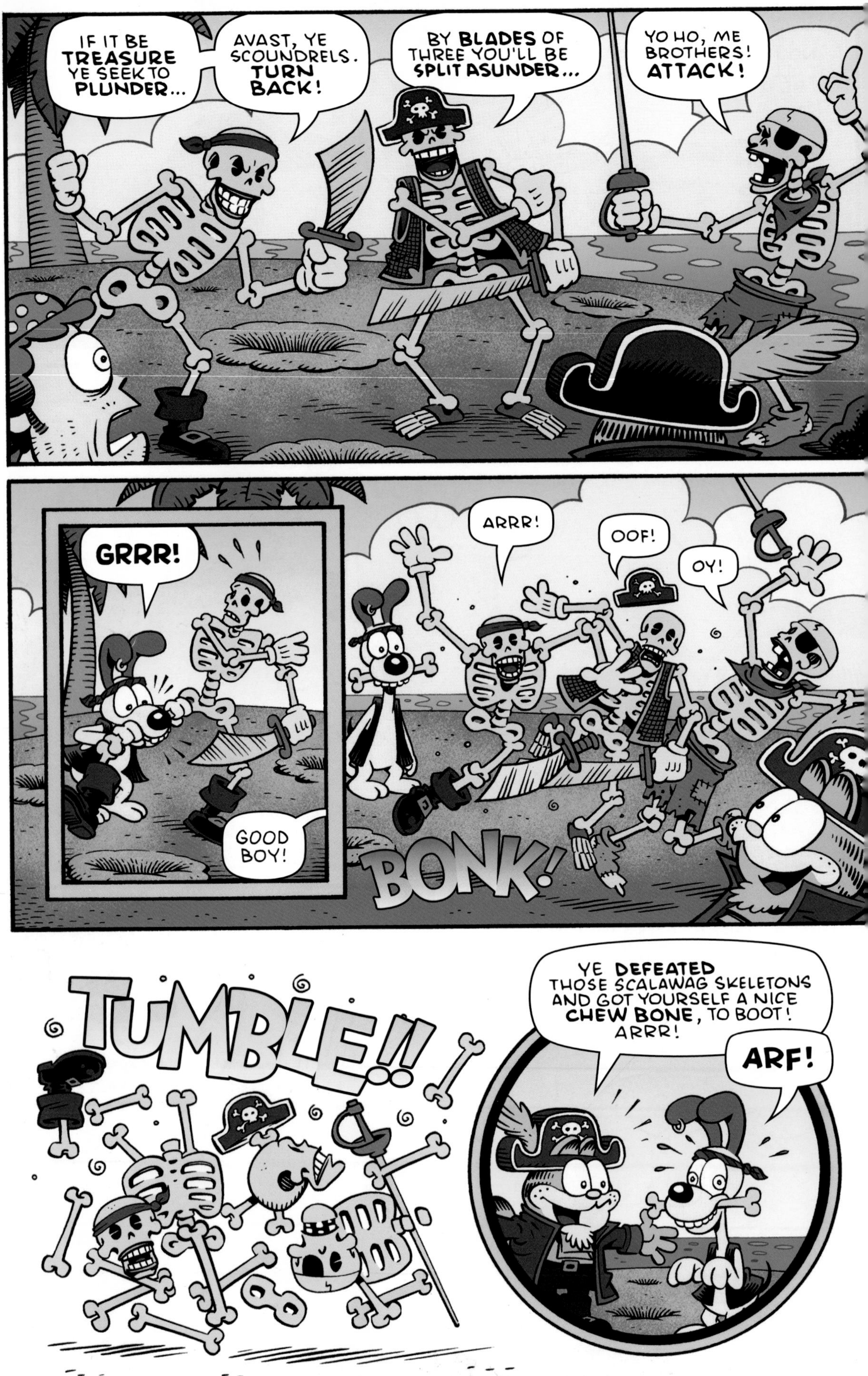

IF IT BE TREASURE YE SEEK TO PLUNDER...
AVAST, YE SCOUNDRELS. TURN BACK!
BY BLADES OF THREE YOU'LL BE SPLIT ASUNDER...
YO HO, ME BROTHERS! ATTACK!
GRRR!
GOOD BOY!
ARRR!
OOF!
OY!
BONK!
TUMBLE!!
YE DEFEATED THOSE SCALAWAG SKELETONS AND GOT YOURSELF A NICE CHEW BONE, TO BOOT! ARRR!
ARF!

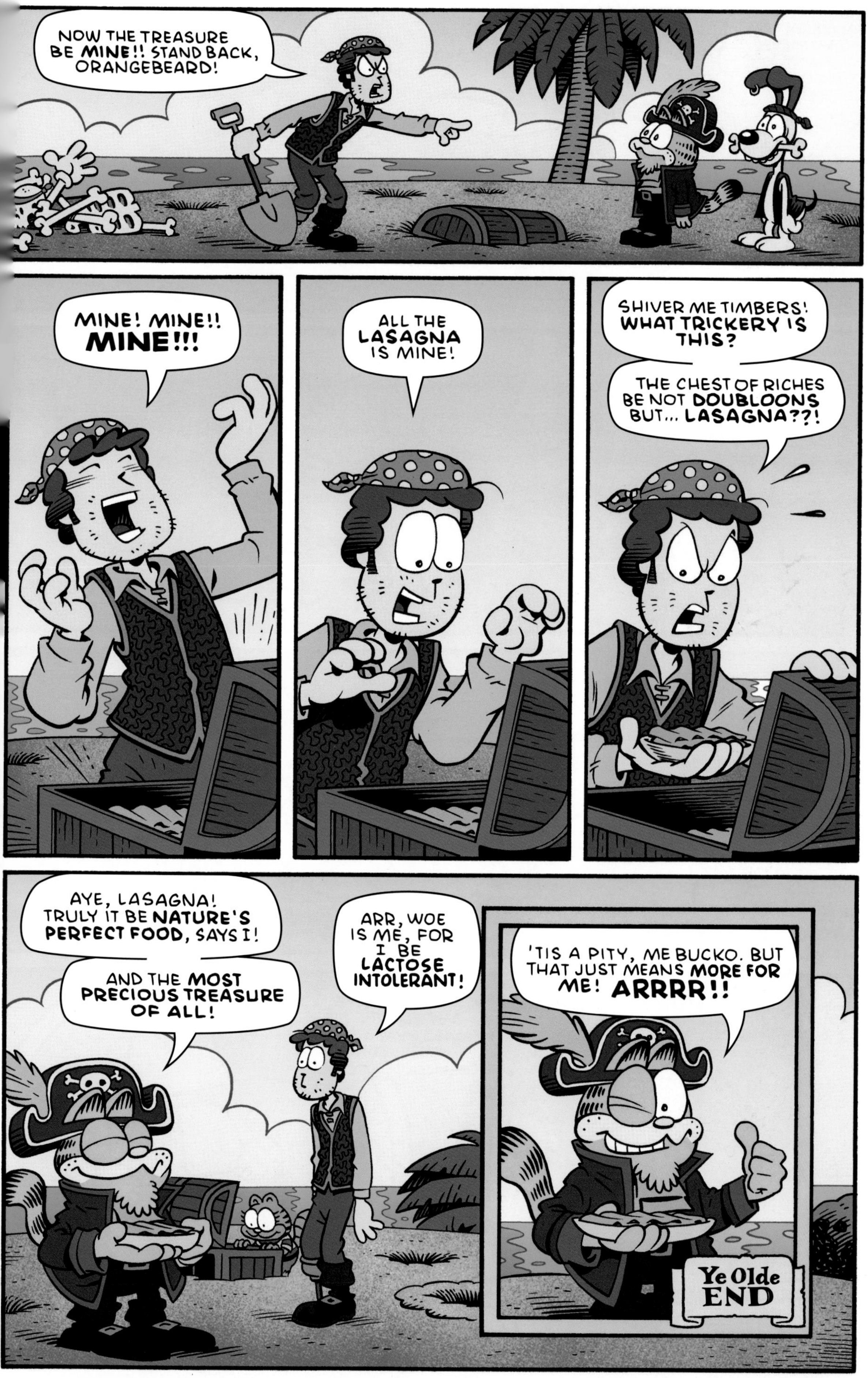
NOW THE TREASURE BE MINE!! STAND BACK, ORANGEBEARD!
MINE! MINE!! MINE!!!
ALL THE LASAGNA IS MINE!
SHIVER ME TIMBERS! WHAT TRICKERY IS THIS?
THE CHEST OF RICHES BE NOT DOUBLOONS BUT... LASAGNA??!
AYE, LASAGNA! TRULY IT BE NATURE'S PERFECT FOOD, SAYS I!
AND THE MOST PRECIOUS TREASURE OF ALL!
ARR, WOE IS ME, FOR I BE LACTOSE INTOLERANT!
'TIS A PITY, ME BUCKO. BUT THAT JUST MEANS MORE FOR ME! ARRRR!!
Ye Olde END

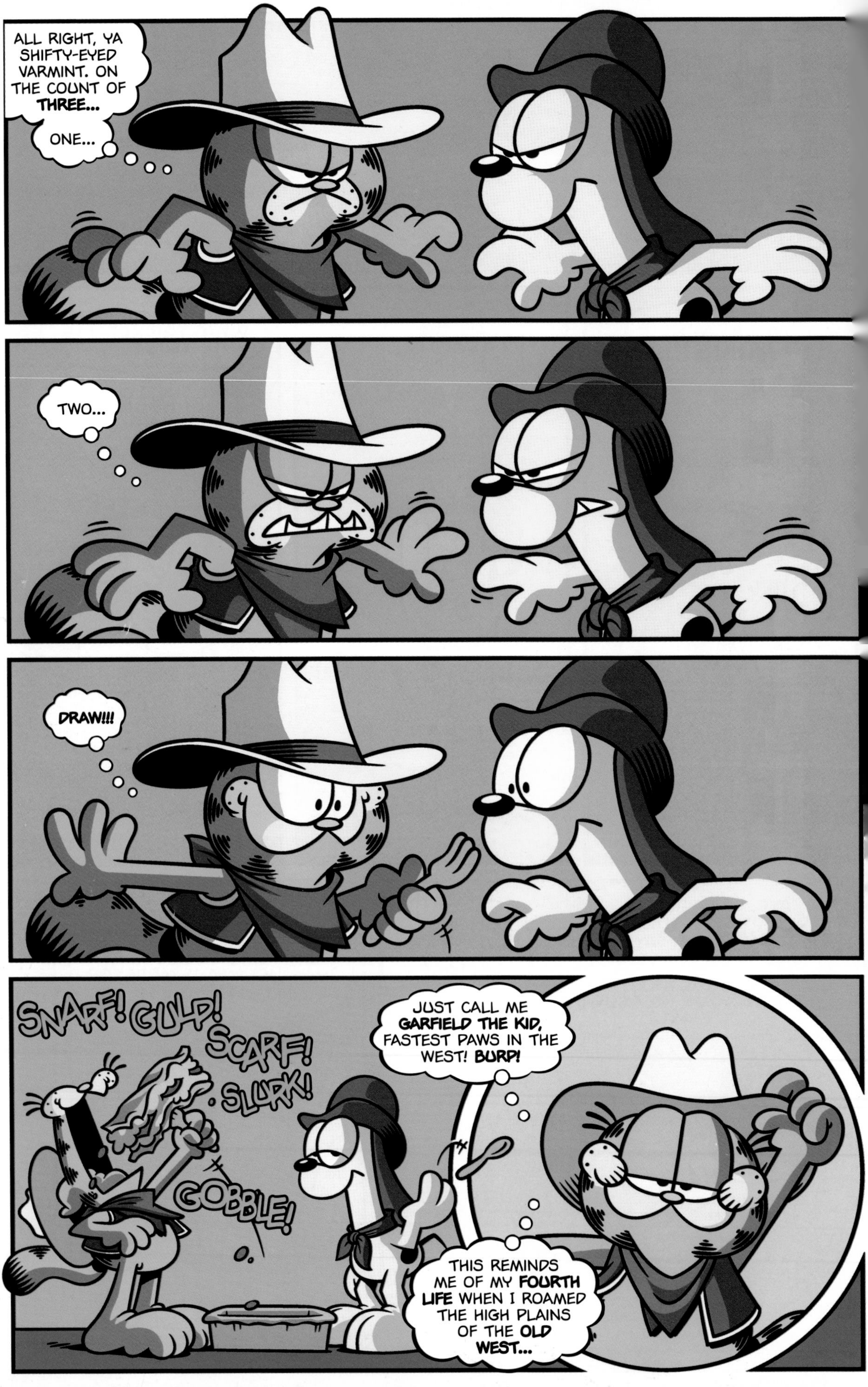
ALL RIGHT, YA SHIFTY-EYED VARMINT. ON THE COUNT OF THREE...
ONE...
TWO...
DRAW!!!
SNARF! GULP!
SCARF!
SLURK!
GOBBLE!
JUST CALL ME GARFIELD THE KID, FASTEST PAWS IN THE WEST! BURP!
THIS REMINDS ME OF MY FOURTH LIFE WHEN I ROAMED THE HIGH PLAINS OF THE OLD WEST...

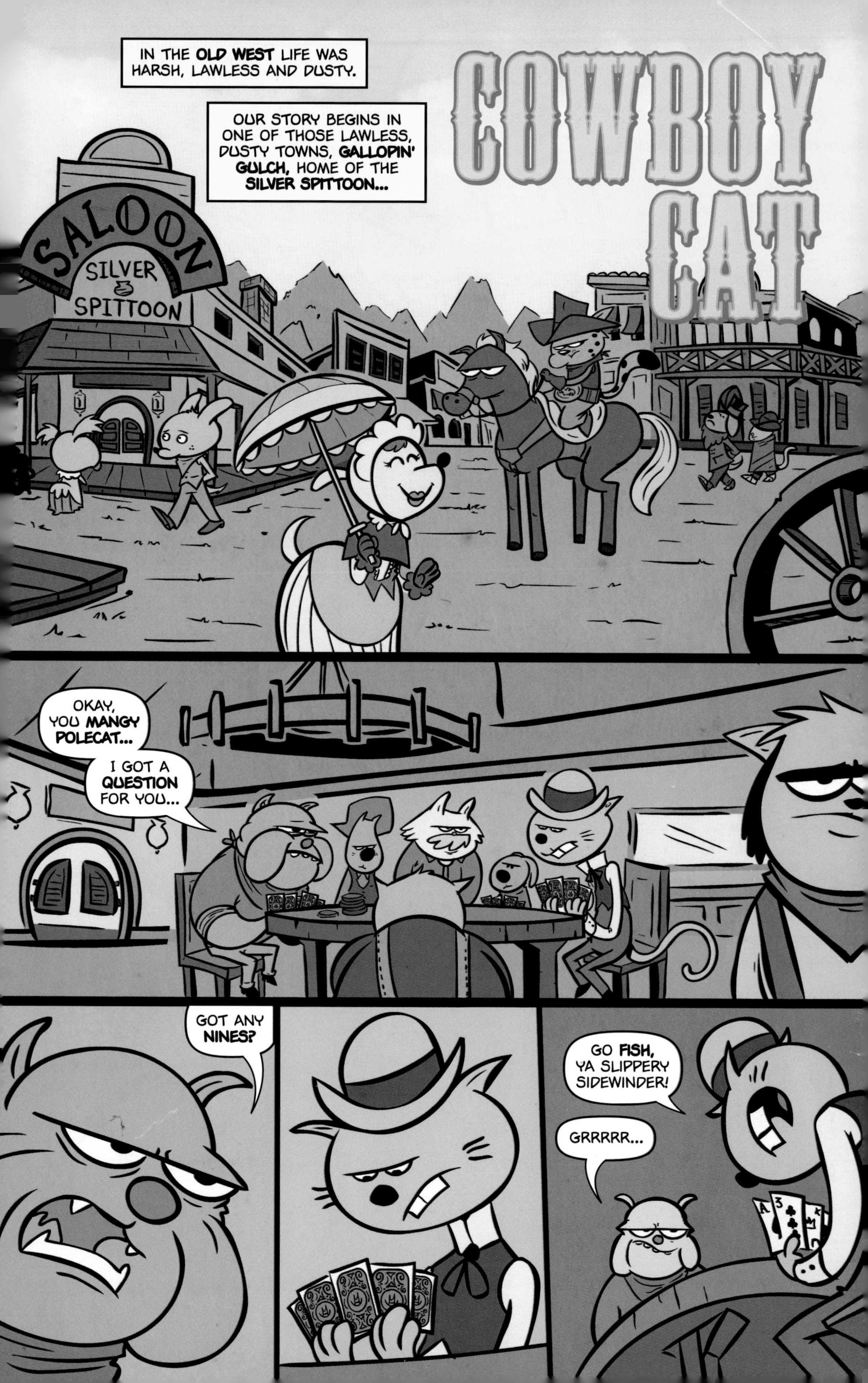
IN THE OLD WEST LIFE WAS HARSH, LAWLESS AND DUSTY.
COWBOY CAT
OUR STORY BEGINS IN ONE OF THOSE LAWLESS, DUSTY TOWNS, GALLOPIN' GULCH, HOME OF THE SILVER SPITTOON...
SALOON
SILVER & SPITTOON
OKAY, YOU MANGY POLECAT...
I GOT A QUESTION FOR YOU...
GOT ANY NINES?
GO FISH, YA SLIPPERY SIDEWINDER!
GRRRRR...

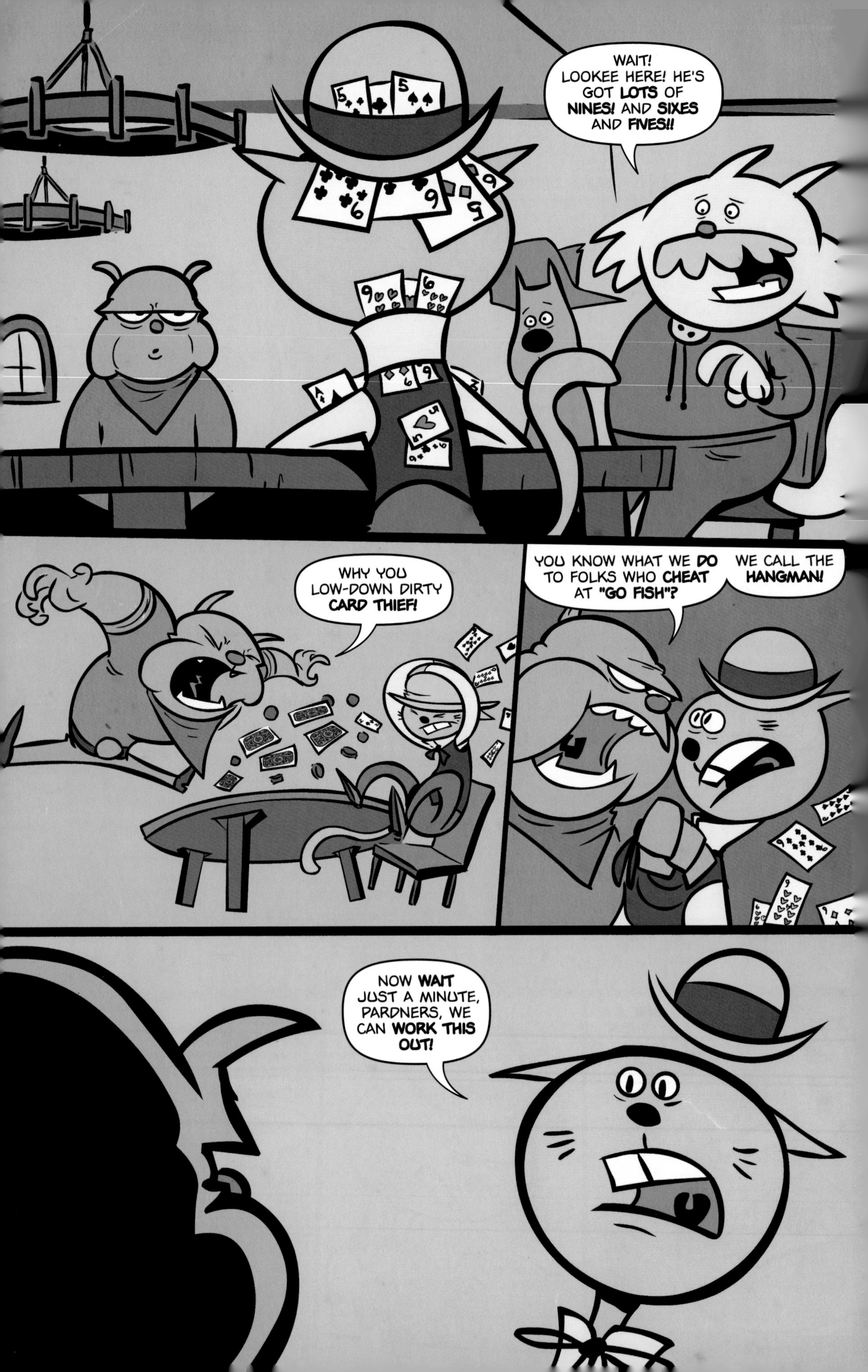
WAIT! LOOKEE HERE! HE'S GOT LOTS OF NINES! AND SIXES AND FIVES!!
WHY YOU LOW-DOWN DIRTY CARD THIEF!
YOU KNOW WHAT WE DO TO FOLKS WHO CHEAT AT "GO FISH"?
WE CALL THE HANGMAN!
NOW WAIT JUST A MINUTE, PARDNERS, WE CAN WORK THIS OUT!

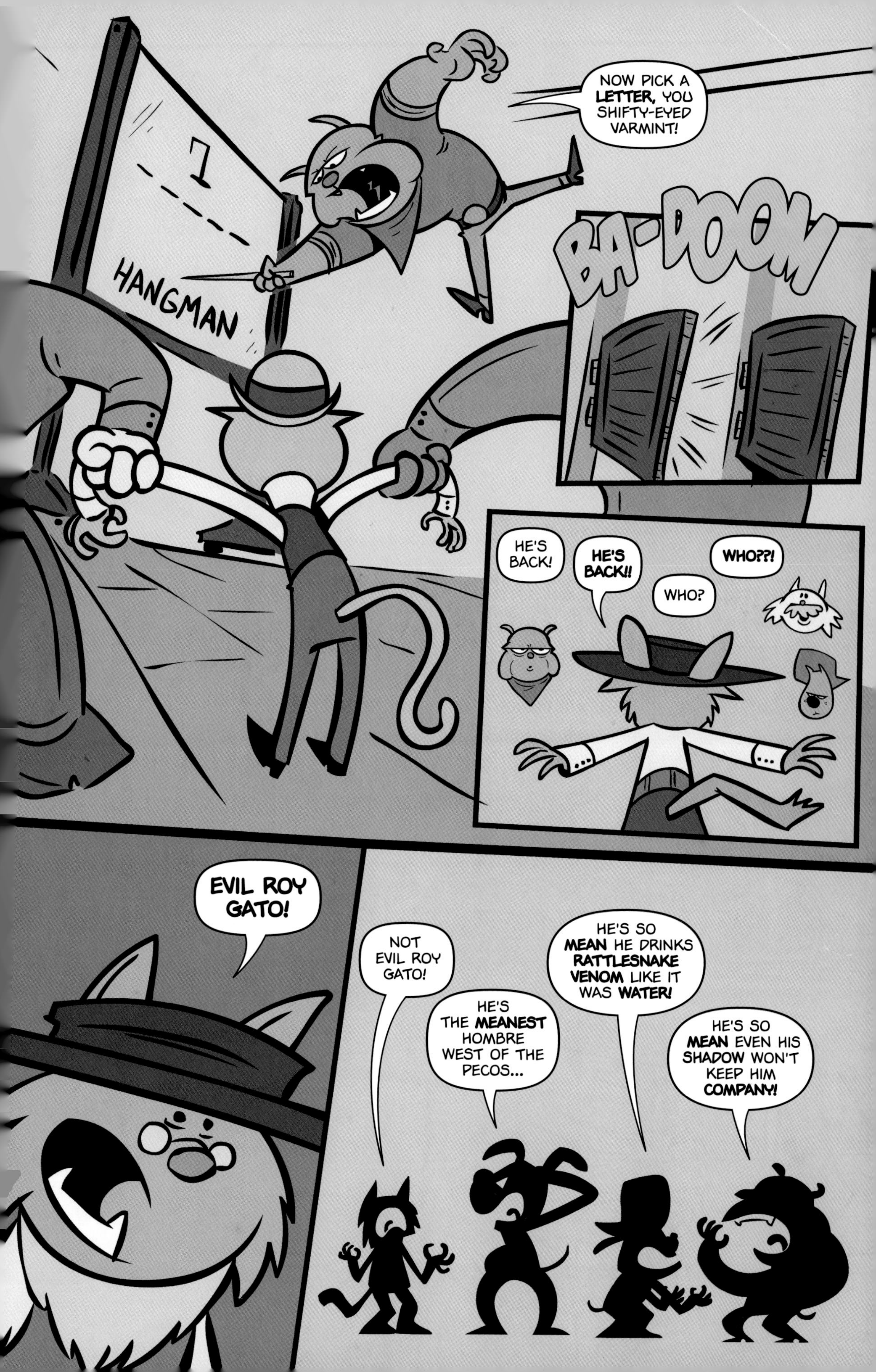

HANGMAN
NOW PICK A LETTER, YOU SHIFTY-EYED VARMINT!
BA-DOOM
HE'S BACK!
HE'S BACK!!
WHO?
WHO??!
EVIL ROY GATO!
NOT EVIL ROY GATO!
HE'S THE MEANEST HOMBRE WEST OF THE PECOS...
HE'S SO MEAN HE DRINKS RATTLESNAKE VENOM LIKE IT WAS WATER!
HE'S SO MEAN EVEN HIS SHADOW WON'T KEEP HIM COMPANY!

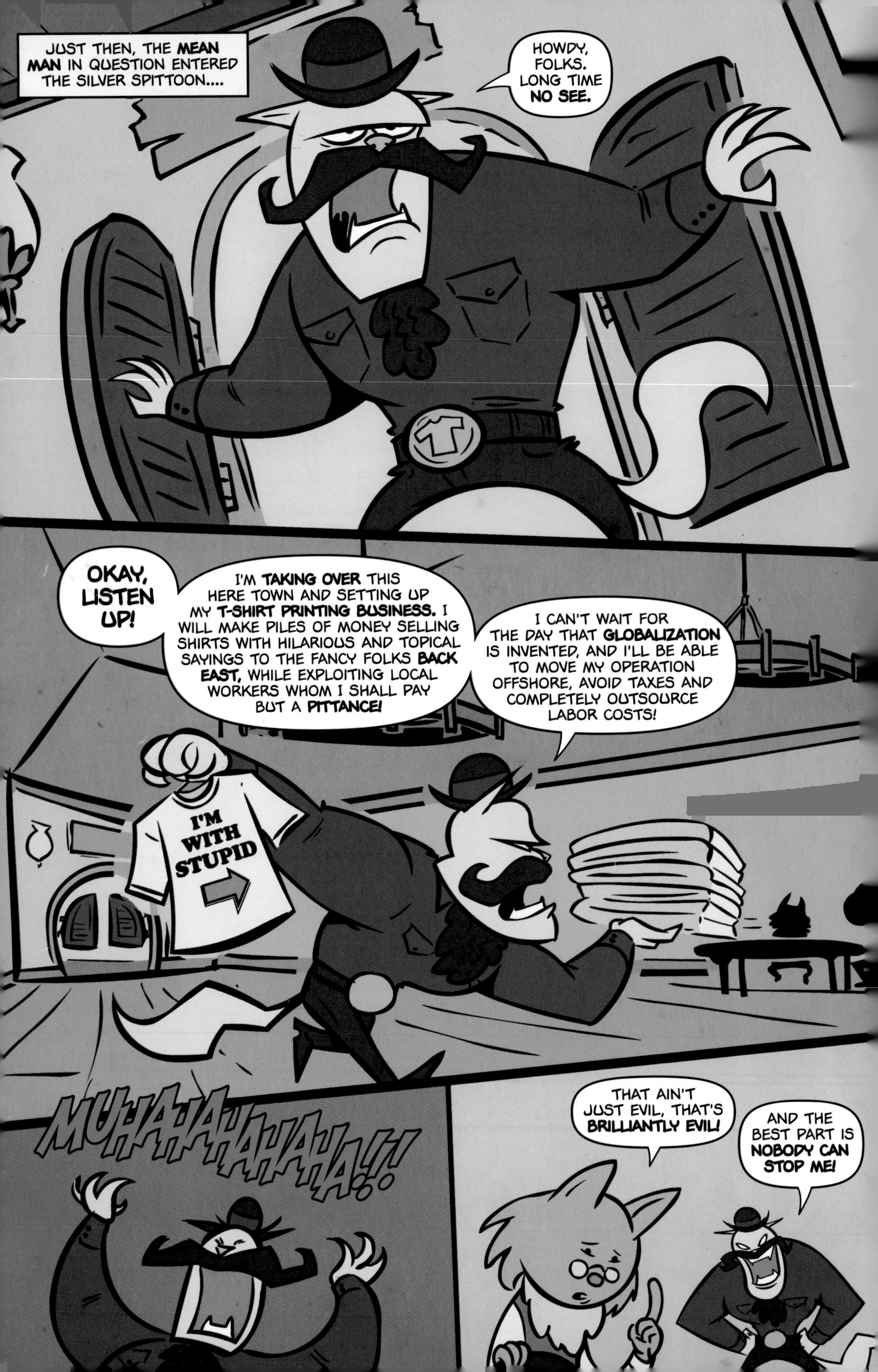
JUST THEN, THE MEAN MAN IN QUESTION ENTERED THE SILVER SPITTOON....
HOWDY, FOLKS. LONG TIME NO SEE.
OKAY, LISTEN UP!
I'M TAKING OVER THIS HERE TOWN AND SETTING UP MY T-SHIRT PRINTING BUSINESS. I WILL MAKE PILES OF MONEY SELLING SHIRTS WITH HILARIOUS AND TOPICAL SAYINGS TO THE FANCY FOLKS BACK EAST, WHILE EXPLOITING LOCAL WORKERS WHOM I SHALL PAY BUT A PITTANCE!
I CAN'T WAIT FOR THE DAY THAT GLOBALIZATION IS INVENTED, AND I'LL BE ABLE TO MOVE MY OPERATION OFFSHORE, AVOID TAXES AND COMPLETELY OUTSOURCE LABOR COSTS!
I'M WITH STUPID
MUHAHAHAHAHAHA!!!
THAT AIN'T JUST EVIL, THAT'S BRILLIANTLY EVIL!
AND THE BEST PART IS NOBODY CAN STOP ME!

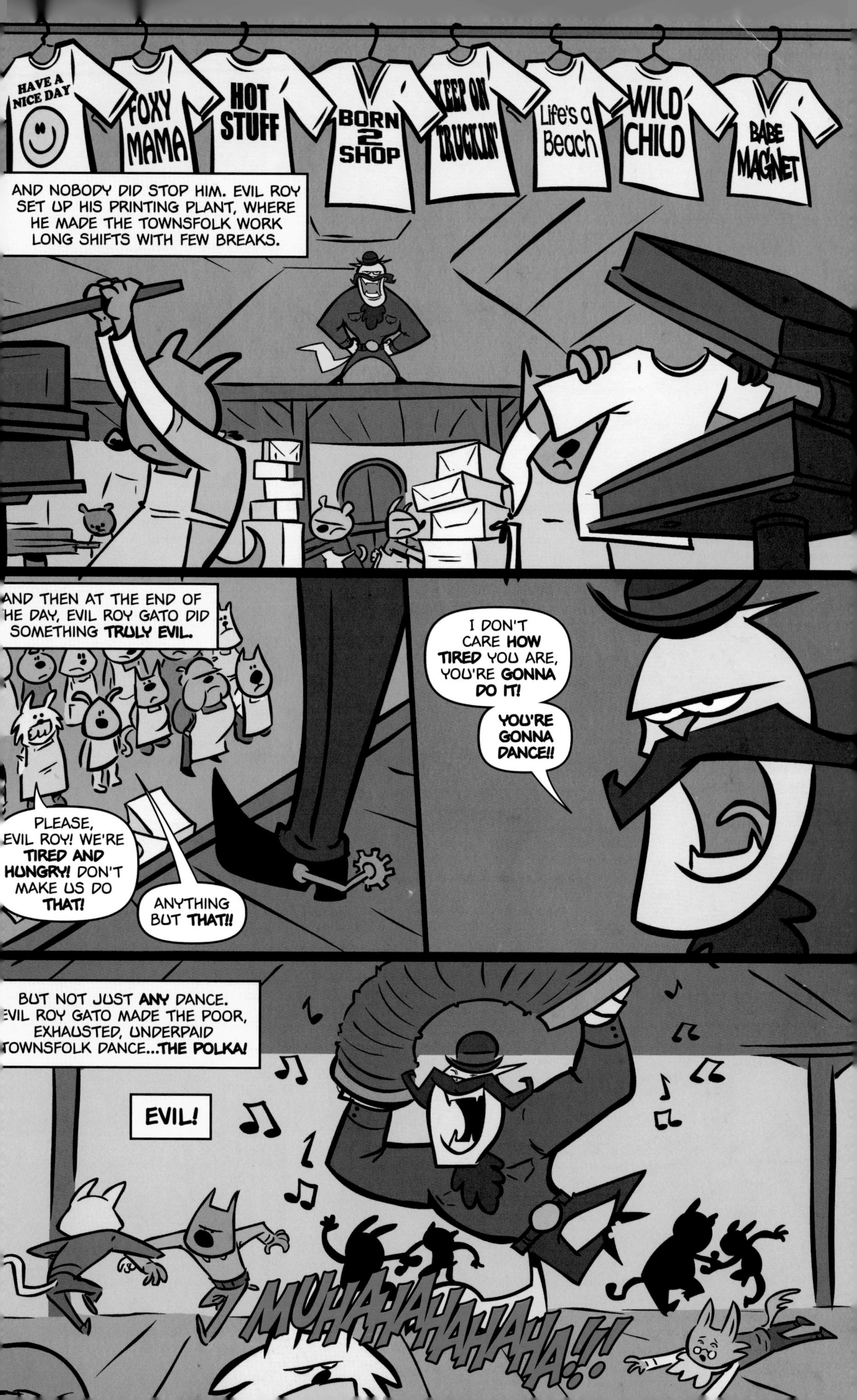
HAVE A NICE DAY
FOXY MAMA
HOT STUFF
BORN 2 SHOP
KEEP ON TRUCKIN'
Life's a Beach
WILD CHILD
BABE MAGNET
AND NOBODY DID STOP HIM. EVIL ROY SET UP HIS PRINTING PLANT, WHERE HE MADE THE TOWNSFOLK WORK LONG SHIFTS WITH FEW BREAKS.
AND THEN AT THE END OF THE DAY, EVIL ROY GATO DID SOMETHING TRULY EVIL.
PLEASE, EVIL ROY! WE'RE TIRED AND HUNGRY! DON'T MAKE US DO THAT!
ANYTHING BUT THAT!!
I DON'T CARE HOW TIRED YOU ARE, YOU'RE GONNA DO IT!
YOU'RE GONNA DANCE!!
BUT NOT JUST ANY DANCE. EVIL ROY GATO MADE THE POOR, EXHAUSTED, UNDERPAID TOWNSFOLK DANCE...THE POLKA!
EVIL!
MUHAHAHAHAHAHA!!!

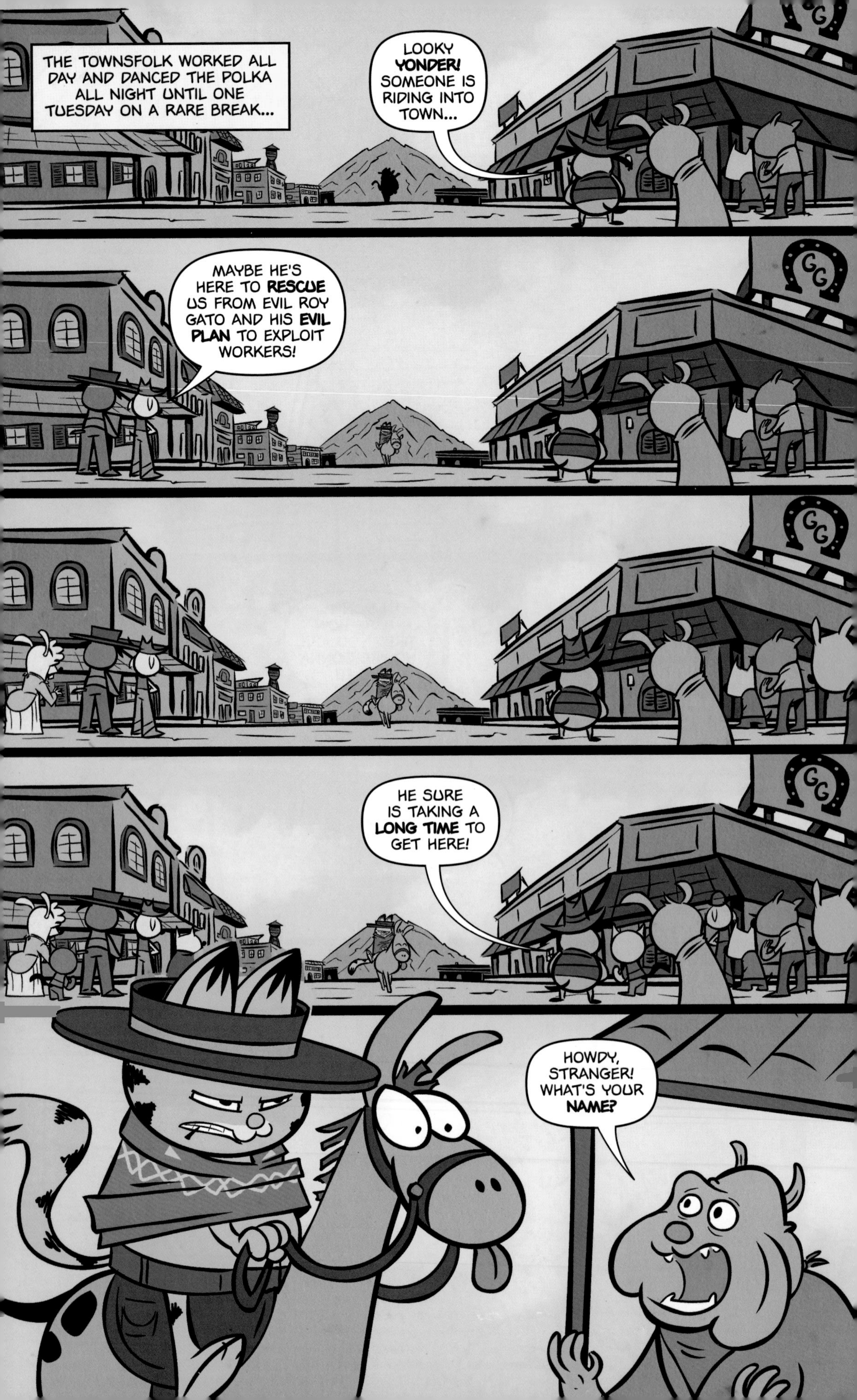
THE TOWNSFOLK WORKED ALL DAY AND DANCED THE POLKA ALL NIGHT UNTIL ONE TUESDAY ON A RARE BREAK...
LOOKY YONDER! SOMEONE IS RIDING INTO TOWN...
MAYBE HE'S HERE TO RESCUE US FROM EVIL ROY GATO AND HIS EVIL PLAN TO EXPLOIT WORKERS!
HE SURE IS TAKING A LONG TIME TO GET HERE!
HOWDY, STRANGER! WHAT'S YOUR NAME?

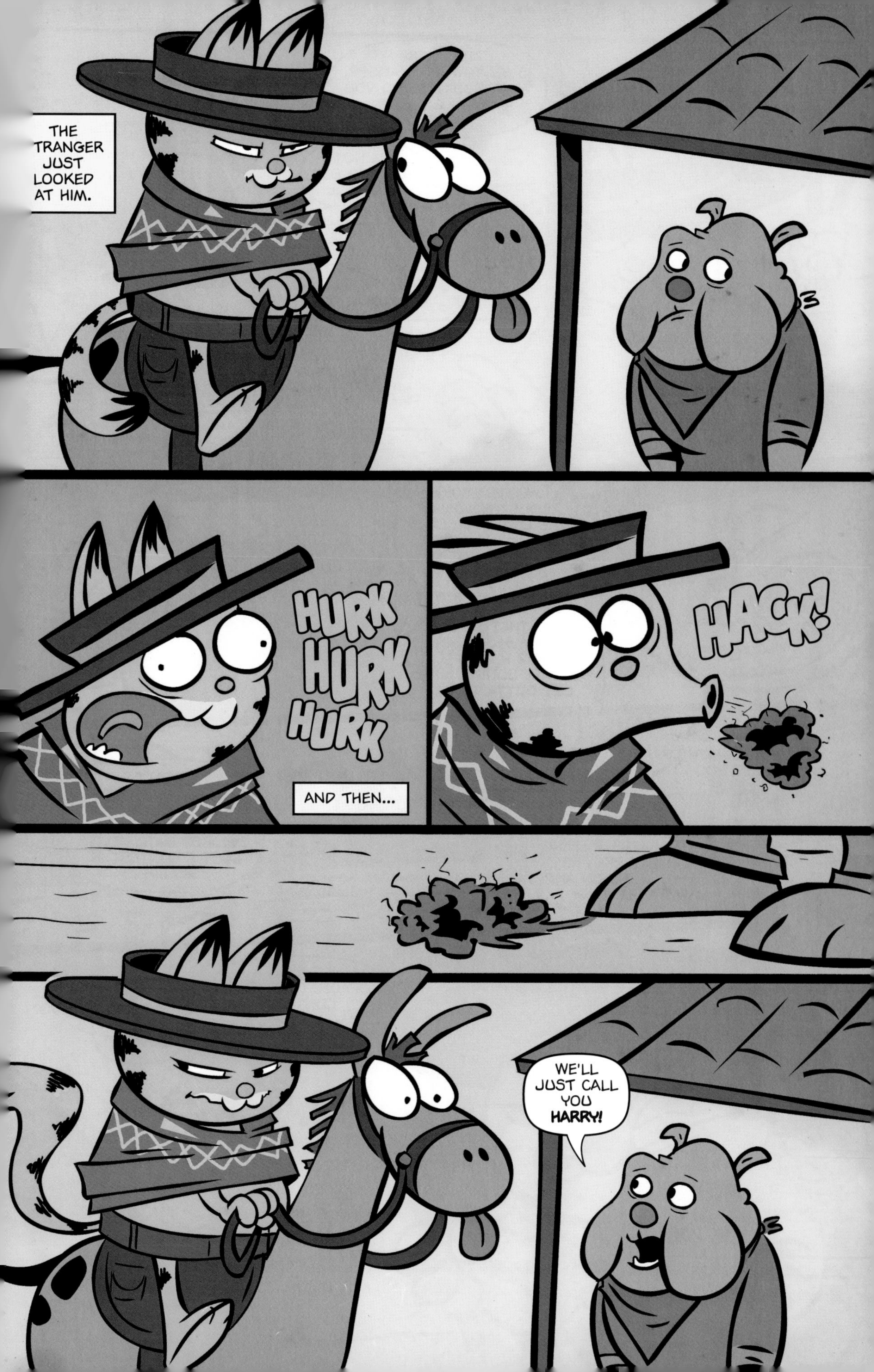
THE TRANGER JUST LOOKED AT HIM.
HURK HURK HURK
AND THEN...
HACK!
WE'LL JUST CALL YOU **HARRY!**

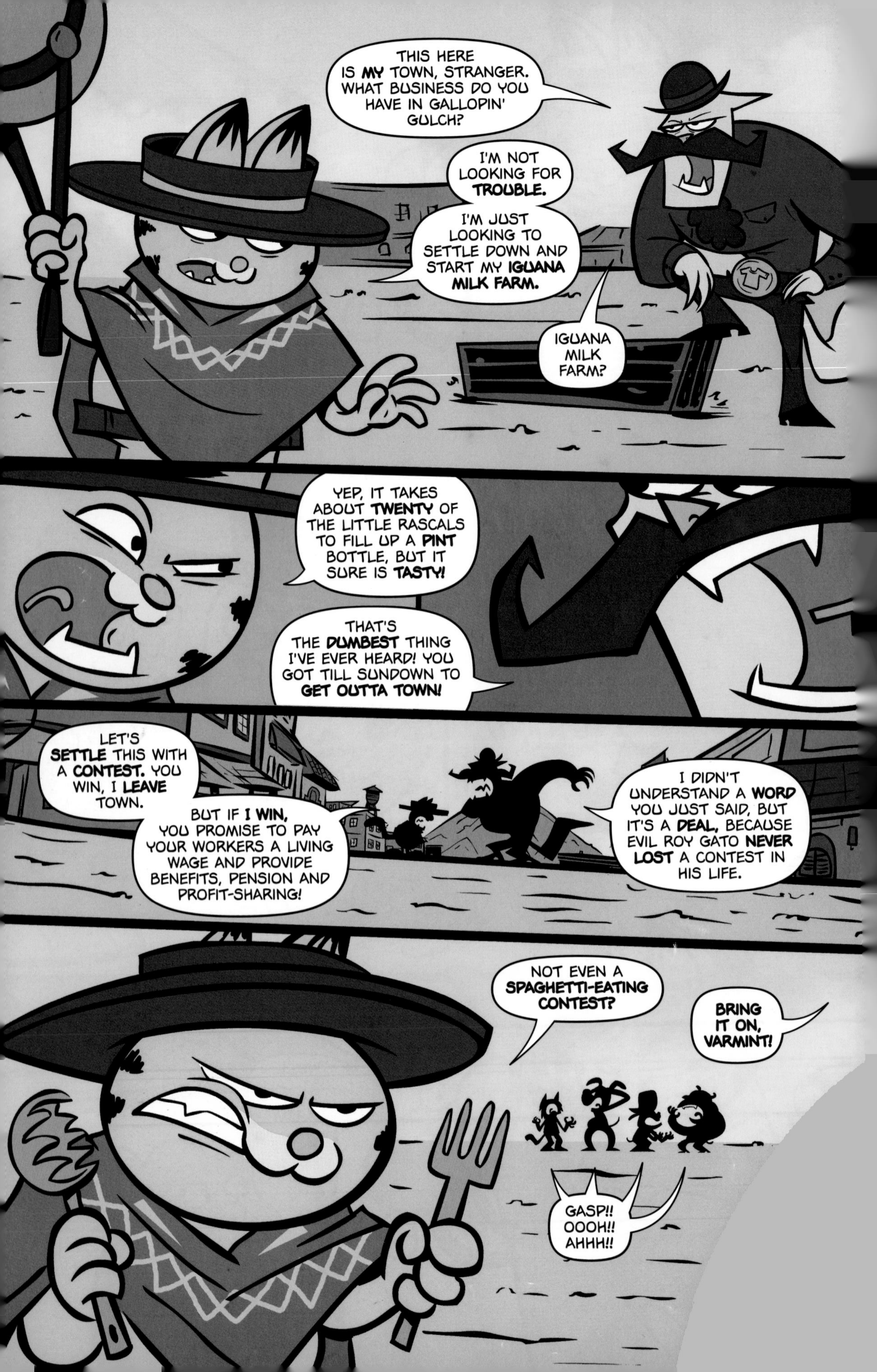
THIS HERE IS MY TOWN, STRANGER. WHAT BUSINESS DO YOU HAVE IN GALLOPIN' GULCH?
I'M NOT LOOKING FOR TROUBLE.
I'M JUST LOOKING TO SETTLE DOWN AND START MY IGUANA MILK FARM.
IGUANA MILK FARM?
YEP, IT TAKES ABOUT TWENTY OF THE LITTLE RASCALS TO FILL UP A PINT BOTTLE, BUT IT SURE IS TASTY!
THAT'S THE DUMBEST THING I'VE EVER HEARD! YOU GOT TILL SUNDOWN TO GET OUTTA TOWN!
LET'S SETTLE THIS WITH A CONTEST. YOU WIN, I LEAVE TOWN.
BUT IF I WIN, YOU PROMISE TO PAY YOUR WORKERS A LIVING WAGE AND PROVIDE BENEFITS, PENSION AND PROFIT-SHARING!
I DIDN'T UNDERSTAND A WORD YOU JUST SAID, BUT IT'S A DEAL, BECAUSE EVIL ROY GATO NEVER LOST A CONTEST IN HIS LIFE.
NOT EVEN A SPAGHETTI-EATING CONTEST?
BRING IT ON, VARMINT!
GASP!! OOOH!! AHHH!!

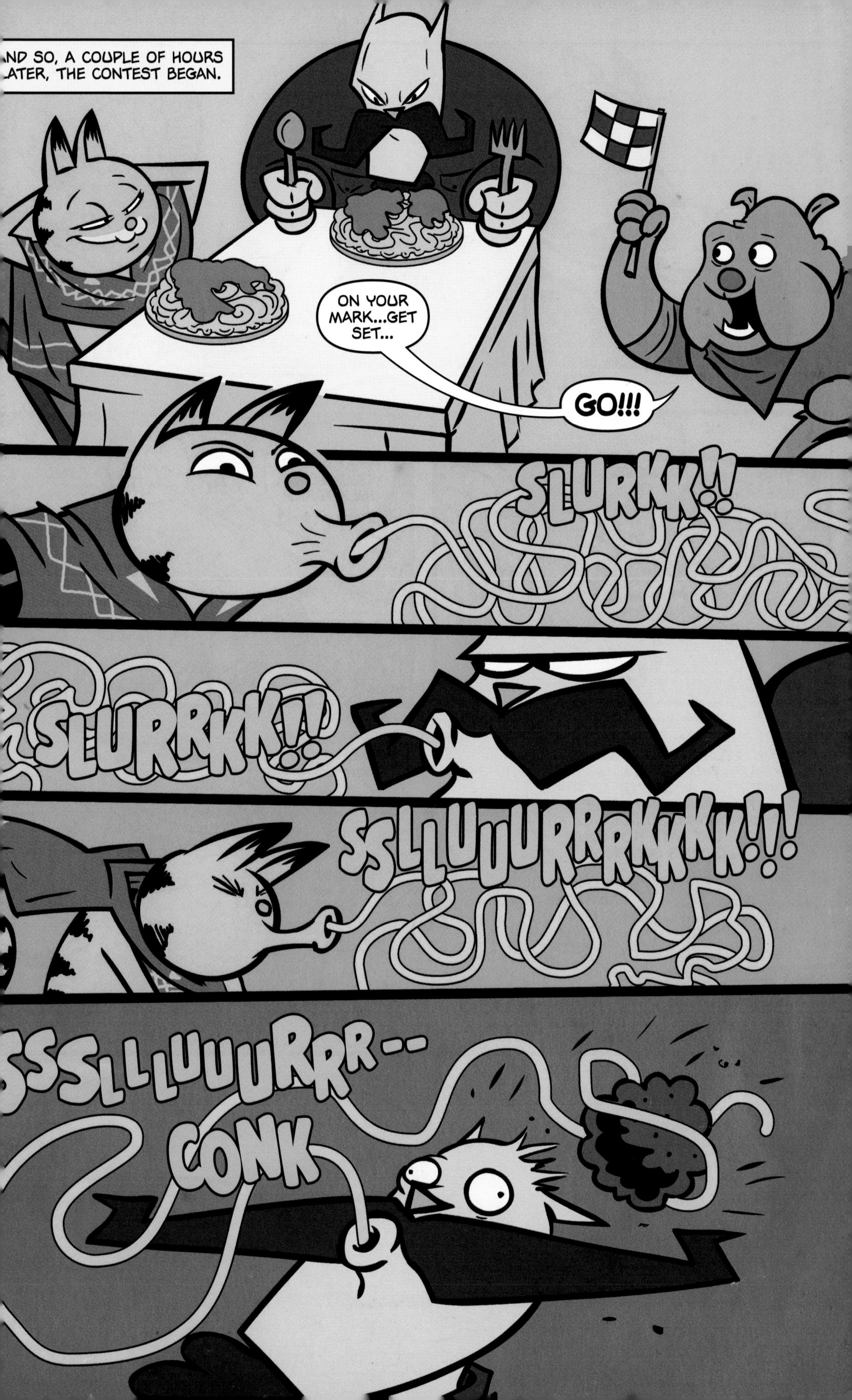
ND SO, A COUPLE OF HOURS LATER, THE CONTEST BEGAN.
ON YOUR MARK...GET SET...
GO!!!
SLURKK!!
SLURRKK!!
SSLLUUURRRKKKK!!!
SSSLLUUURRR--
CONK

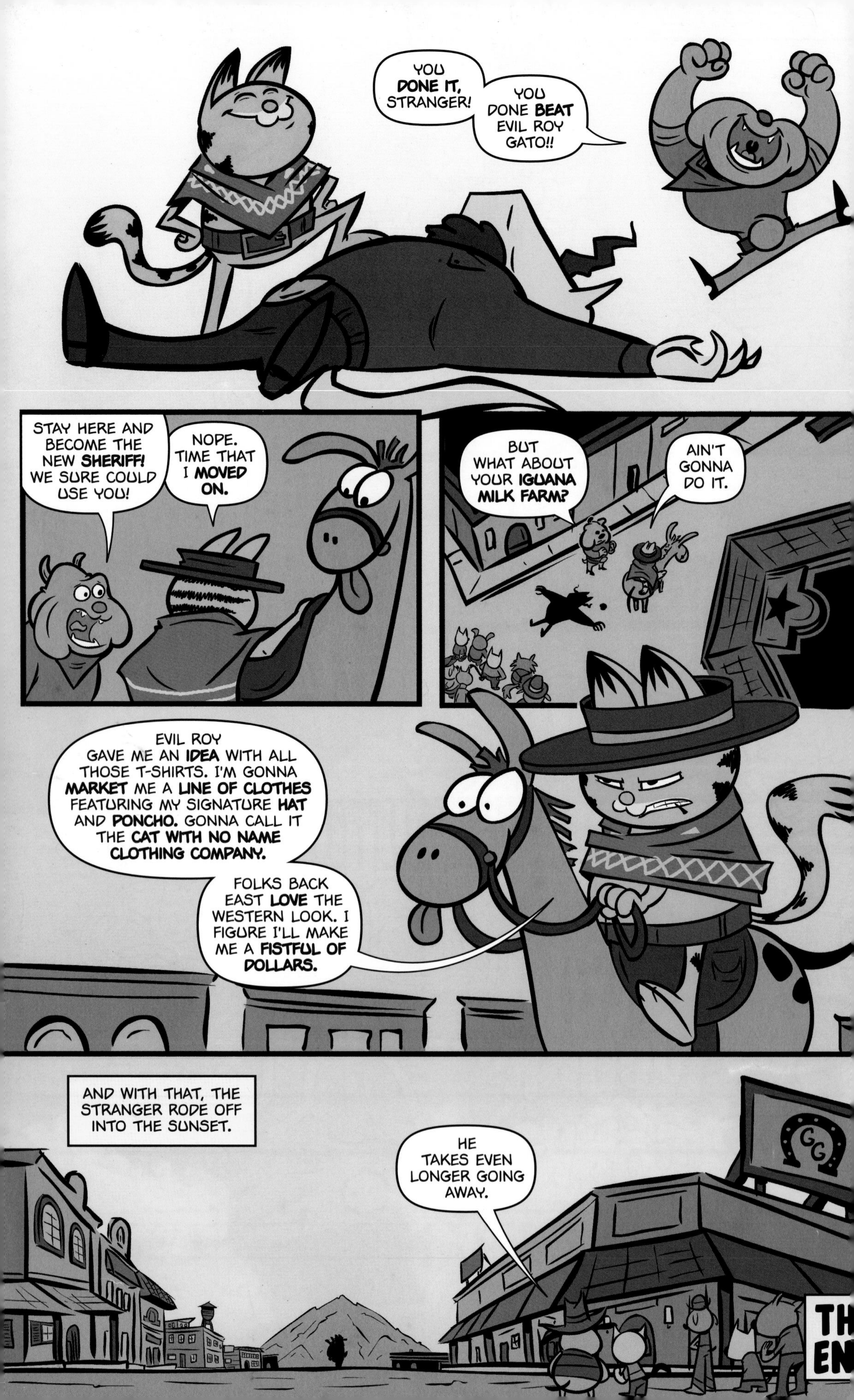
YOU DONE IT, STRANGER!
YOU DONE BEAT EVIL ROY GATO!!
STAY HERE AND BECOME THE NEW SHERIFF! WE SURE COULD USE YOU!
NOPE. TIME THAT I MOVED ON.
BUT WHAT ABOUT YOUR IGUANA MILK FARM?
AIN'T GONNA DO IT.
EVIL ROY GAVE ME AN IDEA WITH ALL THOSE T-SHIRTS. I'M GONNA MARKET ME A LINE OF CLOTHES FEATURING MY SIGNATURE HAT AND PONCHO. GONNA CALL IT THE CAT WITH NO NAME CLOTHING COMPANY.
FOLKS BACK EAST LOVE THE WESTERN LOOK. I FIGURE I'LL MAKE ME A FISTFUL OF DOLLARS.
AND WITH THAT, THE STRANGER RODE OFF INTO THE SUNSET.
HE TAKES EVEN LONGER GOING AWAY.
GG
TH
EN

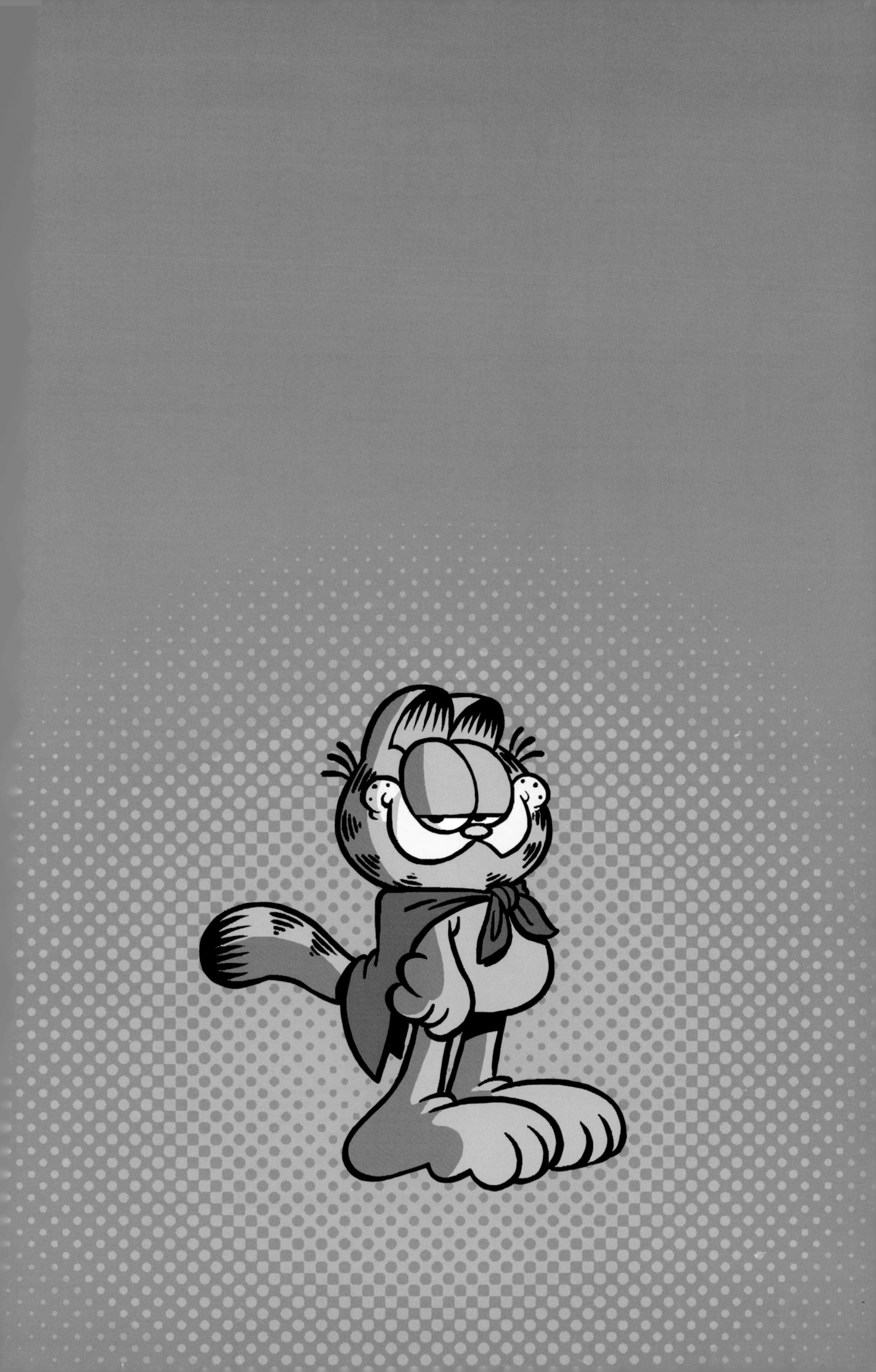

PART 3

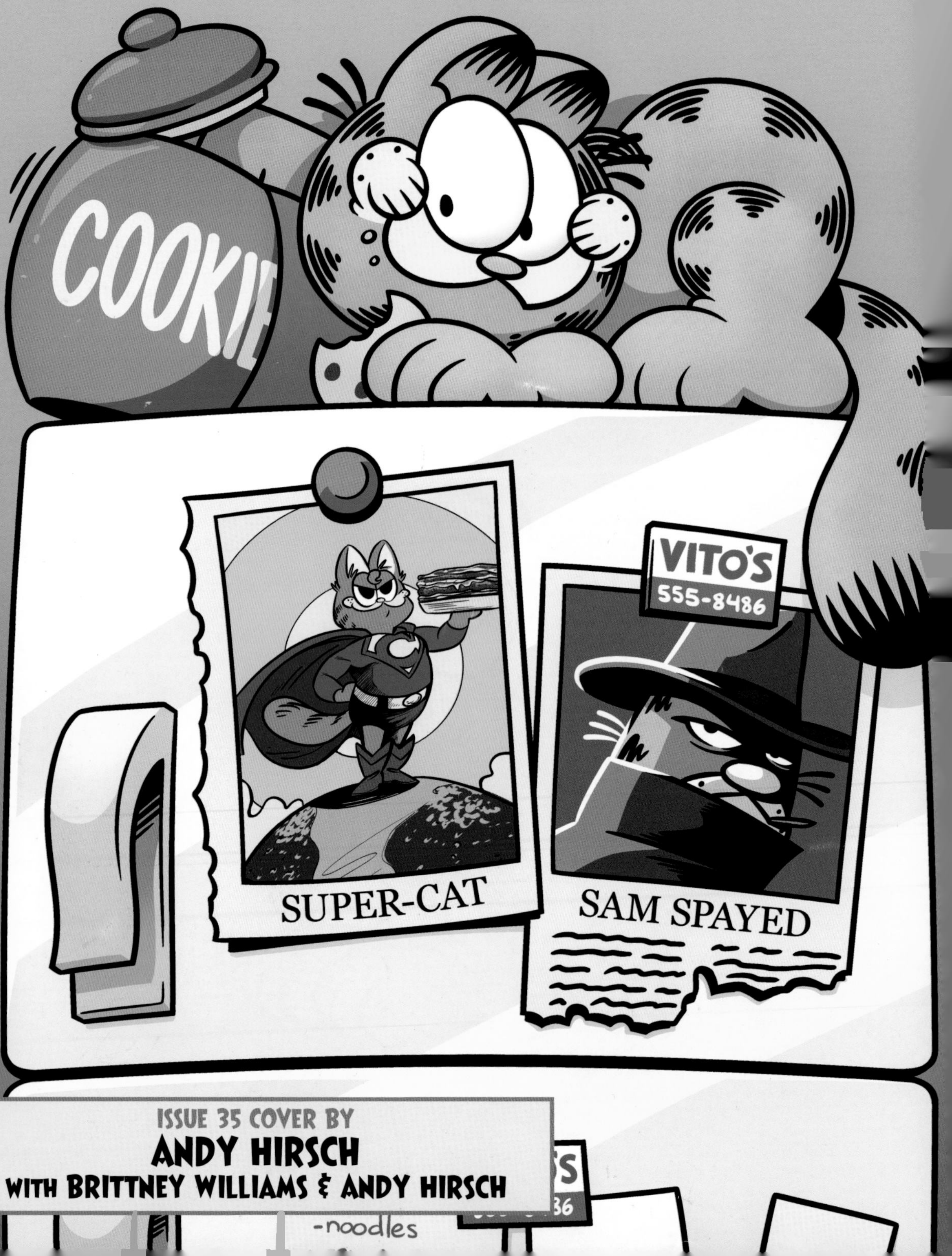
COOKIE
SUPER-CAT
VITO'S
555-8486
SAM SPAYED
-noodles

ISSUE 35 COVER BY
ANDY HIRSCH
WITH BRITTNEY WILLIAMS & ANDY HIRSCH

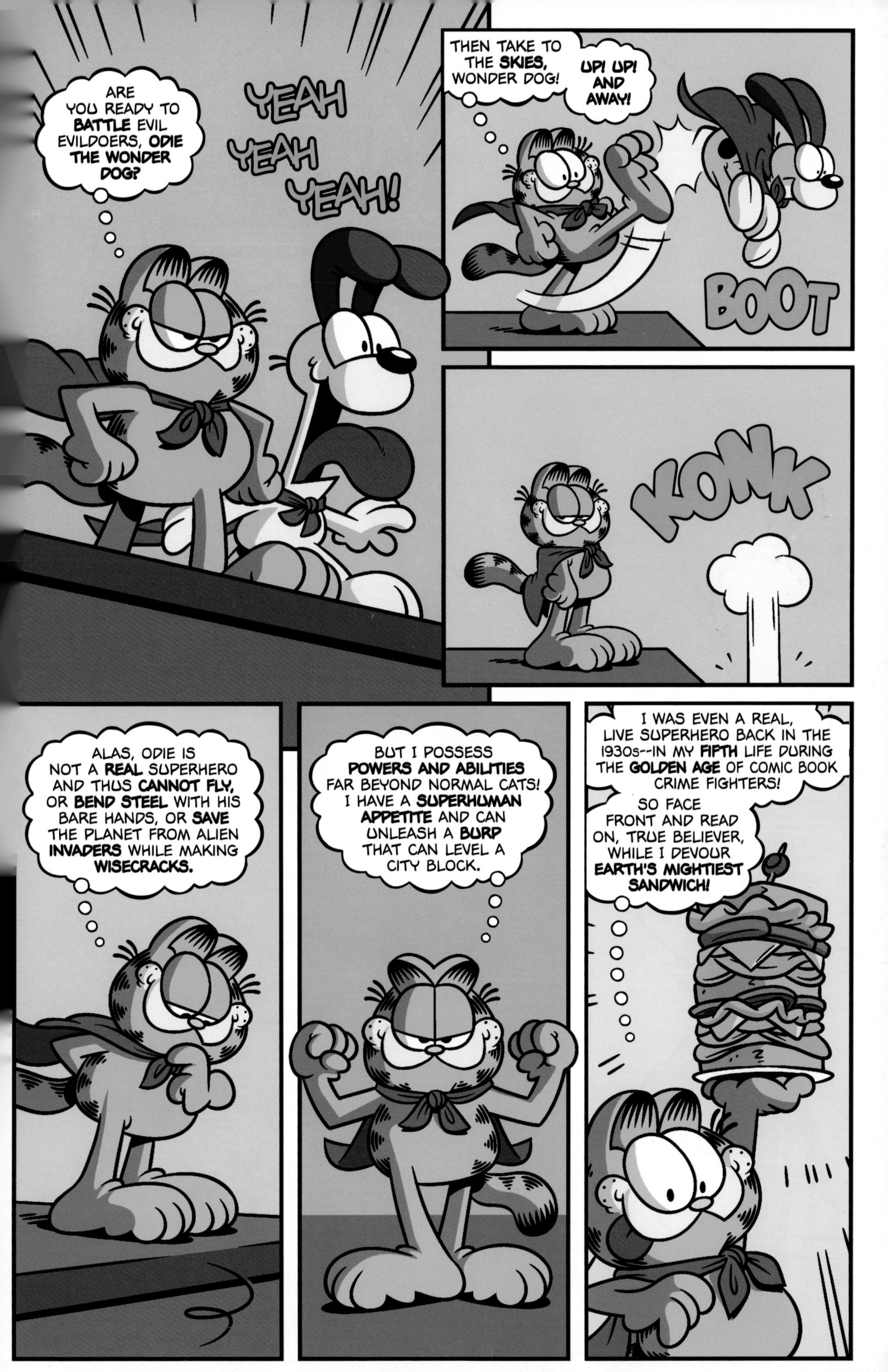
ARE YOU READY TO BATTLE EVIL EVILDOERS, ODIE THE WONDER DOG?
YEAH YEAH YEAH!
THEN TAKE TO THE SKIES, WONDER DOG!
UP! UP! AND AWAY!
BOOT
KONK
ALAS, ODIE IS NOT A REAL SUPERHERO AND THUS CANNOT FLY, OR BEND STEEL WITH HIS BARE HANDS, OR SAVE THE PLANET FROM ALIEN INVADERS WHILE MAKING WISECRACKS.
BUT I POSSESS POWERS AND ABILITIES FAR BEYOND NORMAL CATS! I HAVE A SUPERHUMAN APPETITE AND CAN UNLEASH A BURP THAT CAN LEVEL A CITY BLOCK.
I WAS EVEN A REAL, LIVE SUPERHERO BACK IN THE 1930s--IN MY FIFTH LIFE DURING THE GOLDEN AGE OF COMIC BOOK CRIME FIGHTERS!
SO FACE FRONT AND READ ON, TRUE BELIEVER, WHILE I DEVOUR EARTH'S MIGHTIEST SANDWICH!

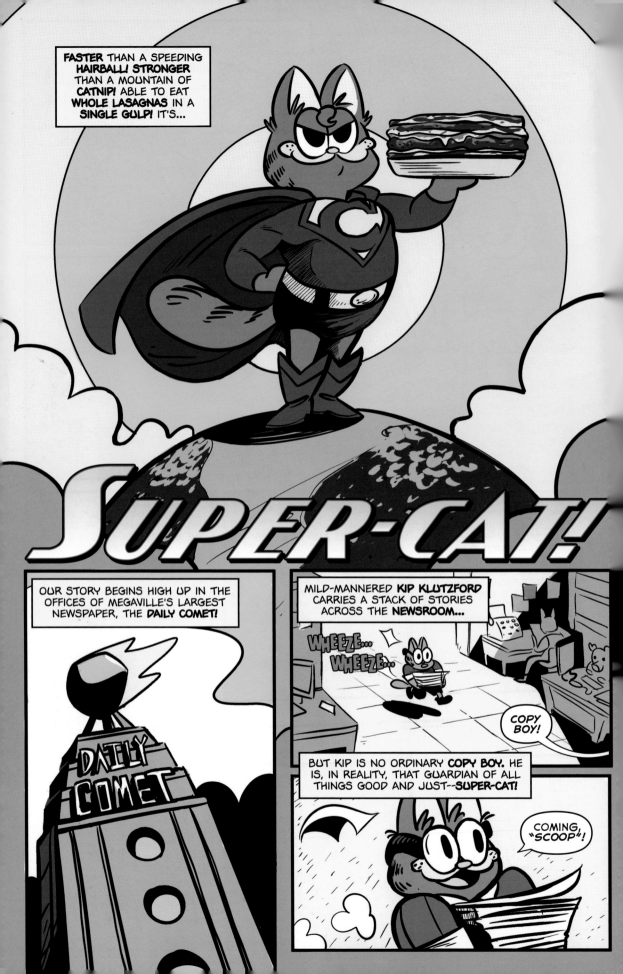

FASTER THAN A SPEEDING HAIRBALL! STRONGER THAN A MOUNTAIN OF CATNIP! ABLE TO EAT WHOLE LASAGNAS IN A SINGLE GULP! IT'S...

SUPER-CAT!

OUR STORY BEGINS HIGH UP IN THE OFFICES OF MEGAVILLE'S LARGEST NEWSPAPER, THE **DAILY COMET!**

DAILY COMET

MILD-MANNERED **KIP KLUTZFORD** CARRIES A STACK OF STORIES ACROSS THE **NEWSROOM...**

WHEEZE... WHEEZE...

COPY BOY!

BUT KIP IS NO ORDINARY **COPY BOY.** HE IS, IN REALITY, THAT GUARDIAN OF ALL THINGS GOOD AND JUST--**SUPER-CAT!**

COMING, "SCOOP"!

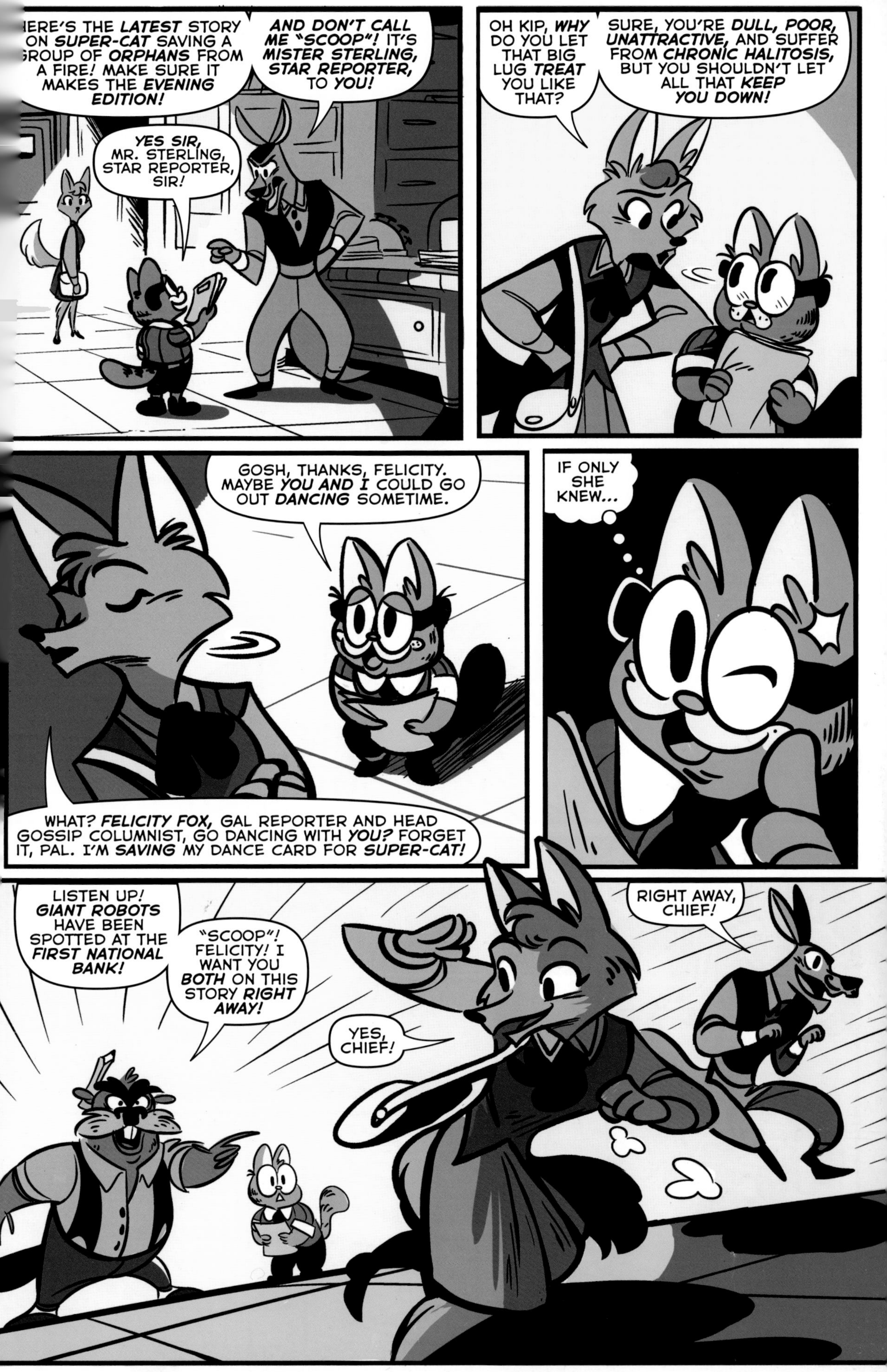

HERE'S THE LATEST STORY ON SUPER-CAT SAVING A GROUP OF ORPHANS FROM A FIRE! MAKE SURE IT MAKES THE EVENING EDITION!
AND DON'T CALL ME "SCOOP"! IT'S MISTER STERLING, STAR REPORTER, TO YOU!
YES SIR, MR. STERLING, STAR REPORTER, SIR!
OH KIP, WHY DO YOU LET THAT BIG LUG TREAT YOU LIKE THAT?
SURE, YOU'RE DULL, POOR, UNATTRACTIVE, AND SUFFER FROM CHRONIC HALITOSIS, BUT YOU SHOULDN'T LET ALL THAT KEEP YOU DOWN!
GOSH, THANKS, FELICITY. MAYBE YOU AND I COULD GO OUT DANCING SOMETIME.
WHAT? FELICITY FOX, GAL REPORTER AND HEAD GOSSIP COLUMNIST, GO DANCING WITH YOU? FORGET IT, PAL. I'M SAVING MY DANCE CARD FOR SUPER-CAT!
IF ONLY SHE KNEW...
LISTEN UP! GIANT ROBOTS HAVE BEEN SPOTTED AT THE FIRST NATIONAL BANK!
"SCOOP"! FELICITY! I WANT YOU BOTH ON THIS STORY RIGHT AWAY!
YES, CHIEF!
RIGHT AWAY, CHIEF!

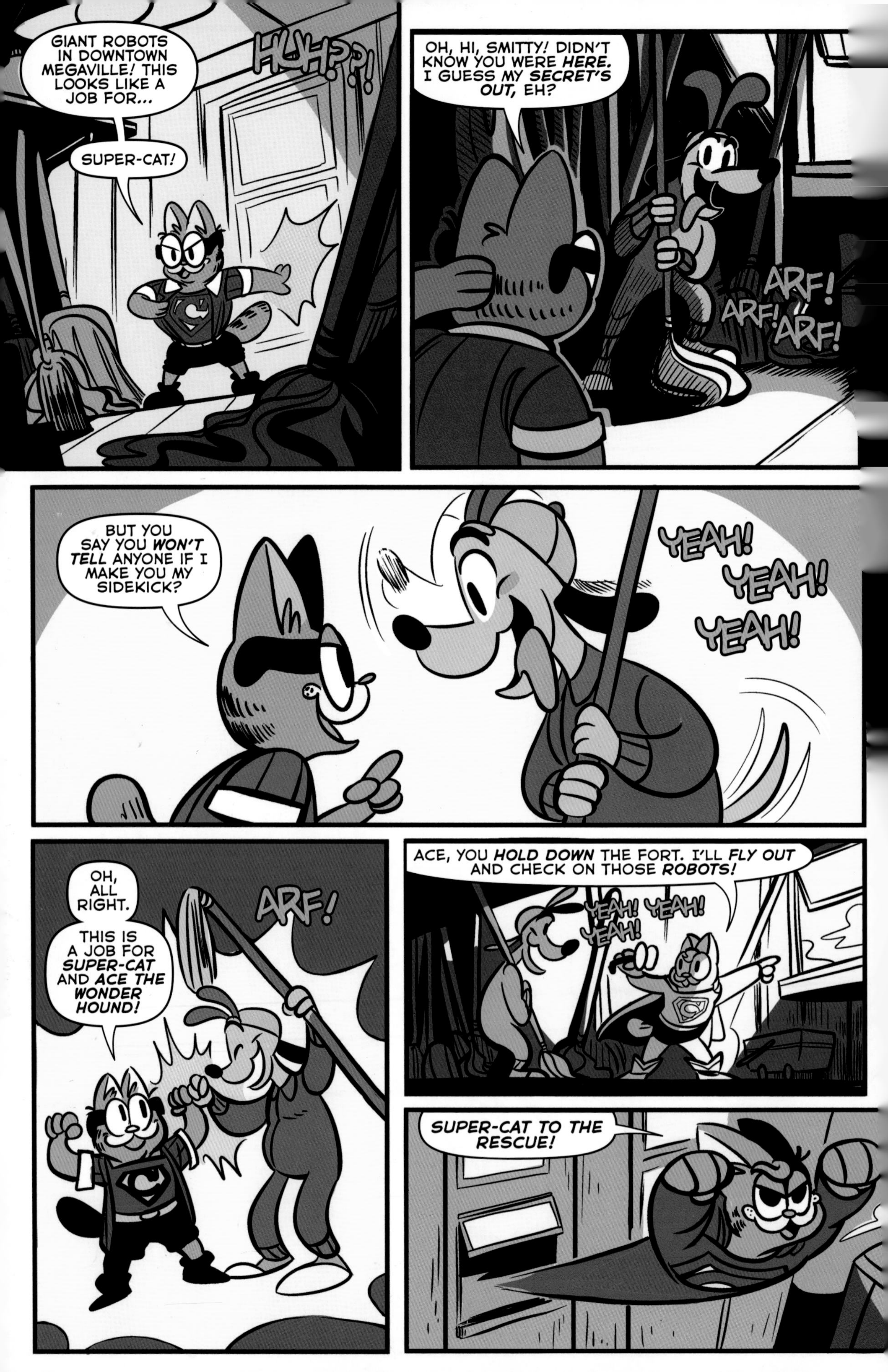
GIANT ROBOTS IN DOWNTOWN MEGAVILLE! THIS LOOKS LIKE A JOB FOR...
SUPER-CAT!
HUH??!
OH, HI, SMITTY! DIDN'T KNOW YOU WERE HERE. I GUESS MY SECRET'S OUT, EH?
ARF! ARF! ARF!
BUT YOU SAY YOU WON'T TELL ANYONE IF I MAKE YOU MY SIDEKICK?
YEAH! YEAH! YEAH!
OH, ALL RIGHT.
THIS IS A JOB FOR SUPER-CAT AND ACE THE WONDER HOUND!
ARF!
ACE, YOU HOLD DOWN THE FORT. I'LL FLY OUT AND CHECK ON THOSE ROBOTS!
YEAH! YEAH! YEAH!
SUPER-CAT TO THE RESCUE!

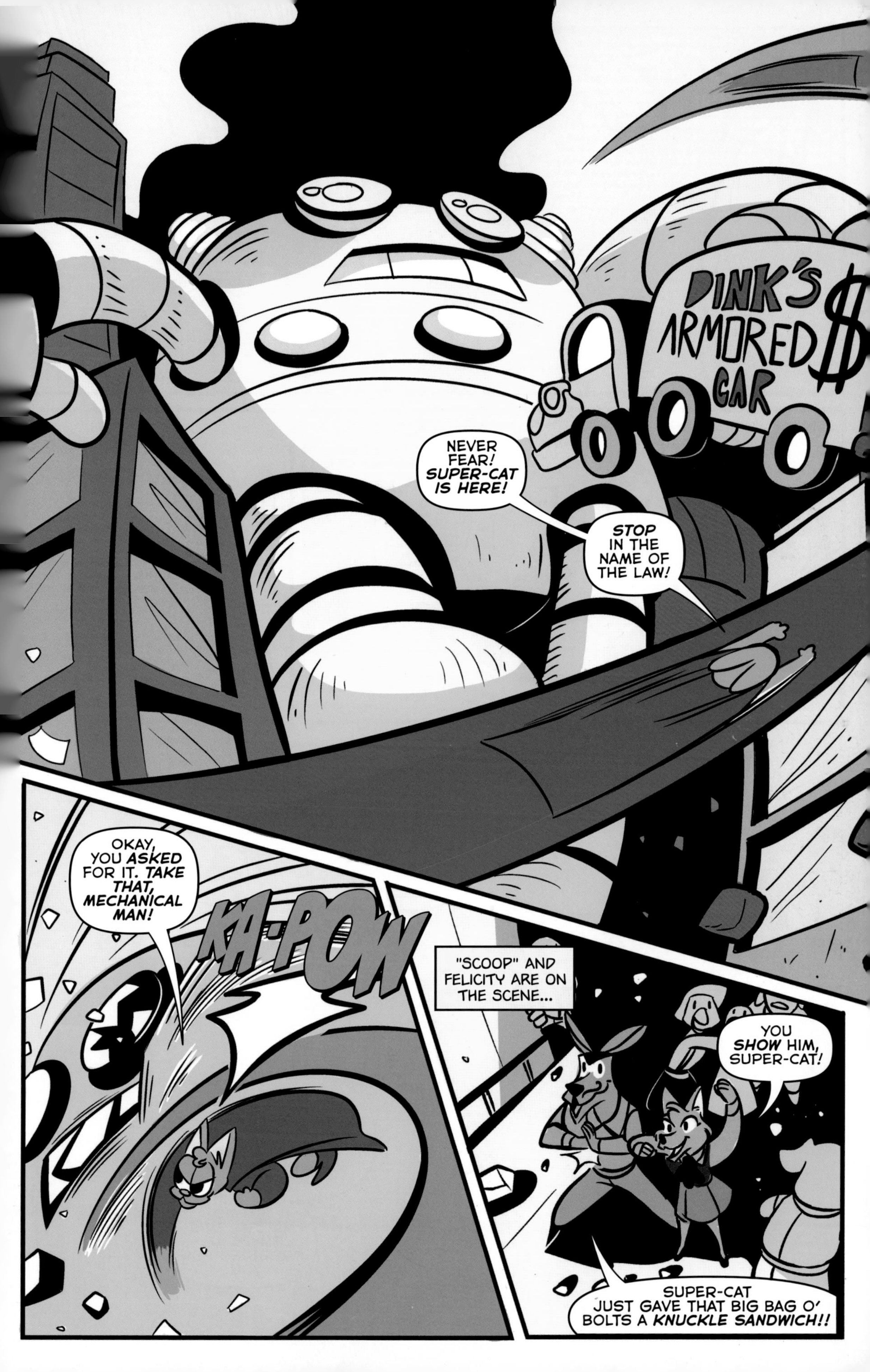
DINK'S ARMORED CAR $
NEVER FEAR! SUPER-CAT IS HERE!
STOP IN THE NAME OF THE LAW!
OKAY, YOU ASKED FOR IT. TAKE THAT, MECHANICAL MAN!
KA-POW
"SCOOP" AND FELICITY ARE ON THE SCENE...
YOU SHOW HIM, SUPER-CAT!
SUPER-CAT JUST GAVE THAT BIG BAG O' BOLTS A KNUCKLE SANDWICH!!

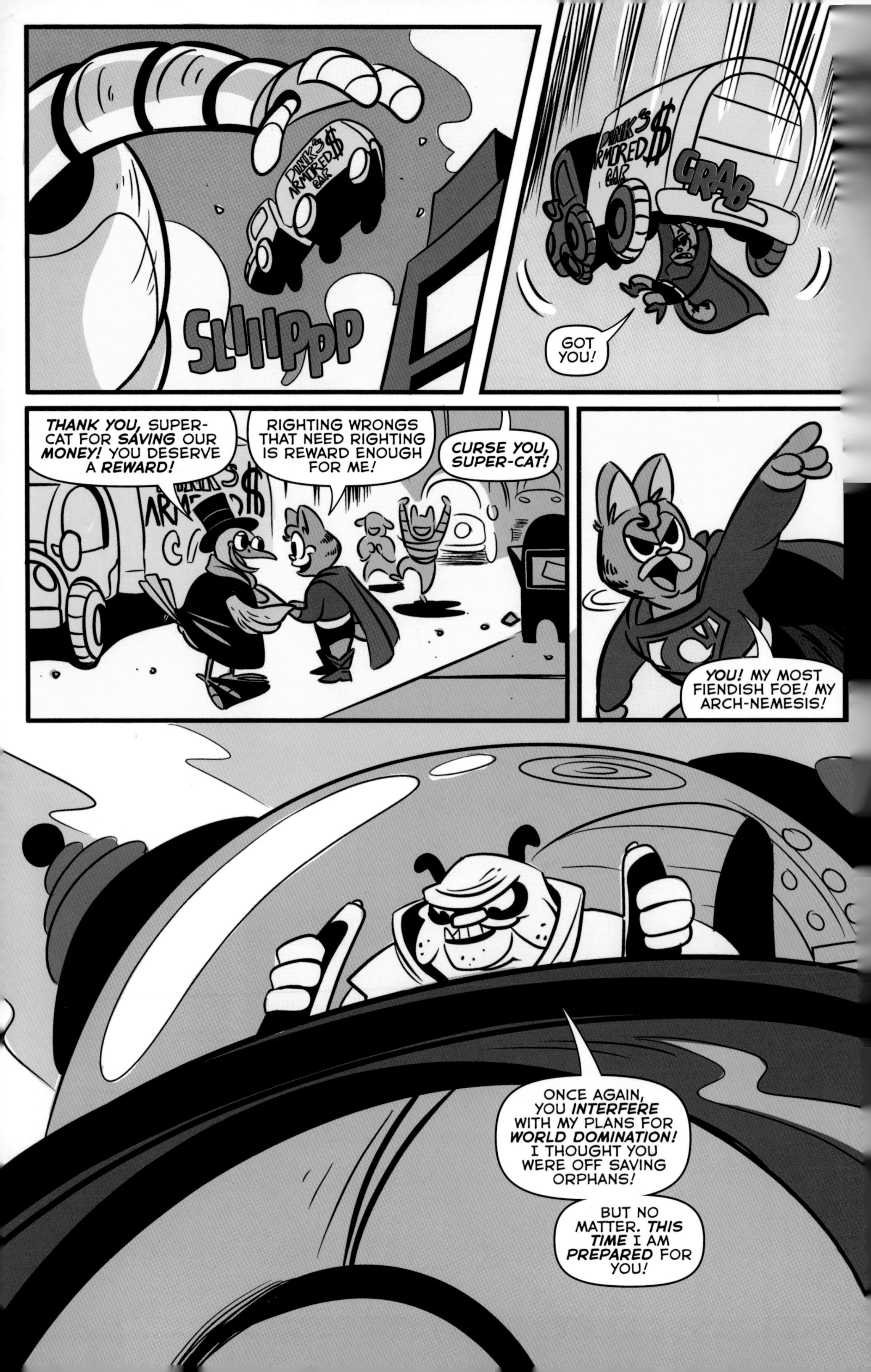

PINK'S ARMORED CAR
SLIIIPPP
PINK'S ARMORED CAR
CRAB
GOT YOU!
THANK YOU, SUPER-CAT FOR SAVING OUR MONEY! YOU DESERVE A REWARD!
RIGHTING WRONGS THAT NEED RIGHTING IS REWARD ENOUGH FOR ME!
CURSE YOU, SUPER-CAT!
YOU! MY MOST FIENDISH FOE! MY ARCH-NEMESIS!
ONCE AGAIN, YOU INTERFERE WITH MY PLANS FOR WORLD DOMINATION! I THOUGHT YOU WERE OFF SAVING ORPHANS!
BUT NO MATTER. THIS TIME I AM PREPARED FOR YOU!

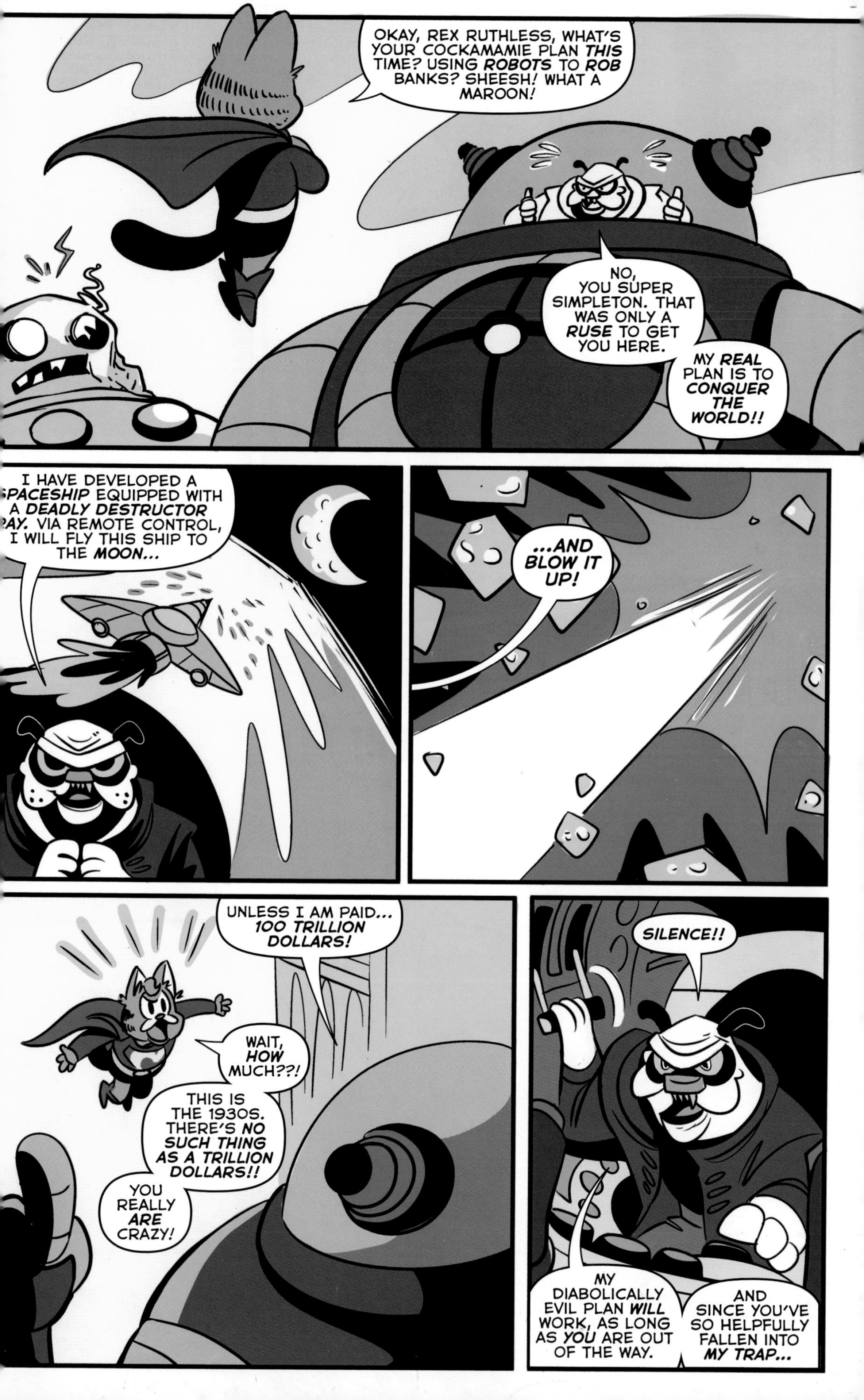

OKAY, REX RUTHLESS, WHAT'S YOUR COCKAMAMIE PLAN *THIS* TIME? USING *ROBOTS* TO *ROB* BANKS? SHEESH! WHAT A MAROON!
NO, YOU SUPER SIMPLETON. THAT WAS ONLY A *RUSE* TO GET YOU HERE.
MY *REAL* PLAN IS TO ***CONQUER THE WORLD!!***
I HAVE DEVELOPED A ***SPACESHIP*** EQUIPPED WITH A ***DEADLY DESTRUCTOR RAY.*** VIA REMOTE CONTROL, I WILL FLY THIS SHIP TO THE ***MOON...***
...AND BLOW IT UP!
UNLESS I AM PAID... ***100 TRILLION DOLLARS!***
WAIT, ***HOW*** MUCH??!
THIS IS THE 1930S. THERE'S ***NO SUCH THING AS A TRILLION DOLLARS!!***
YOU REALLY ***ARE*** CRAZY!
SILENCE!!
MY DIABOLICALLY EVIL PLAN ***WILL*** WORK, AS LONG AS ***YOU*** ARE OUT OF THE WAY.
AND SINCE YOU'VE SO HELPFULLY FALLEN INTO ***MY TRAP...***

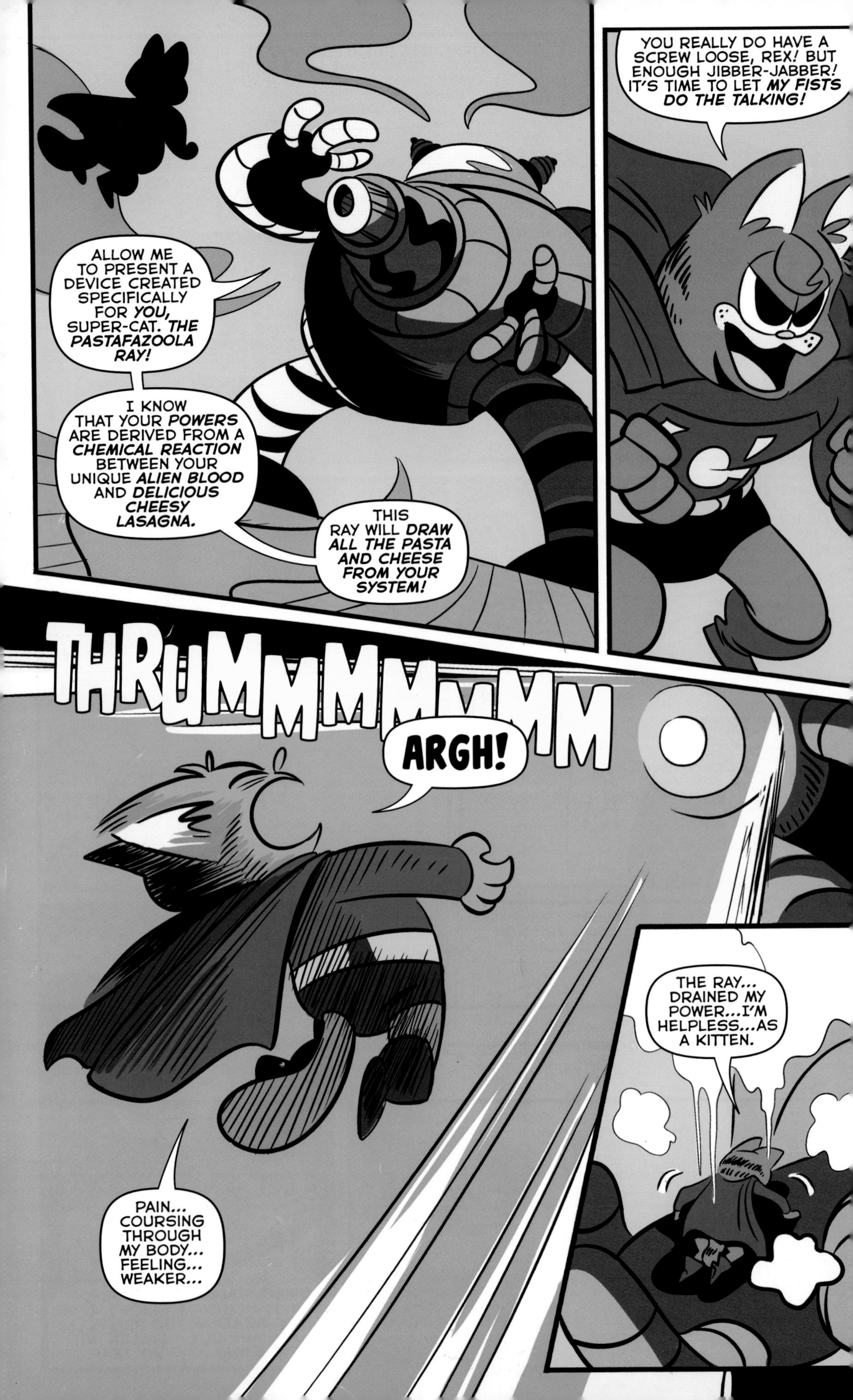
ALLOW ME TO PRESENT A DEVICE CREATED SPECIFICALLY FOR *YOU*, SUPER-CAT. *THE PASTAFAZOOLA RAY!*
I KNOW THAT YOUR *POWERS* ARE DERIVED FROM A *CHEMICAL REACTION* BETWEEN YOUR UNIQUE *ALIEN BLOOD* AND *DELICIOUS CHEESY LASAGNA.*
THIS RAY WILL *DRAW ALL THE PASTA AND CHEESE FROM YOUR SYSTEM!*
YOU REALLY DO HAVE A SCREW LOOSE, REX! BUT ENOUGH JIBBER-JABBER! IT'S TIME TO LET *MY FISTS DO THE TALKING!*
THRUMMMMMMMM
ARGH!
PAIN... COURSING THROUGH MY BODY... FEELING... WEAKER...
THE RAY... DRAINED MY POWER...I'M HELPLESS...AS A KITTEN.

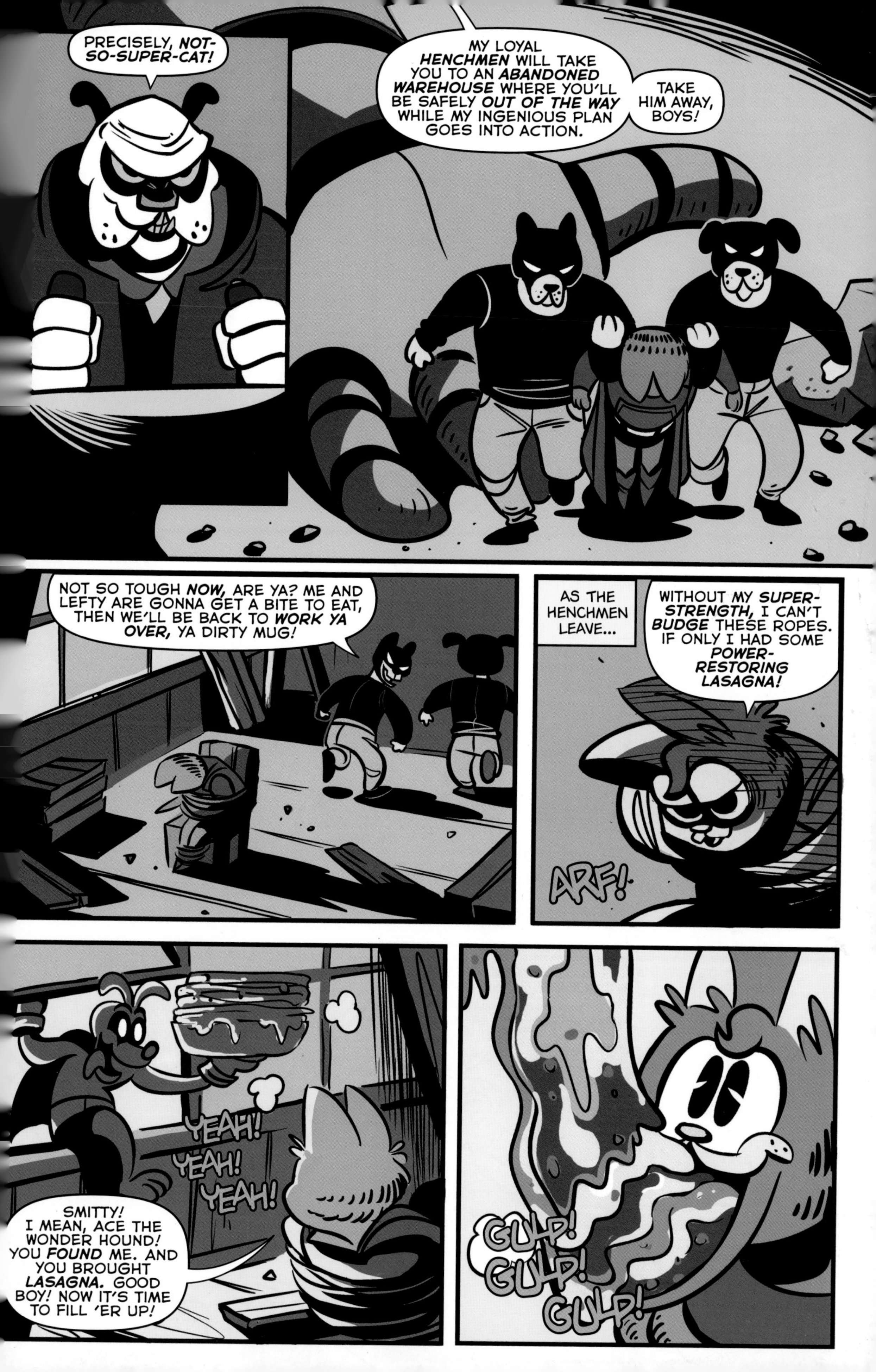
PRECISELY, NOT-SO-SUPER-CAT!
MY LOYAL HENCHMEN WILL TAKE YOU TO AN ABANDONED WAREHOUSE WHERE YOU'LL BE SAFELY OUT OF THE WAY WHILE MY INGENIOUS PLAN GOES INTO ACTION.
TAKE HIM AWAY, BOYS!
NOT SO TOUGH NOW, ARE YA? ME AND LEFTY ARE GONNA GET A BITE TO EAT, THEN WE'LL BE BACK TO WORK YA OVER, YA DIRTY MUG!
AS THE HENCHMEN LEAVE...
WITHOUT MY SUPER-STRENGTH, I CAN'T BUDGE THESE ROPES. IF ONLY I HAD SOME POWER-RESTORING LASAGNA!
ARF!
YEAH! YEAH! YEAH!
SMITTY! I MEAN, ACE THE WONDER HOUND! YOU FOUND ME. AND YOU BROUGHT LASAGNA. GOOD BOY! NOW IT'S TIME TO FILL 'ER UP!
GULP! GULP! GULP!

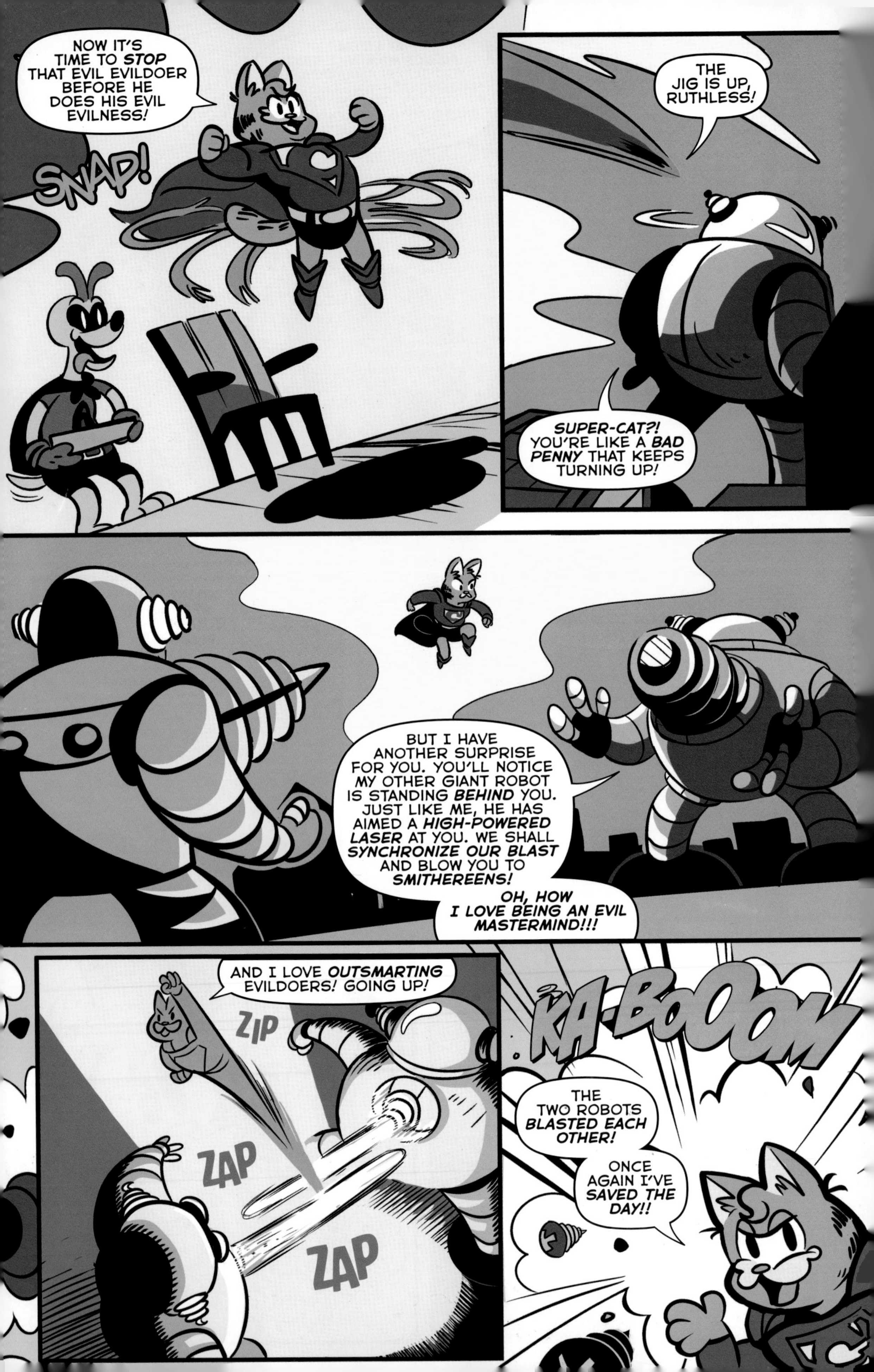
NOW IT'S TIME TO *STOP* THAT EVIL EVILDOER BEFORE HE DOES HIS EVIL EVILNESS!
SNAP!
THE JIG IS UP, RUTHLESS!
SUPER-CAT?! YOU'RE LIKE A *BAD PENNY* THAT KEEPS TURNING UP!
BUT I HAVE ANOTHER SURPRISE FOR YOU. YOU'LL NOTICE MY OTHER GIANT ROBOT IS STANDING *BEHIND* YOU. JUST LIKE ME, HE HAS AIMED A *HIGH-POWERED LASER* AT YOU. WE SHALL *SYNCHRONIZE OUR BLAST* AND BLOW YOU TO *SMITHEREENS!*
OH, HOW I LOVE BEING AN EVIL MASTERMIND!!!
AND I LOVE *OUTSMARTING* EVILDOERS! GOING UP!
ZIP
ZAP
ZAP
KA-BOOOOM
THE TWO ROBOTS *BLASTED EACH OTHER!*
ONCE AGAIN I'VE *SAVED THE DAY!!*

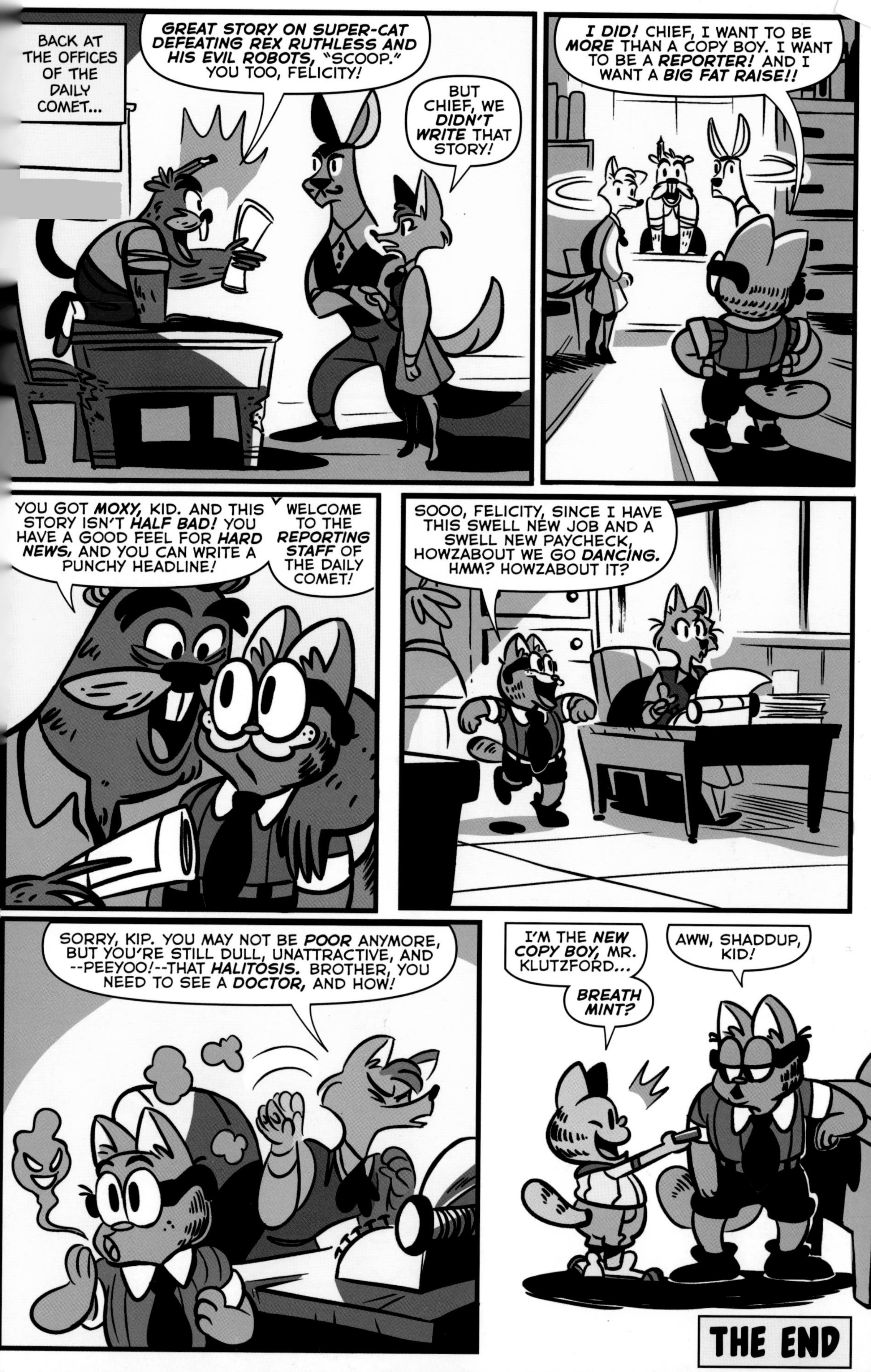
BACK AT THE OFFICES OF THE DAILY COMET...
GREAT STORY ON SUPER-CAT DEFEATING REX RUTHLESS AND HIS EVIL ROBOTS, "SCOOP." YOU TOO, FELICITY!
BUT CHIEF, WE DIDN'T WRITE THAT STORY!
I DID! CHIEF, I WANT TO BE MORE THAN A COPY BOY. I WANT TO BE A REPORTER! AND I WANT A BIG FAT RAISE!!
YOU GOT MOXY, KID. AND THIS STORY ISN'T HALF BAD! YOU HAVE A GOOD FEEL FOR HARD NEWS, AND YOU CAN WRITE A PUNCHY HEADLINE!
WELCOME TO THE REPORTING STAFF OF THE DAILY COMET!
SOOO, FELICITY, SINCE I HAVE THIS SWELL NEW JOB AND A SWELL NEW PAYCHECK, HOWZABOUT WE GO DANCING. HMM? HOWZABOUT IT?
SORRY, KIP. YOU MAY NOT BE POOR ANYMORE, BUT YOU'RE STILL DULL, UNATTRACTIVE, AND --PEEYOO!--THAT HALITOSIS. BROTHER, YOU NEED TO SEE A DOCTOR, AND HOW!
I'M THE NEW COPY BOY, MR. KLUTZFORD...
BREATH MINT?
AWW, SHADDUP, KID!
THE END

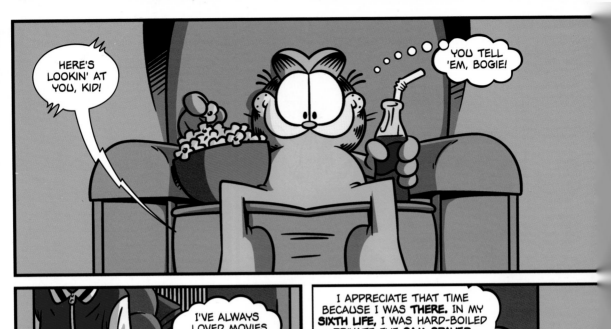

HERE'S LOOKIN' AT YOU, KID!

YOU TELL 'EM, BOGIE!

I'VE ALWAYS LOVED MOVIES FROM THE 1940s. THINGS WERE SIMPLER THEN.

DID YOU KNOW THAT THE WORLD WAS ACTUALLY BLACK AND WHITE IN THOSE DAYS?

I APPRECIATE THAT TIME BECAUSE I WAS THERE. IN MY SIXTH LIFE, I WAS HARD-BOILED PRIVATE EYE SAM SPAYED.

IT WASN'T EASY BEING A P.I. WITH A NAME LIKE THAT, BUT I HAD ALL THE REQUIREMENTS. I LOVED BABES AND BULLETS, AND I LOOKED GREAT IN A TRENCH COAT.

I REMEMBER THIS ONE CASE...IT WAS LITERALLY LIFE OR DEATH. MINE.

I SHOULD HAVE KNOWN I WAS IN TROUBLE BECAUSE IT ALL STARTED ON A MONDAY...

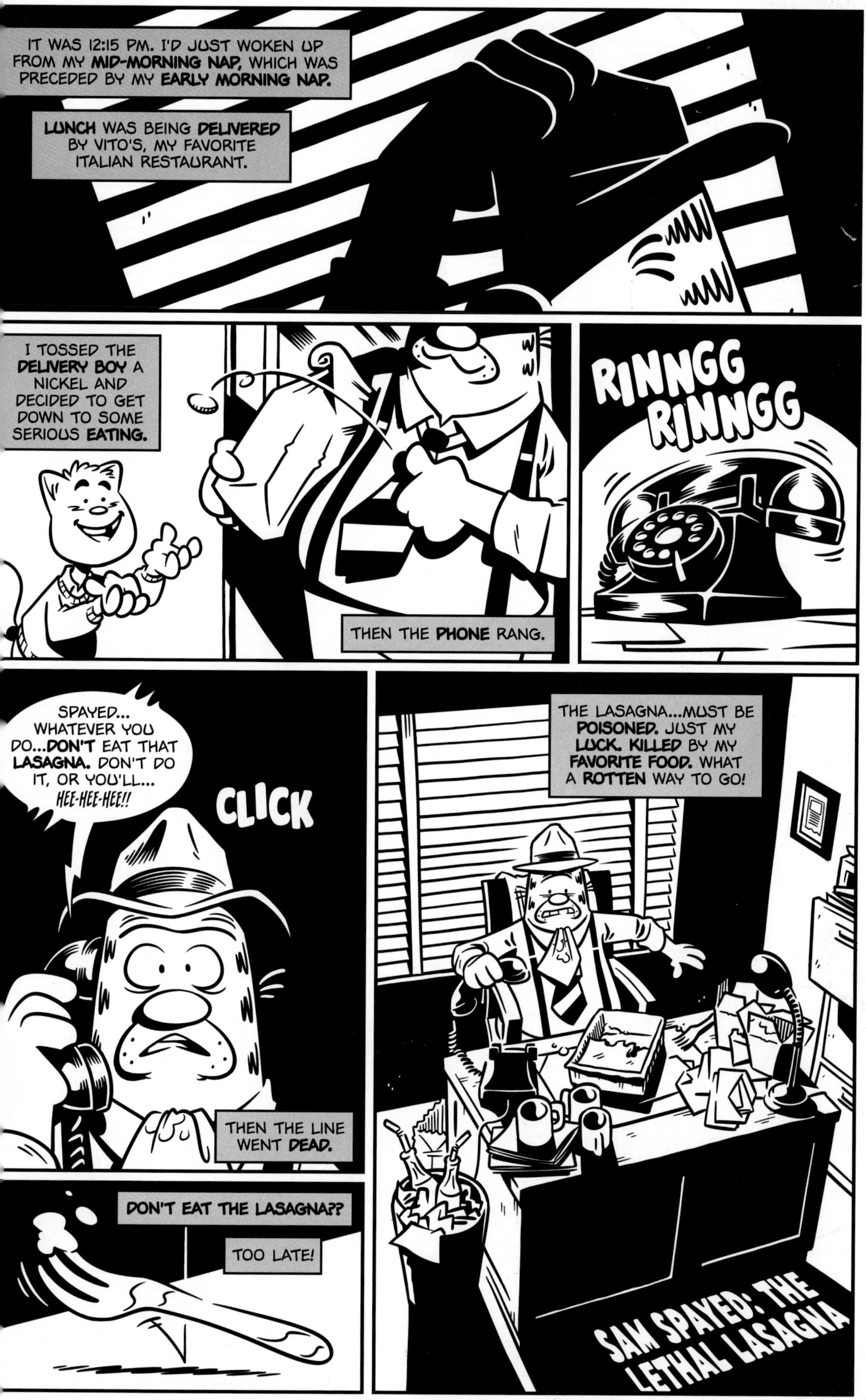

IT WAS 12:15 PM. I'D JUST WOKEN UP FROM MY MID-MORNING NAP, WHICH WAS PRECEDED BY MY EARLY MORNING NAP.
LUNCH WAS BEING DELIVERED BY VITO'S, MY FAVORITE ITALIAN RESTAURANT.
I TOSSED THE DELIVERY BOY A NICKEL AND DECIDED TO GET DOWN TO SOME SERIOUS EATING.
THEN THE PHONE RANG.
RINNGG RINNGG
SPAYED... WHATEVER YOU DO...DON'T EAT THAT LASAGNA. DON'T DO IT, OR YOU'LL... HEE-HEE-HEE!!
CLICK
THEN THE LINE WENT DEAD.
THE LASAGNA...MUST BE POISONED. JUST MY LUCK. KILLED BY MY FAVORITE FOOD. WHAT A ROTTEN WAY TO GO!
DON'T EAT THE LASAGNA??
TOO LATE!
SAM SPAYED: THE LETHAL LASAGNA

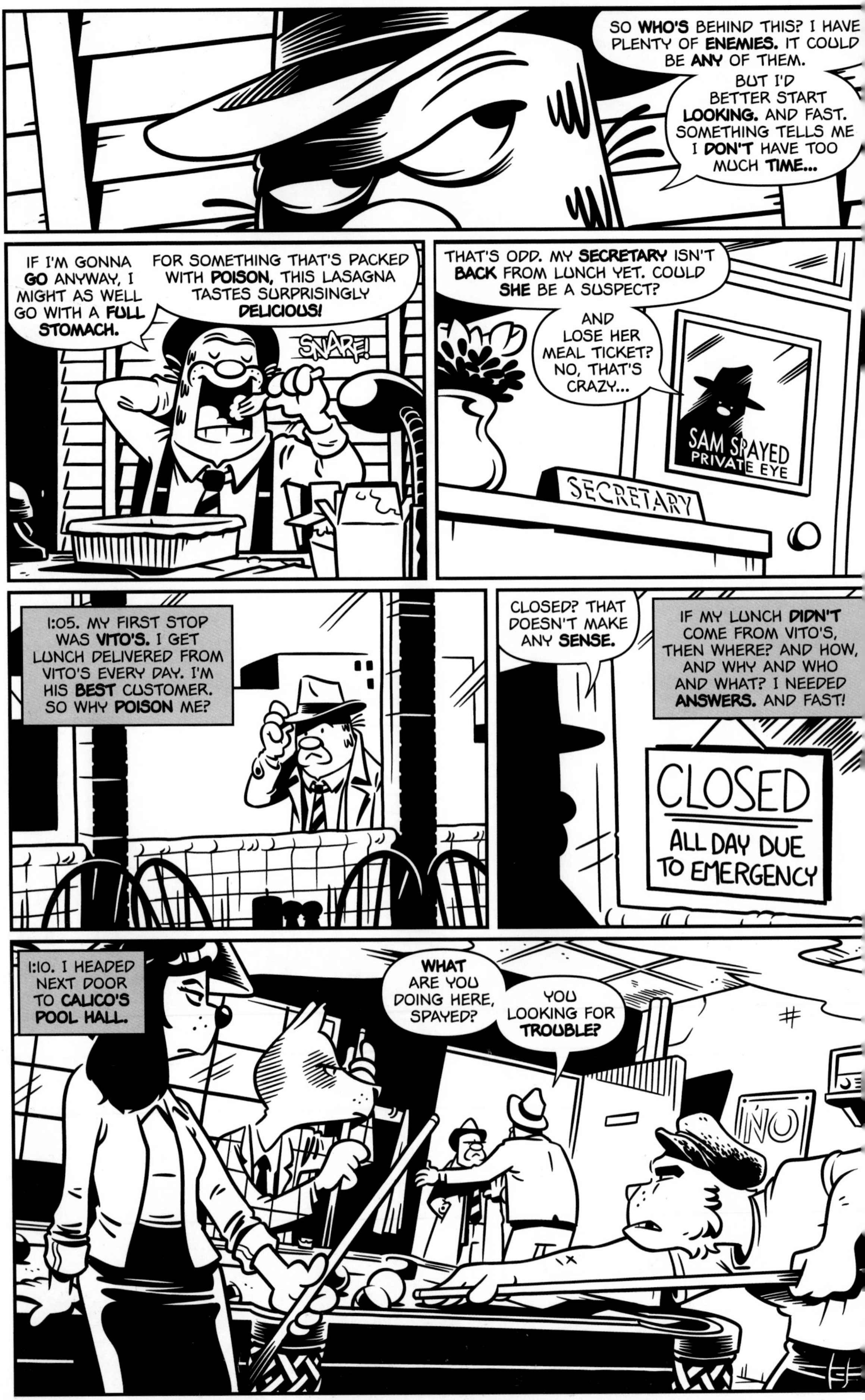
SO WHO'S BEHIND THIS? I HAVE PLENTY OF ENEMIES. IT COULD BE ANY OF THEM.
BUT I'D BETTER START LOOKING. AND FAST. SOMETHING TELLS ME I DON'T HAVE TOO MUCH TIME...
IF I'M GONNA GO ANYWAY, I MIGHT AS WELL GO WITH A FULL STOMACH.
FOR SOMETHING THAT'S PACKED WITH POISON, THIS LASAGNA TASTES SURPRISINGLY DELICIOUS!
SNARF!
THAT'S ODD. MY SECRETARY ISN'T BACK FROM LUNCH YET. COULD SHE BE A SUSPECT?
AND LOSE HER MEAL TICKET? NO, THAT'S CRAZY...
SAM SPAYED PRIVATE EYE
SECRETARY
1:05. MY FIRST STOP WAS VITO'S. I GET LUNCH DELIVERED FROM VITO'S EVERY DAY. I'M HIS BEST CUSTOMER. SO WHY POISON ME?
CLOSED? THAT DOESN'T MAKE ANY SENSE.
IF MY LUNCH DIDN'T COME FROM VITO'S, THEN WHERE? AND HOW, AND WHY AND WHO AND WHAT? I NEEDED ANSWERS. AND FAST!
CLOSED
ALL DAY DUE TO EMERGENCY
1:10. I HEADED NEXT DOOR TO CALICO'S POOL HALL.
WHAT ARE YOU DOING HERE, SPAYED?
YOU LOOKING FOR TROUBLE?
NO

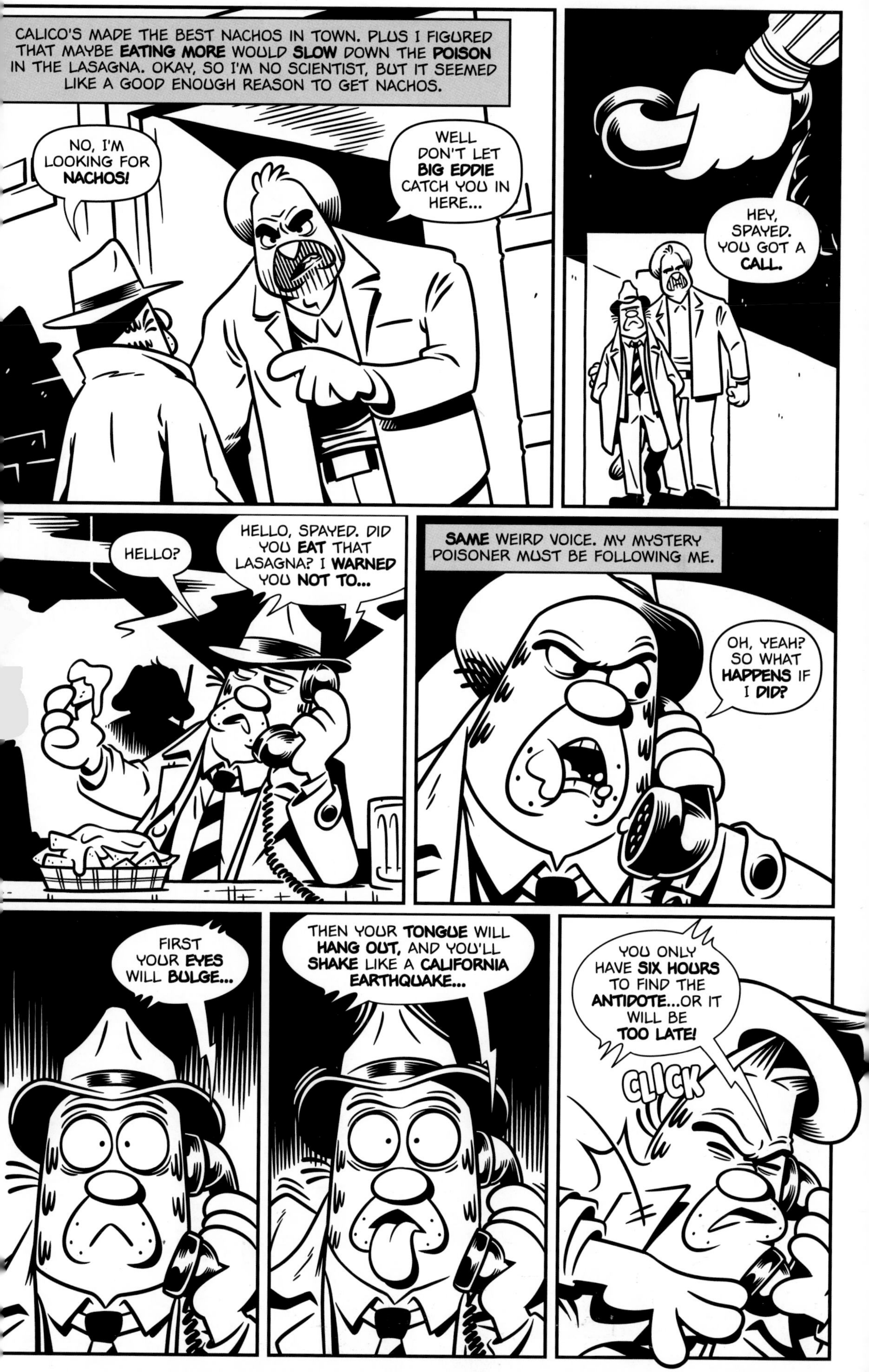

CALICO'S MADE THE BEST NACHOS IN TOWN. PLUS I FIGURED THAT MAYBE EATING MORE WOULD SLOW DOWN THE POISON IN THE LASAGNA. OKAY, SO I'M NO SCIENTIST, BUT IT SEEMED LIKE A GOOD ENOUGH REASON TO GET NACHOS.
NO, I'M LOOKING FOR NACHOS!
WELL DON'T LET BIG EDDIE CATCH YOU IN HERE...
HEY, SPAYED. YOU GOT A CALL.
HELLO?
HELLO, SPAYED. DID YOU EAT THAT LASAGNA? I WARNED YOU NOT TO...
SAME WEIRD VOICE. MY MYSTERY POISONER MUST BE FOLLOWING ME.
OH, YEAH? SO WHAT HAPPENS IF I DID?
FIRST YOUR EYES WILL BULGE...
THEN YOUR TONGUE WILL HANG OUT, AND YOU'LL SHAKE LIKE A CALIFORNIA EARTHQUAKE...
YOU ONLY HAVE SIX HOURS TO FIND THE ANTIDOTE...OR IT WILL BE TOO LATE!
CLICK

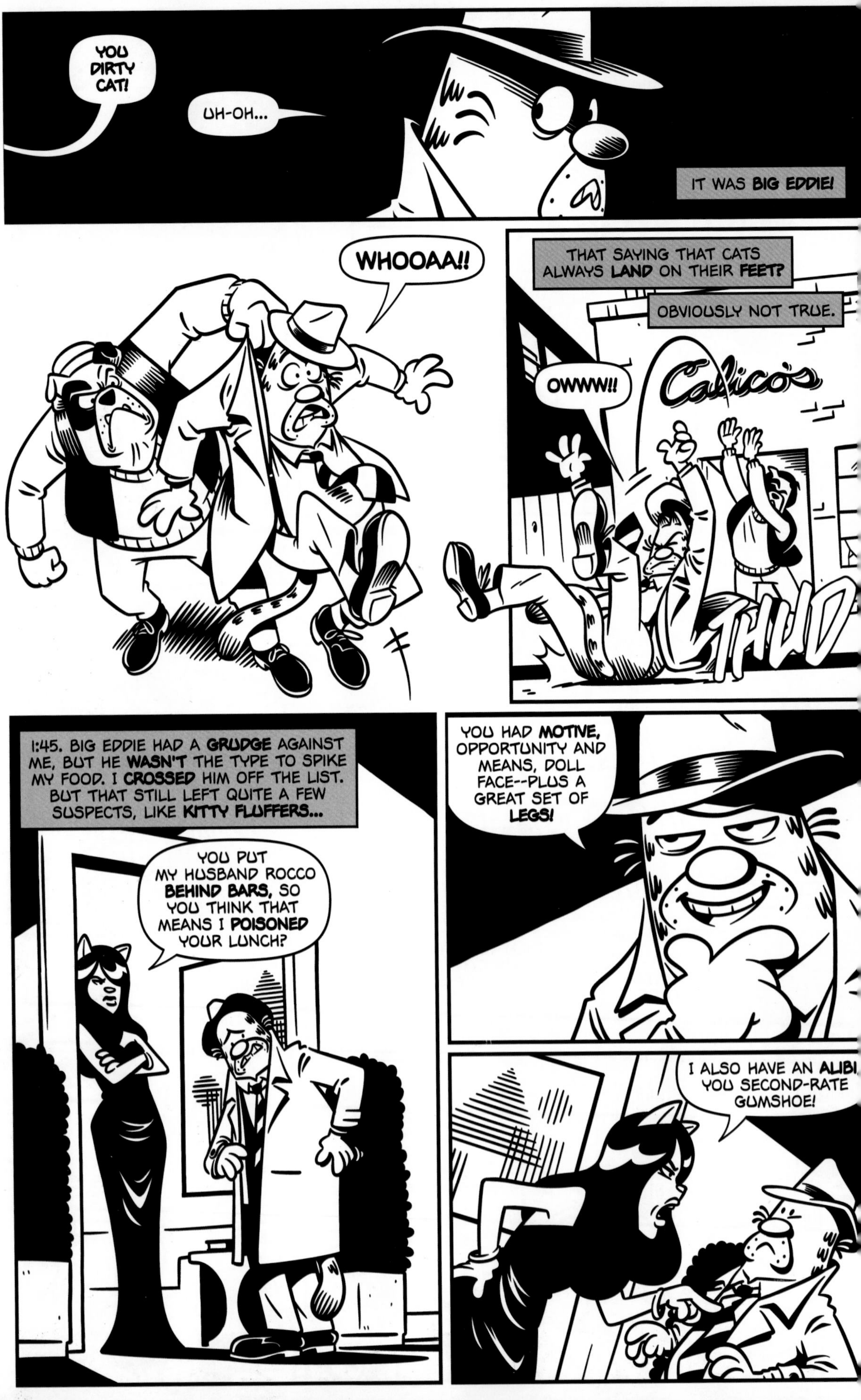
YOU DIRTY CAT!
UH-OH...
IT WAS BIG EDDIE!
WHOOAA!!
THAT SAYING THAT CATS ALWAYS LAND ON THEIR FEET?
OBVIOUSLY NOT TRUE.
OWWW!!
Calico's
THUD
1:45. BIG EDDIE HAD A GRUDGE AGAINST ME, BUT HE WASN'T THE TYPE TO SPIKE MY FOOD. I CROSSED HIM OFF THE LIST. BUT THAT STILL LEFT QUITE A FEW SUSPECTS, LIKE KITTY FLUFFERS...
YOU PUT MY HUSBAND ROCCO BEHIND BARS, SO YOU THINK THAT MEANS I POISONED YOUR LUNCH?
YOU HAD MOTIVE, OPPORTUNITY AND MEANS, DOLL FACE--PLUS A GREAT SET OF LEGS!
I ALSO HAVE AN ALIBI, YOU SECOND-RATE GUMSHOE!

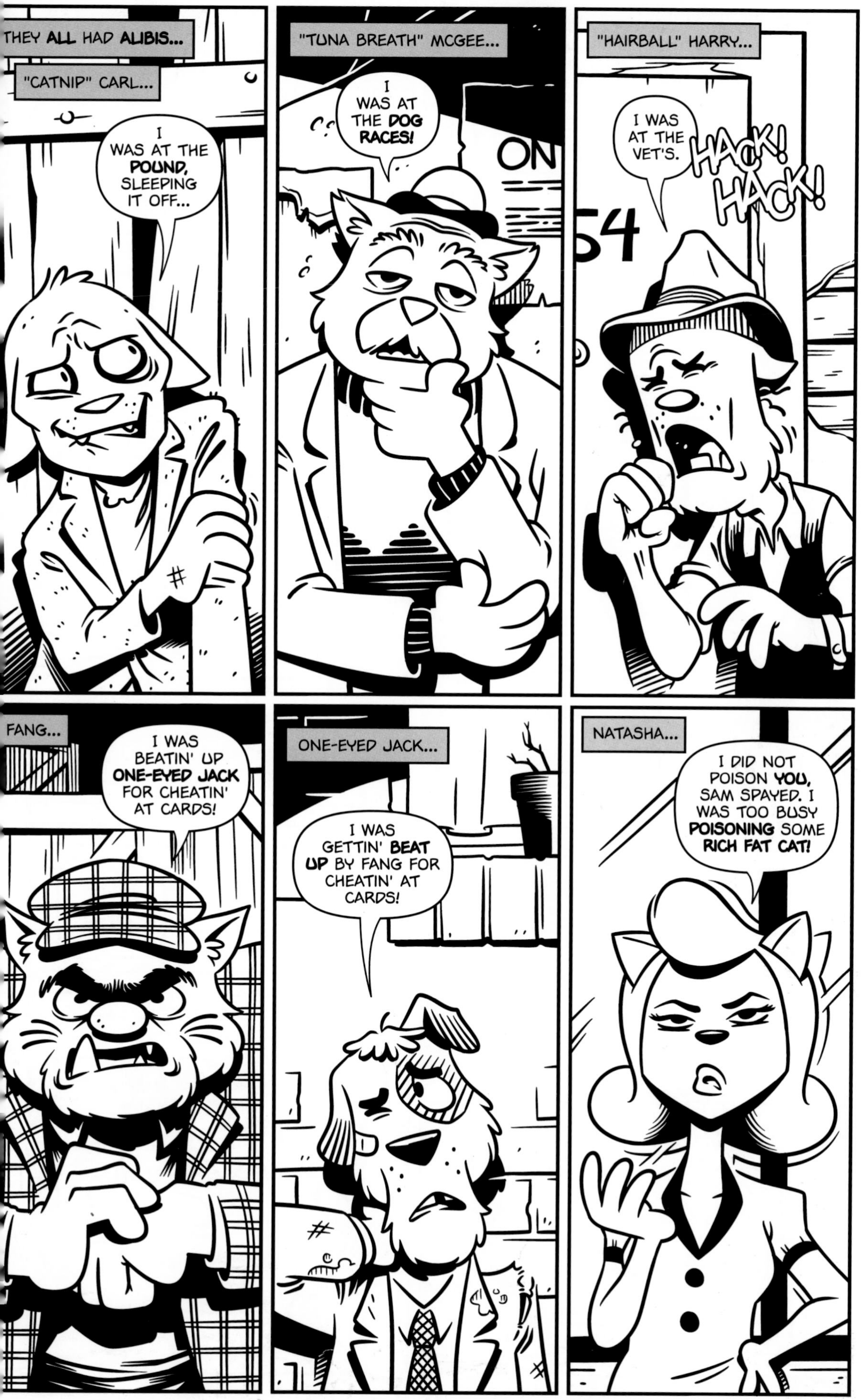
THEY ALL HAD ALIBIS...
"CATNIP" CARL...
I WAS AT THE POUND, SLEEPING IT OFF...
"TUNA BREATH" MCGEE...
I WAS AT THE DOG RACES!
"HAIRBALL" HARRY...
I WAS AT THE VET'S.
HACK! HACK!
FANG...
I WAS BEATIN' UP ONE-EYED JACK FOR CHEATIN' AT CARDS!
ONE-EYED JACK...
I WAS GETTIN' BEAT UP BY FANG FOR CHEATIN' AT CARDS!
NATASHA...
I DID NOT POISON YOU, SAM SPAYED. I WAS TOO BUSY POISONING SOME RICH FAT CAT!

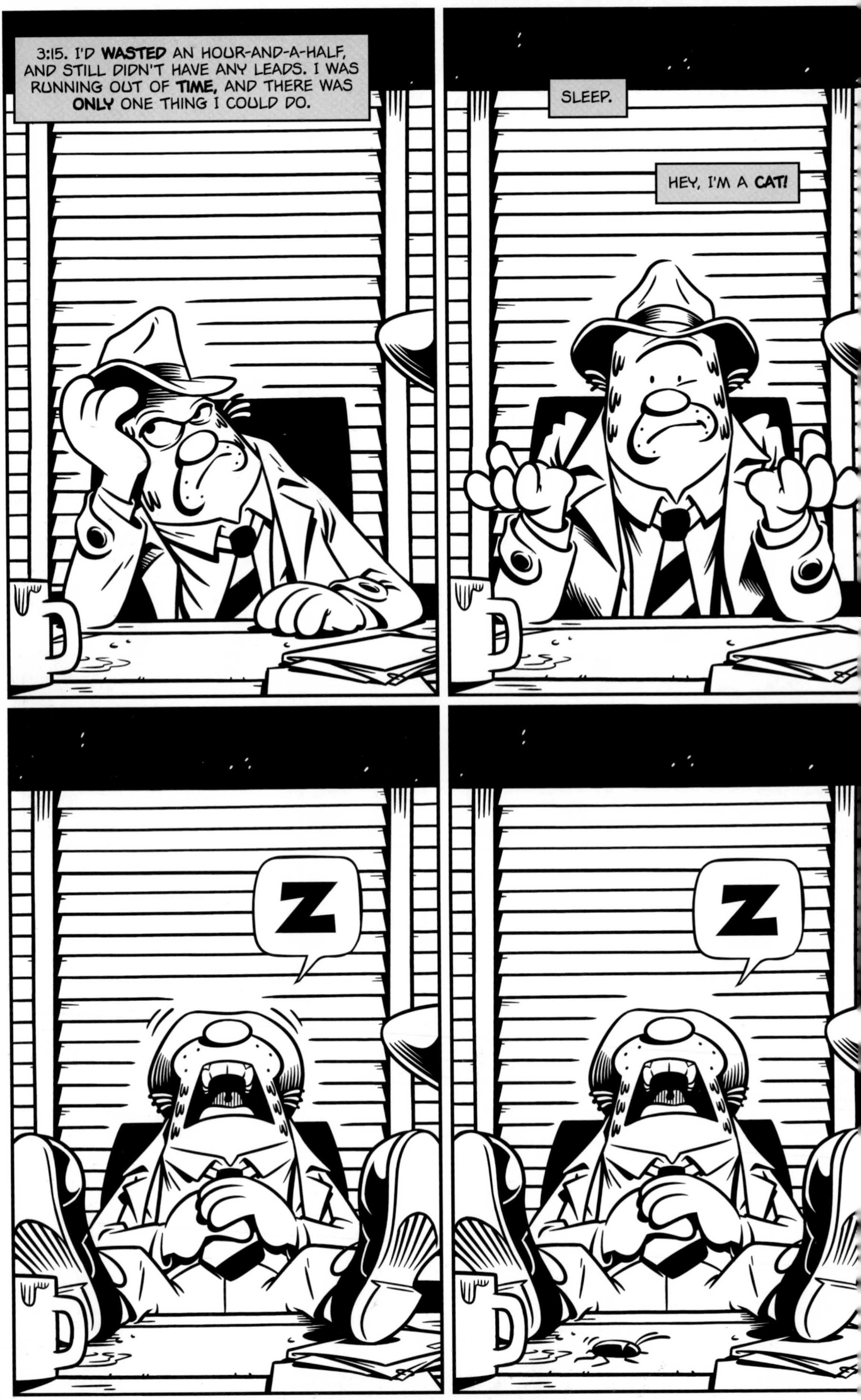
3:15. I'D WASTED AN HOUR-AND-A-HALF, AND STILL DIDN'T HAVE ANY LEADS. I WAS RUNNING OUT OF TIME, AND THERE WAS ONLY ONE THING I COULD DO.
SLEEP.
HEY, I'M A CAT!
Z
Z

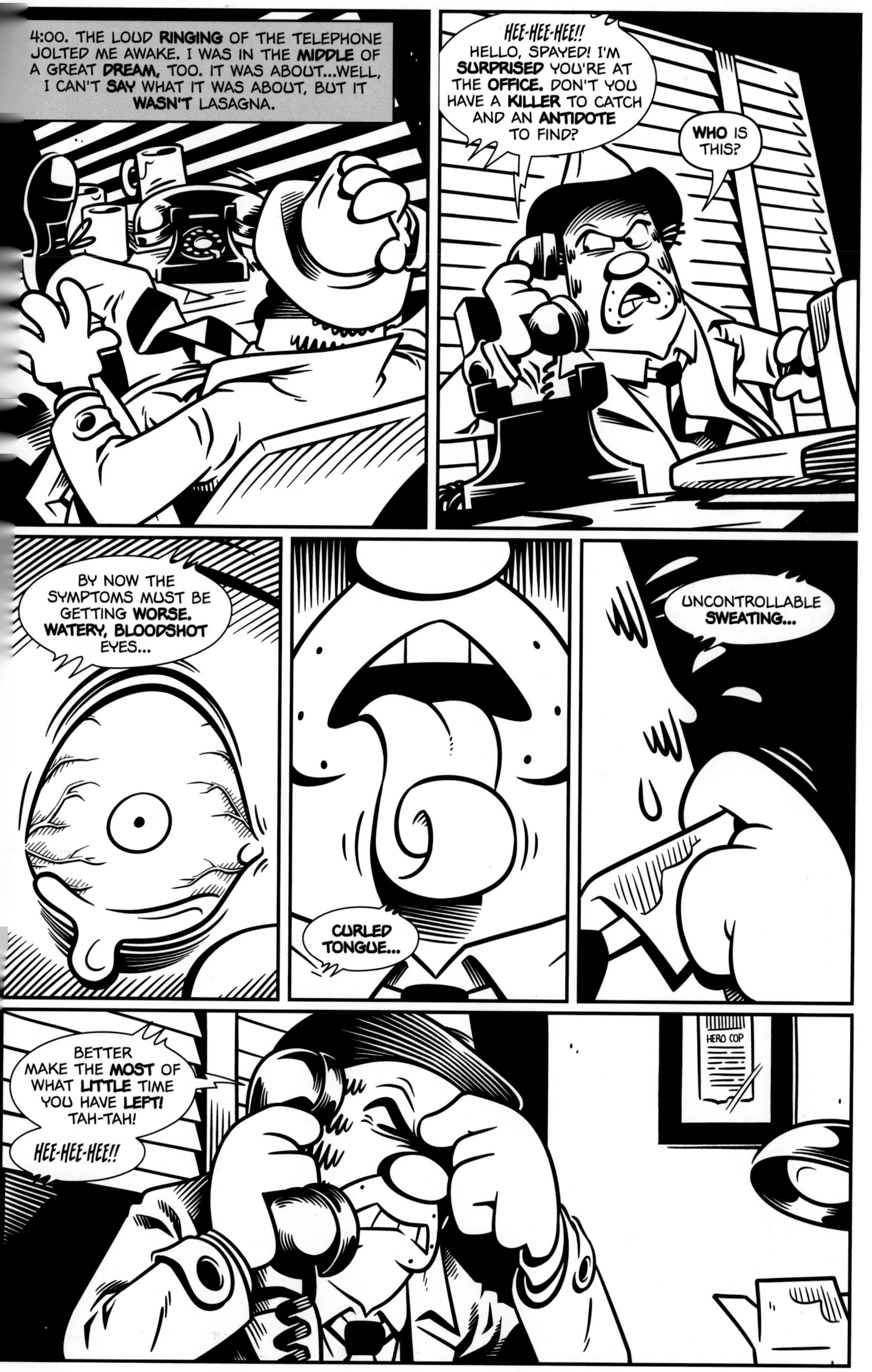
4:00. THE LOUD **RINGING** OF THE TELEPHONE JOLTED ME AWAKE. I WAS IN THE **MIDDLE** OF A GREAT **DREAM,** TOO. IT WAS ABOUT...WELL, I CAN'T **SAY** WHAT IT WAS ABOUT, BUT IT **WASN'T** LASAGNA.
HEE-HEE-HEE!! HELLO, SPAYED! I'M **SURPRISED** YOU'RE AT THE **OFFICE.** DON'T YOU HAVE A **KILLER** TO CATCH AND AN **ANTIDOTE** TO FIND?
WHO IS THIS?
BY NOW THE SYMPTOMS MUST BE GETTING **WORSE. WATERY, BLOODSHOT** EYES...
CURLED TONGUE...
UNCONTROLLABLE **SWEATING...**
BETTER MAKE THE **MOST** OF WHAT **LITTLE** TIME YOU HAVE **LEFT!** TAH-TAH!
HEE-HEE-HEE!!
HERO COP

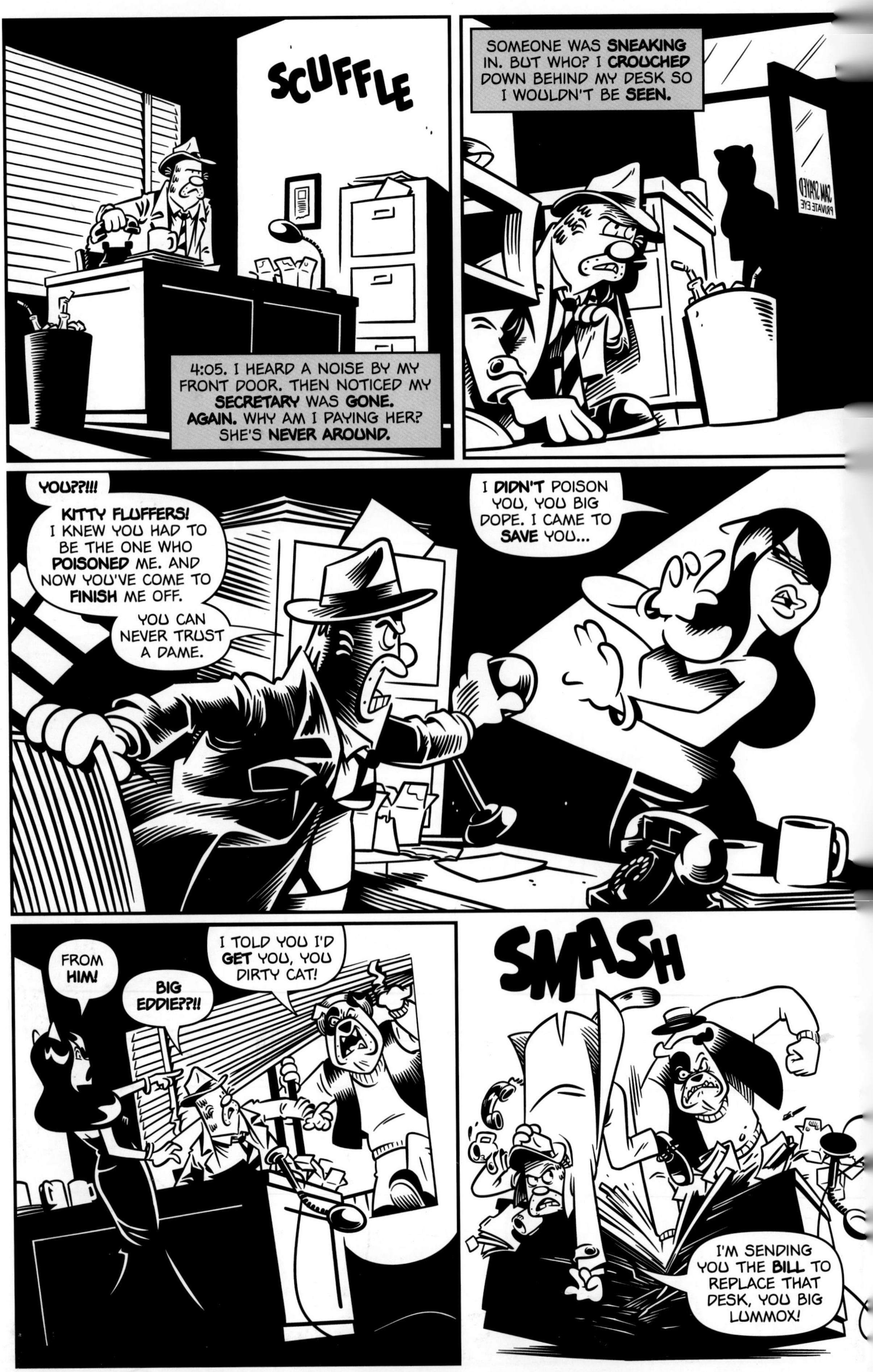
SCUFFLE
4:05. I HEARD A NOISE BY MY FRONT DOOR. THEN NOTICED MY SECRETARY WAS GONE. AGAIN. WHY AM I PAYING HER? SHE'S NEVER AROUND.
SOMEONE WAS SNEAKING IN. BUT WHO? I CROUCHED DOWN BEHIND MY DESK SO I WOULDN'T BE SEEN.
YOU??!!!
KITTY FLUFFERS! I KNEW YOU HAD TO BE THE ONE WHO POISONED ME. AND NOW YOU'VE COME TO FINISH ME OFF.
YOU CAN NEVER TRUST A DAME.
I DIDN'T POISON YOU, YOU BIG DOPE. I CAME TO SAVE YOU...
FROM HIM!
BIG EDDIE??!!
I TOLD YOU I'D GET YOU, YOU DIRTY CAT!
SMASH
I'M SENDING YOU THE BILL TO REPLACE THAT DESK, YOU BIG LUMMOX!

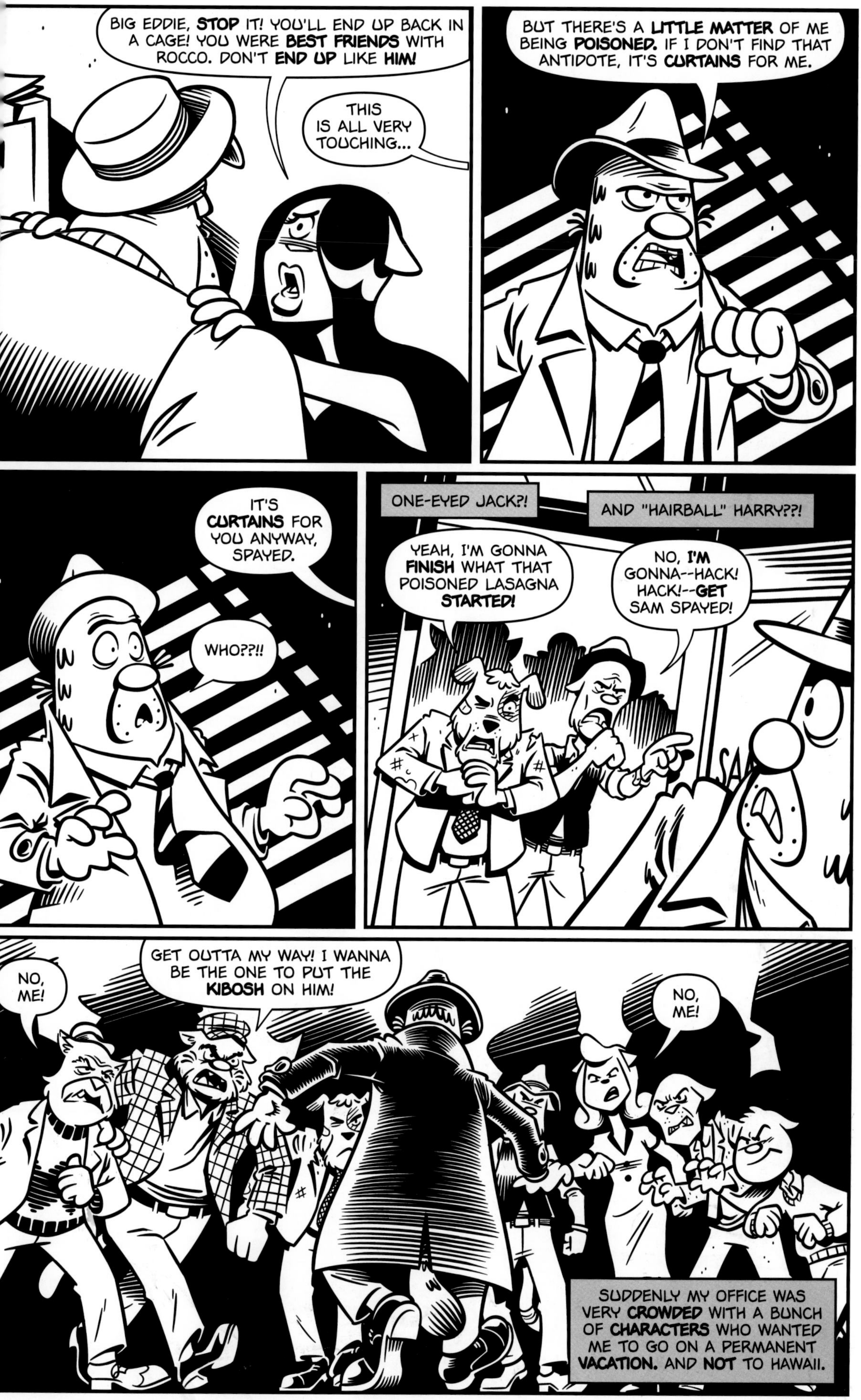
BIG EDDIE, STOP IT! YOU'LL END UP BACK IN A CAGE! YOU WERE BEST FRIENDS WITH ROCCO. DON'T END UP LIKE HIM!
THIS IS ALL VERY TOUCHING...
BUT THERE'S A LITTLE MATTER OF ME BEING POISONED. IF I DON'T FIND THAT ANTIDOTE, IT'S CURTAINS FOR ME.
IT'S CURTAINS FOR YOU ANYWAY, SPAYED.
WHO??!!
ONE-EYED JACK?!
AND "HAIRBALL" HARRY??!
YEAH, I'M GONNA FINISH WHAT THAT POISONED LASAGNA STARTED!
NO, I'M GONNA--HACK! HACK!--GET SAM SPAYED!
NO, ME!
GET OUTTA MY WAY! I WANNA BE THE ONE TO PUT THE KIBOSH ON HIM!
NO, ME!
SUDDENLY MY OFFICE WAS VERY CROWDED WITH A BUNCH OF CHARACTERS WHO WANTED ME TO GO ON A PERMANENT VACATION. AND NOT TO HAWAII.

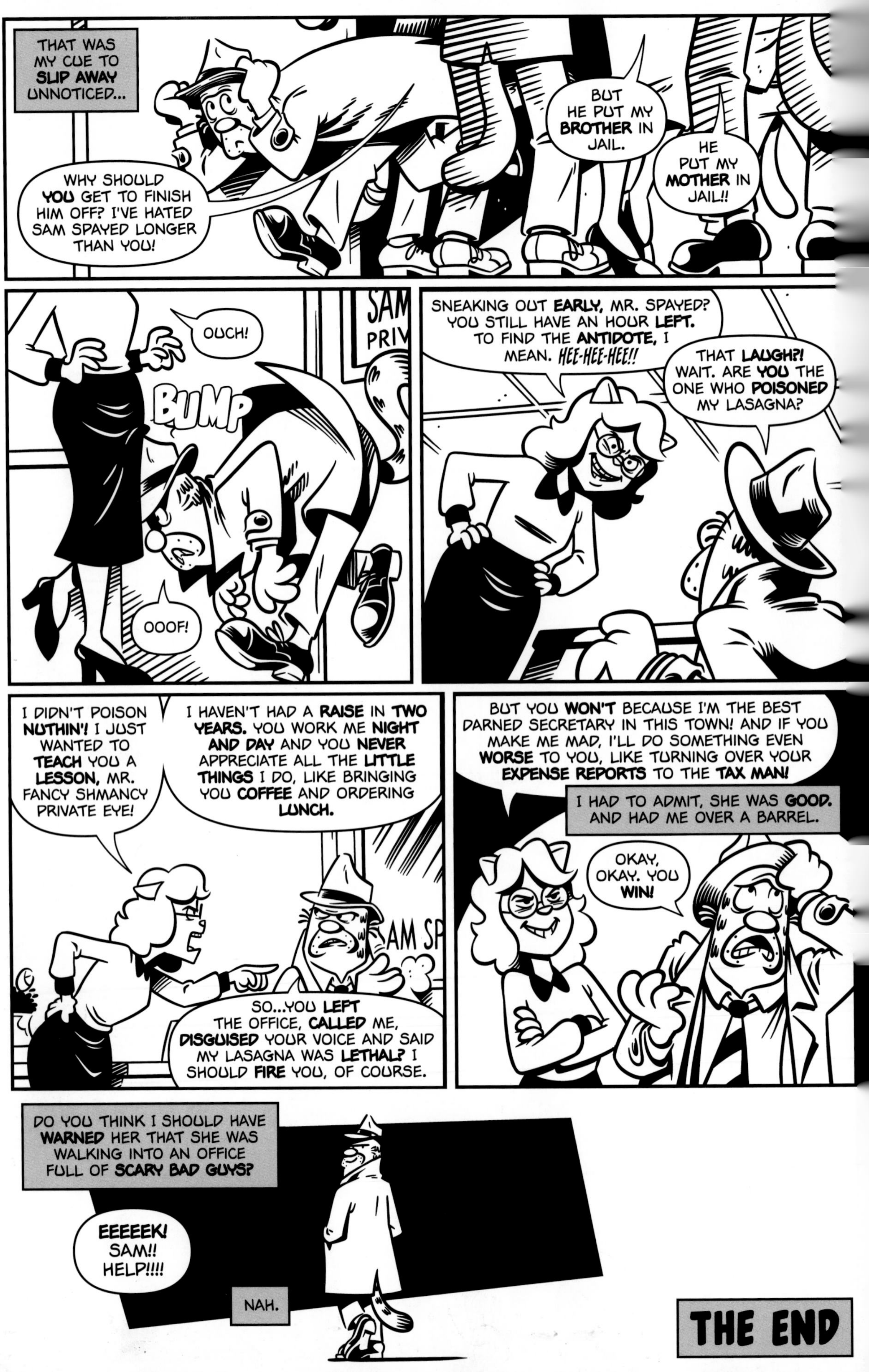

THAT WAS MY CUE TO SLIP AWAY UNNOTICED...
WHY SHOULD YOU GET TO FINISH HIM OFF? I'VE HATED SAM SPAYED LONGER THAN YOU!
BUT HE PUT MY BROTHER IN JAIL.
HE PUT MY MOTHER IN JAIL!!
OUCH!
BUMP
OOOF!
SAM
PRIV
SNEAKING OUT EARLY, MR. SPAYED? YOU STILL HAVE AN HOUR LEFT. TO FIND THE ANTIDOTE, I MEAN. HEE-HEE-HEE!!
THAT LAUGH?! WAIT. ARE YOU THE ONE WHO POISONED MY LASAGNA?
I DIDN'T POISON NUTHIN'! I JUST WANTED TO TEACH YOU A LESSON, MR. FANCY SHMANCY PRIVATE EYE!
I HAVEN'T HAD A RAISE IN TWO YEARS. YOU WORK ME NIGHT AND DAY AND YOU NEVER APPRECIATE ALL THE LITTLE THINGS I DO, LIKE BRINGING YOU COFFEE AND ORDERING LUNCH.
SO...YOU LEFT THE OFFICE, CALLED ME, DISGUISED YOUR VOICE AND SAID MY LASAGNA WAS LETHAL? I SHOULD FIRE YOU, OF COURSE.
BUT YOU WON'T BECAUSE I'M THE BEST DARNED SECRETARY IN THIS TOWN! AND IF YOU MAKE ME MAD, I'LL DO SOMETHING EVEN WORSE TO YOU, LIKE TURNING OVER YOUR EXPENSE REPORTS TO THE TAX MAN!
I HAD TO ADMIT, SHE WAS GOOD. AND HAD ME OVER A BARREL.
OKAY, OKAY. YOU WIN!
DO YOU THINK I SHOULD HAVE WARNED HER THAT SHE WAS WALKING INTO AN OFFICE FULL OF SCARY BAD GUYS?
EEEEEK! SAM!! HELP!!!!
NAH.
THE END

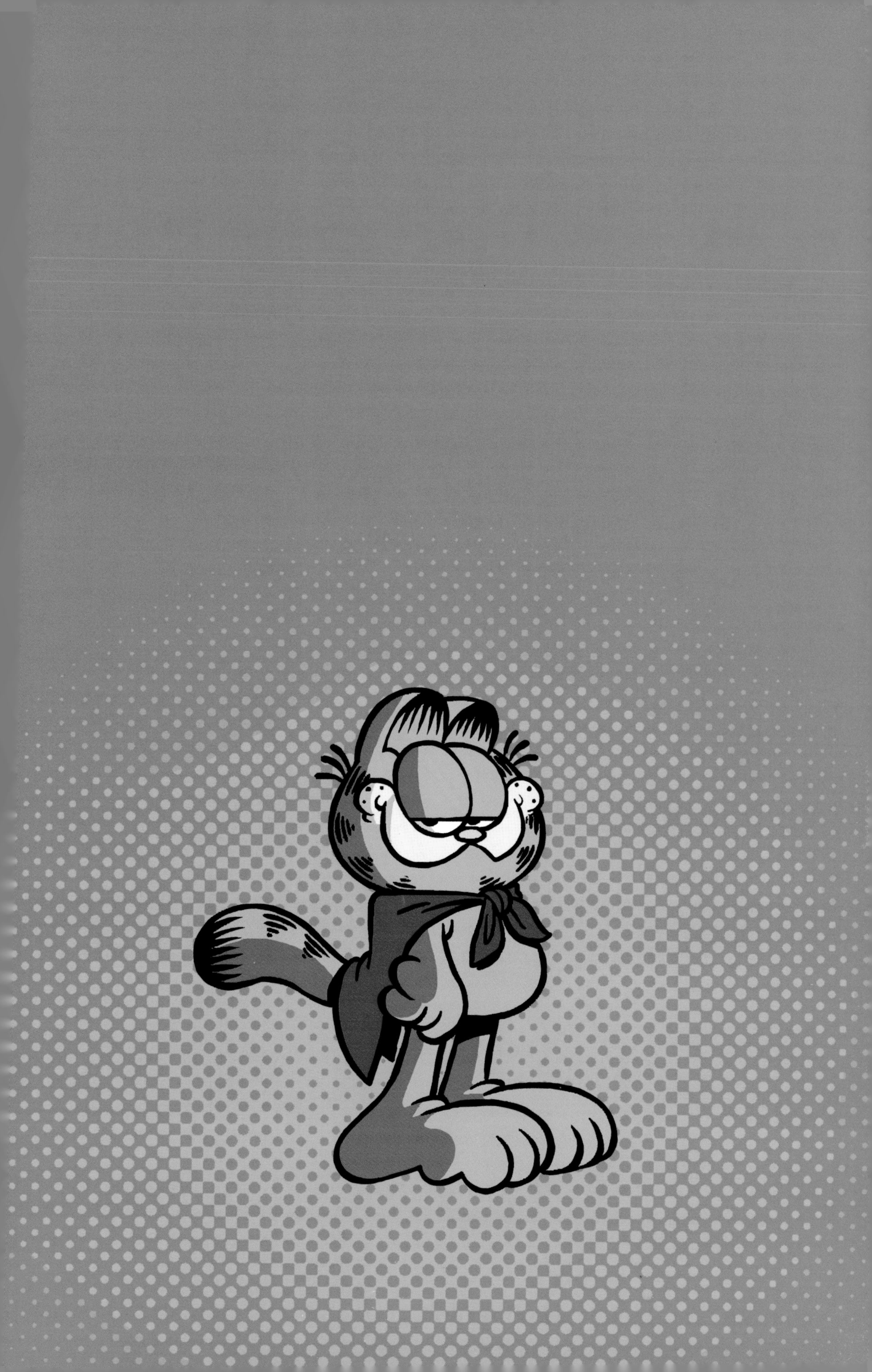

PART 4

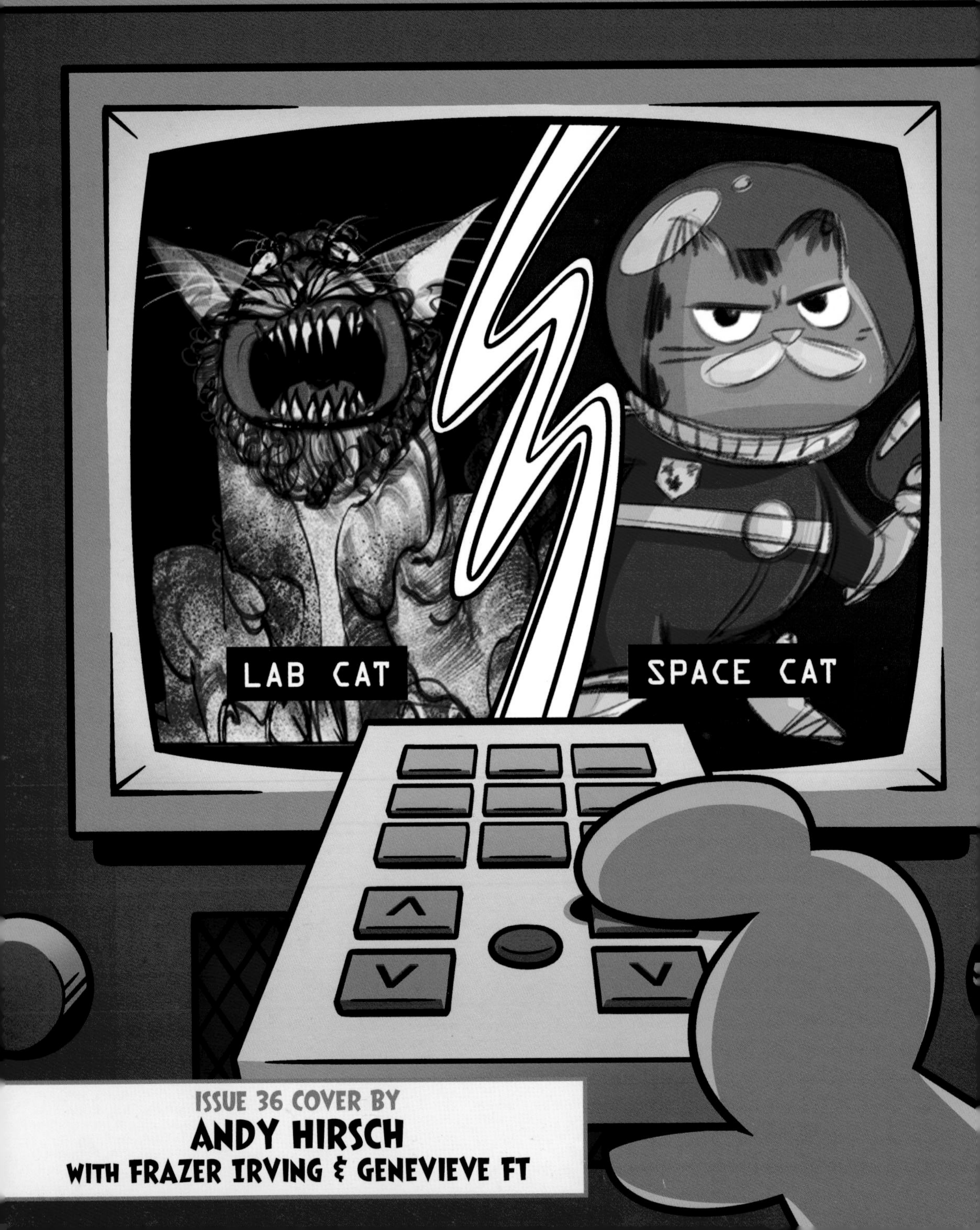
LAB CAT
SPACE CAT

ISSUE 36 COVER BY
ANDY HIRSCH
WITH FRAZER IRVING & GENEVIEVE FT

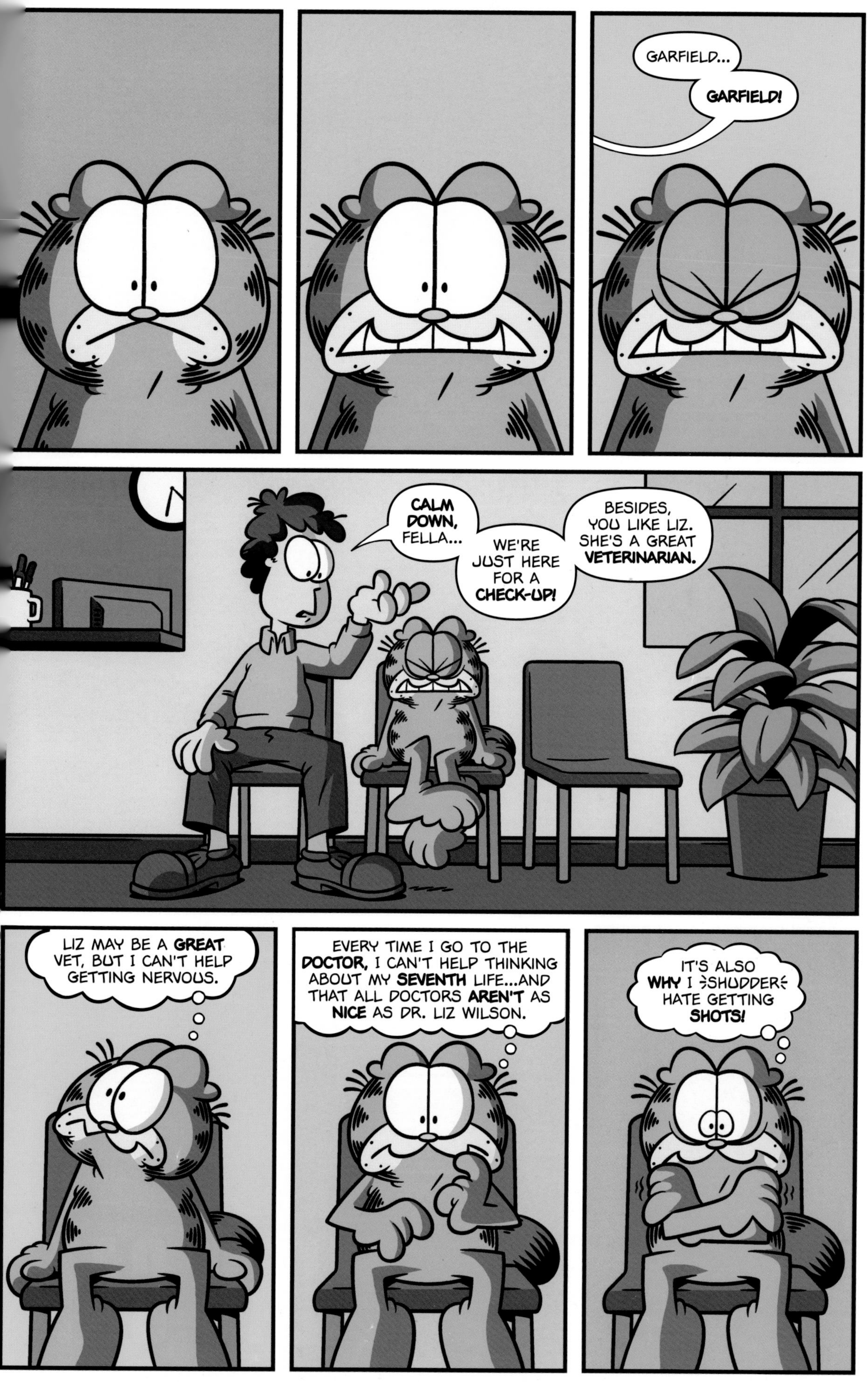
GARFIELD...
GARFIELD!
CALM DOWN, FELLA...
WE'RE JUST HERE FOR A CHECK-UP!
BESIDES, YOU LIKE LIZ. SHE'S A GREAT VETERINARIAN.
LIZ MAY BE A GREAT VET, BUT I CAN'T HELP GETTING NERVOUS.
EVERY TIME I GO TO THE DOCTOR, I CAN'T HELP THINKING ABOUT MY SEVENTH LIFE...AND THAT ALL DOCTORS AREN'T AS NICE AS DR. LIZ WILSON.
IT'S ALSO WHY I SHUDDER HATE GETTING SHOTS!

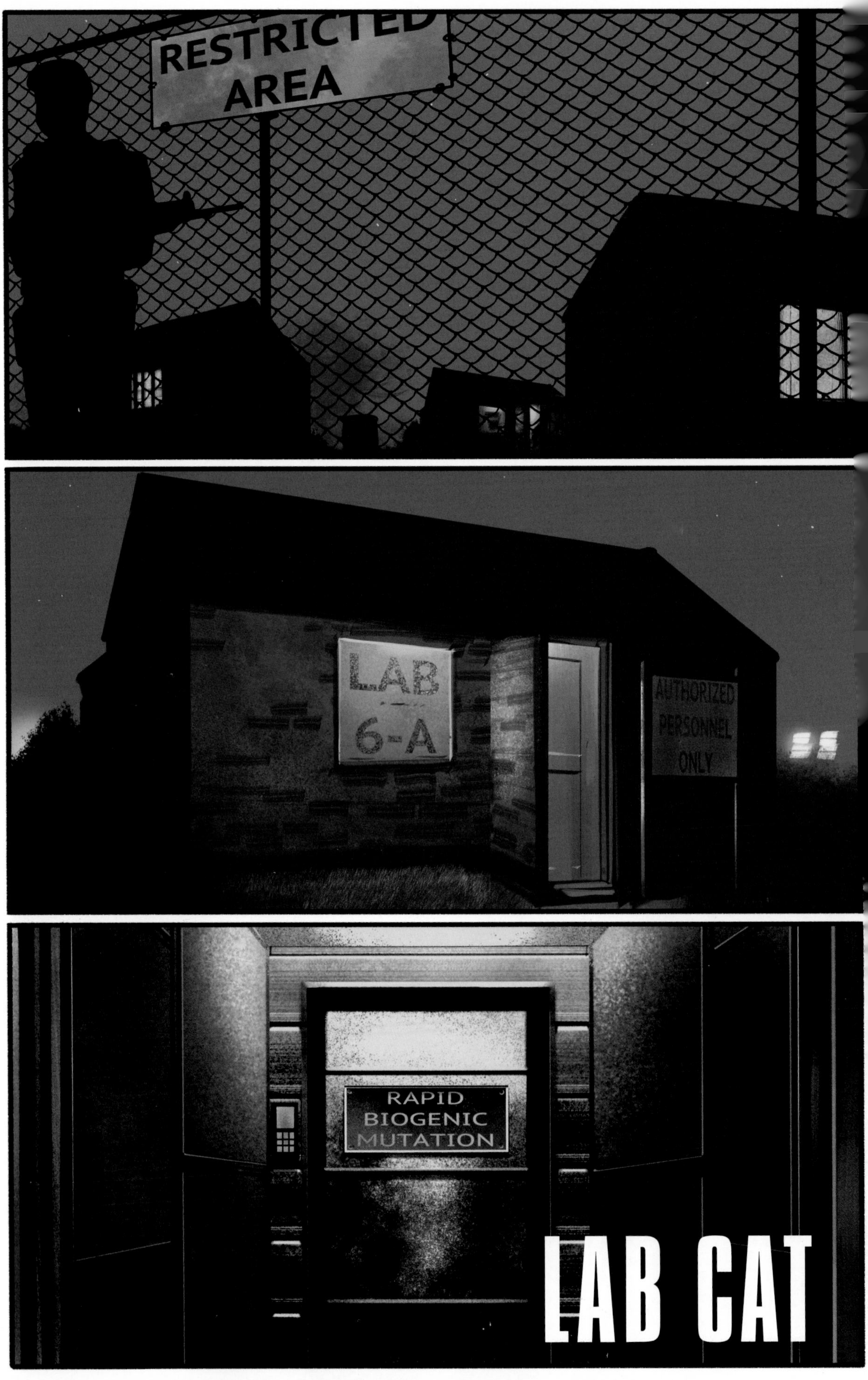
RESTRICTED AREA
LAB 6-A
AUTHORIZED PERSONNEL ONLY
RAPID BIOGENIC MUTATION
LAB CAT

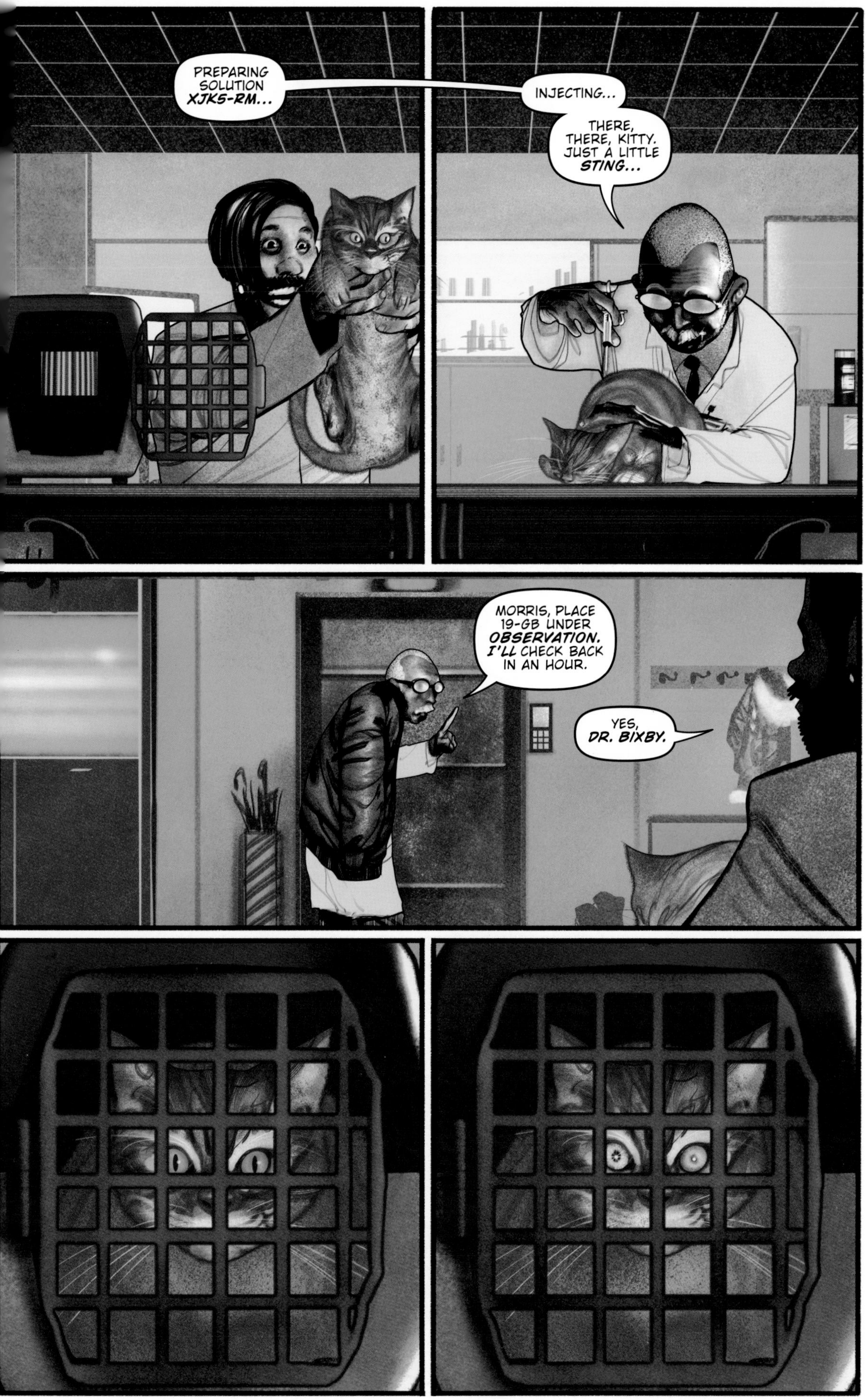
PREPARING SOLUTION XJKS-RM...
INJECTING...
THERE, THERE, KITTY. JUST A LITTLE STING...
MORRIS, PLACE 19-GB UNDER OBSERVATION. I'LL CHECK BACK IN AN HOUR.
YES, DR. BIXBY.

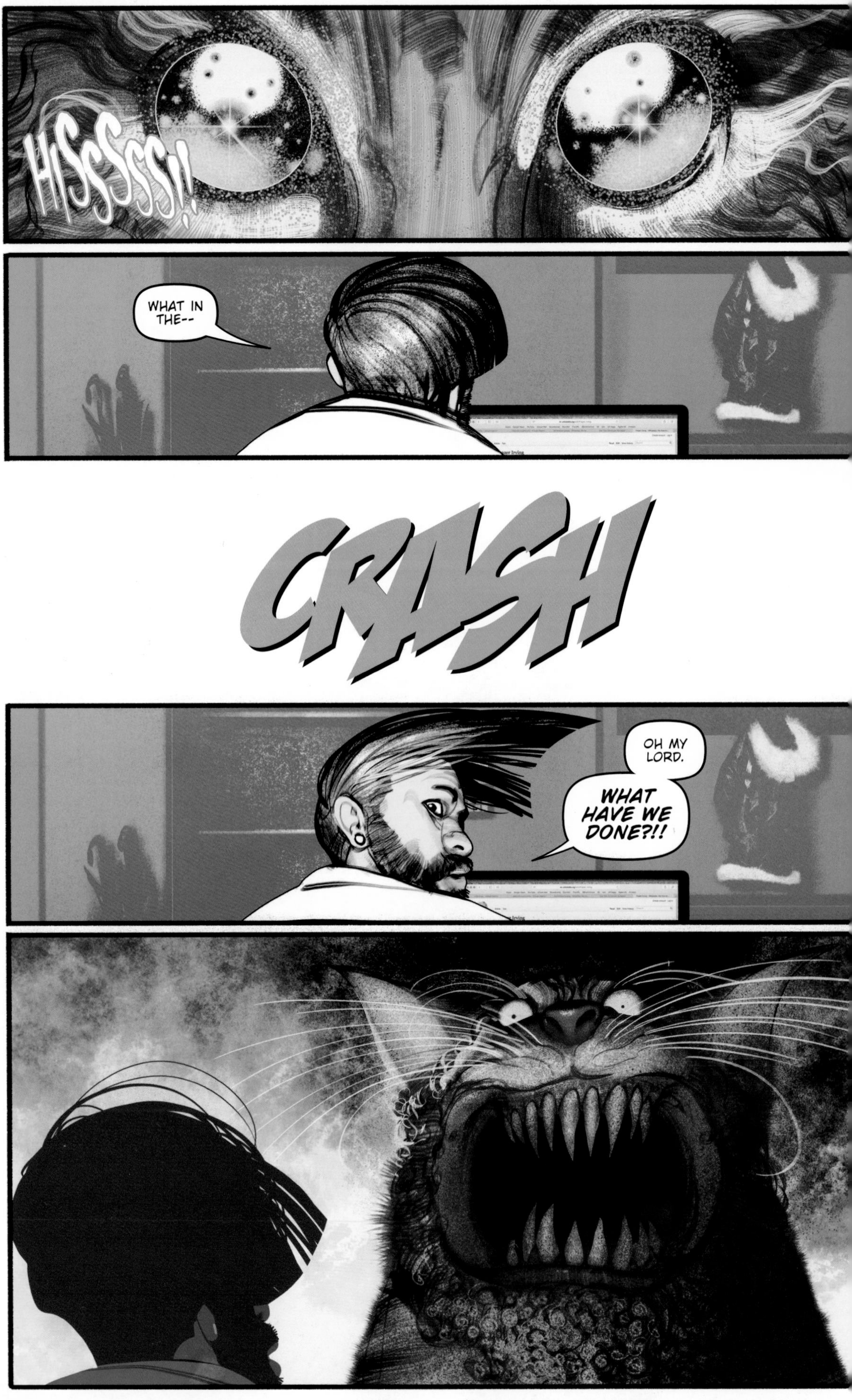
HISSSSS!!
WHAT IN THE--
CRASH
OH MY LORD.
WHAT HAVE WE DONE?!!

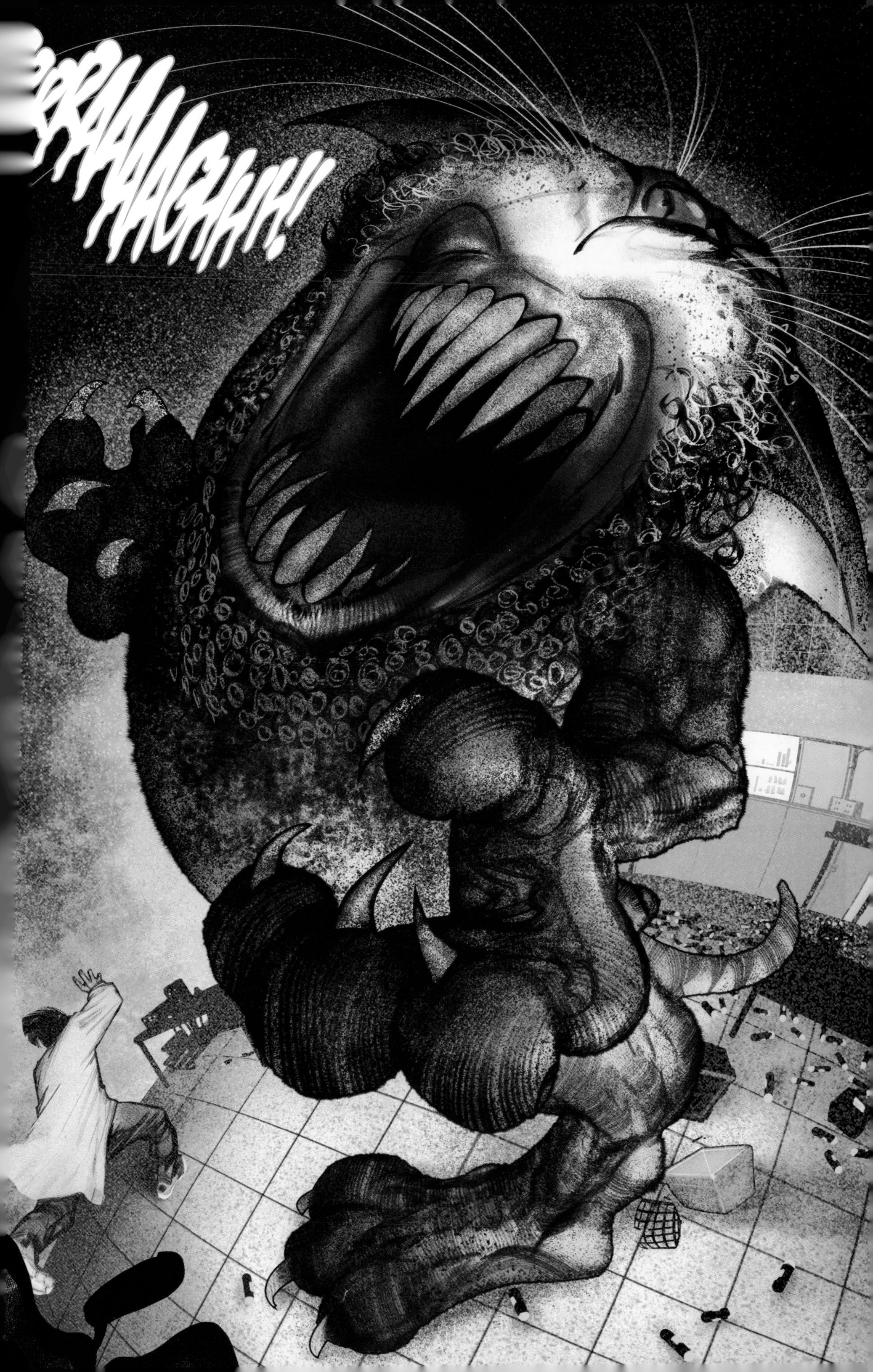
RRAAAAAGHHH!!

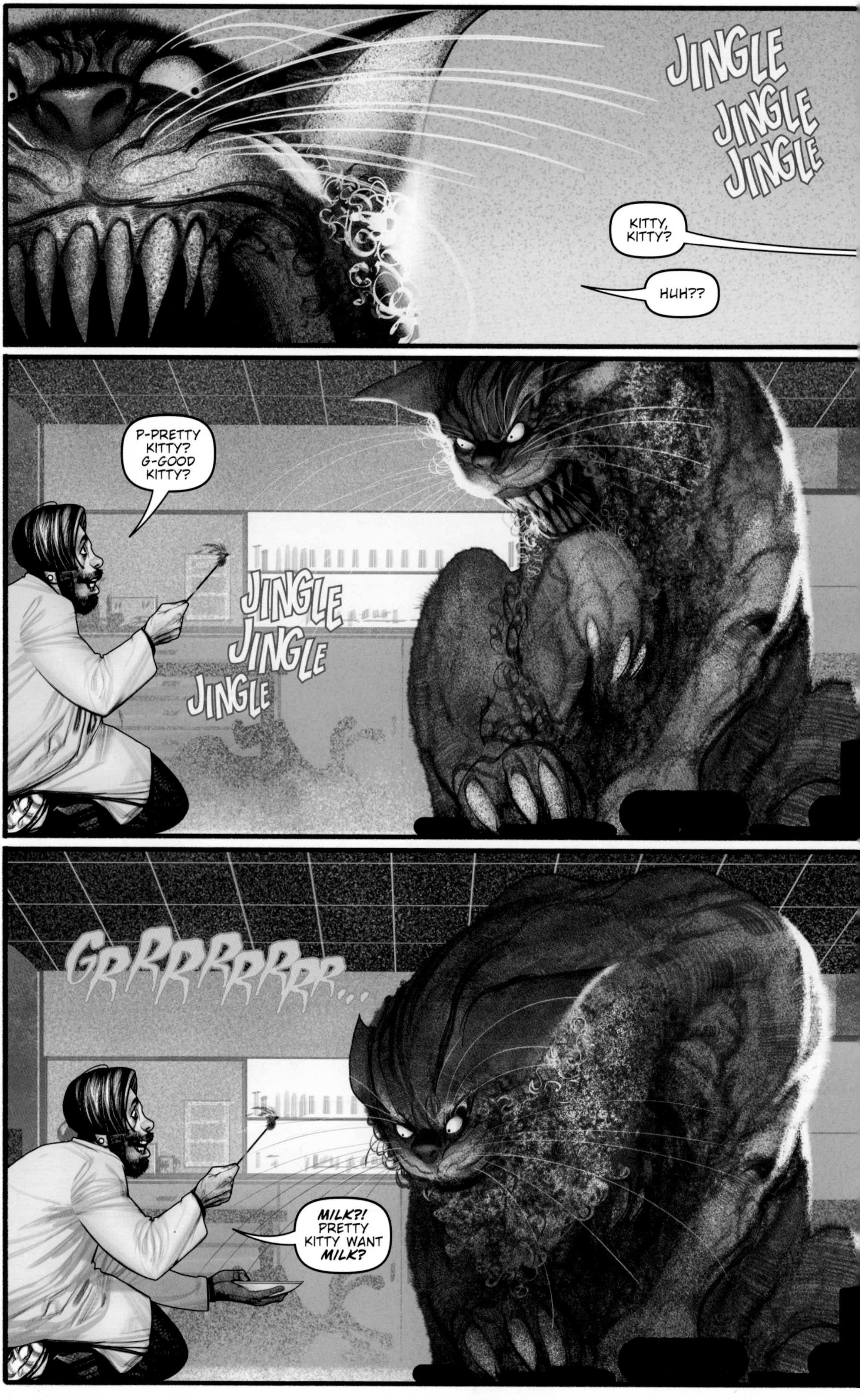
JINGLE
JINGLE
JINGLE
KITTY, KITTY?
HUH??
P-PRETTY KITTY? G-GOOD KITTY?
JINGLE
JINGLE
JINGLE
GRRRRRRRR...
MILK?! PRETTY KITTY WANT MILK?

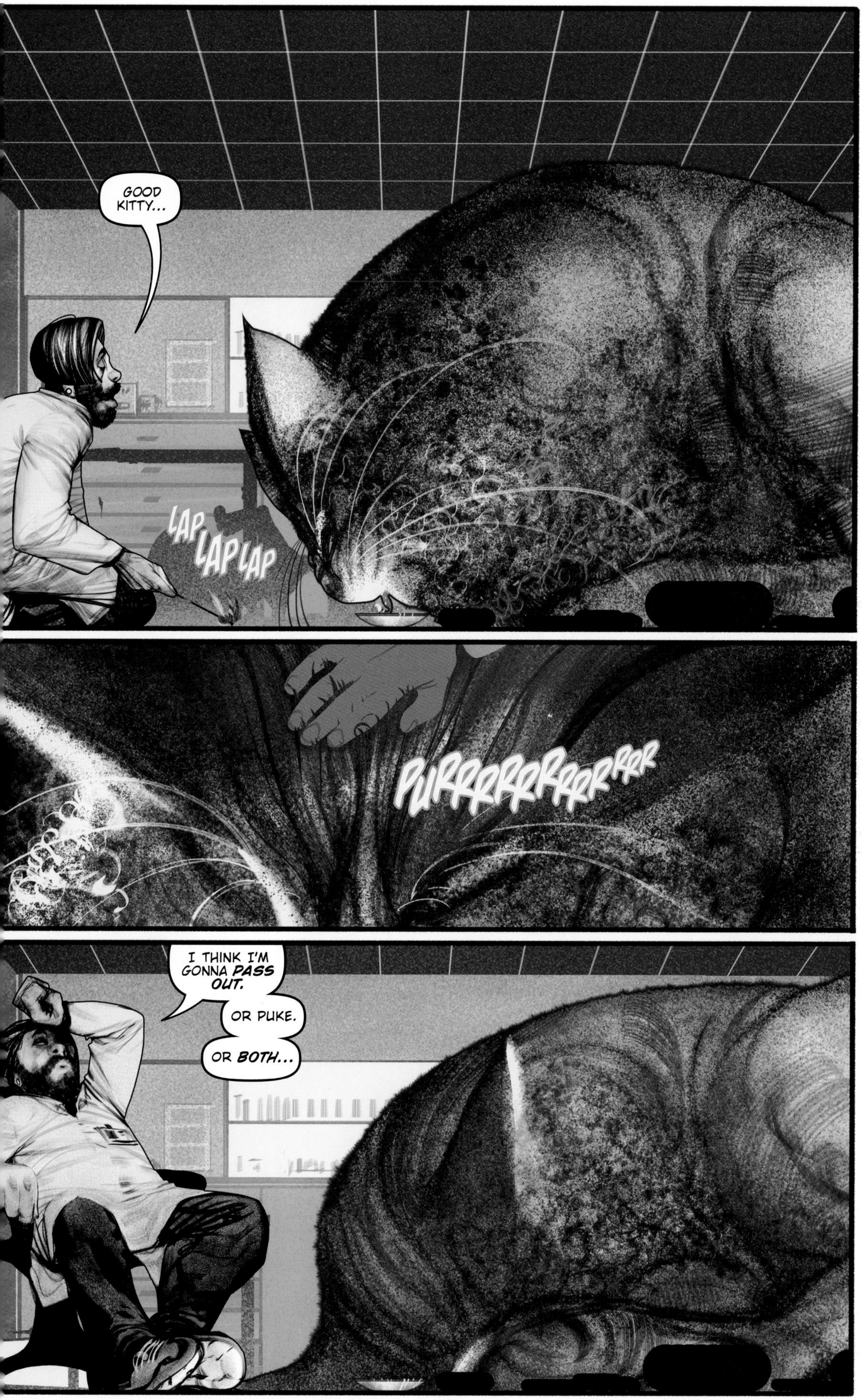
GOOD KITTY...
LAP LAP LAP
PURRRRRRRRRRRRR
I THINK I'M GONNA PASS OUT.
OR PUKE.
OR BOTH...

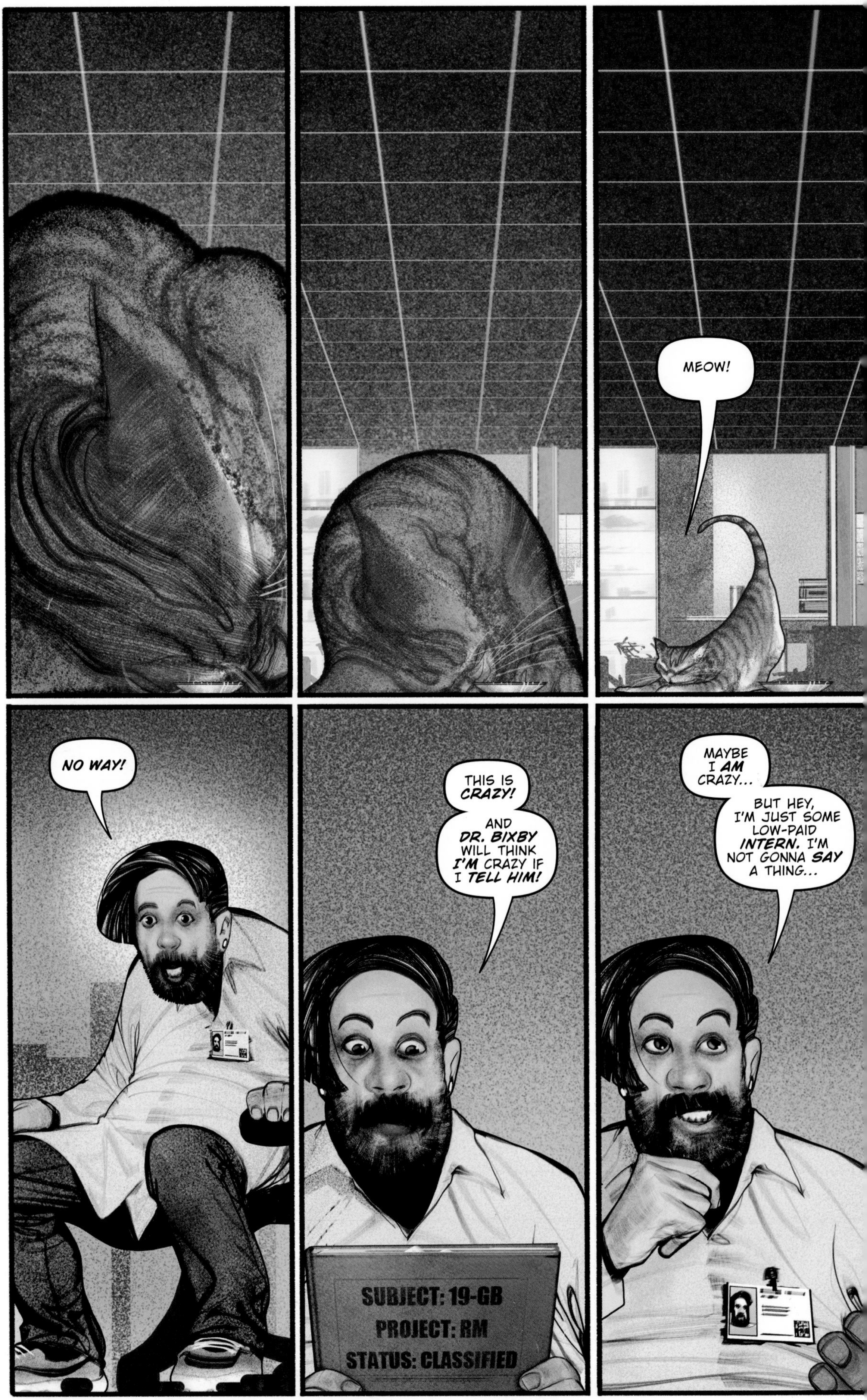
MEOW!
NO WAY!
THIS IS CRAZY!
AND DR. BIXBY WILL THINK I'M CRAZY IF I TELL HIM!
SUBJECT: 19-GB
PROJECT: RM
STATUS: CLASSIFIED
MAYBE I AM CRAZY...
BUT HEY, I'M JUST SOME LOW-PAID INTERN. I'M NOT GONNA SAY A THING...

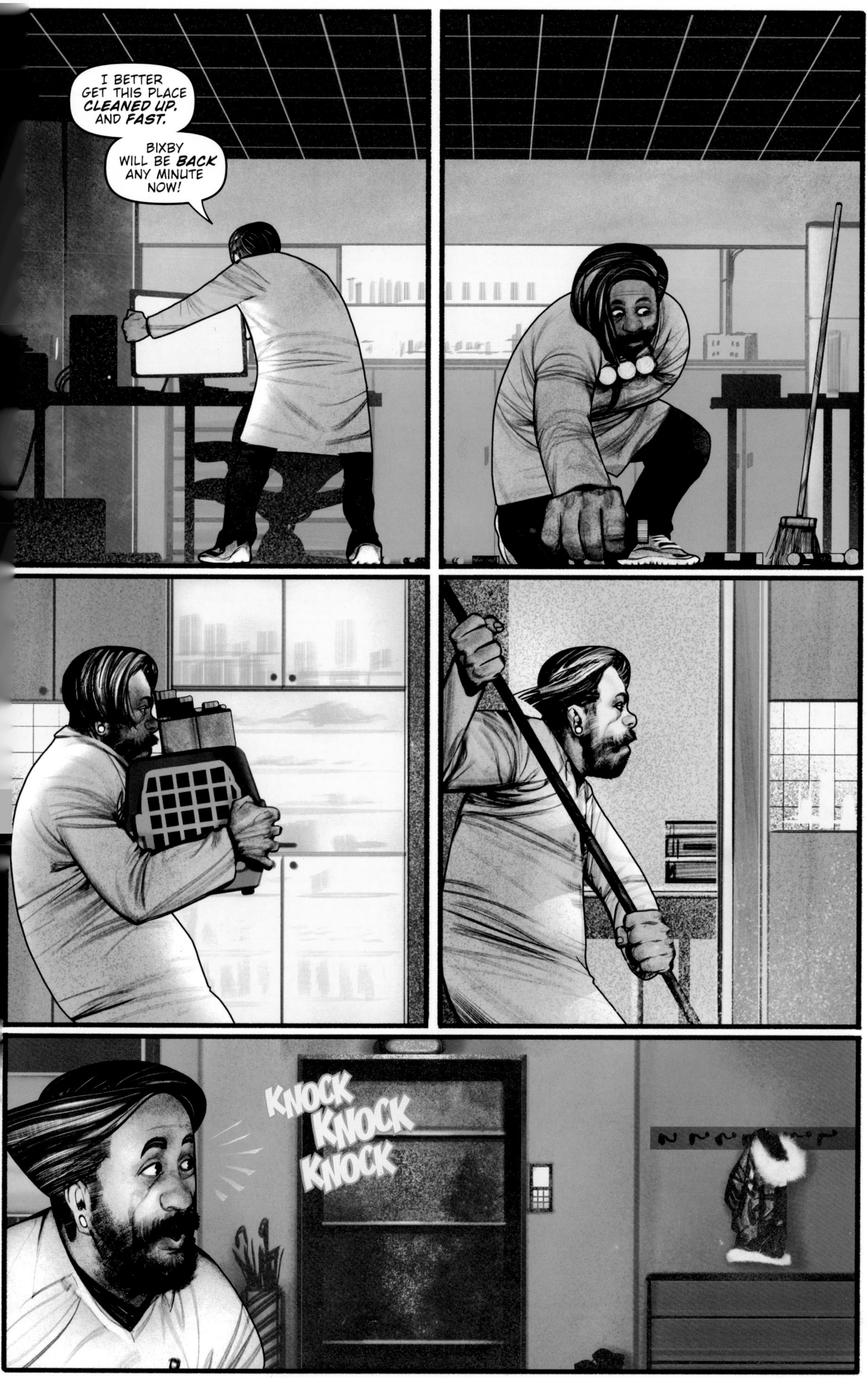

I BETTER GET THIS PLACE CLEANED UP. AND FAST.
BIXBY WILL BE BACK ANY MINUTE NOW!
KNOCK KNOCK KNOCK

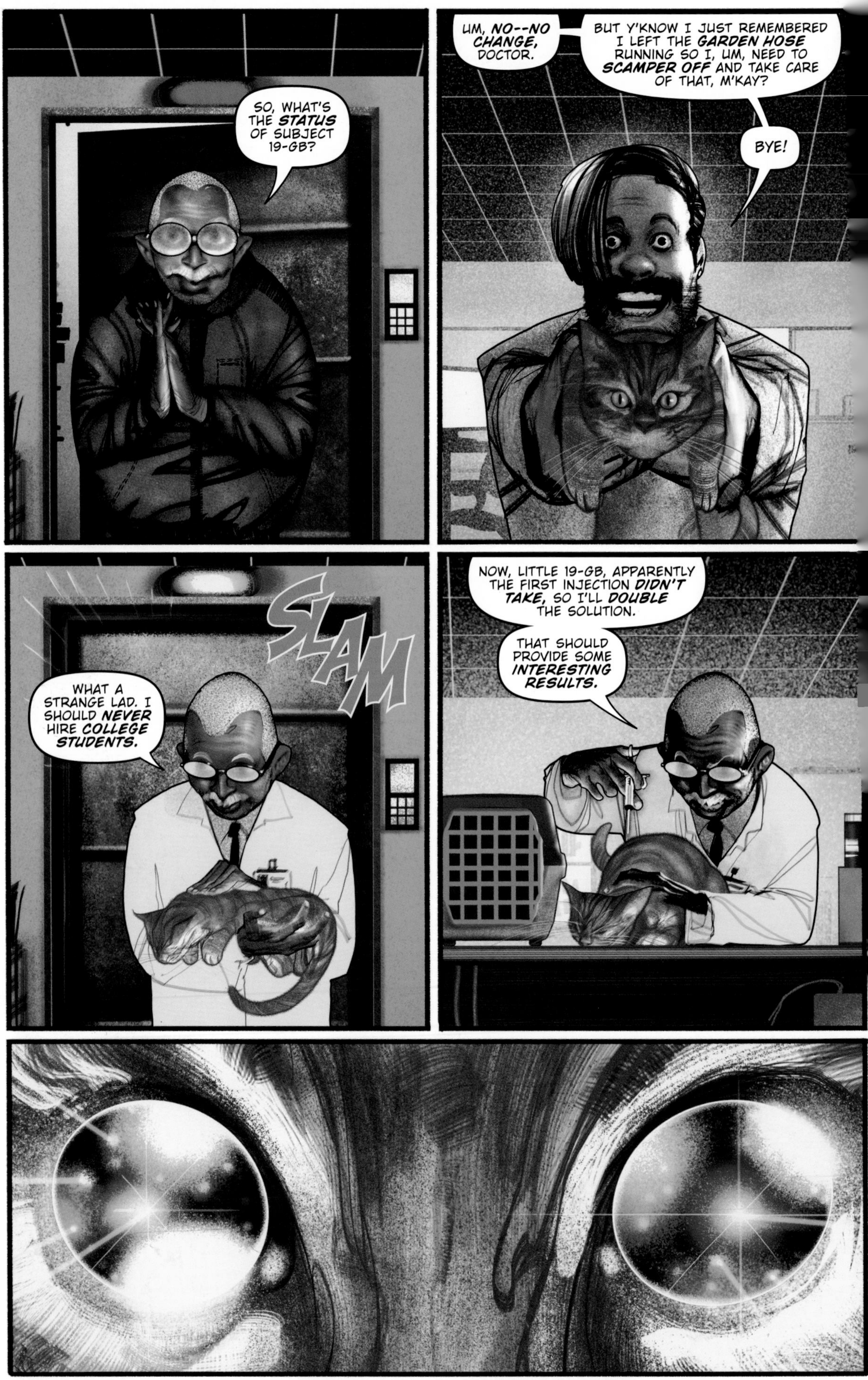

SO, WHAT'S THE STATUS OF SUBJECT 19-GB?
UM, NO--NO CHANGE, DOCTOR.
BUT Y'KNOW I JUST REMEMBERED I LEFT THE GARDEN HOSE RUNNING SO I, UM, NEED TO SCAMPER OFF AND TAKE CARE OF THAT, M'KAY?
BYE!
SLAM
WHAT A STRANGE LAD. I SHOULD NEVER HIRE COLLEGE STUDENTS.
NOW, LITTLE 19-GB, APPARENTLY THE FIRST INJECTION DIDN'T TAKE, SO I'LL DOUBLE THE SOLUTION.
THAT SHOULD PROVIDE SOME INTERESTING RESULTS.

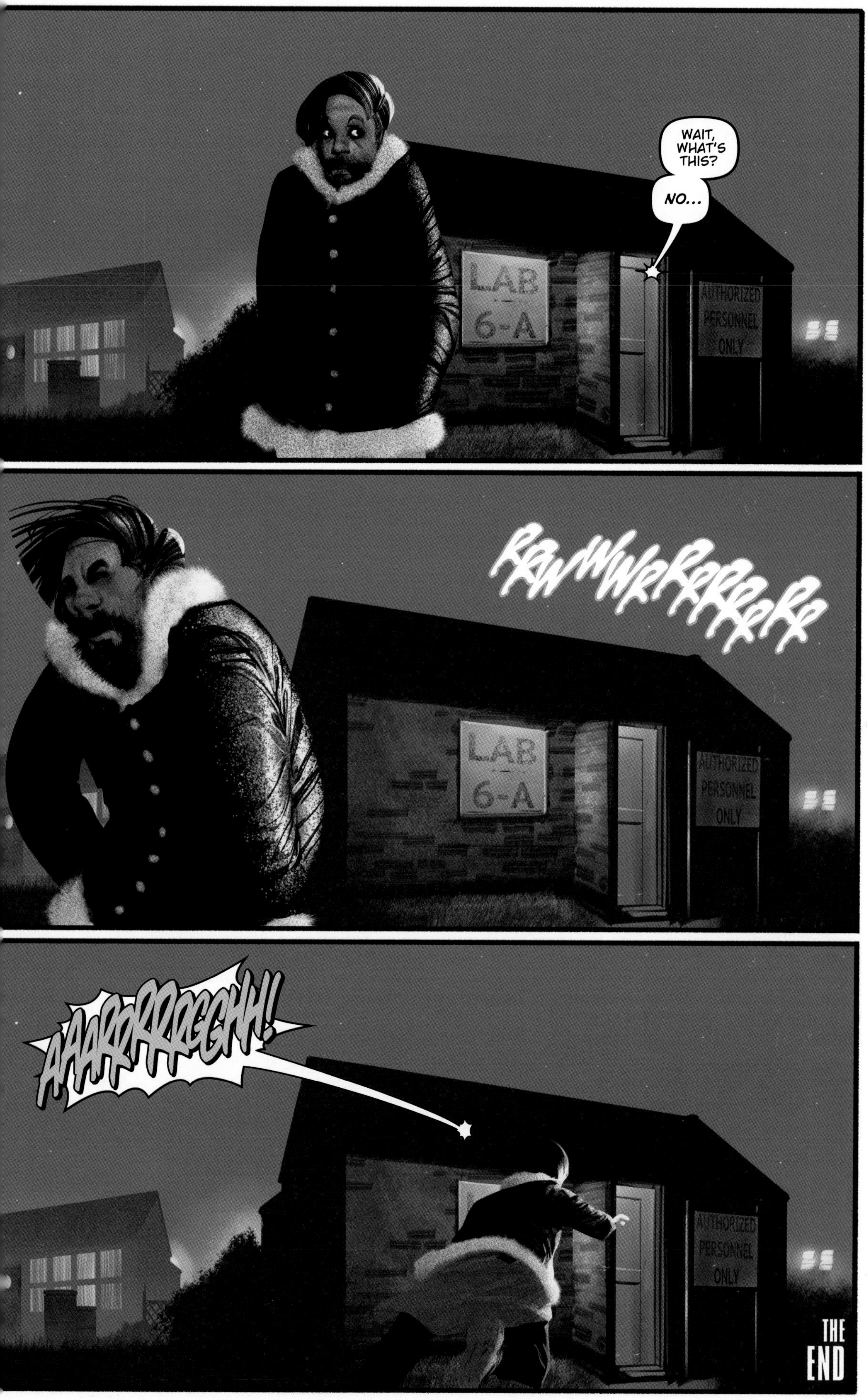
WAIT, WHAT'S THIS?
NO...
LAB 6-A
AUTHORIZED PERSONNEL ONLY
RAWWWRRRRRRRR
LAB 6-A
AUTHORIZED PERSONNEL ONLY
AAARRRRRGGHH!
AUTHORIZED PERSONNEL ONLY
THE END

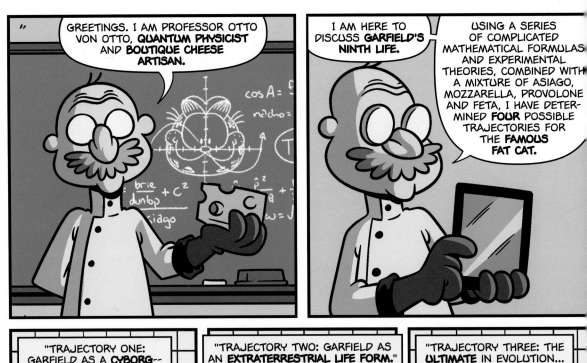

GREETINGS. I AM PROFESSOR OTTO VON OTTO, **QUANTUM PHYSICIST** AND **BOUTIQUE CHEESE ARTISAN.**

I AM HERE TO DISCUSS **GARFIELD'S NINTH LIFE.**

USING A SERIES OF COMPLICATED MATHEMATICAL FORMULAS AND EXPERIMENTAL THEORIES, COMBINED WITH A MIXTURE OF ASIAGO, MOZZARELLA, PROVOLONE AND FETA, I HAVE DETERMINED **FOUR** POSSIBLE TRAJECTORIES FOR THE **FAMOUS FAT CAT.**

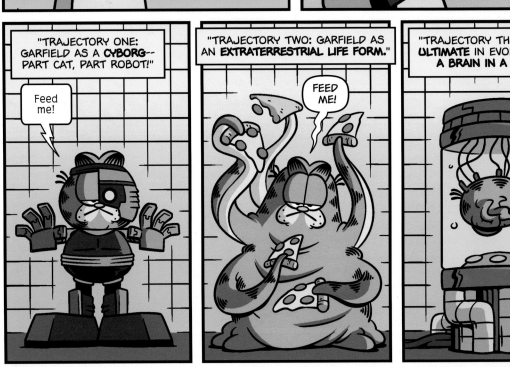

"TRAJECTORY ONE: GARFIELD AS A **CYBORG**-- PART CAT, PART ROBOT!"

Feed me!

"TRAJECTORY TWO: GARFIELD AS AN **EXTRATERRESTRIAL LIFE FORM.**"

FEED ME!

"TRAJECTORY THREE: THE **ULTIMATE** IN EVOLUTION... A BRAIN IN A JAR!"

FEED ME!

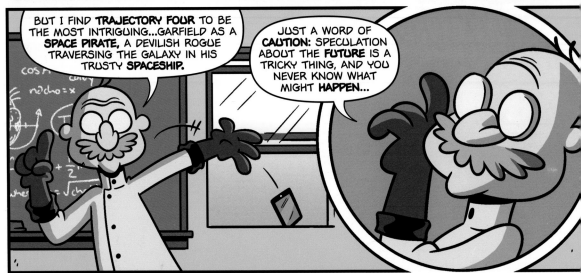

BUT I FIND **TRAJECTORY FOUR** TO BE THE MOST INTRIGUING...GARFIELD AS A **SPACE PIRATE**, A DEVILISH ROGUE TRAVERSING THE GALAXY IN HIS TRUSTY **SPACESHIP.**

JUST A WORD OF **CAUTION**: SPECULATION ABOUT THE **FUTURE** IS A TRICKY THING, AND YOU NEVER KNOW WHAT MIGHT **HAPPEN**...

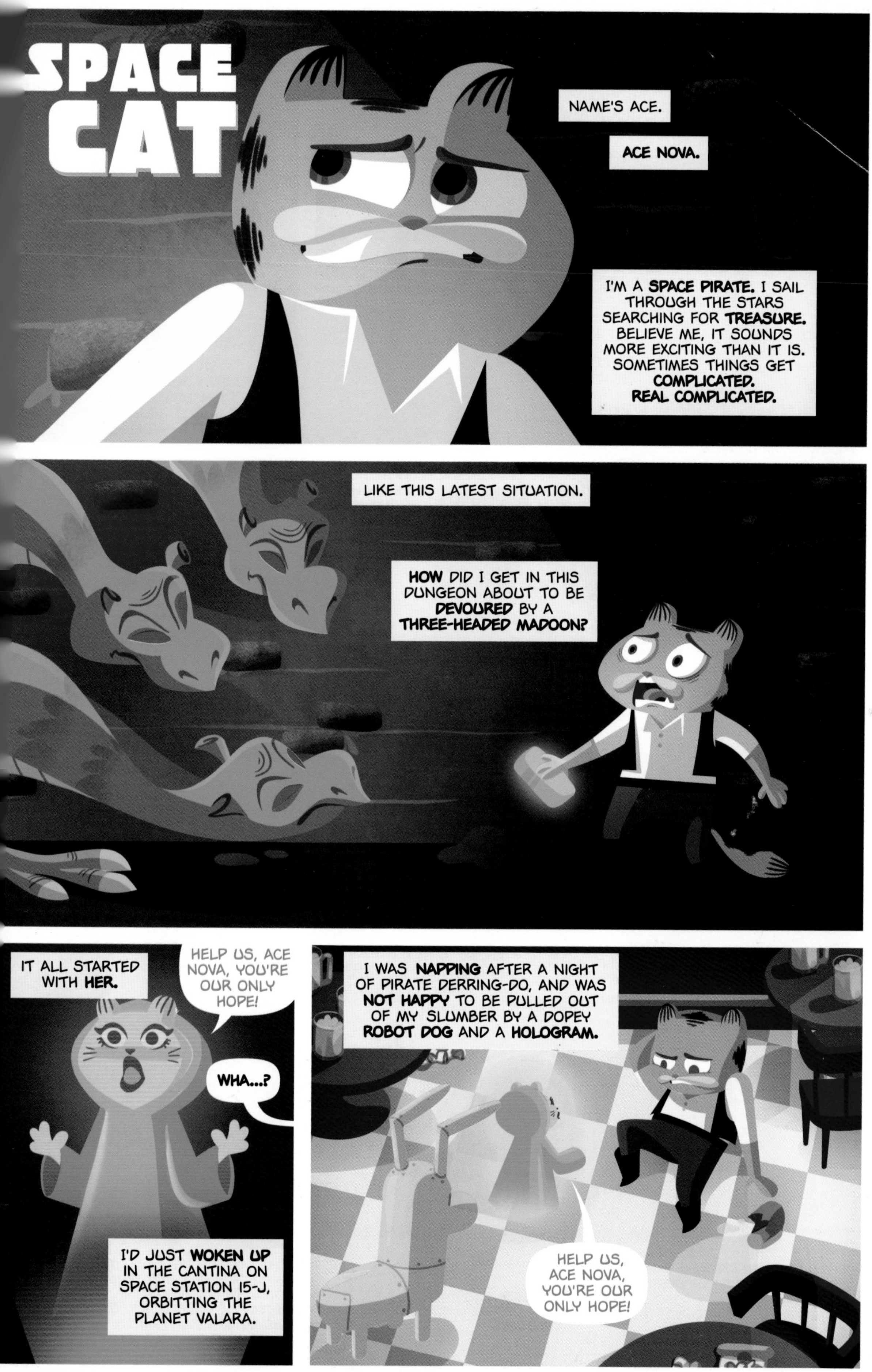
SPACE CAT
NAME'S ACE.
ACE NOVA.
I'M A SPACE PIRATE. I SAIL THROUGH THE STARS SEARCHING FOR TREASURE. BELIEVE ME, IT SOUNDS MORE EXCITING THAN IT IS. SOMETIMES THINGS GET COMPLICATED. REAL COMPLICATED.
LIKE THIS LATEST SITUATION.
HOW DID I GET IN THIS DUNGEON ABOUT TO BE DEVOURED BY A THREE-HEADED MADOON?
IT ALL STARTED WITH HER.
HELP US, ACE NOVA, YOU'RE OUR ONLY HOPE!
WHA...?
I'D JUST WOKEN UP IN THE CANTINA ON SPACE STATION 15-J, ORBITTING THE PLANET VALARA.
I WAS NAPPING AFTER A NIGHT OF PIRATE DERRING-DO, AND WAS NOT HAPPY TO BE PULLED OUT OF MY SLUMBER BY A DOPEY ROBOT DOG AND A HOLOGRAM.
HELP US, ACE NOVA, YOU'RE OUR ONLY HOPE!

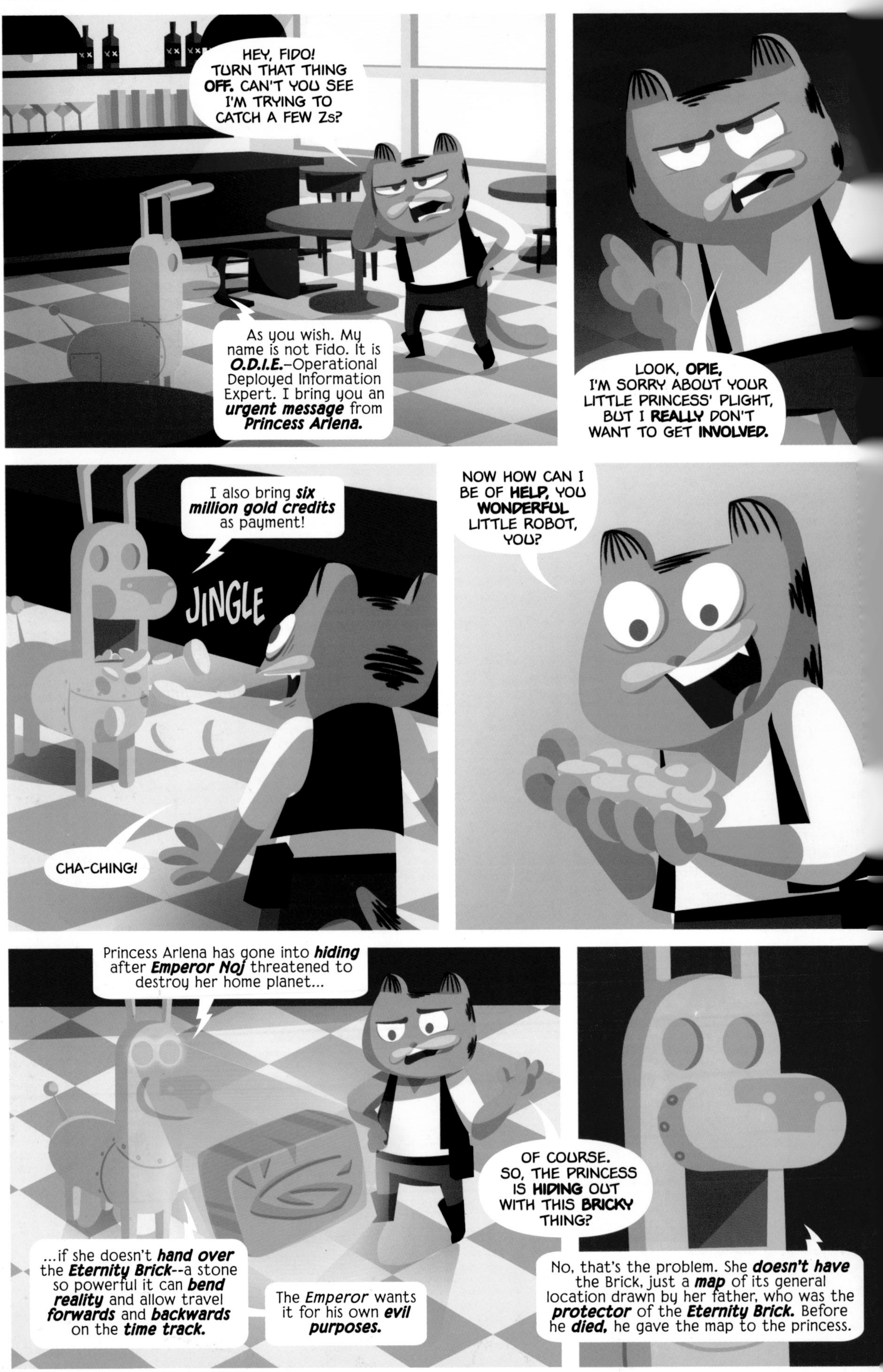
HEY, FIDO! TURN THAT THING OFF. CAN'T YOU SEE I'M TRYING TO CATCH A FEW Zs?
As you wish. My name is not Fido. It is O.D.I.E.–Operational Deployed Information Expert. I bring you an urgent message from Princess Arlena.
LOOK, OPIE, I'M SORRY ABOUT YOUR LITTLE PRINCESS' PLIGHT, BUT I REALLY DON'T WANT TO GET INVOLVED.
I also bring six million gold credits as payment!
JINGLE
CHA-CHING!
NOW HOW CAN I BE OF HELP, YOU WONDERFUL LITTLE ROBOT, YOU?
Princess Arlena has gone into hiding after Emperor Noj threatened to destroy her home planet...
...if she doesn't hand over the Eternity Brick--a stone so powerful it can bend reality and allow travel forwards and backwards on the time track.
The Emperor wants it for his own evil purposes.
OF COURSE. SO, THE PRINCESS IS HIDING OUT WITH THIS BRICKY THING?
No, that's the problem. She doesn't have the Brick, just a map of its general location drawn by her father, who was the protector of the Eternity Brick. Before he died, he gave the map to the princess.

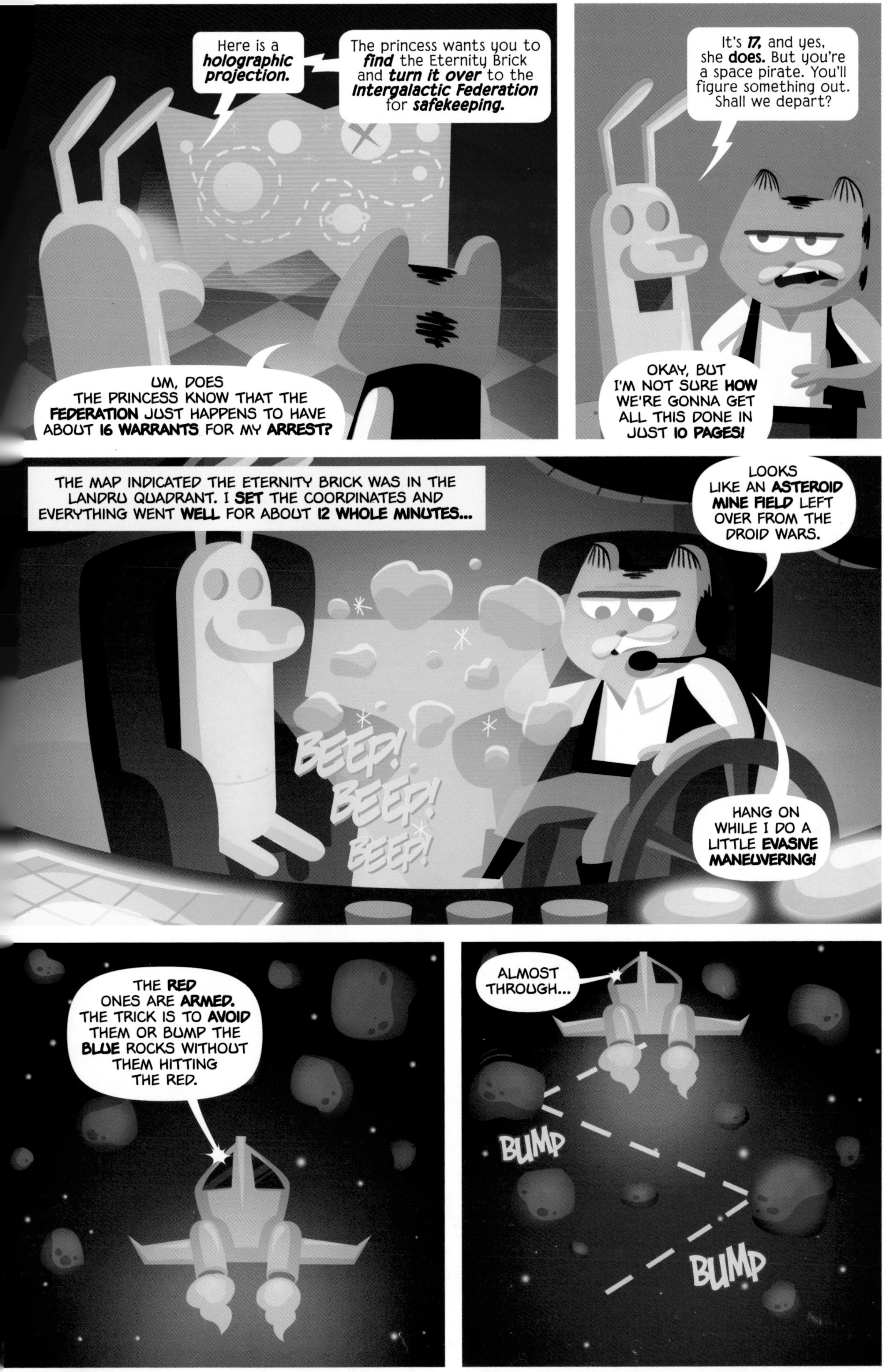
Here is a holographic projection.
The princess wants you to find the Eternity Brick and turn it over to the Intergalactic Federation for safekeeping.
UM, DOES THE PRINCESS KNOW THAT THE FEDERATION JUST HAPPENS TO HAVE ABOUT 16 WARRANTS FOR MY ARREST?
It's 17, and yes, she does. But you're a space pirate. You'll figure something out. Shall we depart?
OKAY, BUT I'M NOT SURE HOW WE'RE GONNA GET ALL THIS DONE IN JUST 10 PAGES!
THE MAP INDICATED THE ETERNITY BRICK WAS IN THE LANDRU QUADRANT. I SET THE COORDINATES AND EVERYTHING WENT WELL FOR ABOUT 12 WHOLE MINUTES...
LOOKS LIKE AN ASTEROID MINE FIELD LEFT OVER FROM THE DROID WARS.
BEEP! BEEP! BEEP!
HANG ON WHILE I DO A LITTLE EVASIVE MANEUVERING!
THE RED ONES ARE ARMED. THE TRICK IS TO AVOID THEM OR BUMP THE BLUE ROCKS WITHOUT THEM HITTING THE RED.
ALMOST THROUGH...
BUMP
BUMP

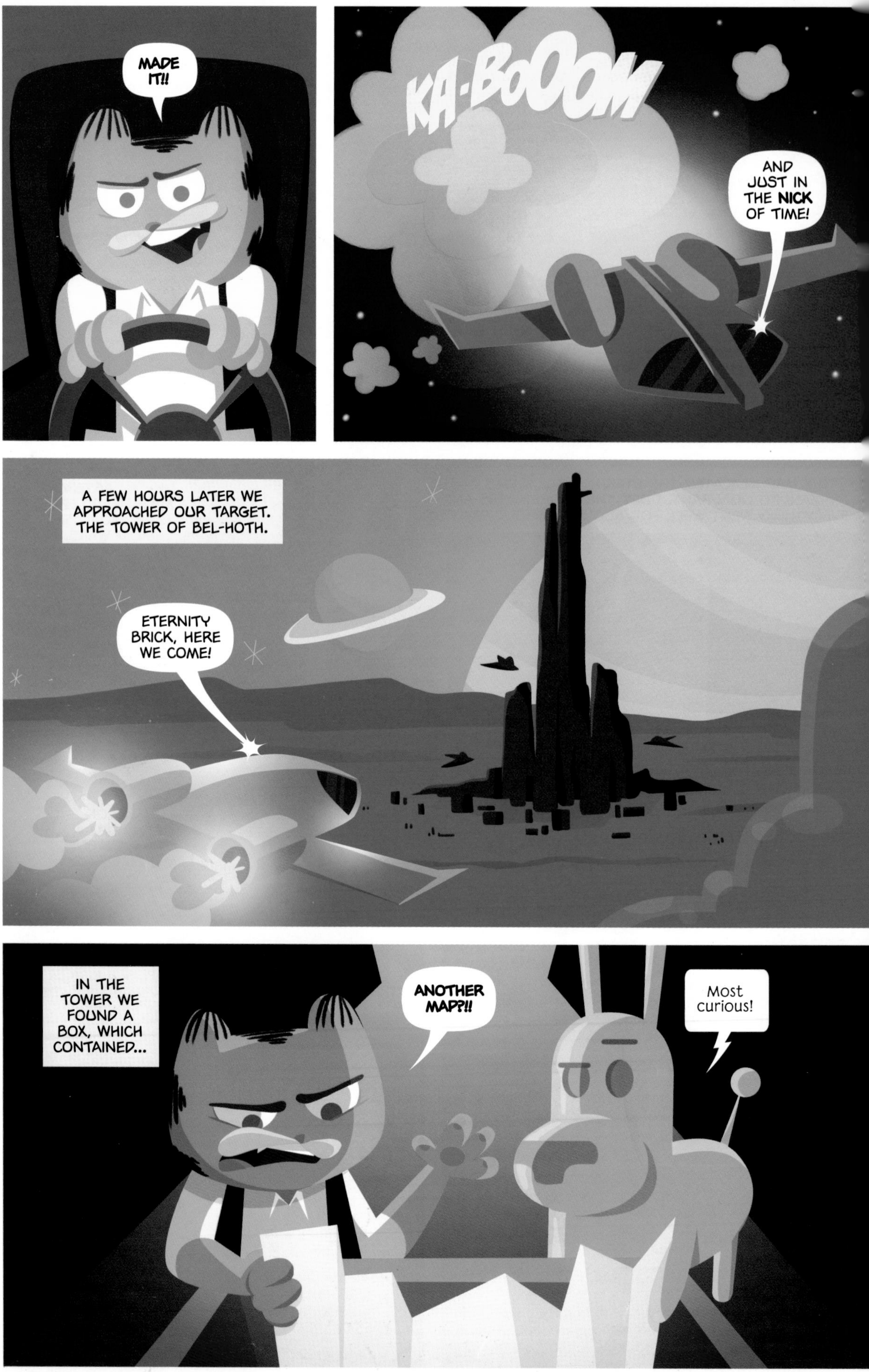

MADE IT!!
KA-BOOOM
AND JUST IN THE **NICK** OF TIME!
A FEW HOURS LATER WE APPROACHED OUR TARGET. THE TOWER OF BEL-HOTH.
ETERNITY BRICK, HERE WE COME!
IN THE TOWER WE FOUND A BOX, WHICH CONTAINED...
ANOTHER MAP?!!
Most curious!

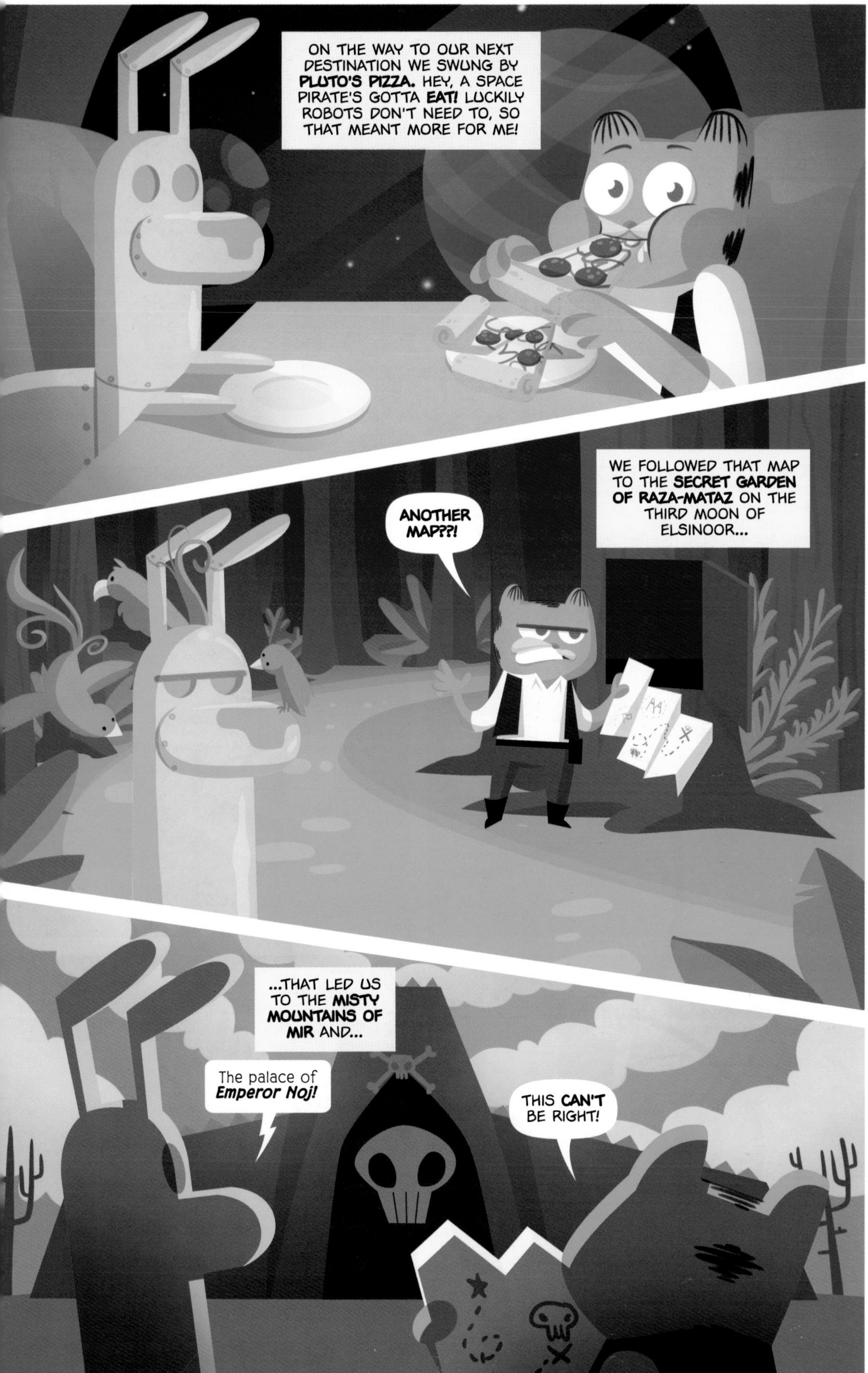

ON THE WAY TO OUR NEXT DESTINATION WE SWUNG BY **PLUTO'S PIZZA.** HEY, A SPACE PIRATE'S GOTTA **EAT!** LUCKILY ROBOTS DON'T NEED TO, SO THAT MEANT MORE FOR ME!
WE FOLLOWED THAT MAP TO THE **SECRET GARDEN OF RAZA-MATAZ** ON THE THIRD MOON OF ELSINOOR...
ANOTHER MAP??!
...THAT LED US TO THE **MISTY MOUNTAINS OF MIR** AND...
The palace of ***Emperor Noj!***
THIS **CAN'T** BE RIGHT!

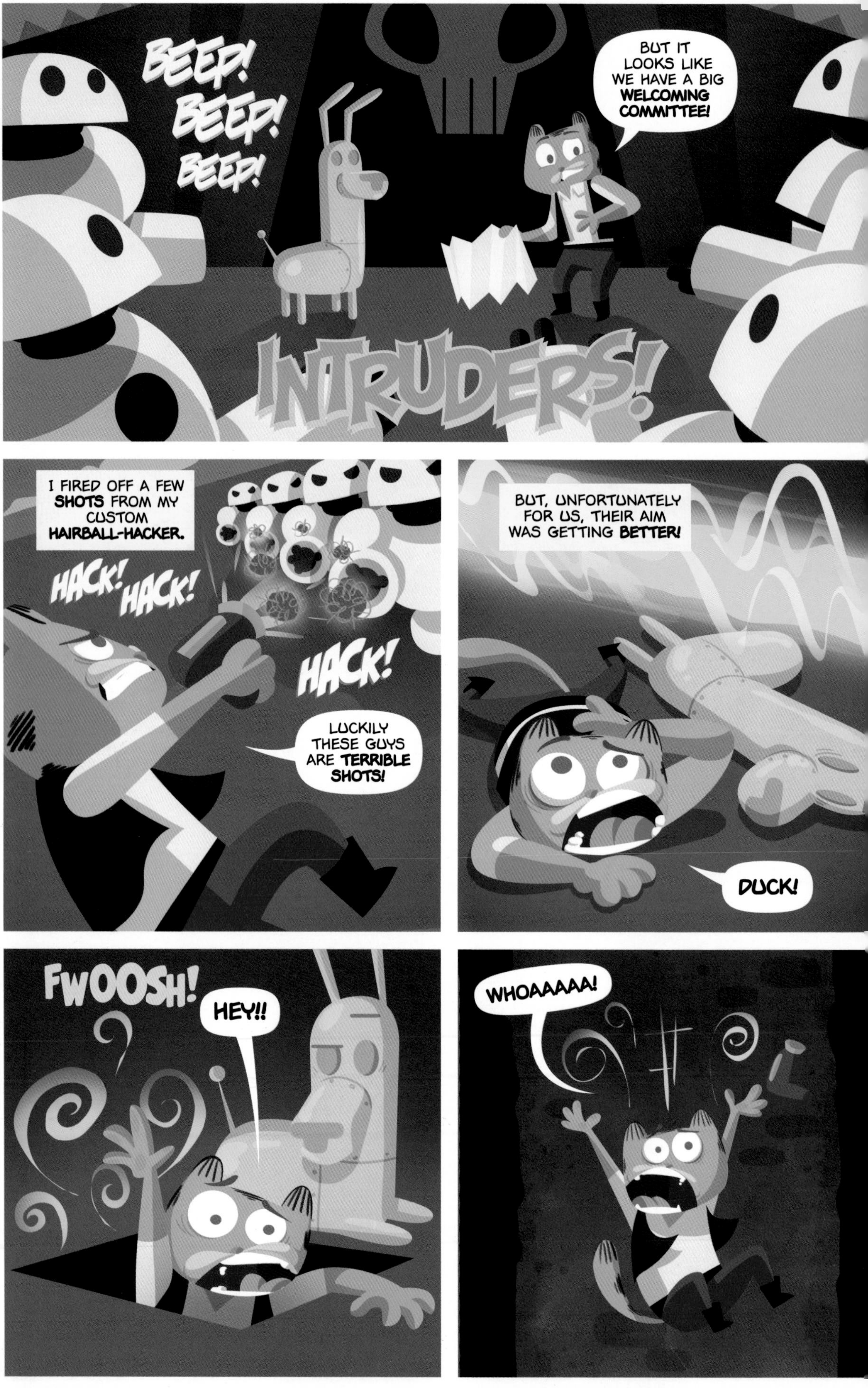
BEEP! BEEP! BEEP!
BUT IT LOOKS LIKE WE HAVE A BIG WELCOMING COMMITTEE!
INTRUDERS!
I FIRED OFF A FEW SHOTS FROM MY CUSTOM HAIRBALL-HACKER.
HACK! HACK!
HACK!
LUCKILY THESE GUYS ARE TERRIBLE SHOTS!
BUT, UNFORTUNATELY FOR US, THEIR AIM WAS GETTING BETTER!
DUCK!
FWOOSH!
HEY!!
WHOAAAAA!

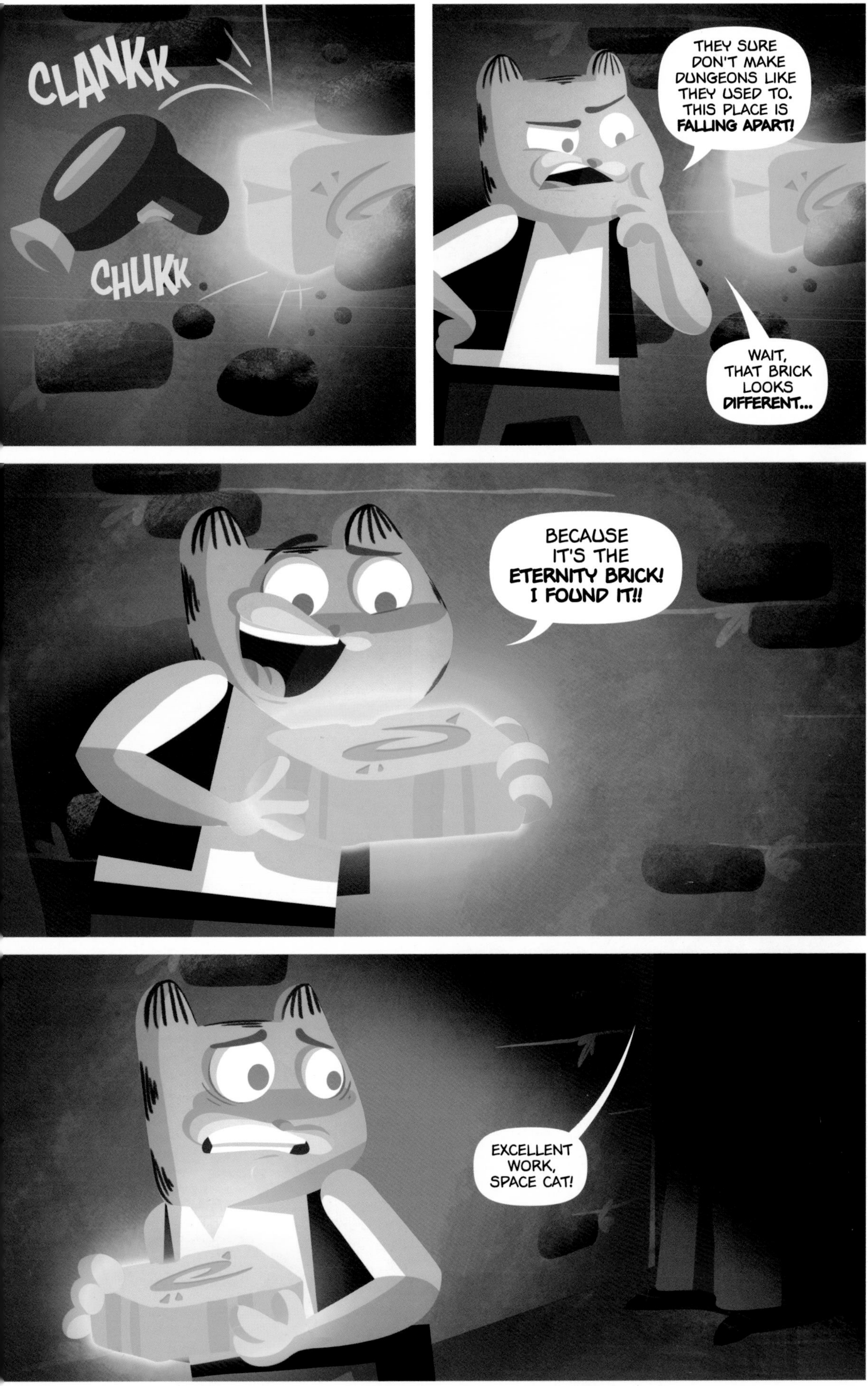
CLANKK
CHUKK
THEY SURE DON'T MAKE DUNGEONS LIKE THEY USED TO. THIS PLACE IS **FALLING APART!**
WAIT, THAT BRICK LOOKS **DIFFERENT...**
BECAUSE IT'S THE **ETERNITY BRICK! I FOUND IT!!**
EXCELLENT WORK, SPACE CAT!

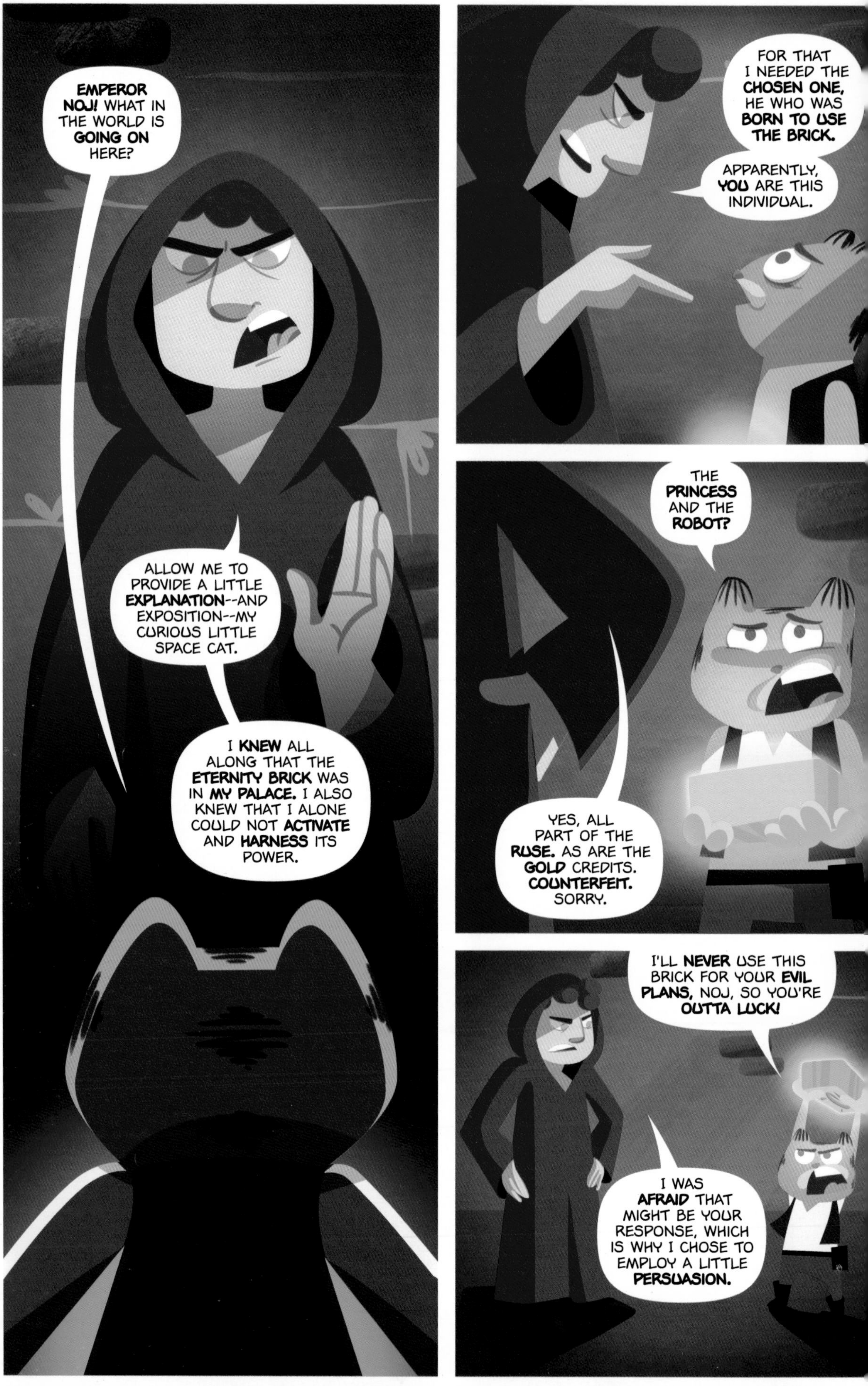
EMPEROR NOJ! WHAT IN THE WORLD IS GOING ON HERE?
ALLOW ME TO PROVIDE A LITTLE EXPLANATION--AND EXPOSITION--MY CURIOUS LITTLE SPACE CAT.
I KNEW ALL ALONG THAT THE ETERNITY BRICK WAS IN MY PALACE. I ALSO KNEW THAT I ALONE COULD NOT ACTIVATE AND HARNESS ITS POWER.
FOR THAT I NEEDED THE CHOSEN ONE, HE WHO WAS BORN TO USE THE BRICK.
APPARENTLY, YOU ARE THIS INDIVIDUAL.
THE PRINCESS AND THE ROBOT?
YES, ALL PART OF THE RUSE. AS ARE THE GOLD CREDITS. COUNTERFEIT. SORRY.
I'LL NEVER USE THIS BRICK FOR YOUR EVIL PLANS, NOJ, SO YOU'RE OUTTA LUCK!
I WAS AFRAID THAT MIGHT BE YOUR RESPONSE, WHICH IS WHY I CHOSE TO EMPLOY A LITTLE PERSUASION.

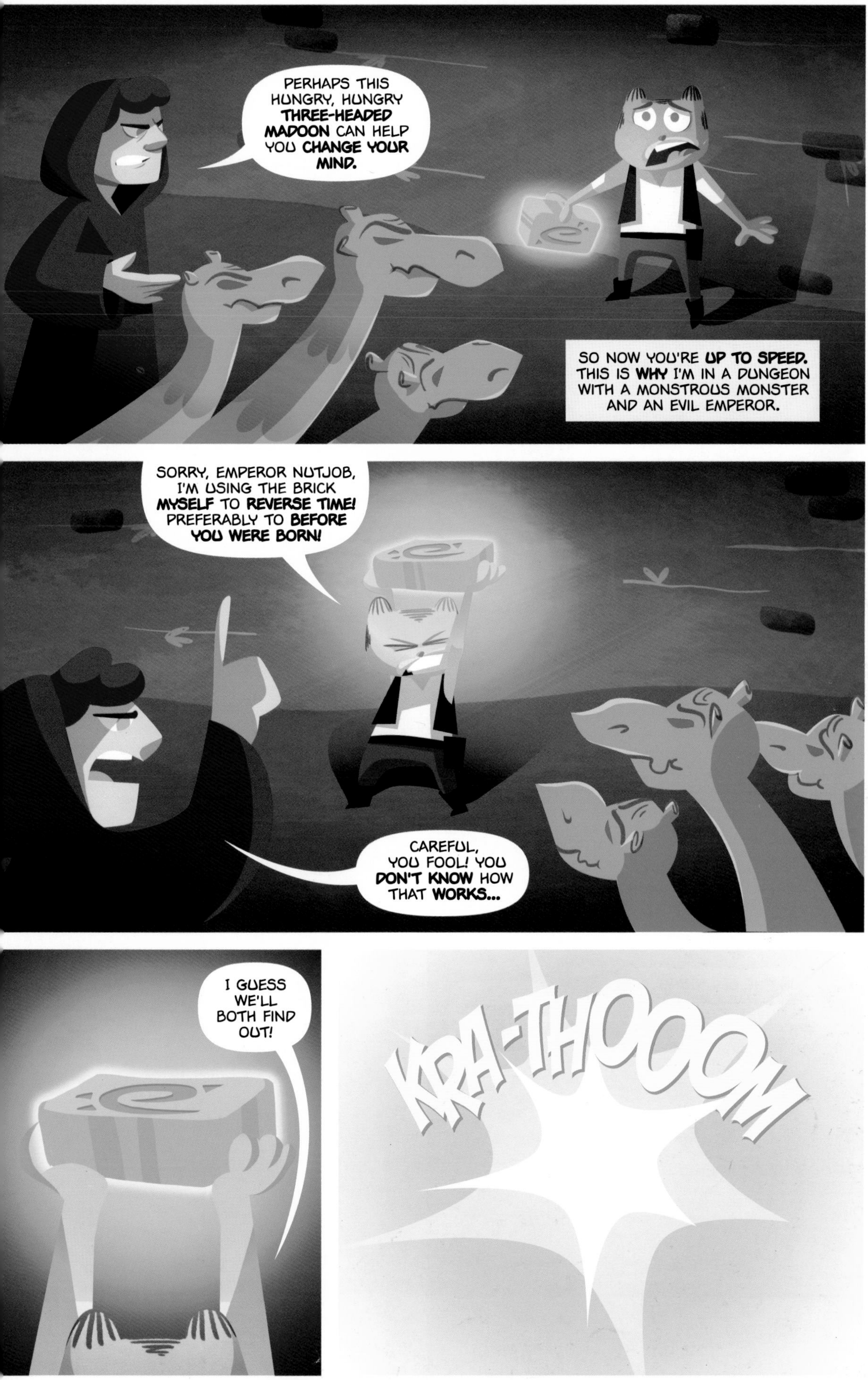
PERHAPS THIS HUNGRY, HUNGRY THREE-HEADED MADOON CAN HELP YOU CHANGE YOUR MIND.
SO NOW YOU'RE UP TO SPEED. THIS IS WHY I'M IN A DUNGEON WITH A MONSTROUS MONSTER AND AN EVIL EMPEROR.
SORRY, EMPEROR NUTJOB, I'M USING THE BRICK MYSELF TO REVERSE TIME! PREFERABLY TO BEFORE YOU WERE BORN!
CAREFUL, YOU FOOL! YOU DON'T KNOW HOW THAT WORKS...
I GUESS WE'LL BOTH FIND OUT!
KRA-THOOOM

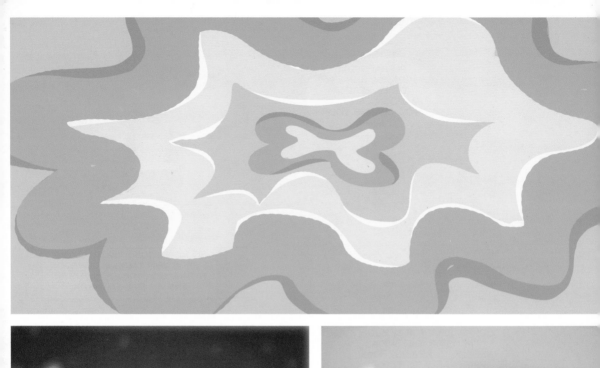

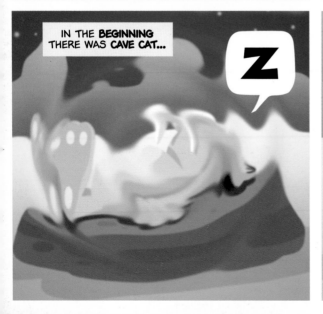

IN THE **BEGINNING** THERE WAS **CAVE CAT**...

Z

LIKE ALL CATS, CAVE CAT LOVED TO SLEEP.

Z

THE END?

COVER GALLERY

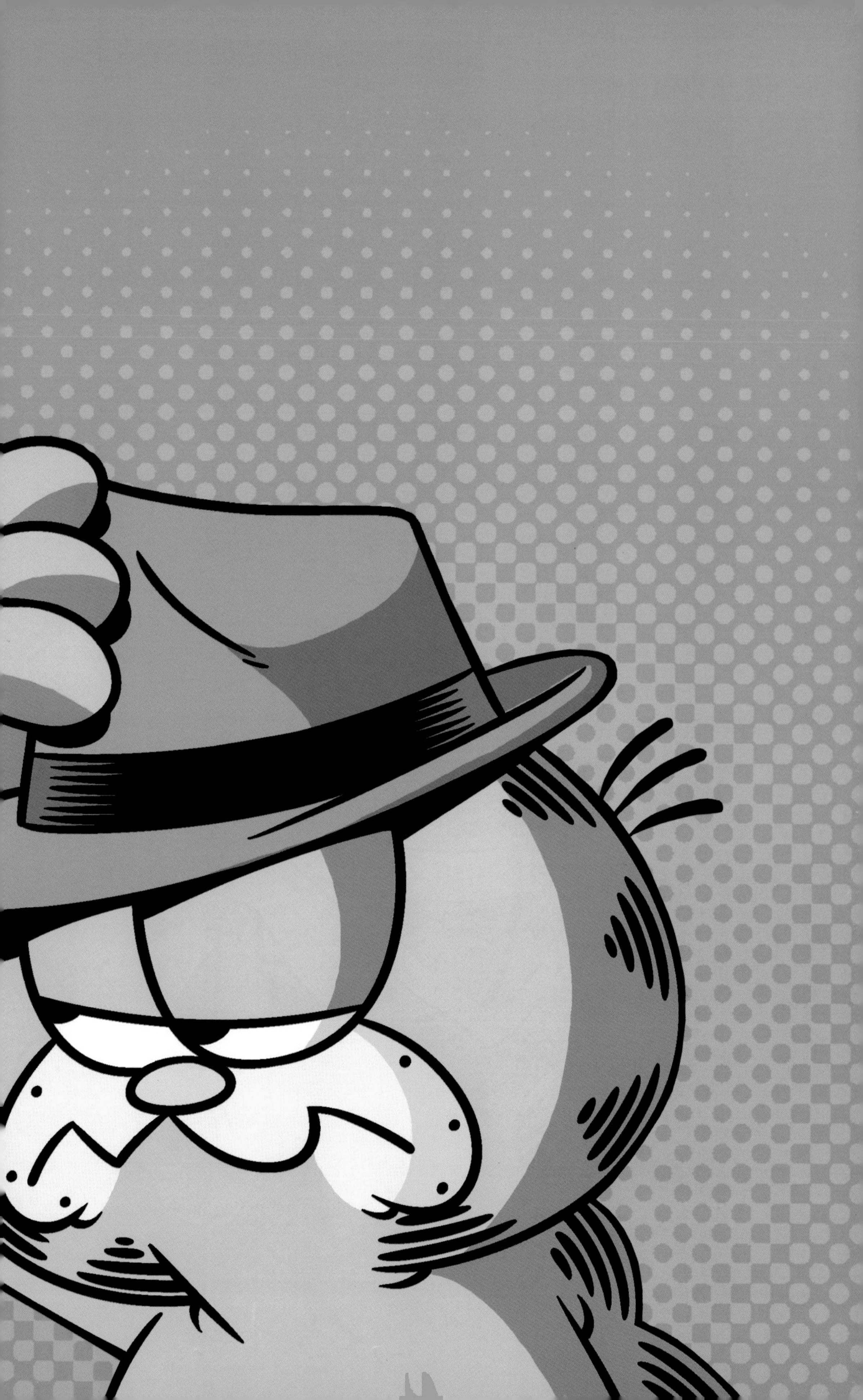

ISSUE 33 VARIANT COVER BY
K. LYNN SMITH

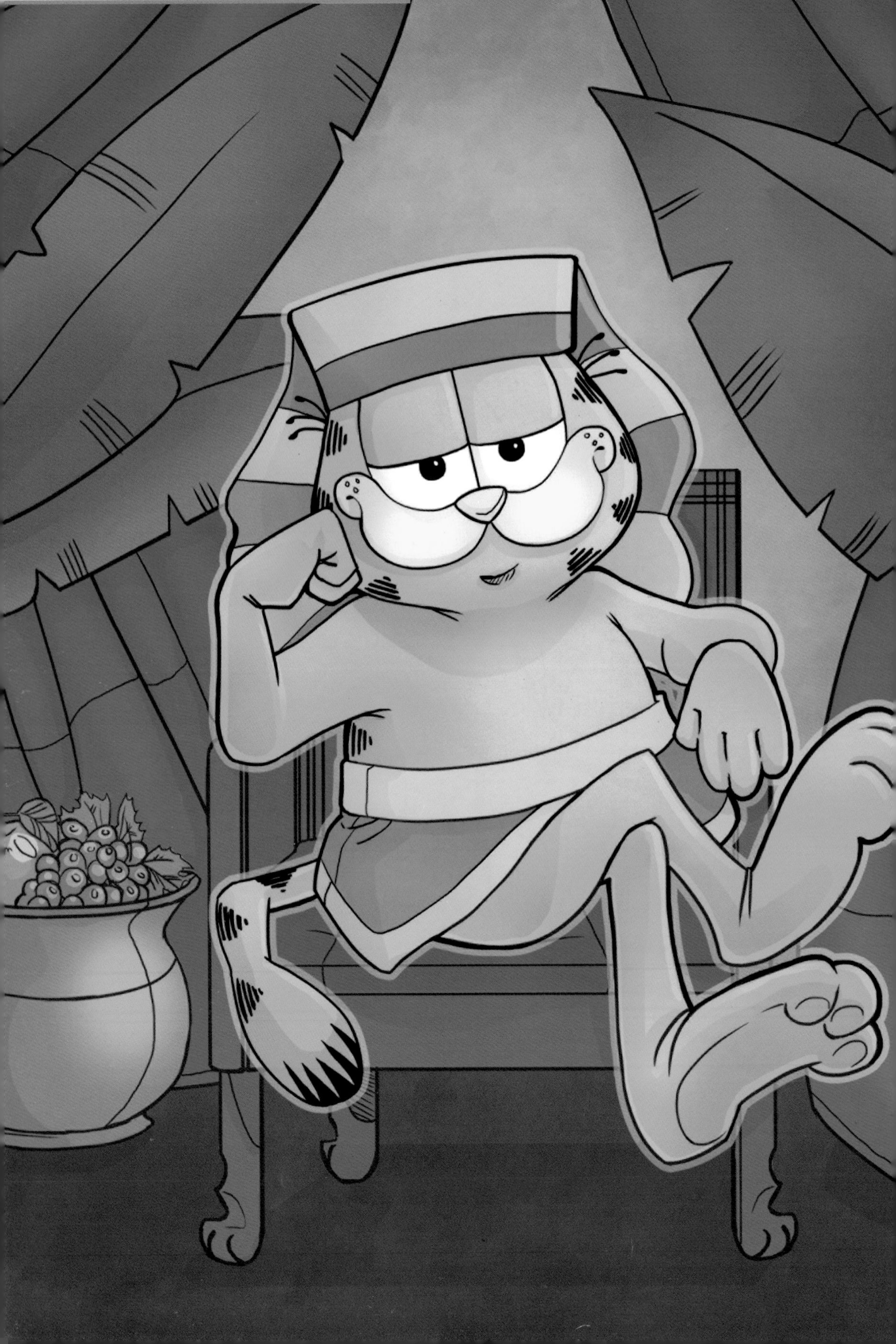

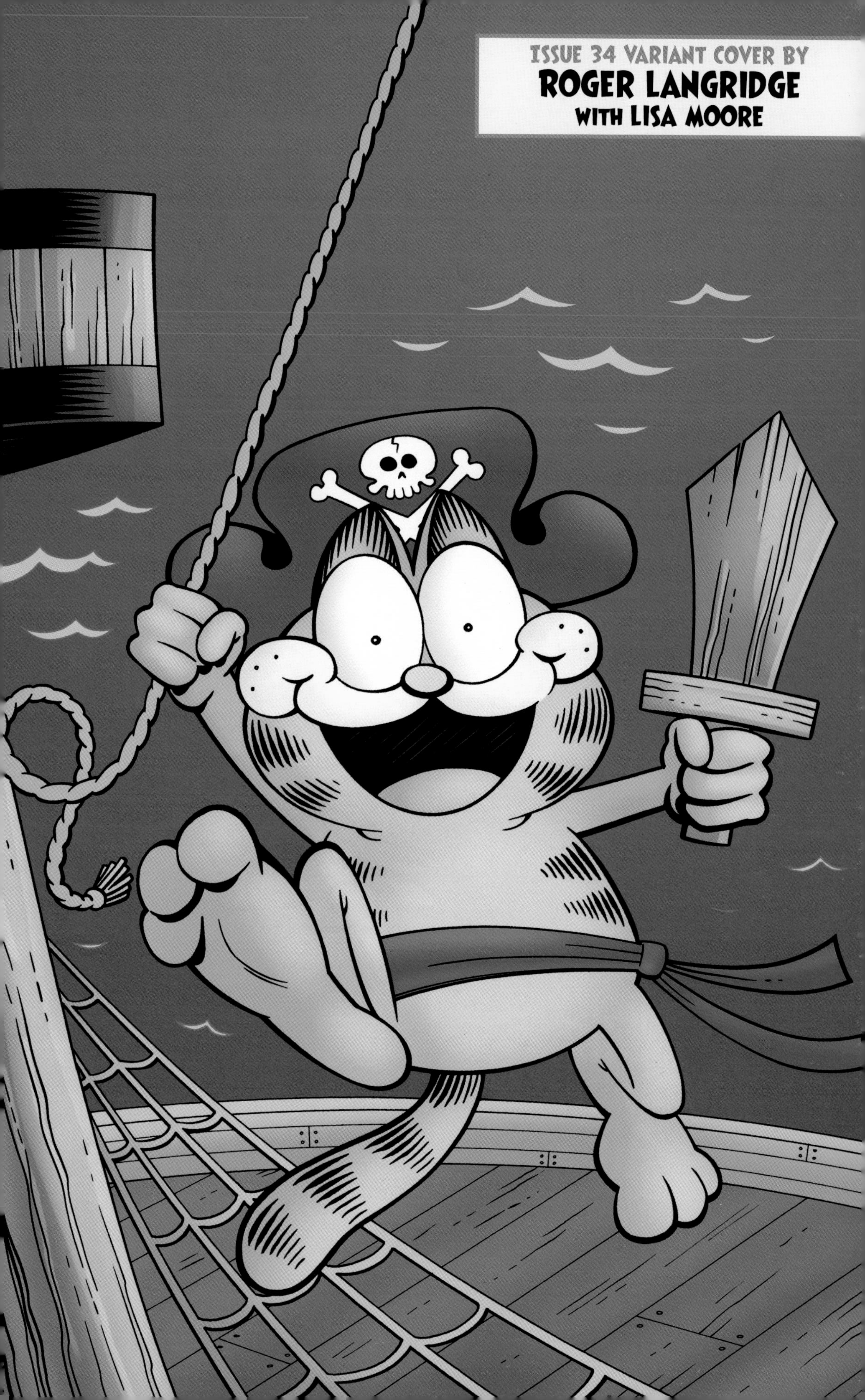

ISSUE 34 VARIANT COVER BY
ROGER LANGRIDGE
WITH LISA MOORE

ISSUE 35 VARIANT COVER BY
ANDY HIRSCH

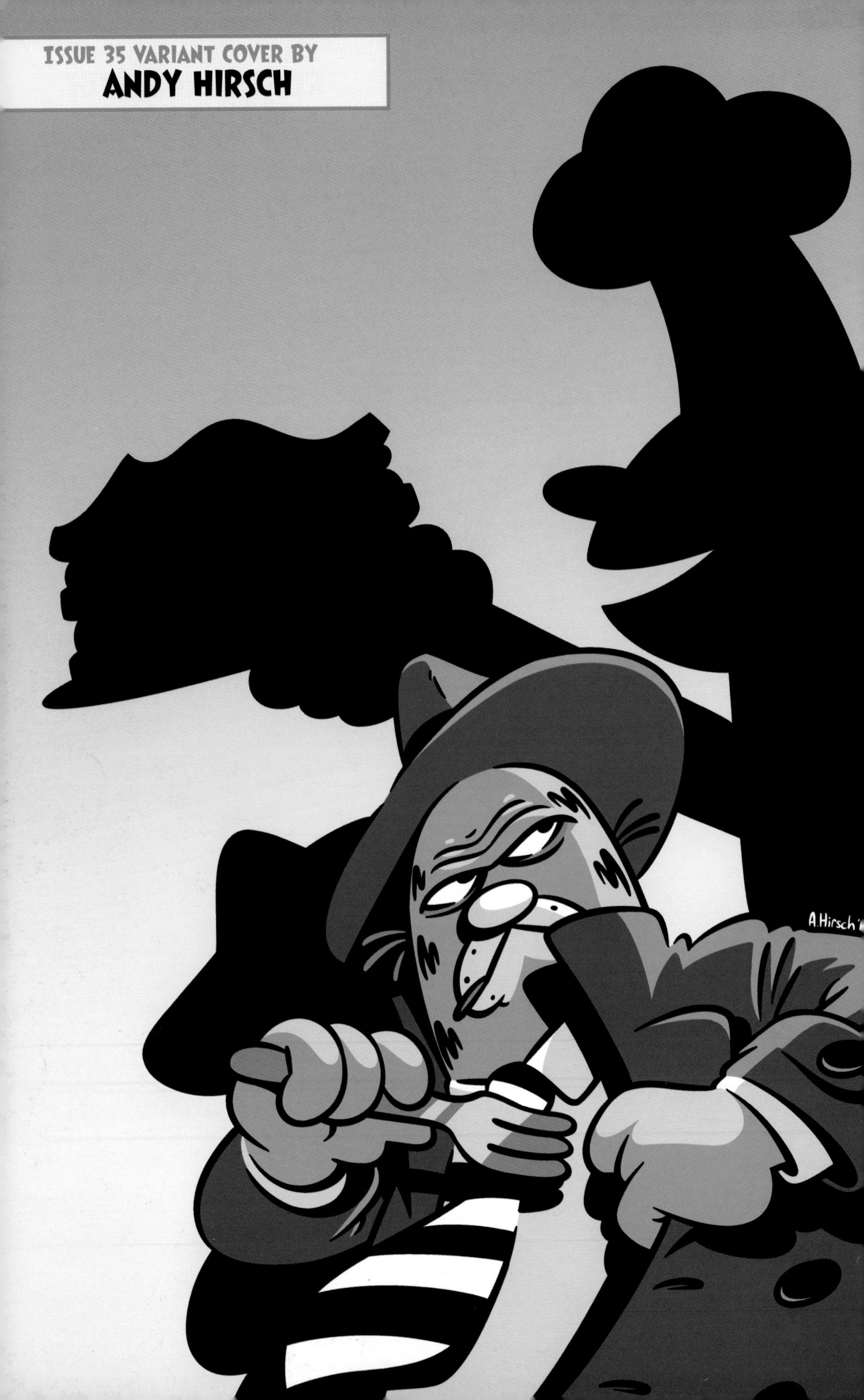
A.Hirsch

ISSUE 36 VARIANT COVER BY
FRAZER IRVING

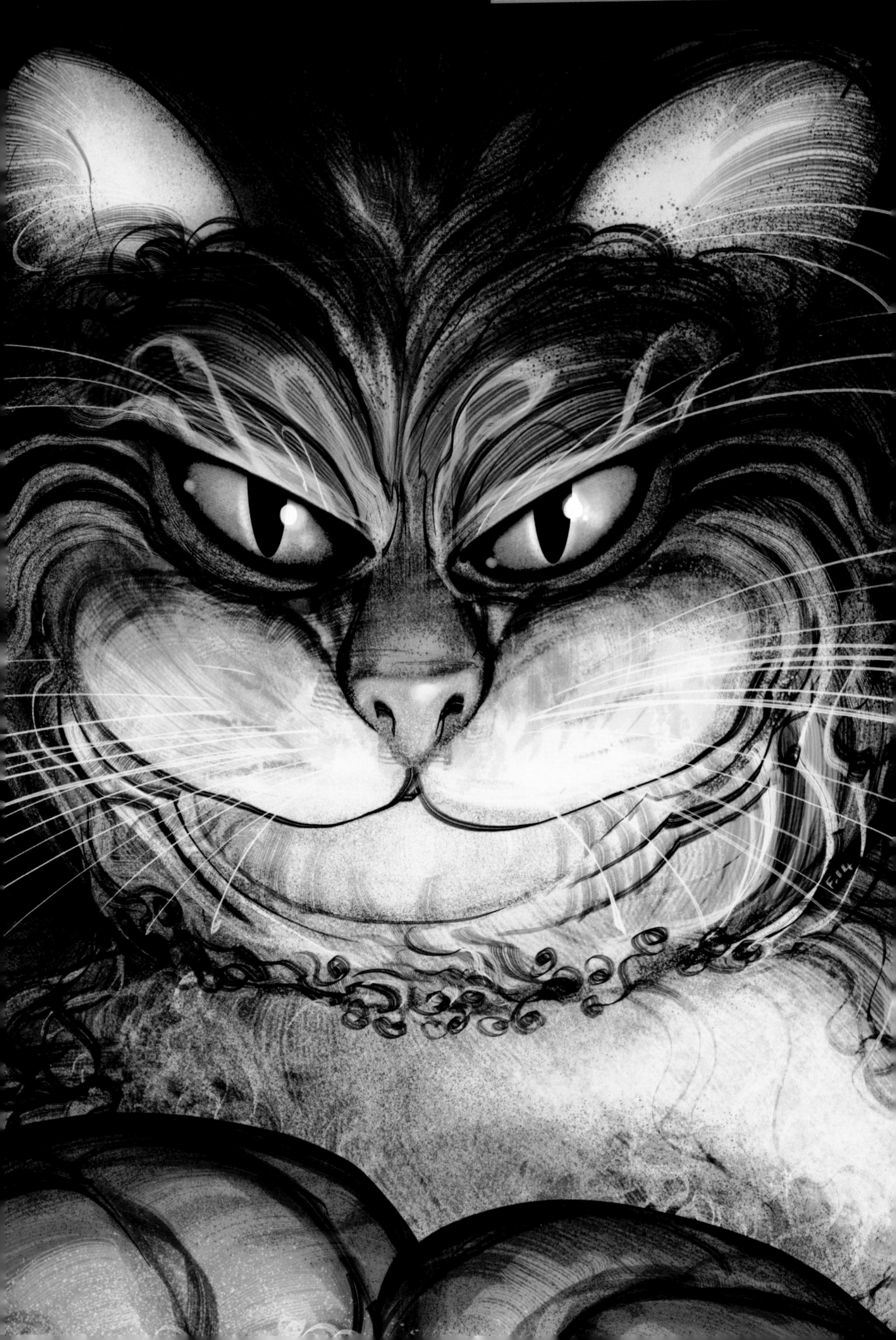

Garfield: His 9 Lives
A Look Back

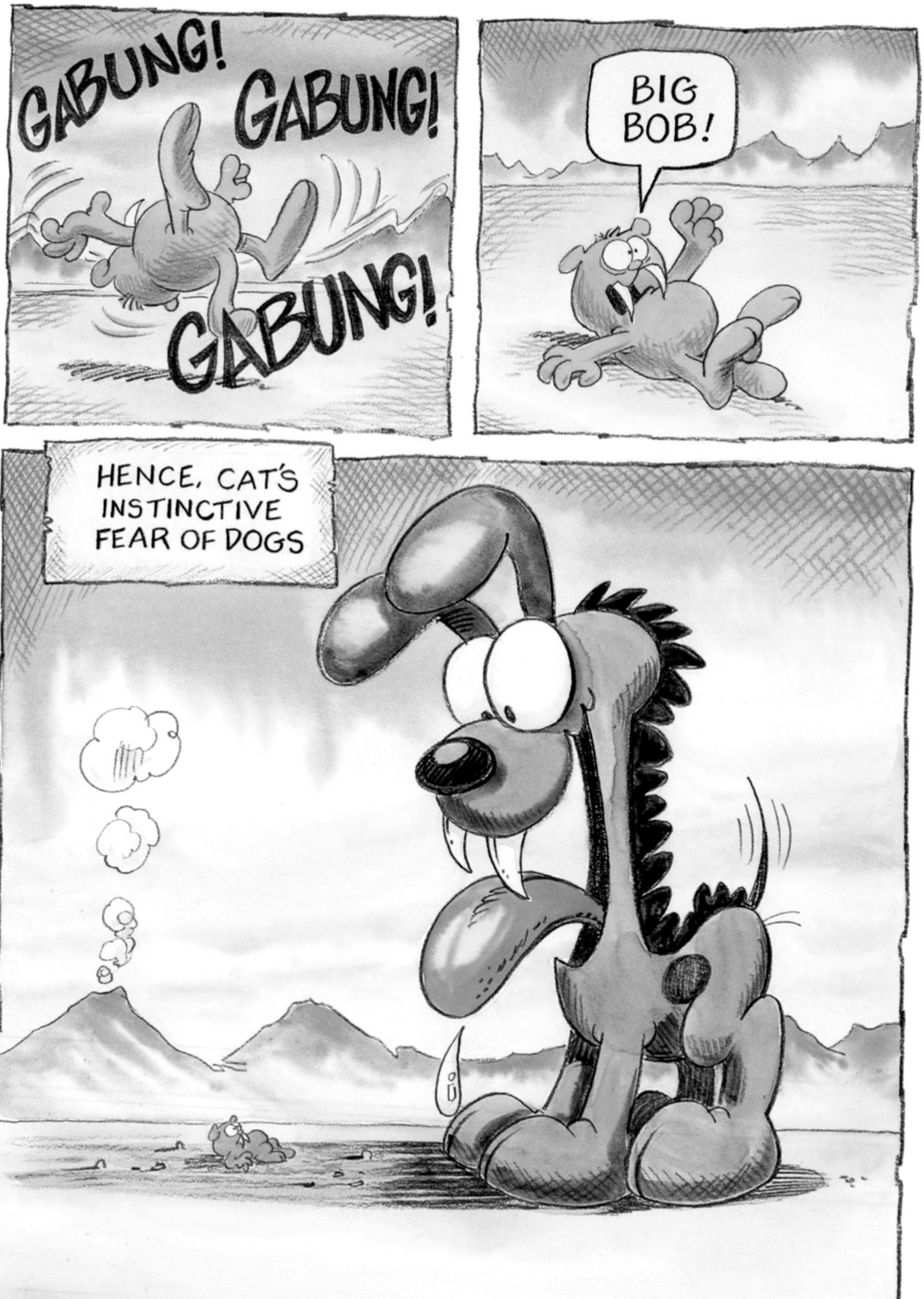
GABUNG! GABUNG!
GABUNG!
BIG BOB!
HENCE, CAT'S INSTINCTIVE FEAR OF DOGS

Original art from "Cave Cat" by
Jim Davis, Mike Fentz and Larry Fentz.
Published in *Garfield: His 9 Lives* by
Ballantine Books in 1984.

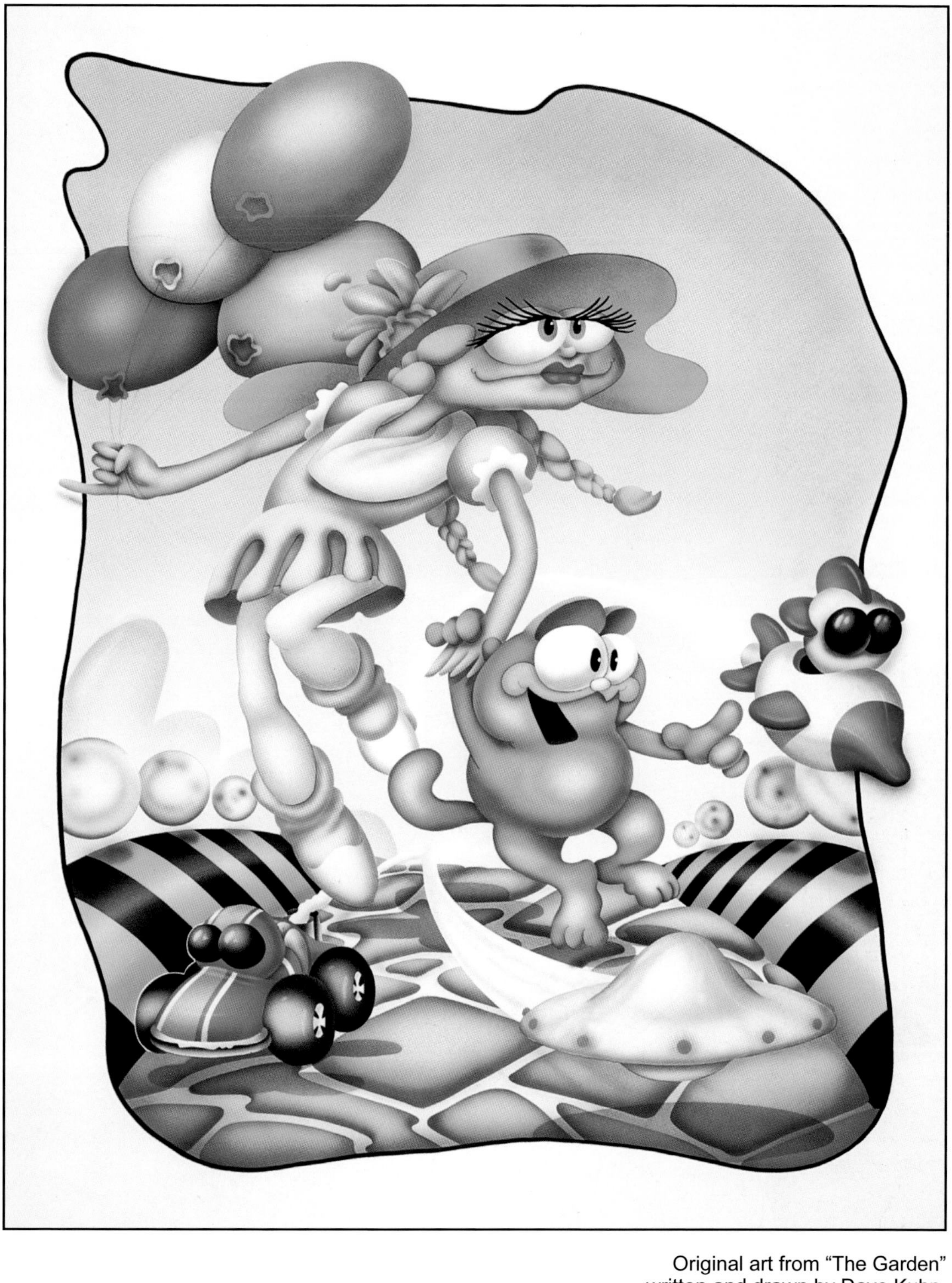

Original art from “The Garden”
written and drawn by Dave Kuhn.
Published in *Garfield: His 9 Lives*
by Ballantine Books in 1984.

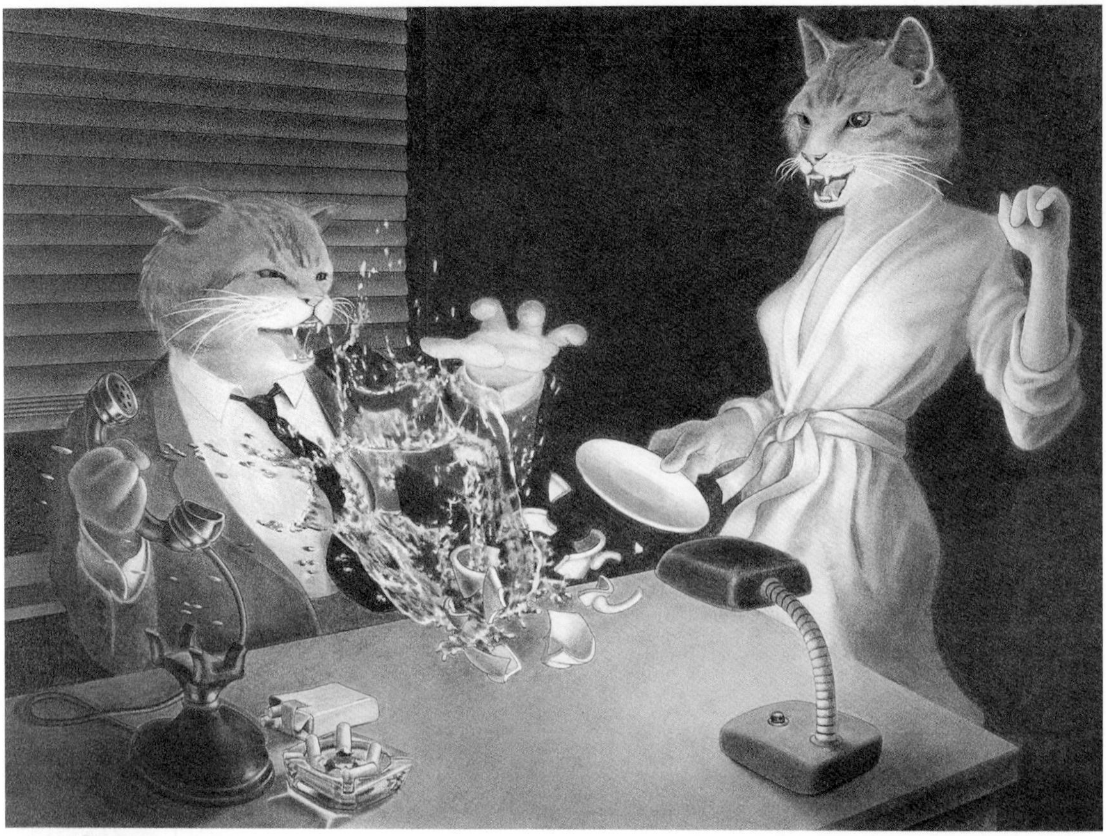

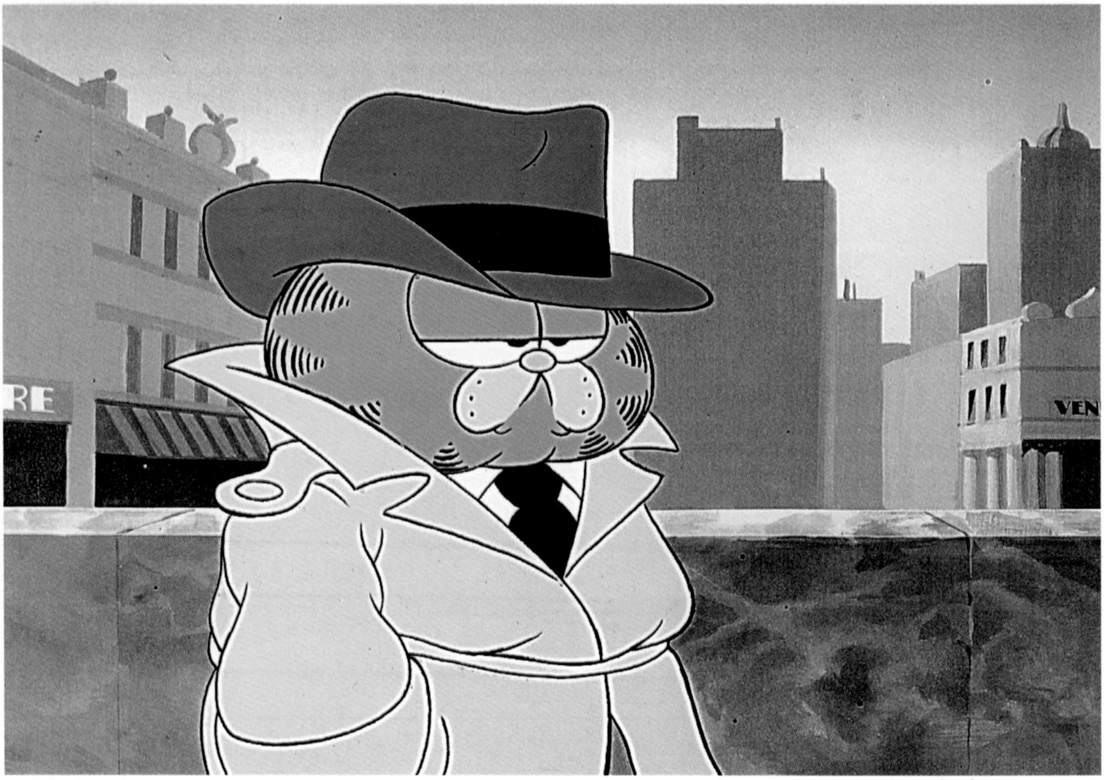

TOP: Original art from “BABES & BULLETS: The Continuing Adventures of Sam Spayed” by Kevin Campbell. Published in *Garfield: His 9 Lives* by Ballantine Books in 1984.

BOTTOM: Animation cell of Sam Spayed from the 1989 Emmy-winning animated TV special “Garfield Presents Babes & Bullets.”

Garfield: His Other Lives

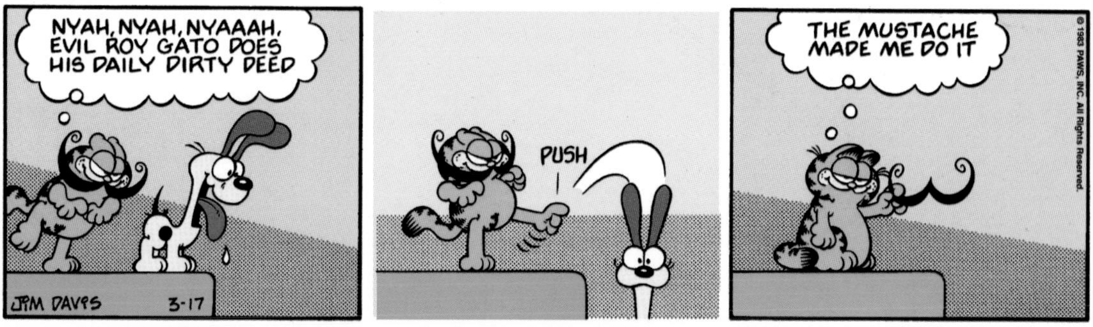
NYAH, NYAH, NYAAAH, EVIL ROY GATO DOES HIS DAILY DIRTY DEED
JIM DAVIS 3-17
PUSH
THE MUSTACHE MADE ME DO IT
© 1983 PAWS, INC. All Rights Reserved.

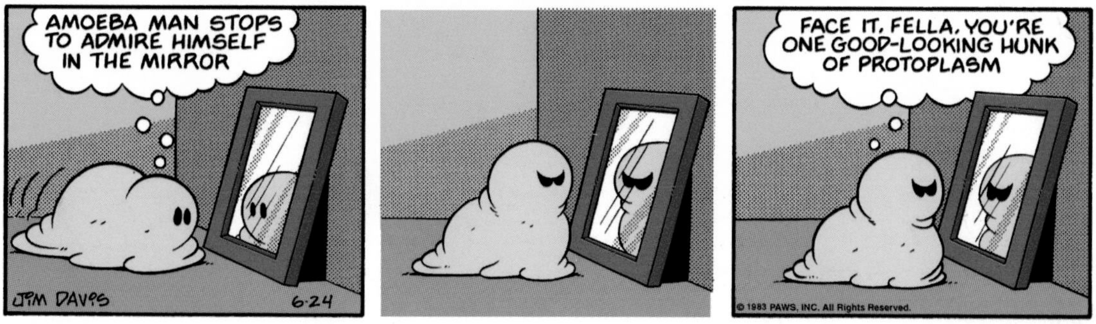
AMOEBA MAN STOPS TO ADMIRE HIMSELF IN THE MIRROR
JIM DAVIS 6-24
FACE IT, FELLA, YOU'RE ONE GOOD-LOOKING HUNK OF PROTOPLASM
© 1983 PAWS, INC. All Rights Reserved.

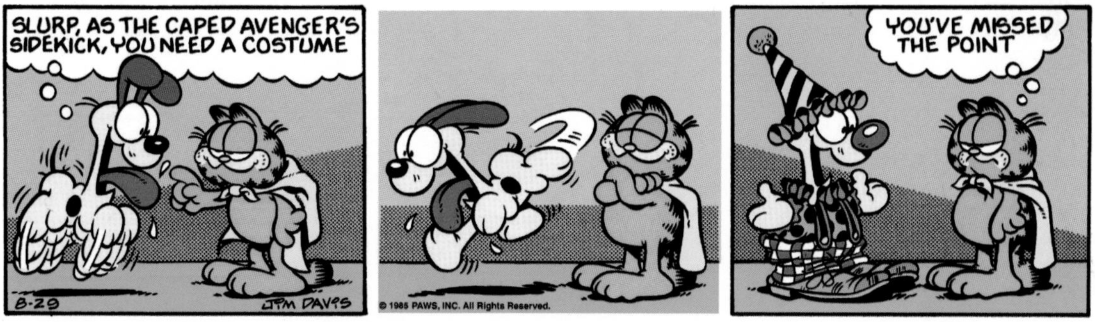
SLURP, AS THE CAPED AVENGER'S SIDEKICK, YOU NEED A COSTUME
8-29 JIM DAVIS
© 1985 PAWS, INC. All Rights Reserved.
YOU'VE MISSED THE POINT

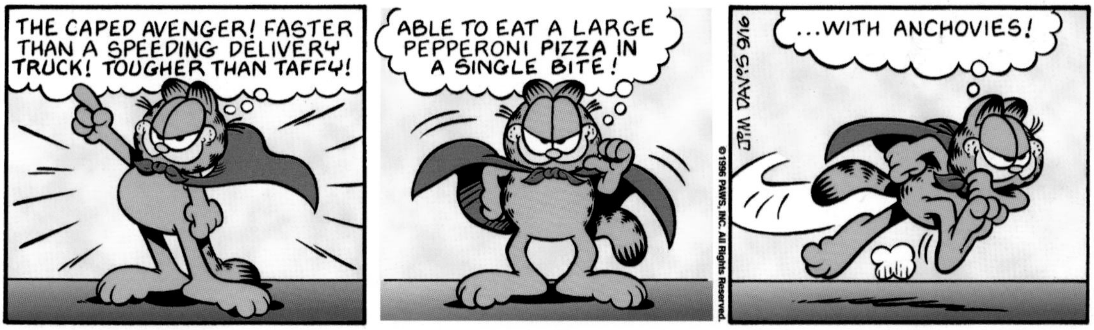
THE CAPED AVENGER! FASTER THAN A SPEEDING DELIVERY TRUCK! TOUGHER THAN TAFFY!
ABLE TO EAT A LARGE PEPPERONI PIZZA IN A SINGLE BITE!
JIM DAVIS 9/16
© 1996 PAWS, INC. All Rights Reserved.
...WITH ANCHOVIES!

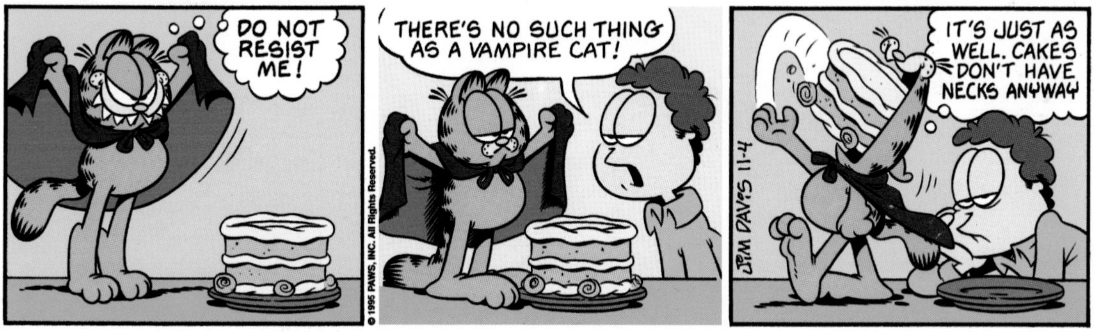
DO NOT RESIST ME!
THERE'S NO SUCH THING AS A VAMPIRE CAT!
© 1995 PAWS, INC. All Rights Reserved.
JIM DAVIS 11-4
IT'S JUST AS WELL. CAKES DON'T HAVE NECKS ANYWAY

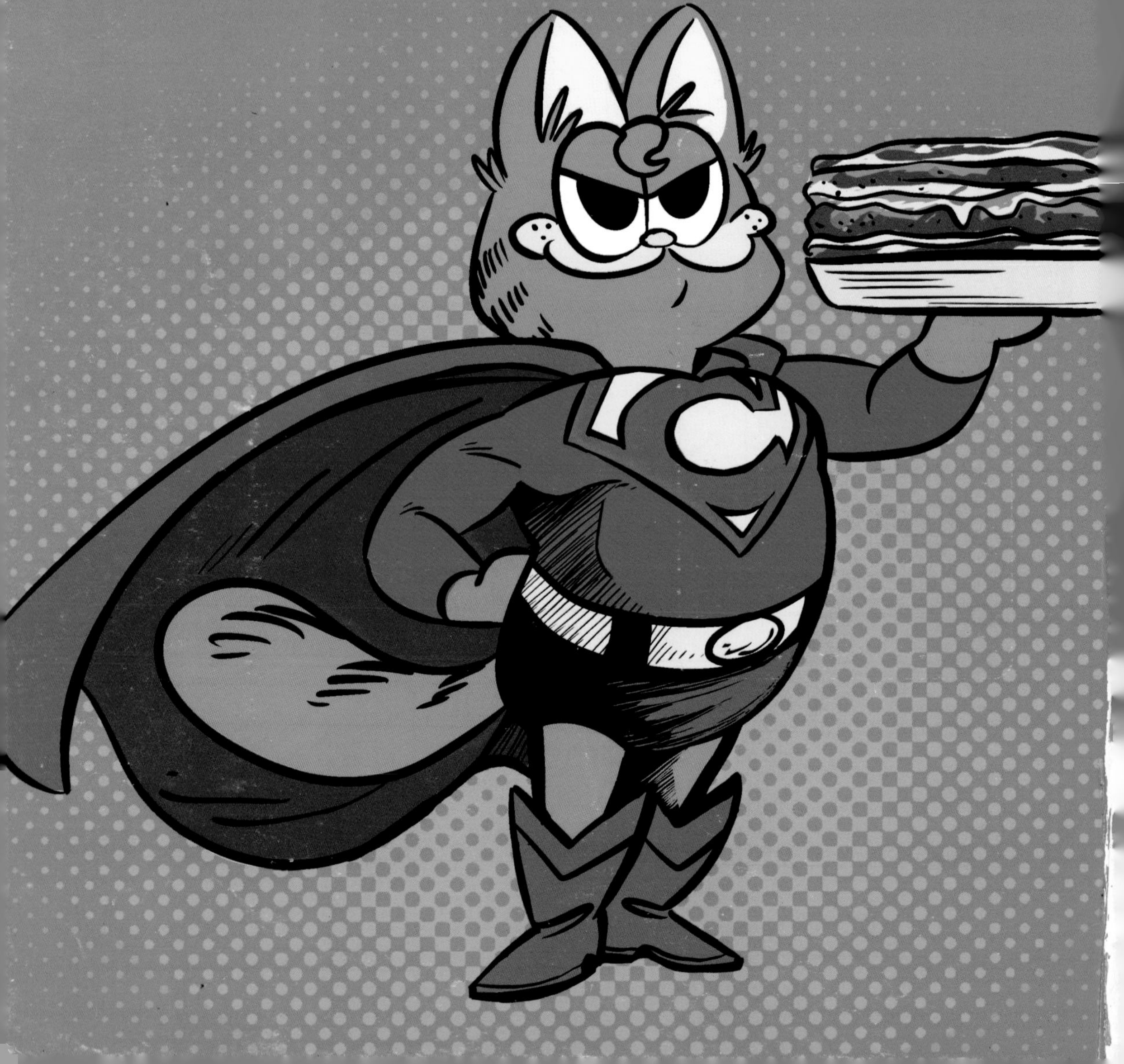